MW00582685

THE QUEEN CITY DETECTIVE AGENCY

ALSO BY SNOWDEN WRIGHT

American Pop

Play Pretty Blues

THE QUEEN CITY DETECTIVE AGENCY

A NOVEL

SNOWDEN WRIGHT

wm

WILLIAM MORROW

An Imprint of HarperCollins*Publishers*

This is a work of fiction. Names, characters, places, and incidents are products of the author's imagination or are used fictitiously and are not to be construed as real. Any resemblance to actual events, locales, organizations, or persons, living or dead, is entirely coincidental.

HarperCollins books may be purchased for educational, business, or sales promotional use. For information, please email the Special Markets Department at SPsales@harpercollins.com.

FIRST EDITION

Designed by Bonni Leon-Berman

Library of Congress Cataloging-in-Publication Data has been applied for.

ISBN 978-0-06-296358-1

24 25 26 27 28 LBC 5 4 3 2 1

To my father,
Who inspired parts of this story,
And to my mother,
For putting up with him

I think you are not altogether American unless you have been to Mississippi; you are not a patriot if you start to faint when somebody breaks her thumb. Anyway, I never faint.

—Renata Adler, *Speedboat*

THE QUEEN CITY DETECTIVE AGENCY

THE MERIDIAN STAR

Wednesday, November 7, 1984 | **High 62, Low 50 - Chance of Storms**

REAGAN WINS REELECTION IN LANDSLIDE!

President Ronald Reagan has retained the highest office in the United States of America. On Tuesday, November 6, 1984, the incumbent Republican defeated his Democratic opponent, Walter Mondale, who served as vice president under former president Jimmy Carter. President Reagan proved that it is indeed morning in America. He carried a whopping forty-nine states, only losing his opponent's home state. His victory, according to one staffer, "will surely pave the way for another four years of progress, growth, and prosperity, except in Minnesota." The reelected president will be sworn into office on January 21, 1985.

"TURNIP" CRACKS UP IN MURDER CASE

A recent hearing pertaining to the murder of real estate developer Randall Hubbard concluded with what those in attendance called a "disgrace to our court system." Lewis "Turnip" Coogan, charged with the murder, hurled expletives at District Attorney Will Pickett, Assistant DA Russell Clyde, and the victim's family. In particular, he expressed outrage toward Hubbard's widow, Odette, also in custody for the tragic murder of her husband. (cont. A4)

POP. OF GREATER MERIDIAN HITS RECORD LOW

Meridian, Miss., once the second-largest city in the state, is now officially the seventh. Recent data confirms a steady, decades-long decline in the population. The seat of Lauderdale County, Meridian remains the principal city in what statisticians call a "micropolitan" area formed by three counties—Lauderdale, Kemper, and Clarke. Mayor Rosenbaum expressed optimism for the city's future, noting the recent expansion of the National Guard complex at Key Field.

YOUR THREE-DAY OUTLOOK

Thursday: Sunny, High 70, Low 60

Friday: Overcast, High 75, Low 62

Saturday: Severe Storms, High 80, Low 65

1

ZIP-A-DEE-DOO-DAH

On New Year's Day of 1985, Turnip Coogan, facing twenty to life for capital murder, decided he'd have to be dumb as a post not to break out of jail, and his mama didn't raise no post. That morning, as usual, the cells were unlocked to give the hundred inmates time to exercise, and due to a current heat wave, one of the trustees had opened a window by the mess hall. Turnip saw his chance. In poor testament to his mother's child-rearing abilities, he didn't bother getting dressed before climbing out the window, and in poorer testament to the intelligence of posts, he forgot the jail was located on the roof of the Lauderdale County Courthouse.

Turnip had nowhere to run, and even if he did, he'd be running there in a tank top, boxer shorts, and one sock.

Before and below him lay downtown Meridian, Mississippi, a railroad hub that billed itself the state's "Queen City" but that had, over recent decades, become more of a countess or baronet. Strip malls in the northern hills, via two fangs, Poplar Springs Drive and Highway 39, had sucked the life out of the city's downtown. What remained included a triptych of hospitals, donut shops to help fill them, churches praying to empty them, and lawyers' offices trying to profit off them. Turnip blamed all those goddamn shit-brained lawyers for his present situation.

One in particular. William *motherfucking* Pickett. On the roof of the courthouse, as the alarm started to whine inside the jail and onlookers in the street below raised hands to brows, Turnip let his half-socked toes hang over the edge, thinking of all he would like to do to that asshole Will Pickett, the district attorney prosecuting his case.

"Take a step on this roof and I jump!" Turnip yelled at the armed guard whose short-brimmed hat bobbed like a fishing float at the top lip of the fixed metal cage ladder twenty yards away.

"You got nowhere to run, Coogan! This ladder's the only way down, besides that window you climbed out of, and there's ten, twelve guards waiting inside it. Come back yonder ways, we forget all about it. All right now?"

"One step, okay? One step and I jump!"

How long had Turnip been on the roof? He couldn't say for sure. The day was turning into a real blue-moon scorcher, even for January in Mississippi, the roof's black tar going glassy, the sun a giant interrogation lamp blasting down on Turnip. In the street three stories below, the crowd had grown. A police blockade cut off traffic. Patrolmen in short sleeves and aviators tried without success to disperse the people on cigarette breaks from the few offices that remained downtown.

Everyone, Turnip figured, was getting pushed around by this godforsaken city. Those folks down there knew a comrade in arms when they saw one. Their hands held to their temples were a salute, not makeshift visors what better to see the fun. Turnip was a hero, a symbol of oppression! If only his mama could see him now.

Soon the crowd even started to chant for him. Turnip's bare shoulders slumped, however, when he realized what exactly they were chanting.

"Jump, Turnip, jump!" yelled the crowd, singsong. "Jump! Jump! Jump!"

With a grunt, Turnip sat on the edge of the roof, letting his legs dangle humpty-dumpty-style. He tried to ignore the chants by plotting his revenge. The prosecution, led by that son-of-a-bitch district attorney, claimed Turnip and an accomplice had killed Randall Hubbard, the rich-ass real estate developer responsible, if Turnip was being honest, for the death of downtown Meridian. Hubbard had built the strip malls draining the life out of this city. Hubbard made millions leasing space to greasy pizza joints, bargain shoe stores, nail and hair salons, liquor stores, dollar stores, record stores, and hippie-dippie head shops.

And what did he do with those millions? Build a house on a hilltop, marry a woman young enough to be his daughter, get fat, go bald, and take out a stupidly sizable amount of life insurance on himself. Of course his beautiful young wife had started to get *notions*.

"I been framed!" Turnip yelled to the crowd below. "That bitch set me up!"

The bitch in question was Odette Hubbard. Turnip never should have trusted her. Last year, she'd hired him as her bodyguard at the rate of $1,000 per week, which was a sight more than what he made driving commercial rigs. Turnip figured she hired him because she knew he was connected to the DM, a deduction he made when, a week after hiring him, she said, "I hear you're connected to the DM."

So, sure, Turnip thought, watching TV crews set up equipment on the street below, he'd made some calls to his people in the Dixie Mafia. Due to his cockfighting side hustle—he'd earned some of the high-ups in the DM piles of money with his secret method of sticking a cocaine-laced Q-tip up his bird's asshole before the fight—Turnip had used code. "Got a hen offering thirty-large for somebody to take out her rooster."

Soon as he got off this roof, Turnip would prove the murder had been Odette's plan all along. He was a patsy. The news crews down there would hold up their mics to his face and he'd spill, goddamn it. Everybody would know the truth—about Odette and the DM, about the Meridian PD and city hall, about the whole goddamn rigged system of this whole goddamn town!

An updraft cooled Turnip's feet and calves. He rubbed the lacerations on his wrists. Last night, he'd tried to get moved to the infirmary by way of a suicide attempt, but when the doctor saw the cuts Turnip had made with a plastic knife, he'd laughed in Turnip's face and said, "Son, you're supposed to cut on the *under*side of the wrist."

In the street, all the cars, whether parked or driving by, seemed to be tuned to Q101. Turnip could hear the radio from their open windows. "Shit," he whispered after noticing what song was playing. When Van Halen's "Jump" ended, the DJ said, "This goes out to you, Turnip. Give those folks downtown a show!" and the song started up again.

Had he only wanted to go to the infirmary? Turnip asked himself, rubbing his wrists, fingering the scabs. No. He'd wanted to go somewhere else, and he couldn't even get that right.

Firemen set up a jumping sheet on the curb, locking the hinges of its circular metal frame and, each spaced a few feet apart, holding it above the hard concrete. They looked to Turnip like kids gathered around a trampoline. He appreciated the white sheet had a red bull's-eye in its center. That way he'd know where not to aim if he took his last step.

Leaning forward, hands clamped to the ledge, Turnip let a glob of spit form against his parched lips. He watched it fall three stories to the sidewalk. *One Mississippi, two Mississippi, three Miss—* Two and a half seconds for three stories. Was that too long a stretch of terror? Turnip would rather die than live out his whole life in prison. Might as well ask for the death penalty, he figured, because he might as well be dead.

He cupped his hands to his mouth. "Somebody stand up and say I killed Randy Hubbard! I want somebody to give me a motherfucking lie detector to prove I ain't killed nobody. I may know who killed the worthless bastard, but I'm not going to rat on nobody!"

From behind Turnip came the voice he wanted most and least to hear at that moment. "I'm coming up, Coogan," yelled Will Pickett. The district attorney climbed over the top rim of the cage ladder. Hands raised, he said, "The man behind me? That's my investigator, Jake. He's armed. I told Jake shoot you dead, you make a move."

"You ugly son of a bitch. I'm sure you'd like that. Get rid of me, easy-peez."

Turnip stood. He looked over the ledge. News cameras scattered through the crowd peered back at him, sound operators beside them, raising boom poles above their heads. He guessed that at a distance of three stories they must be close enough to pick up everything he and Pickett said.

"Did I mention fat?" Turnip asked the district attorney, raising his voice so it would carry. "You are one *fat*, ugly son of a bitch."

Pickett, in pin-striped shirtsleeves, maroon suspenders, and an affected bow tie, said, "Let's go on back inside, all right, Coogan?" His round glasses with cable temples reflected a pair of suns. Sweat drenched his chevron moustache.

"You lied about my plea deal," Turnip said, the tone in the second-to-last word sounding, to his embarrassment, like what it was: a plea. Months earlier, after his offer to turn state's evidence if the capital murder charges were dropped, Turnip had sent a letter to the local paper, declaring his innocence and his unfair treatment by the district attorney. Unfortunately, how Turnip concluded the letter, stating he could not have done more to get the court's attention unless he'd threatened to kill Ronald Reagan, occasioned an entire week of questioning by unamused FBI agents.

"Lewis," Pickett said, using Turnip's given name. He inched closer, hands still raised, the old man behind him still gripping a revolver. "You and I both know we never had a plea deal."

"I ain't killed nobody. You took everything I had when you put me in jail."

Not until he saw a line of wet drops on the roof's tar did Turnip realize he was crying. He wiped his face with the hem of his tank top and, as his boxer shorts ballooned from his thighs and his one sock gripped the ledge, did a chicken dance, flapping his bent arms like two wings and making gobble-gobble sounds. The dance used to bring him luck before cockfights. Now he hoped it would keep the people down in the street from seeing his tears.

"What are you doing, Lewis?" Pickett was now close enough to reach out and touch Turnip. "Think about your lovely wife. Think about that baby you got on the way."

"Baby?"

"She hasn't told you. *Shit.*"

Turnip's wife, Molly, hadn't visited him since he'd been detained at the county's pleasure. He understood. In fact, he was happy she stayed away. At the initial hearing, when Turnip had been ordered to be held without bond, Molly had been shaking as she gave her testimony that she had met Turnip's alleged accomplice in the murder, a DM hit man named Jacob Cassidy. Turnip's heart had crumbled like old corn bread to see his girl so afraid of what Cassidy and the Dixie Mafia might do to her in retaliation for the testimony.

It was for the best, her staying away from the jail, but she could have at least called Turnip and told him he was going to be a daddy. Molly could have at least done that.

"You took everything I have," Turnip mumbled to Will Pickett. "My home, my truck. My family." His voice swelled—out of anger with himself and with this piece of shit who'd made him cry in front of the whole world. "How'd you like it if I took away your family, Mr. Pickett? What if someone killed your wife, your son, that baby in your wife's belly?"

Down below, the group of uniformed police officers began to froth, talking into their radios and making hand signals to other officers. Behind Pickett, the old man with a gun stepped forward. "Easy, Jake," Pickett said. "Lewis was just puffing his chest. Isn't that right, Lewis?"

Turnip, sensing he'd gone too far, started to pace, his motion back and forth on the ledge keeping a lockstep with the motion back and forth in his mind. He was such an idiot. What kind of man couldn't properly send himself to hell? Turnip got dizzy thinking about it. Even his stomach turned on him. A belch filled his mouth, tasting of bitter eggs and toast and coffee.

"How can anyone win in this damn town?" After he stopped pacing, Turnip continued swaying side to side, favoring one heel and then the other. He couldn't help himself. The motion was still going in his head. The bitter taste was still in his mouth. "Game's been rigged my whole entire life."

"Let's go back inside." Pickett stepped forward. He was inches from Turnip's back. He couldn't see his face. "We can sit down and have a little talk about a plea deal. How's that sound?"

"They took everything I have, and I ain't got nothing to lose."

"Lewis!"

To the people in the street below, Turnip, shadowed by the noontime sun and given fluffy white wings by the backdrop of two clouds, didn't jump or fall so much as topple from the roof, arms at his sides and back straight, like a toy soldier nudged forward by a child's finger. Collectively they gasped when his body hit the sidewalk. Parents held hands over their children's eyes. Paralegals, secretaries, and nurse practitioners forgot to agonize, if only for a moment, about their overdue mortgage payments, about the tests that came back positive, about the liens on their Ford Escorts or Oldsmobile Cutlasses or Chevy Chevettes.

The rest of Meridian, Mississippi, did not notice. At Bill Gordon's barbershop, young men thinking of joining up asked for flattops, demonstrating by holding one hand like a mortarboard to their heads, trying to tamp the quiver in their voices. At Merrehope, one of six homes left standing after General Sherman's raid during the Civil War, a group of volunteers from the Junior Auxiliary dusted, polished, mopped, and swept in preparation for the two-o'clock tour. At Weidmann's Restaurant, customers smeared peanut butter on saltines while looking over the menu. At the Threefoot Building, insurance salesmen read the paper while getting their brogans shined. At the Temple Theatre, students from Lamar School, a segregation academy named for the Confederate statesman L. Q. C. Lamar, took advantage of the New Year's Day holiday by waiting in line to see Disney's rerelease of *Song of the South*. A few of them sang "Zip-a-Dee-Doo-Dah" as an ambulance passed, headed to the courthouse to collect the body.

And later that evening, after Will Pickett's pregnant wife and two-year-old son had been startled by a black-and-white police cruiser pulling up to their house—"Only here as a precaution, ma'am," the officers had said—Clementine Baldwin, proprietor of the Queen City Detective Agency, sat in her office to look over a stack of unpaid invoices. She was pouring her third whiskey neat when the phone rang.

"Queen City," she said into the shouldered receiver. "Baldwin here."

"Hello," came a woman's voice, frail but bold, with a hill-country twang. "My name is Lenora Coogan. My son is Lewis Coogan. I'd like to hire you to find the sons of bitches who killed him."

2

QUEEN CITY DETECTIVE AGENCY

Clem Baldwin woke the next day on her ratty office couch, as usual, still fully dressed, as usual, and, unusually, not hungover. After getting off the phone with Lenora Coogan, she'd left her office and walked the six blocks to the courthouse, where the scene of what authorities were officially calling an accident was cordoned off in brilliant yellow plastic. Clem, ignoring the bottle of whiskey tucked in a drawer of her desk, had spent the rest of the night watching TV news reports of the incident, which included unnecessarily and, she felt, unconscionably explicit footage of Turnip Coogan's plummet to his death.

The eerie sight of Coogan's body midair, with his arms by his sides instead of flailing and his legs rigid instead of scissoring, was lodged in Clem's mind as she picked up her partner, Dixon Hicks.

"Morning," Dixon said after shutting the car door, his long blond hair still wet from the shower, his beard smelling incongruously of aftershave. Clem handed him a cup of coffee she'd grabbed at a Super Stop on her way to his apartment complex. "Did you remember the cream?" he asked, an old joke Clem was embarrassed to still find funny.

"Pussies like you can't handle straight black." She used that line every time.

Dixon took a sip of coffee before finishing the routine in his heavy drawl. "You never forget the sugar."

From Clem's beat-down, soft-top Jeep, which she'd inherited after her father took on crop shares at Parchman Farm and which she now drove, she told herself, out of spite more than sentiment, Clem watched stock footage of her past life. It still hurt to see the police department on Twenty-Second Avenue, where, during her rookie year and maybe three of the five subsequent ones, she'd genuinely believed the boys in blue could be man enough to accept a woman. It hurt worse to see Highland Park, site of her career-making and, ultimately, career-ending collar, a serial killer the papers relished calling the Dentzel Carousel Strangler.

"Are you still drunk?" Dixon asked, waving his hand in front of Clem's face.

"What? Shut up. What?"

"I was asking you a question."

"Then ask it again, God's sake. Shit."

Dixon picked a piece of lint from his stonewashed jeans. "Did the Coogan woman say why she called us first?"

"Because we're the best?"

"Goes without saying."

"It was a referral," Clem said. "Apparently, she's godmother to that runaway we tracked down in New Orleans."

New Orleans. Blessed, cursed New Orleans. Without that goddamn city, Clem figured, she'd be out of the job. Its proximity to Meridian, a three-hour drive away, and Meridian's location in the east-central hills of Mississippi, two hours from Birmingham, Alabama, and four hours from Atlanta, Georgia, made Clem's hometown a vital pit stop in the loosely affiliated crime belt of the Deep South, one nourished by Louisiana's most notorious city. Thanks to New Orleans, Meridian had become a constellation, the stars of which included gambling, bootlegging, drug-trafficking, number-running, loan-sharking, election-rigging, racketeering, prostitution, extortion, protection, and assassination.

The more crime, Clem knew, the more people needed surveillance, background checks, and countless other services she and Dixon readily provided. Was your husband cheating on you? Signs pointed to yes, in a town with more brothels than bookstores. Had your business partner embezzled to pay down a string of uncovered spreads? Most likely, given the proliferation of bookmakers and the omnipresence of college football.

"Game time," Dixon said as they pulled into a trailer park on Old Country Club Road, and of course, Clem noted, a banner by the front entrance read BIG EASY RV AND MOBILE HOME VILLAGE—THESE GOOD TIMES CAN ROLL, with purple and gold fleurs-de-lys separating the words.

In the crisp morning air, a reprieve from the recent winter heat wave, sloping brown-and-yellow hillocks, some with overgrown but clearly planed tops, testified to the surrounding pasture's former use as a golf course. Cattle grazed around foreclosure signs noting the possibility to rezone. The trailer park looked new to Clem, though she couldn't say for certain. More and more of them were appearing in and outside of town these days. Clem and Dixon passed a community mailbox hutch, on a column of which was posted a REMEMBER TO LEASH YOUR DOG notice. Its letterhead was from Hubbard Developments.

"Your show, boss," Dixon said when they reached Lenora Coogan's trailer.

After knocking on the door, Clem asked her partner, sotto voce, "Why are you wearing aftershave?" and in response, Dixon furrowed and unfurrowed his brow, rubbed his beard, and said, "Wife says it's scratchy. She read in *Mademoiselle* aftershave works as a moisturizer."

"Hello! You must be the private detectives. Please, y'all, come in, come in."

Lenora Coogan, while leading Clem and Dixon into her living area, pushed a finger to the bridge of her thick plastic glasses with lenses the size of drink coasters and retrieved a pack of Viceroys and a lighter from the pocket of her faded blue duster robe. Her slippers shuffled along a spongy carpet going gray with ash instead of age. She lit a cigarette and sat in a Barcalounger. "Please," Lenora said, motioning to the sofa across from her.

On the sofa, seesawed a few inches higher than her partner by his good ol' boy poundage, Clem took out a notepad and a pencil. Her cop brain did a quick survey of the room, cataloguing the spatial layout of the trailer, looking for signs of pets or boyfriends, determining Lenora's age, height, weight, and real hair color, memorizing the shoe prints on the linoleum in the kitchen, noting the Betamax player on top of the twenty-five-inch TV. A rabbit-ear antenna sat next to an out-of-service cable box. It figured. Clem had spent a few years of her childhood in a mobile home not so different from this one. When these sort of folk hit a lick, the first thing they upgraded was the home entertainment, and when the money ran out, so did the cable subscription. Clem knew but too well the sting of that logic.

"Can I offer you a Sanka? Sweet tea?" Lenora said. "Think I have a pitcher of cherry Kool-Aid in the fridge."

"No, but thank you, ma'am," said Dixon. He always knew when to defuse a situation, Clem had to admit. She'd barely had time to register the comment. "You've a darling home," Dixon continued. "I got kin live out this way. Sure quiet, these parts."

"I'm fine as well," Clem said. Keep it business, she told herself. Nothing personal. "We don't want to take up much of your day, ma'am. Just a few questions."

"Let me guess." Lenora pointed at Clem. She scrunched her eyes like a psychic pretending to peer into the past. "You went to Wechsler."

Clem deadpanned, "Quite a deduction." In her head, she heard lockers slamming and bells ringing, teenage gossip muffled by cupped hands and raised textbooks.

"You know, I was proud, them opening the doors. But I reckon that was before your time."

"Ma'am." Clem leaned forward, pencil pressed to pad. "On the phone you said you want us to find the people who killed your son. What exactly did you mean by that?"

"I meant I want y'all to find the fuckers. That so hard to understand?"

Clem glanced at Dixon. "But, ma'am, your son wasn't killed. He jumped off a roof."

Dixon jerked as though cattle-prodded. "And our condolences for your loss."

"My son didn't jump off anything. Fall? Maybe. Pushed? More like." Lenora Coogan pulled the lever on the side of her recliner like a hangman at the gallows. Her legs were flung into the air, riding the catapult of the footrest. "All I know is he did not . . . he would never kill his self."

"Who do you think did?" Clem asked, answering in her mind, *The sidewalk.*

"His employer, 'course. The DM. Lewis knew too much about their operations for them to let his case go to trial."

Now they were getting somewhere with a bit of grip. During her time on the force, Clem had heard everything and nothing about the Dixie Mafia, how it was *really* just a group of semi-unionized hit men, that it was *actually* a branch of the Italian Mafia from New York City. The Dixie Mafia, according to the most believable stories, moved stolen goods, killed on contract, bribed public officials, and, in general, carried out dirty work for those averse to both work and dirt. To cops, they represented what many cases lacked: causality. If a well-to-do businessman was found dead in his home, bullet to the head, no signs of B and E, no items missing—the DM did it. If an antiques shop went up in flames, a clear case of arson but without any insurance policy to make arson profitable—the DM did it.

"Our thing" did not just become "our thang." Clem had always had a hunch the Dixie Mafia was not only more ruthless but also more organized than its Italian forebears, that its genteel, "lost cause" name was part of its cover. She believed the DM had its own code of silence, a Confederate omertà, one enforced by violence or by money. God knew how many people in the department were in its pocket. Until this moment, though, Clem had never heard a direct, seemingly verifiable admission of the Dixie Mafia's existence.

"What exactly did your son do for the DM?" Clem asked Lenora Coogan.

"Oh, little of this, little of that. A mother doesn't want to know, know what I mean? His work helped keep this roof over my head. But since my little Turnip went to jail, I've had to go on the food stamps! Can you believe? Like I was some damn, uh . . ."

One eyebrow hiked, Clem watched, not without a touch of resigned amusement, as the woman shuffled the deck of words in her head. Clem asked, with the same resigned amusement, "Like you were some damn what?"

"I do know one thing." Lenora put out her cigarette in a standing ashtray next to the recliner. "Turnip handled the little birdies on the DM circuit."

"Little birdies?"

"Cockfights."

Clem scribbled on her pad. "Any known associates? With the little birdies."

"Tell the truth, Clementine—"

"*Ms.* Baldwin."

"Tell a truth, Miss Baldwin, I was never partial to that alley of my son's life." Lenora laced her forehead, her eyebrows knitting together. She swallowed significantly. "Turnip could be hard to love, but he always took care of me. May he find peace at last."

The emotion in Lenora's voice as she spoke those words shook a few drops of bitters onto the sugar cube that was Clem's heart. It was typical, and she knew it. Given the amount of bourbon usually in her blood, Clem liked to think at times such as this one, the melted sugar cube and the bitters turned her into an old-fashioned. The name fit, she supposed. Clem was the same as her own go-to cocktail, old-fashioned—in temperament, in principles, in conduct.

But then Lenora had to go and ruin it with her next words. "Girl, fetch me that photo album on that shelf over there."

Dixon jumped from the sofa. "I got it, I got it," he said, retrieving the album and handing it to Lenora. Afterward Clem could feel him giving her the counterpart necessary for a shared, pointed look, one that in this case meant, *I get it, I get it.*

Bound in worn felt glued to floppy cardboard, the open photo album molded to Lenora's lap like an overfed cat. She flipped its pages in clumps. "Here we go. This is of Lewis and some friends on the circuit. Never met them, don't know their names, afraid."

In the photo Lenora handed Clem, Turnip Coogan, holding a beer and shorn of sleeve, stood next to a pickup, locking shoulders with two other men. Clem checked off boxes in her head, for height, age, weight, and race, all of which fell under the heading of "Unexceptional." Of course, she noted, one of these unexceptional shits had, inked on his forearm, a Confederate flag draped ever so artfully from a cross.

"May I hang on to this?" Clem asked Lenora, who flapped her hand in assent. "Like I mentioned on the phone, ma'am, our rate is two hundred dollars a day."

Dixon, who, ever since a client stiffed them after they orchestrated a honeypot scheme involving a lecherous used-car salesman, an expensive two-way mirror, an even more expensive film camera, and an out-of-work actress, had become overly cautious in such matters, said, "Plus expenses."

After writing a check for the first week in advance, Lenora saw Clem and Dixon to her door. "You know, it's strange," she said, squinting in the daylight.

"Ma'am?" said Clem.

"I'd heard y'all were a colored operation." Lenora nodded at Dixon. "But there's him."

Jesus goddamn Christ. When would this woman stop? She'd started with the cherry Kool-Aid, an offer that was almost comical, it was such a caricature; then she'd made her "deduction" that Clem had gone to Wechsler, one of the first schools for Black children in the state, until it had integrated a few decades back; followed by her close call with whatever derogatory term she'd nearly used in reference to food stamps; after which came her all-too-common, all-too-infuriating use of "girl" when asking Clem to fetch the photo album; and now, for the coup de grace, she'd said *colored* as casually as *God bless you*. A universal truth of the South: the so-called poor white trash, perpetually denigrated by the wealthier white trash for their cheap sugary drink powders, their reliance on public education and federal handouts, their servile positions in the social, cultural, and economic hierarchy, found absurd and misguided reprisal in denigrating the Black people of the South for those very same things.

If Clem weren't so used to this sort of thing, if she hadn't spent her entire life wielding blows, with a dented and nicked shield of armor to show for it, she might have lost her cool with Lenora Coogan. Unfortunately, her partner, usually so adept at alleviating these situations, was less battle-hardened. "I've had just about enough with that kind of language," Dixon said, crimson in the face. "Ma'am, you owe my partner an apology."

"It's okay, Dixon. She's right." Clem turned to Lenora. "Little while back, I decided to desegregate my operation." She smiled at her new client, the same way she had at her partner when, years ago, he'd found the courage to ask why she'd even hired him in the first place. Clem said, "Coffee tastes better with a touch of cream, don't you think?"

It was difficult to be a Black woman in Ronald Reagan's America. It was even more difficult to be a Black woman in 1980s Mississippi. But to be a

Black woman who was also a private investigator in both of those places? Now, that was near about impossible.

Clem Baldwin was a pragmatist at heart. After years of disregard by the white bureaucrats in city hall, scorn from the white housewives and mechanics and prep-school kids she questioned in the field, rejection by white clients, belittlement by white suspects, and, unsurprisingly, if she was being honest, smaller-scale occasions of disregard, scorn, rejection, and belittlement from the Black people she dealt with on a case, Clem came up with a solution.

She needed a prop.

This prop, Clem concluded, had to be completely useless in most circumstances, but, in hers, as handy as locking hubs on a muddy day. In other words, the prop had to be a white man.

The guy needed to have hominy for gray matter and little to no imagination or initiative, the type who wouldn't get in Clem's way on a case but would also, through his being that pervasive and as such inherently unimpressive thing, a white man, lend her the authority she already deserved—wait, correction: the authority she had already *earned*.

Dixon Hicks, whose name said it all, was the fourth person she interviewed for the position. Given Dixon's military background, Clem figured that, in addition to providing a sense of authority for her clients and other people she encountered on an investigation, he might offer the fringe benefit of physicality. On occasion, a runner had to be subdued, an eye blacked, a pinkie snapped, a door busted in. Clem had not, however, planned on a fringe benefit of friendship.

"She's a crackpot, right?" said the white man Clem was still, after two years of working together, surprised to think of as her friend. "I mean, the Dixie Mafia? That's a myth."

"People used to think that about the KKK. Then one ran for president."

They were walking through the marble sarcophagus that was the Lauderdale County Courthouse. After a week of not getting an appointment with District Attorney Will Pickett, Clem had managed to get one with the assistant DA, Russ Clyde. He happened to have an opportune crush on Clem, one she may or may not have aggrandized, strategically or tipsily, by making out with him in the Howard Johnson parking lot last month.

Russ's secretary, who Clem guessed was a former waitress, given she used a check spindle as a memo holder for carbon copies, led them into an office pungent with aerosol deodorant and squash-racket grip.

"Clementine!" Russ said, nearly knocking coffee onto his pleated slacks.

"We're here on business, Mr. Clyde. Call me *Ms.* Baldwin, please and thank you."

"Of course, of course. Have a seat, Miss Baldwin. How can I help you?"

On shelves throughout the office, law books gathered dust. Next to an open window hung a framed photograph of what looked to be either a lily pad or a diaphragm. The handwritten line at the bottom of the photo, noting its provenance in a sexual assault case, almost caused Clem to say out loud, *Ugh*. Instead, she asked, "Your boss doesn't want to meet with me. Why is that?"

"Will's busy these days, and he's given the incident more than enough time with the press. And he's not so self-indulgent to keep harping on his own act of heroism."

"Is it heroic to push a man off a ledge?"

"Listen, I know why you're here, and I know who hired you. Lenora Coogan has been going all over town saying her boy was killed. It's simply not true."

Clem and Dixon had been going all over town as well, asking about the same thing. In the week since they'd been hired, the pair had become bucket-seat scholars on the Hubbard murder. Clem might have considered the case open-shut, if not for some odd, rather fecal discrepancies. It seemed clear that Turnip Coogan had indeed been hired by Odette Hubbard to kill her husband, Randy, a real estate developer making advances through town with small-scale enterprises, your dollar stores, your trailer parks, your gas stations, your fried-chicken stands. The man was hardly a mogul. He didn't seem especially well-liked among Meridian's doctor-and-lawyer caste, the majority of whom had denied him membership at the Lakeshoals Country Club. According to his disconcertingly bribable accountant, Hubbard had leveraged himself to the hilt, and his life insurance policy for half a million dollars, the one his wife wanted to reap, wouldn't have benefited her. It had been used by Hubbard to secure loans to construct a shopping center off Highway 19.

So, the way Clem saw it, you had a rich man who actually wasn't, a wife who wanted insurance money she never would have gotten, and at the center, Turnip Coogan, some half-wit cockfighter who forgot the county jail was located on the courthouse roof, who admitted to having called in a hit but claimed to have canceled it, who may or may not have been connected with a perhaps apocryphal organization thought to be involved with every major crime committed in the South. The whole situation reeked of shit.

"Let me run a few things by you, Mr. Clyde." With her use of that impersonal name, Clem spotted a mournful flinch at the corners of Russ's adoring eyes. She took out her notepad and flipped its pages. "Randall Hubbard had his fingers in quite of few pies, real estate–wise?"

"I think he even owned a pie business."

"Sister Jemima's Homemade Pies. Don't know how the Aunt Jemima people didn't sue."

"Meridian, Mississippi," Dixon said. "Not exactly the capital of the world."

"Worlds don't have capitals. Countries do." Clem could never resist teasing Dixon.

He gave her his signature half eye roll and slight mouth-shrug and said, "What about states?" Dixon, as with Clem's teasing, could never resist pretending to be the idiot she'd originally hired him to be. "Do states got capitals? How about letters? Economies?"

Clem turned back to Russ. "Hubbard was also known to frequent some rough spots." She looked through her notes. "East End Tea Room? John Wesley Hardin Club?"

"And don't forget Ho Jo's," Russ said, referring to the bar at the Howard Johnson in Meridian. His dopey, fawning grin at the allusion to what had happened in the parking lot shriveled when he saw Clem's stern-faced refusal to reciprocate the nostalgia. Russ cleared his throat. "Yes, uh, it's public record that Hubbard had a few altercations at some of the, at some of the, the more disorderly business concerns in town, and usually with what we like to call our *frequent fliers*. Real lowlifes, I'm saying."

"Like what?"

"Certainly not like me!"

"I meant," Clem said, "like what sort of altercations?"

"Oh. Oh. I thought you meant the . . . well, and because I'm talking to a friend, I can divulge that Hubbard, when he visited said business concerns, most often, and for good reason, had a bodyguard with him."

"Armed?"

"He wouldn't be much of one if he weren't."

Clem asked for the bodyguard's name even though she and Dixon had already questioned him. At six foot four and nearly three hundred pounds, that tree had been awful big for nothing to shake out of it. "Turnip said Odette had hired him as *her* bodyguard," Clem said. "Did she ever have an altercation at the East End Tea Room, the John Wesley Hardin Club?"

"A few. Look, what are you getting at here, Clem—Miss Baldwin?"

"I'm wondering if anyone witnessed Turnip or Odette meeting with the man Turnip said he hired for the hit. This, this, what was his name?" Squinting as though to read small print, Clem flipped through blank pages in her notepad.

"Jacob Cassidy."

"That's right, Jacob Cassidy," Clem said, filing in her mind the name everyone she had so far questioned refused to give. As of yet she'd managed to create only a tenuous mental composite of the man. Cassidy, according to those who'd encountered him, was over six feet tall, with shoulder-length hair. He drank bourbon and Coke but also, on occasion, Bloody Marys, "because he was worried about being picked up for drunk driving again." Also, he had two hairline scars, wide-set shoulders, and, as nearly everyone mentioned, "cold blue eyes."

"Any leads on his whereabouts, this Jacob Cassidy?" Clem asked Russ.

"You know I can't say."

"Why did Will Pickett push Coogan off the roof?"

"Stop it, okay?"

"What are your leads on the whereabouts of Jacob Cassidy?"

"Enough."

"Did Will Pickett order his investigator to shoot Coogan when they were on that roof?"

"You're embarrassing yourself."

"So then tell me what you know about the location of Jacob Cassidy."

"It's sad, really."

"Ru-uss."

In response to that word, how Clem had stretched it, hacked its syllable in two, and dropped into contralto, Russ lost all playfulness in his demeanor. He looked so hurt, professionally and, worse, personally. Clem realized she'd crossed an unseen line. She'd gone from coyly badgering Russ to blatantly seducing him. Wasn't that the problem with all decent guys these days? They were okay with you leading them on, but as soon as you did so for purely selfish and cruel reasons, they got offended. Clem didn't know what the world was coming to.

Russ stared at his necktie. He ran his index finger and thumb down the entire length of it as though he were extending the slide of a trombone. "I think I've given you enough information for one day."

"I meant," Clem said, but she couldn't bring herself to add, *no offense*. This was one of the men, after all, who'd put her father away. Then again, Clem had to admit, she was hardly blameless herself in that matter. "Thank you for your time," she said right as Russ's secretary came into the office, her unharried urgency reaffirming Clem's guess she used to be a waitress.

Without noting the interruption, the secretary marched behind Russ's desk, whispered in his ear, and handed him a memo.

Russ, after reading the message, gave Clem an odd look, at once perplexed and suspicious. His face got so constricted it was like staring directly at the point of a Phillips-head screwdriver. "Have a nice day, Clementine."

Outside the office, where the secretary led them, Clem tilted her head at Dixon, letting him know to hold up a moment. She turned to the secretary with her most winning and therefore most counterfeit smile.

"Did you used to work at the Red Hot?" Clem asked, referring to a truck-stop diner frequented as often by her clients as by the people they hired her to investigate. "I would come in late-night."

"I slang coffee at the Waffle House. That must be what you're thinking of."

"Must be it." Clem pointed toward the floor. "I'm in love with those pumps, by the way."

The secretary, looking down, raised her ankle. She pulled up her dress an inch and, clearly flattered, said, "These old things?"

Clem waited until she and Dixon were a block from the courthouse before she looked at the carbon copy she'd slipped off the check spindle on the secretary's desk. It was a message about the results of a toxicology report. "That old bat was right after all," Clem said to her partner, the carbon copy fluttering in her fingers, the horns and engine sputters of street traffic obscuring her words.

Turnip Coogan had been poisoned. He was likely dead by the time he hit the sidewalk.

3

GOOD MORNING, AMERICA

It was morning again in America. On his drive through the outskirts of Slidell, Louisiana, a man who over the years had been known as Jacob Kilpatrick, Jacob Carver, Jacob Longabaugh, Jacob Hanks, and Jacob Cassidy played a game called "Good Morning, America!" His daughter had invented it. After seeing, for the thousandth time, Ronald Reagan's reelection campaign ads on how it was morning again in America, Jacob's little girl, Sue June, grudgingly weaned off her bedtime addiction to *Goodnight Moon*, started to say those three words as a both a fix and a rebuke to her dad's insistence he couldn't read her favorite picture book to her again without losing his damn mind.

Sue June had loved playing the game on car rides. When she saw a cloud that looked like a rooster playing the flute, she'd say, "Good morning, America!" When they passed her favorite snowball stand, the one that did rainbow sprinkles at no extra charge, she'd say, "Good morning, America!"

This afternoon, driving alone for work, Jacob repeated the saying despite not having an audience. He passed a foreclosure sign. "Good morning, America." He passed a deer processing center. "Good morning, America." Near the Twin Span, glittery with broken bottles and lumpy with discarded fast-food sacks, the brands of which were painted on billboards overshadowing traffic, Jacob exited the interstate and turned down a side street, Lake Pontchartrain tracking his passage from residential to commercial, commercial to industrial, industrial to mixed-use, and back again. "Good morning, America." He passed the playground where Sue June had collapsed. He passed the hospital where her leukemia had been diagnosed. He passed the stoplight where he'd sobbed through the news that nothing could be done. "Good morning, America."

Jacob pulled over at a pay phone. He usually preferred the kind with a booth, for the privacy, but he'd done enough driving this afternoon to shake any tails that might be following him.

"It's me," he said after slotting his ten cents and dialing the usual number.

A man coughed on the other end. "Any heat since your last trip to Meridian?" asked Jacob's handler, his voice shagged by God knew how many packs of cigarettes.

"Nada."

"Might be some coming soon. The MPD," said Jacob's handler, drawing out the letters derisively, "up and decided to waste Johnny Taxpayer's hard-earned and run a blood test on Humpty Dumpty."

"Shit."

"Correct. But that's not why we needed to talk. The mother hired a PI, some ex-cop who's meddled in the organization's affairs before."

"Like how?"

"Unimportant. Main thing, it's been decided she can't be allowed any meddling again."

"She?"

Jacob's handler laughed. "Buddy, ol' pal, that ain't even the half of it."

After getting details on the job, Jacob took a route home even longer than his route to the pay phone had been, all while keeping eyes on his rearview. *Meddling.* That word reminded him of Sue June's favorite cartoon, the one about a big dog and a gang of hippie kids who rambled around the country solving mysteries. Whenever they caught the bad guy, who was usually after something as pedestrian but lucrative as real estate, he'd curse "you meddling kids."

Turnip Coogan had been a lot like the fella called Shaggy, always highstrung, whether chemically or situationally induced, and, when Jacob first met him, in search of a dog. Usually a cockfighter, Turnip had been looking to expand into the canine trade, and Jacob had sold him one of his

Dobermans. The next time he heard from Turnip? A phone call offering thirty-large for Jacob to take out a rooster that some hen wanted rid of.

The hen turned out to be Odette Hubbard. Jacob should've known better than to trust that woman. Talk about a piece of work. It served her right to be cooling her dainty, scrubbed heels in county lockup, counting the days until the trial.

In the cab of his truck, Jacob tried to distract himself from the shit show that had been the Hubbard job, including its cleanup, by changing the radio station. It helped as little as the goofballs his doctor at the VA gave him for his stress flashbacks. Outside the city limits, he passed a newly built "retail park," with a liquor store named LIQUOR STORE and a tanning salon named TANNING SALON. Jacob didn't know what the hell was going on with the world. A few years ago, this area had been considered the backwoods. Now it was a riot of commerce. The world had become one goddamn thing after the other: the Tet Offensive in '68, Camille in '69, the boundless line of *llelo* that was the '70s, and now the '80s, a boom time, the TV said, but not boom enough for a new carburetor, or repairs on the plumbing, or a child's health insurance.

The smell of noodles and black bean sauce welcomed Jacob when he walked through the front door. In the living room, he asked his mother-in-law, "*Halmoni, oneul bam TV joh-eungeo eseo?*"

With the clicker she gestured toward the television set. "*Wheel.*"

"You've got the hots for Pat Sajak. Don't even think I haven't noticed."

Jacob found his wife, Min, in the kitchen, stirring a saucepan with a wooden spoon. He hooked his chin over her shoulder and gave her butt a playful squeeze. "'S for supper?"

"Beeswax," she said. "The nunya kind."

"My favorite."

From the fridge, the door to which still, though it had been a year, presented a collage of Sue June's artwork, including Froot Loops glued into the shape of a T. rex and her paint handprint as the foundation for a Thanksgiving turkey, Jacob retrieved a beer. He pulled its tab, closed the door, and stared at a life line, heart line, head line, fate line.

"How was work?" Min asked.

Jacob turned away from the fridge and took a swallow of his beer. "Work's work. You know."

"Foreman still a pain in the ass?"

"Ever and always. We've got a job in Mississippi next week. I may be gone a few days."

Min, holding the sauce spoon with one hand and cupping her other beneath it, motioned for Jacob to have a taste. After he had tried the sauce and nodded in approval, she gave him a peck on the lips and said, "Be sure to miss me."

In the garage, where he told his wife he was going to get some tools, Jacob finished his beer. A sawhorse stood in the corner. Screwdrivers and wrenches hung from a pegboard on the wall. A soup can of screws sat on the worktable. Jacob walked past them.

He used a stepladder to reach one of the ceiling tiles, which he removed, and, groping blindly, found his black attaché case. He replaced the ceiling tile, set his case on the table, and opened it. A kill kit, Jacob's mentor in the DM had called the case when he bequeathed it to his protégé. Jacob double-checked the contents of the kit—his .380-caliber semiautomatic, two walkie-talkies, four boxes of ammunition, handcuffs, Mace, a syringe and a vial of poison, ninja throwing stars, and two sets of brass knuckles—while repeating the name Clementine Baldwin in his mind like an incantation. He shut the case and whispered good morning to America.

4

THE JOHN WESLEY HARDIN CLUB

Only a place like Meridian would have, among its many venues of infamous repute, a bar named for arguably the deadliest gunfighter of the American frontier, a man who killed forty-two people, including one for the sin of snoring too loudly. Clem had to hand it to this town. It wanted to be the Old West when it was actually just the same Old South.

"We going in heavy?" Dixon asked Clem as they pulled into the John Wesley Hardin Club's parking lot.

Clem rolled her eyes at her partner. Of course they were going in heavy.

After retrieving his piece from the glove compartment, Dixon, whose bladder was smaller than a toddler's, excused himself to "take a squirt" behind a dumpster. Clem didn't have the patience to wait for him. She approached the one-story cinder-block building, pea gravel crunching beneath her feet.

The bouncer sat on a lopsided stool by the door, writing in pencil on a folded copy of *The Meridian Star*. He looked like the Michelin Man, with rolls of flesh instead of stacked white tires. "What's a three-letter word for smoked herring?" he asked Clem without looking up from the paper.

"Fuck should I know?"

That united his formerly divided attention, Clem was happy to see. She'd never been a fan of bouncers. They had a tendency to get in her way. This one, after giving her two and a half seconds of droop-lidded analysis, blinked deliberately, sighed deliberately, and said, "We don't allow your kind in here."

Her kind? Clem almost couldn't believe it. "My kind? What is this, the fifties? There a sign on the wall, says, 'No Negroes Allowed'?"

"Huh?" The bouncer got to his feet. "We don't allow *cops* in here, asshole."

"Oh." Blood pooled in Clem's cheeks and forehead. She asked, "Does it matter I'm not a cop anymore?" to which the bouncer made a face that meant, *Once one, always one.*

To hide her embarrassment, Clem took a step back, giving this guy her own two and a half seconds of droop-lidded analysis. She figured he weighed at least a deuce-fifty. It was time to put her boy to work. "Dixon," she called toward the dumpster. "I could use some help over here."

"Coming."

Without turning away from the bouncer, Clem followed Dixon's passage across the parking lot by the crunching of gravel. "This guy giving you trouble?" he asked when he'd reached her side.

Clem couldn't help but smirk at the bouncer. "Lots of trouble. You mind?"

"Nope." Dixon squared himself in front of the bouncer, their faces only a few inches apart. Each thump of bass from the music inside the club matched the heartbeat Clem could feel in both her temples. She forgot to breathe, the tension was so exquisite.

In a deep, sinister voice, Dixon asked the bouncer, "How's your mother?"

"She's doing well, Dix. Thanks for asking." A beatific smile broke across the bouncer's face. "Your family hanging in there?"

"Best can be expected. You know how it is." His smile mirroring the bouncer's, Dixon pointed at the door to the club. "Hey, listen, can we get in here a sec? Got business matters."

Inside the club, where the bouncer allowed them with his best wishes that they enjoy their night, Dixon ticked his head at Clem. "He was my lineman at Meridian High."

Sometimes Clem had to remind herself that Dixon had been the town's boy wonder in his youth, the star quarterback, king of the prom. Then came the draft. Dixon was shipped to Vietnam, while his counterpart from the local private school, the grandson of a state Supreme Court justice, ended up quarterbacking for Ole Miss and now owned half a dozen successful car dealerships and twice as many Domino's franchises.

Dixon's return from the war, according to the stories he told on stake-outs, had been met with a thunderclap of silence. Both his parents having passed away, his mother from cancer when he was still in diapers and his father of a heart attack while Dixon was overseas, the erstwhile boy wonder of Meridian put his green beret and various medals of honor in a shoebox, married his high school sweetheart, and joined the growing ranks of white veterans, some angry, some bitter, many both, applying for a dwindling number of jobs at the steel mill, the lumberyard, the auto plant, and even the manufacturer of audio equipment to which everybody in town had pinned their hope that Meridian would return to its former economic glory. Dixon, Clem thanked God, was "one of the good ones," as her colleagues on the force used to say of a different type of person, oblivious or simply not giving a shit that Clem was standing right there.

As she and her partner walked through the John Wesley Hardin Club, Clem witnessed the opposite of Dixon—an entire room full of people who were not the good ones. Their entitlement curdled and their privilege drained, the men glaring at Clem from their bar tables, through greasy, unkempt hair, had the dangerous look of those caged by a newfound lack of fortune in life. Instead of empathy for their fellow oppressed, especially ones who had been so for centuries, this merry bunch exuded a nearly palpable craving to reclaim the position of oppressor. Clem honestly couldn't tell if their hostile stares owed more to the color of her skin, that she was a woman, or the fact she used to be a badge.

A bit of each, she figured, noting that instead of chips on their shoulders the bar patrons of the John Wesley Hardin Club favored bulges at their ankles. Out of habit Clem pressed her elbow against the bulge of her own piece, a Beretta 92, where it was holstered beneath her shoulder.

"Guess that's why they call them *honky*-tonks," Clem whispered to Dixon, who responded, not unsympathetically, "She says to a born and raised honky."

The club was as unimaginatively designed on the inside as it had been on the outside. Clem supposed people who still considered themselves at war must have been comforted by the aesthetics of a bunker. Calligraphic neon advertising Schlitz and Dixie and Budweiser hung from the cinder-block walls. Fly tape, likely dating from the Carter administration and studded with desiccated fly corpses, dangled from the cork ceiling tiles. In one corner, an old Studebaker of a jukebox played Cream covering Robert Johnson's "Play Pretty Blues."

At the metal-top bar, Clem and Dixon commandeered two stools and, from a bartender with a pharmaceutical gleam to her eyes, ordered two shots of bourbon. Clem said, "I'm looking for a friend of mine," as the bartender sloshed well liquor into plastic shot glasses.

"You don't say."

"He's tall, at least six feet. Shoulder-length hair. He drinks Beam and Coke. Bloody Marys, come time to sober up for the road."

"This friend of yours must be awful close, if you don't know his name."

"Jacob Cassidy."

Clem almost pitied this girl, she gave herself away so quick. At mention of that name, the bartender paused her erratic swiping of the bar with a rag. Her color fell off to a shade of dryer sheet. Her dilated pupils stayed that way, only more noticeably, with her eyes widened.

"When's the last time you saw him?" Dixon asked, filling Clem with pride. He'd been with her long enough to have noted the same tells.

The bartender swallowed gum she hadn't been chewing. "Not for a while. Cassidy hasn't been here since, I don't know, since Christmastime. Maybe New Year's?"

"Any regular associates?" Clem said, already reaching for her coat pocket.

"Nope."

After slipping it from her pocket, Clem placed a $20 bill on the bar. "Ever see him with Odette Hubbard or Turnip Coogan?"

"Who?"

With a face full of smile and a smile full of teeth, Clem said, "You must have confused me for a soft fucking touch."

The bartender snatched up the twenty. "Okay, fine. I saw him with Turnip. But, hey, listen. Molly didn't have nothing to do with it. Please don't start trouble. I got her this job."

Molly? To find that LP, Clem flipped through the record crate of her mind, cheap plastic slipcovers buffeting cheap plastic slipcovers. Nothing came up under *M* except for Miranda, the rights Clem was happy to no longer have to read, and Dr. Sam Mott, her orthodontist back in junior high. She checked *J* and *W* and *H* for John and Wesley and Hardin, to no avail. Finally, Clem found a Molly right where she should have started her search all along—under *C*, for Coogan.

According to what Clem knew, Turnip and his wife had been estranged at the time of his death. Molly Coogan was on Clem's list of people to question, to be sure, but far from the top. Now it turned out she worked at the very club where Turnip had met with the man who more than likely murdered Randall Hubbard. There had to be a connection.

"Don't worry," Clem told the bartender. "We won't start any trouble. We just want to ask Molly a few questions. What's her section?"

Clem scanned the women in the part of the club pointed out by the bartender, ignoring the overserved, underdressed ones seated around the tables, skipping the even more overserved, underdressed ones dancing between and on the tables, until she spotted a tall girl with ginger hair carrying a drink tray and wearing an apron over a significantly pregnant belly. She really was just a girl. Clem guessed she was no older than twenty-five.

"Mama Coogan told me y'all might come 'round," the girl said after Clem and Dixon approached her and asked if they could talk about her husband. She led them to an empty table in a corner of the club. "I only get five minutes for breaks."

"We'll be quick," Dixon said. "But you really should stay off your feet. How far along?"

"Twenty-six weeks."

"That all? I would've guessed—"

"Molly," Clem said, verbally kicking Dixon in the foot. He had a thing about pregnant women. And old people. And babies. And every goddamn dog he'd ever met. Clem said to Molly, "What would you say was the last time you saw your husband?"

"Oh, the arraignment. I just couldn't bring myself to visit him in jail."

"And it was during the evidentiary hearing you testified to having met the man Turnip hired to murder Randall Hubbard?"

"Yes, ma'am."

"Clem's fine."

"Except I didn't say in court Turnip hired Jacob. I know for a fact he did, but I've seen what the DM does to finks." Clem's neck tightened at the reference to the Dixie Mafia. An admittedly grown-ass woman, she was a touch embarrassed by her excitement in wondering, Could the boogeymen be real? Her embarrassment was aggrandized all the more by the second part of her internal query: And did the boogeymen have a *union*?

Her Southern accent as syrupy as freezer vodka, Molly said, "Turnip bought a Doberman pincer from Jacob, how they first met. He thought there was more money in dogfights than cocks."

"Pins*ch*er."

"Huh?"

"Never mind."

"But I wouldn't let Turnip fight Chekov. I love that dog. He's my precious little boy."

"Named after Anton?" Clem asked.

"Pavel. My brother named him. Huge *Trek* fan. He'd go as a different character every Halloween. One year he went as Uhura, if you can believe it. *That* got some looks."

They were getting off topic. Clem had to realign this girl's attention. Over the next fifteen minutes, nary a damn given for the time constraints of her break, Molly Coogan described how her "shit-ass" of a husband, "blinded by that Hubbard woman's tits," had hired Jacob Cassidy. The original offer was $15,000. Cassidy had planned to do the job in the courthouse, with a needle and poison, "just prick him in the ass like it was nothing, and wait for him to die," but Odette, believing she and Randy might reconcile, called it off. Another snag to the hit? Randy Hubbard had hired extra bodyguards, including ones for each of his two children from a previous marriage. "Like his own private football team, armed to the teeth. I heard his boy even kept a pistol in his backpack, which, knowing this town, made him peculiar as a tick on a mangy dog," Molly said, a statement Clem was versed in Meridian's society and culture well enough to know to be true. It might have even been an understatement.

Obviously, from what Molly told Clem and Dixon, any potential reconciliation between Odette and Randy Hubbard shriveled, with Odette giving her lawyer an eight-page letter detailing the numerous times Randy beat her, and with Randy giving his own lawyer a letter that requested, if he died, a full autopsy. At that point, Molly told Clem and Dixon, Odette found a revitalized passion for her husband's untimely death. She offered Jacob $30,000 for the hit, and agreed to pay Turnip $250,000 for setting everything up. "Except she called it off *again*, on the day of, if you can believe," Molly said. "Jacob had already gotten to Meridian with his partner, and I heard him say to Turnip, he said, 'Turnip, I've come to take care of business.'"

"Did you say *partner*?" Clem asked. This was the first she'd heard of Cassidy having a partner.

"Yuh-huh. He said his name was Flynn. Jacob said he was his cousin."

Dixon leaned forward, tilting at what Clem hoped wasn't a windmill. "Did you get a look at him?"

"He had brown hair. Little guy. I'd say he was twenty-two, twenty-three."

The geometry was all wrong with this case. Clem couldn't get a handle on its shape. Over the years, she'd come to think of the problem as isosceles, with two strains of reasoning of equal length leading to a disproportionate conclusion, either too wide or too narrow. Say you were a cop who believed in justice but forwent that belief because you believed in justice too much, and say you first decided to become a cop because the man you idolized more than anyone turned out to be a criminal. Voilà! You were now a private detective. Two strains of faulty but oddly logical reasoning—denouncing justice because it was an impossible standard, becoming the opposite of a criminal because you were raised by one—leading to a conclusion that wasn't equilateral: choosing the job of neither cop nor crook, a warrior for truth more than justice, vindication more than truth, but only if your price could be met, the checks cleared, and expenses were covered.

With this case the conclusion was similarly disproportionate. Odette and Randy had reached a stalemate in their marriage and in its sad dissolution, each holding written evidence against the other, Randy with his letter to his lawyer, Odette with her letter about Randy's abuse. Odette wanted the insurance money, yes, but Randy, if he feared for his life enough to write that letter to his lawyer, must have told her that the money would be tied up with his company, out of her reach, in the event of his death. That had to be the reason Odette called off the hit. So then how and, more important, why did Randy S. Hubbard end up with two bullets in his shoulder, four in his back, and one in his head at approximately 11:00 P.M. on March 27, 1984?

Now to that geometry with two sides of equal length and one not, the Queen City detectives had to add a heretofore-unknown accomplice named Flynn.

Clem, sitting across from the wife of the man who originally called in the hit, reminded herself of still another property unique to isosceles triangles. Their base angles always pointed back toward the vertex point.

"How much do you know about how your late husband made a living?" Clem asked Molly.

"Turnip hauled freight for Pathrite."

"I'm talking about his other living."

"Other kind of living is there?"

"Are you aware of any supplementary income your husband was involved in?" Clem, spotting confusion in Molly's face, decided to come right out with it. "What can you tell me about the Dixie Mafia?"

A flinch. That was all Clem needed to see. But the girl hadn't flinched a muscle, which meant she was used to talking about the DM and her husband's involvement. Clem was getting close.

"You hear stories," Molly said, calm as a coma patient. "Drugs. Break-ins. Burn-downs. The birds. Turnip was deep in the birds, I know you know. Mama Coogan said she told you. It was the DM, his circuit. Bunch of good ol' boys. Their flag isn't the one with fifty stars, you follow?"

"I follow."

"Their daddies taught them to pop a clip, line a sight. Deer first. Quail. Ducks. Government taught them the rest."

"Military?"

"College wasn't really an option. *You* know."

Clem, sighing in her mind instead of out loud, said, "I went to college."

"For serious?"

Dixon asked, "Was Jacob Cassidy in the DM?" He laid a forearm on the table exactly halfway between Clem and Molly, a hairy, sinewy, pale line in a division symbol.

"You'd have to ask Jacob."

At the same moment Molly said those words, her gaze wandered beyond the area where they were sitting, the look on her face one that Clem first mistook for disgust with these recreationally racist, joyfully obtuse patrons of the John Wesley Hardin Club. Clem quickly realized her error. The look on Molly's face after she mentioned Jacob expressed a saying that, when true, Clem had always thought, was disconcertingly accurate: *Speak of the devil.*

The first bullet hit the wall behind Molly, erupting gray shards of cinder block. Clem, recognizing the sound of a semiautomatic, melted time, a trick she'd learned at the academy. By fully welcoming the launched rocket that was her heart rate, she was able to heighten her sensory focus to the extent that time seemed to melt, the world downshifting into slow motion.

An ashtray that had been knocked off the table by Molly's excited hand hung frozen in the air by Clem's knee, lipstick-stained cigarette butts revolving above it. Gunshots—one, two, six, twelve—overlapped into a ceaseless, deafening boom. A dotted line like a sentence in Braille was slowly stenciled into the wall, pulverized cinder block flying from each bullet hole. Only after Clem had jumped at Molly, pushed her to the floor, rolled on her back, and drawn her piece did the velocity of the world return to normal speed.

The ashtray clattering by Clem's elbow sounded like a trigger being pulled.

5

MPD

Hours after the shoot-out, which ended without casualties, only scrapes and bruises and minor cuts, Clementine Baldwin sat in an interrogation room at the Meridian Police Department. She was the only person from the altercation who'd been taken in for questioning, despite likely having been the only person at the John Wesley Hardin Club whose firearm had been properly registered.

Not to mention, Clem thought while twisting her wrists inside their cuffs, she didn't have a record and, in fact, was a former officer of the law.

Clem smirked at the two-way mirror. Years earlier, when she was on the other side of that glass, she'd hated how suspects tended to smirk at the mirror. Now it seemed the only expression her face would muster. Clem wondered who might be looking back at her. Some newbie who didn't know she used to be a badge? That seemed most likely. She still had friends in the department. Unfortunately, one of the few detectives who was very much not her friend opened the door and, whistling, *whistling*, sat down across from her.

"How's it going, T. C.?" asked Detective John Poissant. It pissed Clem off how much that joke always pissed her off. In her partnership with Dixon, she was obviously Thomas Magnum, minus the sports car and moustache and shorty shorts.

"Going well, Pissant."

"Poissant. *Detective* Poissant."

John Poissant had only recently returned to the status of "Detective" John Poissant. Clem had been responsible for his getting busted two grades. Hence their less-than-amicable rapport. The son of a bitch had beaten a suspect nearly to death, after all. The suspect was Clem's collar, which made him sort of like a child to her. Never mind the suspect had murdered an actual child.

"Still getting confessions down in Cellblock QT?" Clem asked, referring to a defunct laundry room in the basement, with broken Maytags lined against the walls, mop buckets standing vigil in the corners, and blood splatters on the ceiling from a vice officer and former Golden Gloves champion known for his temper and vicious uppercut.

"Always with the cute bullshit, Baldwin. Now why in fuck were you at a place like the John Wesley Hardin?"

"Trying to figure out who killed Turnip Coogan, i.e., doing your job."

"Oh, come on. Turnip died from a severe case of sidewalk."

Clem watched herself smirk in the two-way. "That's not what the toxicology report says. The matter, Poissant? Captain still not trust you enough to keep you in the loop?"

"Sneaky-ass PIs. You stole the report? I swear, Mississippi needs to start requiring y'all to be licensed."

"We're not beauticians. *Their* state licensure is rigorous. Priorities, I guess."

The sallow overhead light reflected in his balding pate, Poissant leaned back in his chair, buckled his hands across his suspendered belly, stretched his unshaven face into an amused grimace, and said, "Cute."

Again with the *cute*. How did Southerners manage to turn any word with four letters into a four-letter word? Southern white women began the evolution of *cute*, using its malleable number of syllables to describe everything from A-line dresses to their best friend's baby to a cocktail napkin printed with IT'S WINE THIRTY, Y'ALL! Southern white men then acted like Southern white men. In the prison of their pathetic masculinity, they sharpened the word into a shiv. Clem had been stabbed by it so many times. Her ass was cute. Her attitude was cute. She should quit being cute. "Show me that cute smile."

Poissant put his arms on the cheap card table between him and Clem. "Did you get eyes on the shooter?"

"Enough with the cute pose. We both know who it was and why I was in his sights. Your next moves? Get on the horn, put out a BOLO for Jacob

Cassidy, and then tell me how he managed to break *into* a jail located *on top of* a courthouse and poison a prisoner."

A dial in the trash-ridden, coffee-ringed control room inside Poissant's mind seemed to rotate from "Super-Hard-Ass" to "Semi-Hard-Ass." He slumped forward. "We think it was put into his food. No solid leads with the kitchen staff. Custodial? Maybe."

"What do you know about a man named Flynn?"

"Flynn?"

"Possible accomplice on the Hubbard murder."

"First I'm hearing the name. Cassidy acted alone, we think. We thought."

"Do y'all think, have y'all thought the DM might be involved?"

Whatever professional camaraderie Poissant had been starting to show Clem suddenly shut down. He turned back into just about every cop she'd ever met. He turned into an embodiment of the department itself. Crossing his arms, with a face as featureless, blocky, and plum-colored as the exterior of a strip club, Poissant said, "The DM is a fairy tale."

The door of the interrogation room swung open. "Jesus Christ, John. You've got her in cuffs?"

In the doorway stood one of Clem's best friends from her years on the force.

Samantha Bellflower had been a patrol officer in the same cohort as Clem, and through their shared ambition to make detective in record time, as well as being the only two women of the MPD not in dispatch or the secretarial pool, they quickly grew as close as the stripes they each wanted on the sleeves of their dress blues. Half Native American, Sam had grown up on the Choctaw reservation outside Philadelphia, Mississippi. She and Clem were often referred to by other officers as cousins or sisters, because *obviously,* she and Clem tended to say in response, any two people who weren't blindingly white *had* to be related. A gentle pat on the officer's invariably prominent gut helped for emphasis.

In the years since Clem had given up her shield, Sam had ditched the starched polyester of patrol for a detective's wrinkled sack suit, but she still took neither guff nor shit. Clem could see that fact as Sam entered the interrogation room, told Poissant where "it" could be shoved, apologized to Clem for not getting there sooner, and unlocked her handcuffs.

Poissant stood, propping himself against the table with his fists. "Oh, ho, ho! Samantha and Clementine, Clementine and Samantha. Peas in a fucking pod. Back in the sack again, uh? Hey, Sam, tell me something. What's that thing the little Dutch boy stuck his finger into?"

"Your mother?"

The department's rumpus room, where Sam led Clem by the arm—for show, Clem hoped—had, unsurprisingly, not changed since the days when Clem used to clean house at the poker table. Some plainclothes she didn't recognize was sleeping one off on a secondhand-sectional-turned-modern-art with the reds, yellows, and greens of spilt hot-dog condiments. At a buckled laminate table, an old-timer waited for his pension to vest with either the crossword or the word find in a folded copy of *The Meridian Star*. Clem, intimate with the brain trust that was her old department, could only surmise it to be the word find. Guys like these could spot *sneakers* in a jumble of letters, but try asking for an eight-letter word that meant "Generic Reebok" or "Collective Converse."

"Coffee?" Sam said, waggling her flask at Clem. Without waiting for an answer, she poured shots of bourbon into two coffee cups.

Pick-me-ups in hand, the two of them sat in their usual spot, a wide, varnished windowsill that overlooked downtown Meridian. "How's tricks, Baldwin?" Sam sipped her drink. "Civilian life boring as they say?"

Clem downed her bourbon in a single gulp. "If you call it boring to get shot at with a MAC-11 in the middle of a crowded nightclub, sure."

"You could tell it was a MAC-11 just by the sound? Fuck, you're good."

Out the window, the midnight sky gnawed at the silhouette of Meridian, the town's landmarks more like tooth marks: that notched sliver of the Threefoot Building, on the sixth floor of which Clem's father had operated his jewelry trade, legitimate and illegitimate; the blocky hunks of Rush, Anderson, and Riley, three hospitals that served as many counties; those semicircles of the northern hills, growing more prosperous and populated by the day; those ragged gaps of the downtown business district, each getting wider whenever a white shop owner got "nervous" about the "wrong element" they saw moving in next door; and the square knob that was Weidmann's Restaurant, established in 1870, where Clem's grandfather, in his crisp, white waiter's jacket, used to sneak her peanut butter and crackers, but only if she sat in the stock room, for fear she'd displease his regular customers, same color as his jacket, on whose tips he so desperately relied.

"Did you know this land used to be hunting grounds?" Clem said to Sam.

Sam poured another round into their cups. "Still kind of is, Ms. Just Got Shot At."

"I'm serious. I read about it. The Choctaw had a village nearby named Koosa Town, and they called this land we're looking at Alamucha. It was their hunting grounds. Then they were 'coerced' into giving it all up in the Treaty of Dancing Rabbit Creek."

"Fascinating." Sam took a draw of bourbon. "Please, Clem, explain to me more about my people."

"I know. I'm sorry. I'm an ass."

"You're right about one thing. We are most definitely in hunting season."

Clem's throat grew hot, both from the whiskey and from the complete accuracy she sensed in how Sam had phrased it. They were in hunting season. "What do you mean by that?" she needlessly asked.

"It's like every day we've got a new murder one. Grand larceny? And forget possession. That's kiddie shit. It's all about trafficking. Coke, scag, pot, bennies, tranqs. Captain still blames Camille, if you can believe. When was that storm, fifteen years ago? All the top brass saying hordes of small-time perps moved up here after their trailers got blown to shreds?"

"August 17, 1969. Landfall."

"That brain of yours. I mean."

To hear about the acts of crime rising across town poked a finger into Clem's mind's eye. She didn't care a whit about crime, not anymore, not after her stint with the people who purportedly fought against it, but because of her vocation, she also relied on that very thing. Crime bred secrets. Secrets bred suspicion. Clem's business? Uncovering secrets and allaying suspicion. The crime behind it all? That was no longer her problem. Crime could go fuck itself.

Still, Clem had a job, a paying job, and it just so happened to involve homicide. "Who do you like for the Hubbard murder?"

"Clementine Baldwin. Always after the angle, trying to find your man."

"So you know it was a man."

"Cassidy is the prime suspect, but we're not ruling anyone out." Sam raked her fingers through the glossy black hair that always drew stares, then looked at Clem with the brilliant blue eyes that never failed to sustain those stares. Girl knew her gifts, Clem had to admit. "Mind, this is not my case," Sam said. "That son of a bitch Will Pickett had me taken off. He told Cappie he wanted someone 'more seasoned' on it. Translation: someone with a dick. Translation: someone who will completely bungle this case. The MPD way, right, babe?"

"It's only part of why I left, but an important part. Corner-piece important."

In the pulp paperbacks Clem had devoured as a child, novels with hard-boiled prose masking a soft-boiled heart, people were always "cutting" their eyes at each other. "He cut his eyes at the lovely creature who had strolled into his office to destroy his life." "She cut her eyes at this poor fool asking if she came here often." Clem never understood the phrase—did it mean to look at someone sideways? To glare at them through narrowed eyes?—until she saw Samantha Bellflower enact it.

Sam looked at Clem sideways, glaring through narrowed eyes. "I have noticed one thing."

"Yeah?"

"Remember that case in Neshoba, those Freedom Riders in '64? Three of them went missing. Two Jewish, one Black. So, obviously, I mean, obviously, it couldn't have been racially motivated, huh?"

"I remember."

"This is after my dad left the tribal police, moved to Philadelphia PD. We still lived on the rez."

Clem had heard the backstory a thousand times. Sam's father hated the limitations of his jurisdiction, so he moved to the department in Philadelphia, Mississippi, where, albeit now able to handle felonies, he faced the limitations of his race imposed by the white wall of the blue code.

Sam continued, "The Feds come down. Three civil rights workers go missing, they've got to swing that DC bait and tackle around, right? Except, lo and behold, these Mississippi cops aren't exactly accommodating. Crazy, right? Back then my dad wasn't prom king of the department, as I know you know. Still, he had eyes, he had ears, okay? And so Dad starts to notice something. Whenever his department brought someone in for questioning, they'd end up letting them go, naturally, but as these suspects were walking out, cops with let's say a certain animosity to certain colors of people would shake that suspect's hand."

"Oh, no."

"Smart-ass." Sam lowered her voice to a nearly theatrical whisper. "It's the way they shook hands. Dad noticed that their pinkies would always interlace."

As she shrugged her chin, what Dixon called making her grumpy Muppet face, Clem raised her hands and tried to clasp them. "Like this?" she said, in response to which Sam pushed Clem's hands back into her lap and said, "Not where people can see. Fuck's sake, girl."

"What?"

"You didn't let me get to my point." Again with a flavor of theatricality, Sam looked around the rumpus room, the other occupants of which were still passed out or in search of random words. She turned back to Clem and whispered, "Ever since the Hubbard thing, I've noticed some of the boys around here giving each other that same handshake."

The tip was weak, Clem knew, but noteworthy. She squirrel-cheeked it for later.

Outside the station, where Sam escorted her, Clem spotted Dixon in the parking lot. He was leaning against the hood of her Jeep, and he'd apparently been doing so for a good, long while. His body obscured the word, an obnoxious one, in Clem's opinion, that was painted on all the hoods of this particular model. ADE was covered up, so it now read RENEG.

"Hey, Dixie Cup!" Sam yelled from under the station's front awning. "You take care of my girl, okay?"

"She's the one took care of me tonight. I should be a colander about now."

After Clem said bye to Sam and hopped in the driver's seat of the Jeep, she had trouble getting the key to slide into the ignition. Her hands, which she'd managed to keep under control since the incident to avoid embarrassment during the interrogation, started to tremble. She'd never been shot at before that night.

"It's all right," Dixon said after she got the Jeep started, as she reached for but failed to grasp the gearshift. "You handle the clutch; I'll handle the stick. Okay? *Clutch.*"

Clem pressed the clutch, and Dixon shifted to first. "Clutch." Clem pressed the clutch, and Dixon shifted to second. "Clutch." Clem pressed the clutch, and Dixon shifted to third.

6

CONFEDERATE DRIVE

Confederate Drive was so damn typical. Molly Coogan hated living on it, even though she didn't have to pay rent, at least not while she stayed in her brother's shotgun house.

Christopher's house wasn't even technically on Confederate Drive. It sat at the dead end of an unnamed gravel road that doglegged from the drive near the Confederate Army cemetery that inspired its name. The seclusion helped with the business enterprises her brother and husband got involved in on those decreasingly rare occasions when their legitimate jobs failed to cover the bills or their favored teams failed to cover the spread.

The day after she lost her own legit job—apparently bar owners didn't like it when their waitresses got shot at while chatting with private investigators—Molly found a glad distraction from her unemployment by handling what remained of one said business enterprise. She stood in the middle of the chicken pen in her backyard, tossing feed to the hens and roosters Turnip had raised as sparring partners for his prize fighting cocks. They cluck-clucked near her feet, pecking their little beaks at the grain on the ground, feathers and dust rising in the air.

"Don't you worry, my wee ones," she said. "Mom'll keep the geek away."

The afternoon was chilly, even for January in Mississippi. Green, fringed pine trees banked the blue sky overhead, gray clouds drifting between them, aimless as these birds gobbling up their supper. Molly put away the feed bucket and wiped off her hands on the front of her dress. Her belly was getting bigger by the day. For a moment, she let her hands rest on top of it, thinking how her baby was similar to the chickens all around her: fatherless.

Ever since her husband fell to his death, these birds had been left without their first true parent, the father who took care of them, as lovingly, as thoughtfully, as kindly as he, Turnip, had not taken care of his wife.

Good fucking riddance, Molly reminded herself, walking back to the house. The same as how she alone would be a far better parent to the chickens, Molly, alone, would be a far better parent to the child coming into this world in fourteen weeks. Turnip would have made for as shitty a father as he had been a husband. Molly didn't need him, with his dumb plans and ugly temper, with his skirt-chasing and plot-holed denials.

All Molly needed to raise her child was money, just enough to live on for a few years; she wasn't greedy, and as fate would have it, if her plan unfolded squarely, Turnip, that deadbeat, would provide the money from his well-deserved, fortuitously timed grave.

Inside the shotgun house, where a propane unit oozed heat and a ceiling fan tossed it about the room, Molly retrieved a Nehi from the fridge, took a quick swallow to quench her annoyingly persistent craving for artificial-grape flavor, and let her gaze float around the dining/kitchen/living area. Look at this place! Sometimes she couldn't believe she'd ended up in such a shithole. An outdated calendar from a farm-supply shop dangled on the wall. Those unmistakable orange rectangles of Nabs peanut butter crackers sat in a bowl on the coffee table, the closest thing to a nutritious snack to be found anywhere in this so-called house.

Molly had been meant for better things. When she was a little girl, before her father's portfolio took a turn and her mother's inheritance was left to her grandfather's mistress, Molly's family had lived in one of those imperial, decadent mansions on Poplar Springs Drive, the kind with a servants' entrance, ancient brick walkways, fireplaces in the bedrooms, and a sizable mortgage note. They "had land" in the county, which was Meridian-speak for owning acreage as a deer camp and a tax shelter. Back then Molly went to Lamar Elementary, the one private school in town. She loved Lamar, with its healthy cafeteria food and gleaming hallways, its pageants and recitals and sui generis "special" celebrations. Molly's favorite of those celebrations was called Tacky Day. Every student dressed up in their "tackiest" clothes, outfits typically mined from their parents' closets, relics of some bygone era. Molly would come to school in her mother's embroidered bell-bottoms, her father's flower-child poncho, hoping to win that coveted title of Tackiest Student.

Years later, after her family could no longer afford the tuition and she'd been forced to transfer to the public school, where for the first time in her young life she took classes with kids who were not white, Molly reflected back on Tacky Day with a far more analytical eye, and she realized a pattern in those who were chosen by the teachers as the Tackiest Students. They weren't the ones in loud, mismatched colors, old-fashioned cat's-eye glasses, garish cloche hats, or sizes five times too big. They were the ones in overalls with a single gallus hanging down. They were the ones in the name-tagged jumpsuits of gas-station attendants or the lacy pinafores of live-in housekeepers. Their clothes weren't gaudy, dowdy, or shabby, but cheap, low-class, *poor.*

Tacky Day was really Poor People Day, which, ironically, Molly thought as she turned on the television in her brother's shotgun house, made it a perfect example of what Southerners regarded as "tacky" behavior. Maybe she was better off now anyway.

"Welcome to *Live at Five,*" the news anchor said to Molly and the rest of WTOK's broadcasting area, "bringing the latest news from your city, your nation, your world."

In a frayed love seat, Molly tried to avoid dwelling on her joblessness and all the other circumstances, not the least of which being the fact she'd nearly been shot dead by an assassin who may or may not have been aiming for her, that had led to her hiding out at the dead end of an unnamed gravel road that doglegged from Confederate *Can You Believe This Shit* Drive.

The top of the broadcast began with Reagan's inauguration for a second term, scheduled for January 21, less than two weeks away. Although she told people she was and, more often than not, genuinely considered herself a Republican, Molly had voted for the other guy, Mondale. She had made that choice partly out of deference for her brother and what their parents called his "plight," partly out of concern for the issue exemplified by the second story of the broadcast. "This year marks the thirtieth anniversary of the death," said the anchor, "of Emmett L. Till, who was brutally murdered near Money, Mississippi, on August 28, 1955. Events to mark the occasion are being planned statewide. Governor Allain, addressing pushback from certain legislators, remarked that these events will be ones of healing for such a dark moment in our state history. More info will be forthcoming on these cele—excuse me—these *commem*orations. John, how's our weather looking for the weekend?"

Molly doubted she'd even know about Emmett Till if she hadn't transferred to Meridian High. It was hardly the sort of thing taught at a place like Lamar. Despite her resentment at having to attend a public school, Molly hadn't held it against her classmates, many of whom, white and Black, were still her friends. A falling tide sinks all boats, she had figured, then and now. Sure, Reagan had helped certain tides and boats rise, but not her tide, not her boat.

Still, Molly thought, watching commercials with Juan Valdez wandering about Colombia picking coffee beans, Dom DeLuise hawking personal computers, and a New York Mets player warning folks against drugs, at least she *had* a boat, so to speak, being white. Her Black friends, treading water, had only two choices in facing the economic tide manipulated by that geriatric moon called the Gipper: sink slowly or drown quickly. The least Molly could do? Vote for Mondale, such a sad sap he lost every state except the one he was from, managing to snag the extremely lucky number of thirteen electoral votes.

The most Molly could do didn't involve her friends. A girl had to look out for herself every now and then, especially when that now or then happened to coincide with the creation of a *whole new person*. Was it so wrong to use Turnip's death for his child's gain?

From the gravel road outside came the microwave-popcorn sound of a truck pulling up to the house. Molly went to the window. Out of his mud-flared 4x4 with duck boots lodged upside down between the cab and saddle toolbox, a whip antenna secured to the tailgate, headlamps scabrous with dead gnats, and a winch dangling its hook like a parched tongue stepped Molly's younger brother, Christopher. He raised his cap to run a dirty hand through his sweaty blond hair. He slapped dust from his camo long-sleeve and his dip-stained Carhartts. Across the lawn, back from his afternoon squirrel expedition in the pine woods, bounded Chekov—their previous family dogs had been named Kirk, Spock, Bones, and Sulu—who greeted his favorite uncle with a thorough chin-licking. Chekov followed Christopher to the front door and into the house.

"So?" Molly asked, blindly patting Chekov's head while staring at her brother as he removed a tallboy from the fridge. "What'd you find out?"

Christopher shortened the contents of the tallboy by a few inches. "The hit wasn't on you."

"Who, then?" Molly managed to ask, despite now being a puddle on the floor.

"That PI woman."

"Just her? Not the partner, too?"

Christopher shrugged. "Chop off the head."

In drastic need of a cigarette she could not have, Molly sat down at the kitchen table. The hit wasn't on her. Thank *effing* God! Christopher sat across from her, enjoying his beer, another thing she could not have. Molly asked, "How do you know this? Did you see Cassidy?"

"Guy like that on a job? He won't show his face until it's done." Another sip of the tallboy, hacking away at its height. "I asked around at the ranch."

The "ranch," which neither Molly nor, as far as she knew, any woman had ever seen, existed only in her imagination, dread, wonder, fascination, and animosity. A kind of barracks for the Dixie Mafia, according to less-than-wholly reliable hearsay, the ranch was located somewhere in Kemper County, at an abandoned factory or fish camp or golf range or cotton gin. It served as an informal gathering place, replete with pool tables and dartboards and rotating beers on tap, a Cheers where rednecks plotted their next pathetic score. Turnip had used its facilities to raise and train his brawler birds, ofttimes spending entire weeks out there, leaving Molly alone, broke, but oddly relieved. As long as he was at the ranch, she didn't have to listen to his harebrained schemes. As long as he was at the ranch, she could live her life as the Lord divined, free of man, independent of husband.

"Has she come snooping around?" Christopher asked Molly. "The PI woman?"

"Why would she?"

"Oh, I don't know. Maybe because you threw me under the bus, told her Cassidy had a partner?"

"Christopher," Molly said, pulling out the name like a piece of gum stuck to her shoe. "I didn't tell her you were his partner. You know I'd never do that. Under the bus?"

"Right. Right. *Flynn* was his partner. *Flynn* is going to be cooling his heels in county lockup by the end of the week. Still can't believe you used that name. 'Molly's the one with imagination,'" Christopher said in his eerily accurate imitation of their mother's voice.

He was speaking the truth, Molly had to admit. She should have come up with a better fake name to give the private detectives. Flynn had been the name of Christopher's good friend for some time. When Molly was telling the detectives about Cassidy's partner, in order to keep them focused on the case, Flynn had been the first name that came to her. It was stupid, but not the end of the world. How would they ever figure out the connection?

"Why'd you even have to tell them Cassidy had a partner in the first place?"

Molly laid her hands flat on the table. "So they can do their job, idiot. Why else would I have convinced Mama Coogan to hire them? They have to prove that Turnip was killed. If they don't, then his death was suicide, and Pathrite's life insurance doesn't pay shit."

Seventy-five thousand dollars, Molly had calculated and recalculated at least a dozen times since Turnip's death, would last her, after taxes, approximately three years and four months. It would buy thousands of Huggies, hundreds of jars of Gerber, dozens of onesies, a car seat, a stroller, and God knew how many stuffed animals and jacks-in-a- box and bouncy balls and coloring books and those giant plastic keys that rattled.

"I didn't have nothing to do with Turnip falling off that roof," Christopher said. "What I'm saying is why did the PIs need to know Jacob had a partner?"

"We've got to chum the water." Unable to resist any longer, Molly grabbed her brother's tallboy and took a sip, a teensy, tiny one, nothing that would hurt the baby. "If they give up, we're screwed."

"*We*, huh? I'm not seeing much of a 'we' if I get busted for Hubbard's murder."

"Christopher," Molly said, the word a rubber band she snapped at him. "Did you kill Randy Hubbard?"

"No! I've told you hundred million times. Odette called it off last minute!"

"Then you've got nothing to worry about. Meantime, do me a favor and grow a pair."

That shut his trap. In a mild temper-tantrum sort of way, his perennial teapot-tempest move, Christopher stomped off to the bathroom, from which Molly could hear the shower start to run. This whole plan had been such a long shot. When Molly had convinced Turnip's mother that something seemed odd with Turnip's fall, that he was not the type to have killed himself, that maybe she should hire someone to look into it, Molly had known nothing about the poison. That tox report the PIs had found was better than a winning scratch-off!

If only Mama Coogan had told her about the report *before* Molly talked to the private investigators the other night, she never would have spilled so much about the DM and Jacob Cassidy and his partner, "Flynn." But she wasn't going to tell her brother about that little screwup. They just had to hold steady. They had to keep their noses clean, their lips shut, their eyes on the prize. The detectives were hired to find out who'd killed Turnip, after all, not who'd killed Hubbard.

A car horn honked outside the house, prompting a perfunctory bark from Chekov. From the window, Molly saw a BMW with a man in a business suit behind the wheel. "Don't wait up," Christopher said, in a clean T-shirt, jeans, and his good boots. He kissed Molly on the cheek.

"Hey, look at me," Molly said. "Condoms. Got it?"

"Yeah, yeah."

"Did you hear me?"

"I heard you. God!" Christopher said before loping out the front door, running across the yard, tapping the car hood, and leaning through the driver's-side window.

Molly turned away. Her baby brother was going to catch that new disease going around if he wasn't careful. "Suppertime?" she asked Chekov, who thumped his tail in affirmation.

7

PLUS EXPENSES

Half a dozen miles south of Confederate Drive, Clem wandered the streets of downtown Meridian, followed and surrounded and confronted by half a dozen Jacob Cassidys. They were everywhere. One of them sat on a park bench pretending to read *The Meridian Star*, his eyes peering over the top edge of newsprint, watching her step around a puddle. Another stood beneath the alcove of a recently condemned apartment building, his hands in his pockets, clutching the cool, thoroughly oiled steel of a semiautomatic.

Jacob Cassidy winked at Clem as she waited for the WALK sign to turn white. Jacob Cassidy smiled at Clem as she passed him crossing the street. Jacob Cassidy wore track pants and a guayabera shirt. Jacob Cassidy wore a business suit with rolled sleeves. "Spare change?" said Jacob Cassidy, huddled against a graffitied brick wall, draped in a filthy blanket, and when Clem didn't answer, Jacob Cassidy grumbled, "Keep walking, bitch."

"I'll sit at the counter," Clem told the hostess after she ducked into Weidmann's Restaurant. She hoped the girl didn't notice her voice's ragged edge.

It was six o'clock on a Thursday. The dinner crowd was light, mostly families, with the parents staring at the celebrities framed on the walls, the children knifing peanut butter onto saltines. Tablecloths green as billiard felt fluttered in the breeze sent down by ceiling fans set to a low winter speed. Mounted glass-eyed deer heads kept a vigilant watch over plates of black-bottom pie.

At the lunch counter, separated from the dining area by a brass-railing partition, Clem ordered an ice water, regretting the restaurant's lapse on its liquor license, knowing coffee wouldn't help ravel the dropped yarn bobbin of her mind.

"Here you go."

"Thanks."

"Menu?"

"Water's fine."

And it was. The cold water calmed Clem. She downed half the glass. *Keep walking, bitch.* That guy on the street had been right. Clem needed to keep walking. She needed to keep moving forward. To stop was to die. Clem's cases were her cattle prods. They were the carrots at the ends of sticks.

But the jolt of a cattle prod hurt worse than hell. Nobody actually liked to eat carrots.

In her four years as a PI, Clem had been punched in the face as many times as she'd had a door slammed in it. She'd been shot at by hit men, and she'd been hit on by big shots. Her knee never healed right after a run-away teen swiped it with his dad's Ford Pinto. The countless instances of infidelity she'd witnessed through a telephoto lens had ruined her to the very idea of a lasting relationship. She needed reading glasses from staring at microfiche, and she woke most mornings reaching for the gun under her pillow. Nerves? On their last legs. Liver? Putting in its notice any day now. Savings? Tapped out long ago. To calculate the money her clients had stiffed her would require an accountant she could only afford with the money her clients had stiffed her.

And for what? Yes, well. The occasional case came with heartening perks.

During her four years as a PI, Clem had tracked down lost children, spouses, siblings, and parents. She'd retrieved stolen cars, pets, deeds, and, three times, in cases involving former high school couples who'd lost touch, hearts. Clem had helped lock up a husband who whipped his wife with an extension cord, a father who struck his children with golf cleats. She'd helped put away a mother who dosed her daughter's IV with fecal matter, a wife who framed one husband for the other's murder. Even "un-successful" jobs had the potential to be a success. Clem had saved marriages by finding out that *her* tennis instructor was gay, that *his* secretary had no interest and in fact hated his guts. A number of business partnerships avoided dissolution when Clem discovered the actual embezzler had been the in-house attorney all along.

At least the pay is shit, Clem told herself while staring at a glass of water she begrudgingly saw as half-full. She drank the last of it, turning to Weidmann's front door, from which appeared the only person in the MPD who Clem still considered a friend.

"Yeah, I'm late," Samantha Bellflower said. She sat on a stool next to Clem. "What, they run out of whiskey?"

"Revenge of the ABC board," Clem said.

"Or the greed of. They used to be cheaper to grease than the city council."

After ordering a cup of coffee, Sam placed a manila folder on the counter and with her middle finger pushed it toward Clem. "I should start charging you for all these little favors," she said.

The file on the Hubbard murder was thin. Clem tamped the urge to tear into it by looking around Mississippi's oldest restaurant: its exposed-brick walls and maroon-tiled floor and stamped-tin ceilings, those crocks of peanut butter on each table, a Weidmann's tradition since World War II, when there had been a shortage of dairy butter and crackers still needed a spread. Clem didn't look at the portrait of her grandfather on the part of the wall with other past employees. Clem didn't look at the door to the stock room where her grandfather used to make her stay as a girl, hidden from the prying, capricious eyes of his regulars. "Randall Hubbard tried to buy this place," she said to Sam. "The whole building. He was going to chop it up into cheap housing."

"Interesting."

Uninterested, Sam dropped a couple of quarters next to her half-empty cup of coffee. "You were right about Cassidy having a partner," she said. "We got a nosy neighbor saw *dos* men parked in a Toyota near Hubbard's house the night of."

"Fuck me running."

"That was a college thing, swear to God."

"What'd the partner look like?"

"Neighbor's with the sketch artist now." Sam stood from her stool. "I'll keep you posted."

Clem, watching her former colleague and only friend leave the restaurant, did mental backflips at such fantastic news. Flynn was real! Talk about a break of luck. Even if his name was an alias, Cassidy's partner "Flynn" could be the kind of lead that, in Clem's experience, loosened the lid whenever the pickle jar of a case had been sitting in the back of the fridge too long. Flynns banged the lid with a spoon. Flynns wrapped a rubber band around the lid to give it better grip.

Hubbard file in hand, an invigorated Clem strode across Weidmann's, toward an outside world in which there existed only one Jacob Cassidy. On a table next to the door sat the Treasure Chest. Whenever she'd come here as a girl, Clem would jealously watch from a crack in the stock-room door as the kids who'd cleaned their plates got to choose a piece of candy from the famous chest: Tootsie Rolls, suckers, Pixy Stix, Smarties, Runts, bubble gum, those Saf-T-Pops with the loop handles.

Clem picked out a root beer sucker. Her hand still trembled, but it was getting steadier.

8

TO HUNT A SNIPE

The root beer sucker was gone by the time Dixon stopped by her place with a burger and fries. Clem lived next to the Meridian Junior College, behind a Burger King that used to be a McDonald's that used to be a Burger Chef that used to be a Krystal. She had not been able to stomach ground beef, mustard, ketchup, or even American cheese since she'd moved into her apartment.

Her partner had no such qualms. He never failed to pick up a burger when he visited her apartment for work. Dixon was scarfing one down now, seated on her couch, leaning over the coffee table. Clem didn't really mind. She was so used to the smell from the restaurant she could hardly register its physical antecedent's trespass into her home. "Get you a bib?" Clem asked Dixon, watching sesame seeds silt down into his beard.

"I'm good."

To avoid any gloppy fallout of condiments, Clem slid her stack of files on the Coogan case closer to her end of the coffee table, careful not to knock over her bourbon. She took a sip and opened a file. It contained photos she and Dixon had taken of Hubbard's house, well after dark, so they could jump the crime-scene tape undetected. The place had been untastefully opulent, the idea someone who'd grown up poor had of how rich people lived, its sunken center room ensconced in shag carpet and overcrowded with floor clocks and antique globes and potted plants, the kitchen gleaming with cream-colored appliances and elaborately wainscoted cabinetry that clashed with the minimalist light features and untreated windows.

Clem flipped to the photo that had been the hardest to take. On the morning of March 28, 1984, after not showing up for a scheduled meeting at his office, Randall Hubbard had been found by his secretary slumped against the baby grand he was reportedly skilled at and known to play for his frequent late-night party guests. His milk-white sports jacket, on the back of which he'd bedazzled I LOVE AMERICA in purple and gold rhinestones, had turned pink from the four bullets in his back and the two in his shoulder. From the piano strings hung clods of skull, brain, and hair the final bullet had knocked free of his head.

Although the body wasn't in the photo Clem had taken, she could see it there, Hubbard's five-foot-ten, 230-pound frame splayed atop the ivory keys, his blond hair permed with blood, parted forever by a .38 Special.

How old were his children from his first marriage? Clem tried to recall. Twelve and eight. Christ almighty above. At least that night they'd been staying with their mother in Louisiana. At least they'd been spared the scar of finding their father in that condition.

"Here's where I keep tripping up," Clem said to Dixon. "Guy's sitting at home, playing some ditty on the piano. He's even got his cocktail, worked his way through half of it, starting to feel that Absolut. Was the piano so loud he didn't hear someone enter the house? And why wasn't the front door locked?"

"Maybe he felt safe," Dixon said. "Growing up we never locked our doors."

"But the guy was outfitted. Sam said they found his piece sitting on the piano bench, next to his vodka rocks with lime. You don't have a loaded nine-millimeter handy if you're feeling safe."

"And there's the jewelry."

"Right!" Hurriedly, feeling that rush of being onto something, Clem opened another file, where she found a list of the items of jewelry recovered from Hubbard's body after his murder: a ring with nine diamonds, a gold watch with eight diamonds, a C-link gold bracelet, another bracelet made of sterling silver, and a silver chain necklace with a four-carat diamond. "Cassidy is a professional, right? A hit man, not a thief. But is anybody professional enough to pass up this level of goods? The sheer loot he had on his person was like a fucking storybook dragon's lair."

Dixon leaned back on the couch, letting his gaze drift ceiling-ward.

"Hubbard was known as the flashy type, yeah? Those diamonds. That god-ugly jacket."

"Uh-huh."

"What if these," Dixon said, waving a hand at the list of jewelry, "are the items Cassidy and his partner *left behind*?"

"Meaning, they took some, maybe a lot, but left enough so nobody'd bother to look into what was missing?"

"Nice not having to cover your tracks whenever you try and move them."

"Hubbard had to have insurance on everything. We get that master list, it's just a matter of figuring out who they used to move them." Clem's excitement waned when she realized the height of that order. "Which is damn near impossible. God knows how many fences are operating throughout the state. Throughout the South, even. Could be anyone."

"There is somebody comes to mind who could help us out." Dixon canted an eyebrow.

"No. *No.* Absolutely not. No way. And fuck you for even suggesting that."

Four years had passed since the last time Clem saw her father. Throughout her childhood, she had thought of him as a well-respected lapidary, goldsmith, silversmith, horologist, diamond setter, and gem dealer, the law-abiding, churchgoing proprietor of Baldwin Gems. Then, when Clem was in fourth grade, her father "went on vacation" for a year and a half, and Clem, whose mother had passed away during her birth, had to live with her aunt, uncle, and cousins in a mobile home far different from the immobile one her father's illicit transgressions had afforded.

On his release, Lauder Baldwin swore to his only daughter as persuasively and vehemently as she later assumed he must have to the parole board that he had learned the error of his ways, that he would never again risk losing the most precious thing in his life. The most precious thing believed him. She believed him throughout high school. She believed him during her enrollment at a university paid for with the profits from stolen goods. She believed him after she joined the force. She believed him up until the day she convinced her captain to let her be a part of the sting operation that brought down Baldwin Gems.

"It's just a suggestion," Dixon said. He plucked a fry from the greasy paper wrapper on the coffee table. "If it were me? I'd want to see my only daughter. If it were me."

"But it's not you. You wouldn't be here if you were a criminal and a liar."

Clem, to avoid wondering which she hated more, that her father had broken the law or that he had lied to her, finished her bourbon. The drink vanquished the last of her shakes from earlier that evening. At the bar across the room, Clem poured herself another, downed it, and "made like shampoo," the phrase Dixon often used to admonish her. *Rinse and repeat.*

"Don't even say it," Clem preempted her partner as she sat back down on the couch, fresh drink in hand. She grabbed one of his fries.

While savoring the saltiness, Clem stared at the photos spread across the coffee table, the ones from the crime scene, Hubbard's now-and-probably-long-to-be empty house. She found herself, perhaps due to the Magritte-style confluence of the photos lying on her coffee table, staring at one *of* a coffee table. In a further nod to Magritte—Clem supposed that art history course she took freshman year was at last paying off—she noticed, while her own cocktail sat on one, a cocktail napkin lying on the coffee table in the photograph.

"At lunch yesterday, Sam told us Hubbard's nine-millimeter was sitting on the piano bench, didn't she, right next to his drink?"

Dixon nodded. "Vodka rocks with lime, she said. His go-to."

"Then whose drink," Clem said, pointing at the napkin on the coffee table, "was sitting here?"

Eyes scrunched, Dixon leaned toward the photo. "His? Hubbard's relaxing on the couch, and when he heads to the piano, he takes his drink, leaves the napkin."

"How often have you left behind your cocktail napkin?"

"Makes you think I use *cocktail* napkins? They'd look awful silly wrapped around a High Life."

He had a point. "You have a point," Clem said. She drank to it. The Cocktail Napkin Theory, as she began to call it in her head, seemed very much *her,* a theory that hinged on perhaps the most Clementine Baldwin clue in the history of clues, one rooted in booze and how it's served and how it's drunk.

But wouldn't an as-yet-unknown actor solve the problems and loose ends of Jacob Cassidy being the killer, how Odette Hubbard had supposedly called off that hit? The marital troubles, death threats, bodyguards, and insurance money had always felt to Clem a touch too clean, a bit too pat. What if all that domestic bullshit was the car wreck beside the road distracting them from the semi barreling their way for a head-on collision? Clem pitched her partner the idea.

"If I'm a dog choosing which tree to bark up," Dixon said, clearly exhausted, ready to go home, "am I going to choose the tree that *might* have a nice, juicy squirrel in it? Or am I going to choose the tree that I *know* has a hit man who I *know* shot at me in a nightclub a few days ago?"

Again he had a point. Drink in hand, Clem stood from the couch and walked to the sliding glass doors that led onto her closet-size second-story balcony. Out the glass doors sprawled one of the many parking lots for the junior college, prehensile newspaper clinging to phone poles, a bluish-green glare from the mercury-vapor streetlights beating back the evening's moonglow. The parking lot was moated by gas stations and discount stores and quickie lubes, what the city councilmen called growth, development, but what in the blue-green of the mercury vapor appeared more like cancerous growth, more like malignant development.

On the edge of the parking lot lay the parcel of land that Hubbard had planned to develop into a shopping center. Incredible, Clem thought. A man's death may well have been the result of a goddamn, god-awful shopping center. Talk about the '80s in a nutshell! If Hubbard hadn't overleveraged himself to develop the center, he wouldn't have needed to take out a life insurance policy to secure the loan. If Hubbard hadn't taken out the insurance policy, his wife would've had no incentive, at least not a monetary one, to call in the hit.

"*Cheers* is filmed before a live studio audience," came a voice from the TV.

Clem, jolted from her mind's peregrinations, turned away from the glass doors, back toward the living room, where Dixon was now holding the clicker. He stared at the TV, either annoyed, bored, or, most likely, some combination thereof. "Don't mind me," he said. "Keep doing your gaze-out-the-window thing. I'm just checking to see what's on tonight."

"Uh-oh. Is Grumpy Dixon back?" Clem sat beside him on the couch. "I missed Grumpy Dixon. He's so much fun. Grum-py Dix-on, Grum-py Dix-on."

"You really are hilarious."

"Did we miss that new show with the guy from *I Spy*?"

"By an hour. Cosby's on at seven."

At the bar where everybody knew your name, Sam, Norm, Cliff, and a few of those unnamed regulars—Clem guessed not *ev*erybody knew your name—were heading out for a fishing trip. Diane convinces them to take Frasier, who didn't spend much time outdoors as a kid. On the trip, the gang tricks that poor, brainy psychiatrist into going on a snipe hunt, and they leave him in the woods, holding a bag, waiting for them to scare a mythical, nonexistent "snipe" out of the bush. Back at the bar, Frasier bursts through the door, filthy and tired, except instead of being furious, he's grateful. He loves hunting for snipes! The camaraderie with his peers and communing with nature made him feel alive! At the end of the episode, Frasier convinces the gang to go back out to the woods, where, he reveals to Diane, he plans to turn the tables, leaving them to hunt for what he quickly figured out during his own hunt was a fictitious creature.

"I guess what I'm saying," Clem said to Dixon as the credits rolled, "is what if Cassidy and the DM are snipes? Are we looking at this case backward? Are we on a snipe hunt?"

"Snipes are real. They're hard to catch, camouflaged. They hide in plain—"

Before Dixon could finish, the doorbell rang, though not once, as was common, but three quick times. The partners exchanged a look. "You expecting anybody?" Dixon asked, already on his feet.

"Calm down. It's probably just a neighbor, wants to borrow some sugar."

"Like you keep any baking supplies on hand." Despite his joke, Dixon wasn't behaving in a jokey manner. He walked to the coatrack across the room, reached into his jacket pocket, and removed his Smith & Wesson. The image of it made Clem's fingers twitch, as if guitar strings were tied to each of them and the gun barrel had strummed a tune, one from a song called "A Foretoken of Violence (Be Careful with Your Life)."

"You're overreacting," Clem told Dixon. "Jesus."

"Don't call me that. It inflates my ego."

In the foyer, followed by Dixon holding his revolver, Clem paused at the door. Everything was fine, she told herself. Everything was hunky-dory. It was some delivery guy who'd gotten the address wrong. The doorbell rang again, another three quick times in a row, followed by an even more frantic series of knocks. Thud-thud-thud-thwack.

Clem looked at Dixon. She pressed her back to the wall, perpendicular to the door. Dixon did the same against the opposite wall. He held his revolver in both hands, aimed toward the floor. Clem bobbed her head one, two, three times and, casually as possible, called out, "Who is it?"

"Clem, it's Russ. I just heard about what happened at the John Wesley Hardin. Could you let me in? I'm worried sick."

Only when she released her breath did Clem realize she'd been holding it. Dixon, tucking his piece in his belt, gave Clem a smirk that said, *It seems somebody's the popular one,* before heading back into the living room. Clem unlocked and opened the door.

Assistant DA Russ Clyde rushed inside and wrapped his arms around Clem. "Dear God, Clem, are you okay? Why didn't you tell me? I have to find out you've been shot at from some patrolman?"

"I'm all right." Clem withdrew from the uninvited hug. "I said I'm fine."

Daunted by neither Clem's tone nor her language, body as well as verbal, Russ patted her shoulders, wrists, and elbows for injuries, like a mother whose child had fallen off their bike. Clem found it equally annoying and endearing, intrusive but kind of sweet, and she was also annoyed with herself for finding it even partly endearing. "Are you sure you weren't grazed?" Russ said. "Did they check for a concussion? Those can be hard to diagnose."

"Wow. Law school *and* medical school. You're quite the learned fellow."

Russ drew back and performed a pantomime of "harried," emitting an air-rifle report of a sigh, touching his fingers to his lips, squinting at Clem with concern, and, in conclusion to his Oscar-worthy performance, placing his hands on his hips. Yeah, yeah, Clem thought. The guy was adorable.

"Come on inside," she said, pantomiming "resigned." "I'll buy you a drink."

In the living room, Russ said hello to Dixon, who had thoughtfully put away his revolver and just as thoughtfully put on his jacket. "Headed out so soon?" Clem asked her partner as she handed Russ a bourbon he hadn't requested. She sipped her own fresh one.

"It's getting late. Mrs. Hicks will start to worry." Dixon turned to Russ. "Good seeing you, ADA Clyde."

While zipping his jacket, Dixon, out of Russ's sight, lowered his eyes toward Clem's glass and then raised them to meet her gaze. He said, "Fly straight, Wild Turkey," to which Clem responded in the most appropriate way she could imagine: by flipping him the bird.

On July 6, 1981, *The New Yorker* ran a Talk of the Town piece titled, "They Call Her Ms. Tibbs." The piece purported to concern a series of murders by strangulation in a Mississippi city "more modern than Faulkner's postage stamp" but "inhabited by the same stamp of criminal, your charming outlaws, your irascible goons, your violent, racist brigands and wretches so essential to the Southern Gothic." Despite its purported subject, the piece focused less on the "Dentzel Carousel Strangler" and more on the young Black woman who caught him—to the overwhelming resentment of the young Black woman's overwhelmingly white, overwhelmingly male colleagues in the MPD.

Clem despised every aspect of the piece, including that atrocious excuse for a title, but after Dixon had left her condo and she found herself alone with Russ Clyde, she acceded to the accuracy of a particular line from it. "Baldwin only uses one drawer of her dresser, one shelf of her fridge, and one frame of her mind: solve the case, no matter what it takes."

In her kitchen, wearing what she knew to be the third-to-last pair of clean socks from the drawer where she kept her socks, underwear, and T-shirts, retrieving a beer from the shelf in her fridge where she kept beer and leftover pizza, the only items in her fridge, Clem wondered for the millionth time if she was missing something in the Coogan case.

"Here you go," she said to Russ in the living room, handing him the beer and taking his glass of bourbon. "I totally forgot you're not a whiskey guy."

Clem sat next to Russ on the couch and poured his bourbon into her glass.

"You've got quite the spread here," Russ said. He nodded toward the files on the coffee table.

"Housekeeper's year off," Clem said, shuffling the photos and various documents into their manila folders, hidden from prying eyes. You could never be too cautious.

"I couldn't help but notice copies of what looked to be official police evidence. You and Samantha Bellflower are still close, huh?"

Taking a cue from Sam, Clem cut her eyes at Russ, narrowing and angling them. "Hey, hey, I was joking," he said, raising the white flag of his palms, calloused by squash rackets and three-woods, Clem didn't have to be a PI to deduce. Russ said, "You're right. None of my affair."

"Girl's got to protect her friends."

"You're welcome for the toxicology report, by the way. I absolutely have not gotten an ounce of shit for that."

"No idea what you're talking about."

"I wonder, though. I mean, most of this stuff?" Russ waved a hand at the files. "Most of this involves the Hubbard murder. Aren't you investigating the murder of Turnip Coogan?"

What about the moon tonight had compelled all these white men to stop by Clem's place and make so many annoyingly valid points? Russ was right. Clem had been focused a bit too much on the wrong murder. Lenora Coogan had hired her to find her son's killer, not Hubbard's.

But Clem had her reasons. Whoever killed Hubbard most likely poisoned Turnip. Simple! Logical! The quickest route from point A to point B was a straight fucking line. Clem most definitely did not care about catching the person who'd taken away the father of two innocent children, a boy and a girl, ages twelve and eight. The notion of some cold-blooded killer roaming free most definitely did not lodge in Clem's mind like a pebble in her size tens. She was all about business, not justice, and the Hubbard murder was business. She didn't care that Turnip was a criminal. She didn't care that Hubbard was innocent. She only cared about the paycheck, calculated to cover her going daily rate, plus expenses.

After explaining that to Russ succinctly as possible, by telling him to go fuck himself, Clem stood from the couch and meandered to her turntable across the room. She flipped through her collection, past *Imperial Bedroom* and *Remain in Light*, past *Dirty Mind* and *Songs in the Key of Life*, past *Off the Wall*, *She's So Unusual*, and *Street Songs*, until, almost choosing *Synchronicity* but deciding that "Murder by Numbers" was too on the nose, she went with *Never for Ever*. Kate Bush and all her pixie whimsy flooded the room.

"I can go if you want," Russ said, there on the couch in his shirtsleeves and suspenders, his loosened tie and still-creased pants. The guy either didn't have a heavy beard or he'd shaved before coming over.

Clem returned to her seat next to him. "You just got here."

"I'm glad you're okay." Russ sipped his beer. "But you could've called."

"And what would you have done if I had?"

"Rattle my saber? Crack the whip?"

"Whip, huh?"

"That's not . . . You know what I meant." Staring at the label of his beer, which he'd nearly peeled clean off, Russ shuffled his feet against the wall-to-wall frieze carpet.

"Y'all *can* blush," Clem said, her smile languid but distinct, serpentine.

"Stop it."

"I meant lawyers. You've got to have a heart first, right?"

"You could have been killed, Clem. Let me make some calls. I can get a black-and-white stationed right outside. I worry about you here all alone."

Black-and-white. Talk about on the nose. Although for the most part Clem had only dated Black men, she'd gone through, while in college, one of those college phases she'd heard about, except hers didn't involve creative writing, sustainable farming, carob, or the belief that Mississippi might elect a Democrat, but rather a series of white graduate students with monosyllabic names. None of them treated her poorly. They were courteous and attentive. After the phase, though, Clem realized that to Pierce, Ford, and Grant she'd been nothing but a feather in their cap, a notch in their belt, a People I Have Dated bingo card's winning entry: BLACK GIRL.

And of course, Clem thought as she got Russ another beer and poured herself another bourbon, the square on that figurative bingo card would've been marked by one of those round plastic *tokens*.

"To Turnip," Clem said, clinking her fresh drink against Russ's fresh beer.

Russ wasn't all that bad. Most guys in his position vibrated entitlement. They gave off a low-level frequency that told people not who they were but that other people did not matter to them. Russ had no such vibrations and gave off no such frequency. His calm carried, communicable as a cold. To Clem's mind, that made Russ something of a miracle, especially given what she knew of his upbringing in the Mississippi Delta.

It had been a life shot through with moonshots, she'd heard, one in which he wanted for nothing and was obligated to care for even less. Russ Clyde was technically Russell Clyde VII. His family had parlayed the profits from its quintuple-digit acres of Mississippi Delta farm land into a very un-Mississippi-like diversity of blue-chip stock holdings. The Clydes owned a villa in Gstaad, a brownstone in New York, a town house in New Orleans, and Lord could say how many apartments around the country occupied by loafer nephews and layabout nieces, "just till they got on their feet." On the day his father, Russell Clyde VI, shoved off to that great big delta in the sky, good ol' number seven would inherit the patriarchal scepter.

"Why Meridian?" Clem asked Russ, the bourbon in her tongue collapsing the syllables of her hometown into something like *murder*. "Of all the places you could go, of all the things you could be, why assistant district attorney in Meridian, Mississippi?"

"You can't get the big job until you do the little one." Russ paused. "Plus, I figured in a place like this I could be of some good."

"Some good?"

From the turntable across the room, Kate Bush's voice careened through a series of high notes. A digital clock on wall read the time as a quarter till ten. Russ angled his body on the couch so that he faced Clem. "Did I ever tell you about my first day on the job?"

"Nuh-uh."

"I'm new to Meridian, right? Born and raised in Greenwood, college and law school at Ole Miss, I don't know this place. It's lunchtime. I head out to the street, walk around, spot this burger joint, looks halfway decent. Le Saloon."

"Oh, Jesus."

"Don't get ahead, okay?" Russ said. "So, I'm thinking, Le Saloon. It's got that French article—how bad could it be? I walk in, and it's bad. We're talking bikers, thugs, all breeds of ne'er-done-well. But I figure, hell with it. What am I going to do, run for the tall timber? No, ma'am. So I sit at the bar, order a burger and fries. The bartender, he's acting kind of squirrelly, nervous. He goes into the kitchen, where I see him talking to this older guy—the cook, I figure. They keep looking back at me."

"I hope you didn't eat that burger."

"Let me finish." Russ took a swig of beer. "The old guy steps out, asks if I'm Russ Clyde, the new assistant DA. I tell him, 'Yes, sir,' and he asks me to step back in the kitchen for a moment." Another swig for effect. "Now, am I nervous? Of course I'm nervous! But this guy is older, put-together, no visible yard ink. We head to the kitchen, and he offers his hand. Hamilton Delacroix, his name. He owns Le Saloon and, I'll later find out, half the goddamn town."

"Never heard of him."

"That doesn't surprise me. He's a low-profile type." Gingerly, drawing out the motion, Russ placed his empty beer bottle on the coffee table. "We're in the kitchen at Le Saloon, and Hamilton says I'm welcome to eat there anytime I want, but I've got to eat in the kitchen, not at the bar. I ask why, and he says he's got high expectations of me. 'Look out there,' he says, taking me by the shoulder, pointing at those thugs in the joint. 'Within a year, I am expecting you to've put away at least half those guys. When you start putting them away? That's when they figure out who you are, and that's when one of them puts a shank in your gut. My conscience cannot abide.' His exact words. 'My conscience cannot abide.'"

In need of a refill, Clem walked to the bar across the room, trying to parse the story she had just heard. What did it have to do with why Russ had moved to Meridian in the first place? A gulp of bourbon, as she sat back down on the couch, helped her find the answer. "You wanted to be a gunfighter," Clem said to Russ, "so you loaded your wagon and moved to a town full of gunfighters."

"Nutshell, I suppose."

"It's nuts, is what it is."

It was also true, Clem understood now, after what had happened at the John Wesley Hardin Club. In the Wild West of Meridian, Mississippi, every moment, every interaction, every second of the day bore the potential for gunfire. Cordite lingered about the air of this town like a paper mill's hydrogen sulfide did in others. The smell reminded everyone of the past that wouldn't perish, a past apparent not only in that smell but in the tangle of abandoned rail spurs, the shudder in your feet at the approach of a locomotive, the shriek of steam as the Queen City Limited barreled down the Magnolia Co. redline.

"ADA Russell Clyde," Clem said. "The man who shot liberty's valence."

Russ gave a polite chuckle and then took on a polite tone. "Clem, I want you to know I'm not some hothead vigilante cowboy." He brushed lint off his pants. "I really am sorry about what happened with your dad. But we had to pursue the drug charges. It's my duty of office."

He was referring to the raid on Baldwin Gems, during which the police team discovered, in a floor safe covered by a bright yellow rug Clem had woven for her father in home economics, three kilos of uncut Colombian flake. The additional charges against Lauder Baldwin tripled what would have been a fairly easy stretch at Parchman Farm.

Clem, who never could wrap her head around the fact her dad had kept that hideous rug with a giant smiley face on it, said to Russ, "Let's not talk about that. I don't want to think about that. Besides, I kind of have a thing for hothead vigilante cowboys."

Russ made finger guns, grinned sheepishly, and went, "Pow, pow, pow."

"Dork."

"Guilty."

Where were Clem's manners? "You need another," she said, grabbing Russ's empty and, despite his protests, bringing him a fresh beer. "I have to say, Russ. You do surprise."

"Pleasantly, I hope," he said, with a cute little hop in his voice. His feet again did that shimmy-shuffle thing against the carpet.

"Ceci n'est pas une pipe."

"Excuse me?"

"Just a saying I heard in art class."

The frog of her thoughts jumping from one lily pad to the next, Clem found herself returning to the Cocktail Napkin Theory. It scratched at the inside of her skull, some creature with claws trapped in her subconscious, desperate to see the light of day. Apparently still hewing to its origins in Magritte, the Cocktail Napkin Theory felt like something Clem would have scribbled *on* a cocktail napkin, a crazy idea, a ludicrous invention.

Though was it actually all that ludicrous? Yes, Jacob Cassidy and his recently confirmed partner were clearly the prime suspects, the best leads, but what did it hurt to entertain the idea of someone else having been there, someone dangerous enough to have pulled the trigger and, frighteningly, smart enough to have covered their tracks, leaving only a cocktail napkin as evidence?

It had to be an individual Hubbard knew reasonably well, if he felt comfortable enough to play the piano with them in his house. Clem said, "Did y'all find prints of any familiars that stood out? I'm not talking family. More like business associate, that sort of thing."

"On the Hubbard case?" Russ asked. "I can check. You don't think it was someone other than Cassidy, do you? He's our man. It's slam-dunk. Who else could it be?"

An urgency in Russ's tone tripped an alarm system proprietary to, in Clem's experience, the children of recidivist criminals: Don't. Trust. Anyone. "It's nothing," she said, waving a hand that seemed to skip every other frame, a glitch in the film stock. "My wild hairs. You know me."

"Trying to."

"Yeah?"

His steady gaze focused with Clem's unsteady one, Russ inched forward, and when Clem reciprocated, he inched forward again. He certainly was taking his time, she thought, recalling the first time they'd kissed, in the Ho Jo's parking lot after a particularly happy hour. Clem parted her lips as Russ, that nervous goof, that shy gunfighter, parted his own.

The impact of their mouths seemed to trip a breaker instead of an alarm. Pain jolted through Clem's lips, chin, teeth, and cheeks, followed by an audible pop. Both she and Russ jerked away from each other, raising a hand to their respective mouths. "Ouch!" Russ said. He shuffled his feet in confusion. "What was that?"

Clem pointed at the carpet. "Static."

The next morning, Clem woke involuntarily alone—Russ had claimed, while leaving her place after the static zap, that *he*'d had too much to drink, the polite doofus—and was greeted by her neighbors having a row on the other side of her paper-thin walls. They were worried about the black-and-white police cruiser that had been parked across the street for hours.

9

ODETTE

Later that morning, driving with Dixon to the courthouse, Clem attempted to explain why Russ was an asshole. "Everybody in my building is Black. A police cruiser to us means cops, and to us cops rarely mean something good. My neighbors were going crazy! Cops knock on your door, they're not there to make sure everything's okay. Trust me. Cops will do everything they possibly can to make sure everything is very much not okay."

"You do realize you used to be a cop."

"So I should know."

"But Russ meant well," Dixon said. "He was trying to look out for you."

"Go tell Miss Wallace in 4B that. She's had it in for me ever since I moved into the building, and now she thinks I'm running a crack den. Fucking Russ."

Cup of coffee in hand, steam billowing across his wry expression, Dixon took a sip. "Did you?" he asked.

"What? Of course not. Shut up."

The courthouse seethed with that quiet rage born out of bureaucracy, lawyers whispering to clients, clients muttering to lawyers, the squeak-squeak of leather soles on marble floors echoing against the fractured ceiling. Down a corridor, a baby wailed. "Shh, now," the Black mother cooed as her white lawyer said in his Southern accent, "No judge I ever met will buy the claim you were *paid* to walk around such a well-to-do street with your child crying. My sister-in-law's in real estate, and I mean, she would but *ne*ver!"

Clem loathed this place and its vitiated nostalgia, redolent of an era when that idiot Atticus Finch thought he could win a rigged game, when you needed a tool to open a can of beer, when small-time felons didn't wind up as small-time sidewalk smears after doing a Greg Louganis off the roof.

At least the beer cans had gotten better, Clem thought as she walked into the sheriff's office. She handed her ID to the clerk on duty. "My partner and I would like to speak with Odette Hubbard. I believe she's one of your trustees."

The clerk, some kid with a pentimento of acne scars layered beneath his acne, pocketed the $100 bill Clem had folded around her ID, nodded at a door across the room, and said he'd see what could be done. Five minutes later, after Clem and Dixon did their best to get comfortable in a storage space barely able to fit the eight filing cabinets already occupying it, let alone eight filing cabinets plus two people, Odette Hubbard walked in, maxing out the space's capacity.

Her two-tone hair, blond with five inches of brown at the roots, fell down the front of her bright orange jumpsuit, the hair a testament to the number of months she'd been locked up, the jumpsuit a testament to her good behavior during those months. She propped the top sides of her wrists against her cocked hips, letting her fingers jut behind her like the plumage of a yardbird. "And who the shit are you two supposed to be?"

Offering her hand, Clem introduced herself and Dixon. "We'd like to ask you some questions."

"We're meeting in here, I'm guessing y'all aren't exactly sanctioned by the sheriff's office." Odette took a pack of cigarettes from her pocket. "What's in it for me?"

"Chance to clear your name," Clem said, lighting the cigarette for Odette. A classic PI trick: Keep a matchbook on you at all times. The Old Hollywood manners of lighting someone's cigarette for them disarmed that person before an interview. In need of prints? Hand your suspect the matchbook and let them light the cigarette themselves. "Clark Gable over here," Odette said as Clem shook out the match.

Dixon found fold-out chairs propped between the filing cabinets. Once they were seated, the three of them looked to Clem, sitting almost knee to knee, without the bulwark of a table, like a group therapy session after the funding had been pulled. The fluorescent light did no one any favors. A roach scurried into an air vent. A puff of hair wafted into a corner.

"A trustee, huh?" Clem said. "Must be nice. What detail they got you on?"

"*Nice.*" Odette blew smoke toward the ceiling and ashed on the floor. "Do you know how long I've been in? Since August. *August.* But yeah, it's real nice I'm allowed to do some filing. It's positively swell."

"How many trustees they got total?" Dixon asked. It was a good question, one that made Clem proud of her partner. She loved when his thinking synced with her own. Jail trustees were inmates who, because of good behavior, were allowed to handle certain tasks, such as mopping floors, washing dishes, doing laundry, and taking out the trash. If everything went by the book, the trustees were supervised at all times by a deputy, but in Clem's experience, everything rarely went by the book, especially in this rancid town.

An unsupervised trustee could just about do as they pleased. They could pocket extra bars of soap, or bring in contraband to sell, or watch TV after lights-out, or sprinkle poison in another inmate's food.

"Fifteen trustees total," Odette said.

Dixon asked, "And how long have you been one?"

"Since August."

Clem said, "Thought you said you were booked in August."

"Sheriff trusts my type, I guess. Why they call us trustees."

"Type?" Dixon asked.

"You know, nonviolent. Well-behaved."

In other words, Clem thought, the sheriff trusted pretty white women from the right side of the proverbial tracks—tracks that, due to Meridian's roots as the junction of the Southern Railway and the Mobile & Ohio Railroad, were more than proverbial. Never mind if the pretty white woman was accused of hiring a hit man to kill her husband. Never mind if an inmate whose testimony could've led to her conviction had been awaiting trial in the very same jail.

"Did you ever come in contact with Turnip Coogan?" Clem asked. "Before his fall."

"No, and it's a good thing I didn't. Son of a bitch is the reason I'm here."

"Are you saying you would have harmed him if you could?"

"My daughter is seven years old and alone without her mother. My son is nine years old and alone without his mother. I'm saying I would have *killed* Turnip if I could."

Shit. That tossed Clem off the trail. Guilty people did not tend to declare they wished they could have committed the crime. Unless this woman was exceptionally sly, which Clem doubted, she did not poison Turnip Coogan, whether out of retaliation for his having talked or out of fear he might talk further. Still, she had to know something, even if she didn't know that she knew.

"How long were you and your husband together?" Clem asked.

"Me and Randy, let's see, we got together back in seventy-five, I think."

"First marriage?"

"Second. But it might as well have been the first. My first husband had the marriage annulled. Scrubbed the records clean."

"Why?" asked Dixon.

"I dropped out of high school and left home at an unadvisedly early age. I met a man in his thirties. I fell in love with him. Weird thing about men in their thirties? They don't like it when they find out their supposedly eighteen-year-old bride is actually fourteen."

"Whoa," Dixon said with his entire face. "Great balls of fire."

"At least he wasn't my cousin."

When Clem was a girl—younger than fourteen, of course, and very much unwed—she would often imbue everyday objects with talismanic powers: a chipped marble, a bird feather, a pop-top, some old domino she found in a gutter. Later, while on the force, she'd learned to treat information the same as those objects. Clem pocketed the revelation about Odette having been a child bride. You never knew what could heat up a case after it went cold.

"So you met Hubbard in 1975 or thereabouts," Clem said to Odette.

"He was still based in Biloxi then."

"What brought him to Meridian?"

"'Don't knock opportunity.' That's what Randy used to say. He saw opportunity in this town."

"That makes one," Clem said.

"People don't get rich off rich people." Odette stubbed out her cigarette on the floor. "They get rich off poor people. According to Randy. This town's got a lot of poor."

"How'd y'all meet?" Dixon asked.

"Back then Randy hadn't gone out on his own yet. He still worked for DLD. Dixie Land Developments."

"*Dixie* Land?" Clem asked, a growly voice in her head warning it was nothing. Blatant clues usually led nowhere. Regardless how imbecilic its upper management, the Dixie Mafia wouldn't name one of its shell companies "Dixie Land." There may be an X in the word, but it never, ever marked the spot. Ask any cop worth their shield. Hell, ask any cop who wasn't worth it, which happened to be most of them, Clem would heartily concede.

"They're based on the gulf, from New Orleans to Panama Shitty. Randy's from New Orleans, so he knew how to handle those gulf folks. Excuse me. *Was* from." Odette looked at the ceiling, as though putting in drops, the whites of her eyes Mylared in tears. Clem figured it had to be an act. Some people instinctually knew how to perform grief.

"He wasn't with them long," Odette said. "Shooting star, that man. His side hustles had side hustles. Dixie Land was holding him back. Look away, look away, right? Plus, it never really sat well with Randy, working for an organization that's connected."

"Connected to what exactly?" Dixon asked.

With a shrug of her shoulders tucked inside her tone of voice, Odette said, "The Matrangas."

A chasm opened on the floor, dark and endless and dank, a nothingness that echoed fathoms deep. Clem teetered on the edge of it. What had she gotten herself into? The Matranga crime family had been flourishing in New Orleans for more than a century. Although Clem supposed they shouldn't frighten her any more than the Dixie Mafia, the Matrangas occupied a tiny part of her mind locked in amber, forever in childhood, still afraid of the closet monster and the Sowashee Creek witch.

Clem's arrested development with regard to the Matrangas owed mostly to the period when she lived with her aunt Myrtle and uncle Hersh while her father was doing his first bid. Aunt Myrtle and Uncle Hersh, hardly political, idolized the figurehead of the government, the man who held the highest office and on whom they had fastened all their hopes. On the day Kennedy was assassinated, a frightening pall swept across their home, the pall that comes with the once-unimaginable notion that hope has breathed its last.

In Clem's mind, then as now, the Matrangas' alleged involvement cast them in that same frightening pall. They may have killed the president of the United States! And not just any president. They may have killed the best if not the only good one to hold the office since Mr. Lincoln.

"Did Randy maintain any ties with the Matranga crime family?" Clem asked Odette as she mentally forced the chasm at her feet to seal. It slowly shrank to a pinhole. "That is, after he departed this Dixie Land Development and started his own company."

"Oh God, no. Randy? He was straight as an arrow. His friends, though . . ."

"Mm?"

"Randy liked to play the badass. He was always taking me to the East End Tea Room, Nelva Court, Charters, the John Wesley Hardin."

Dixon said, "Heard of it," and his grin lasted approximately 0.258 seconds after he glanced at Clem and double-took the flat, cold rebuke in her expression.

"Rough joints, is what I mean." Odette got another cigarette going. "He always had a gun on him, though I doubt he ever pulled a trigger. And the bodyguards? Mostly for show, made him feel like a big man."

"Is that why he would slap you around?" Dixon asked, his voice and demeanor suddenly grim. Clem knew how much he hated men who beat women. Drunk for a father. With a gentle bob of his chin and gentler lift to his eyebrows, Dixon said, "To feel like a big man?"

Smoke crept out of Odette's mouth, an upside-down Victorian mourning veil. "Love taps. What he called them. Love. Taps." Odette's eyes histrionically brightened as she said, "Randy wrote me a poem this one time. He was a fan*tas*tic poet. Want to hear the last bit?" She cleared her throat with the same histrionics. "'When you call forth my taps of love so eagerly / My heart rises up like troops at reveille.'" She shrugged. "Rhymes."

"Are these love taps why you had him killed?" Clem asked. She ignored the critical look Dixon gave her in response.

"I did not have him killed," Odette said. "Tried to? Sure. But I called it off."

"Why?"

"It wouldn't have done me any good. Did you know he bought a yacht couple months before? But was it all paid up? Nuh-uh. Installment plan. Like how my mom used to buy Christmas presents. Layaway. I probably would have inherited that debt and tons more. Broke motherfucker. 'Put it on credit!' The American way. The American *Express* way."

It seemed Clem was right. Odette had called off the hit when she realized she wouldn't have inherited any of the life insurance policy. The economics had to shake out to countenance murder, trickle-down or not. "Did you have any interaction with Jacob Cassidy?" Clem asked.

"That all went through Turnip."

"What about Flynn?"

"Who?"

"Cassidy's partner."

"Far as I know, Cassidy didn't have a partner. At one point, though, Turnip did say something about 'keeping it in the family.'"

"Whose family? Turnip's family?"

Before Odette could answer, the door to the room inched open, and through it appeared the clerk with acne pockmarks. "Time's up, y'all," he whispered. "Boss man just got back from lunch. Odette, wait a minute until after they've gone before you leave the room."

"Thank you for your candor," Dixon said to Odette after the clerk had left.

Odette leaned back in her chair, thumbing her cigarette butt. The cherry lay burning on the floor. "Turnip's mother hired y'all, right? To find who killed her boy?"

"That's correct," Clem said.

"And so you think whoever killed Randy must have also killed Turnip."

"It's very much a possibility."

"But what if not?" Odette said. "Say you nab Turnip's killer. You give up on looking into Randy's? His killer goes free?"

"It's all about the job," Clem said. "Nothing to do with justice. I'm sorry."

"Ever take on two cases at the same time?"

"Well."

After asking Clem and Dixon's daily rate, Odette reached down the neck of her jumpsuit. She removed a wad of bills, crumpled from having been squeezed between her bra and chest for God knew how long.

"Randy was a son of a bitch, and I'm glad he's dead," Odette said, counting the bills, "but his being dead is the reason I'm in here and not with my children."

"Odette, we can't. It'd be a conflict of interest."

"I'm hearing a harmony of interest. You said so yourself, the two cases are connected. Why not get twice the pay for a single job? That's all it is to you, right? A job."

"But the ethics."

"You're worried about ethics, give Turnip's mother a discount. I don't care." Odette handed Clem a bundle of hundreds. "All I'm asking is a week or two. If you don't find Randy's killer, okay. But if you do find who murdered the father of my children? There's a thousand-dollar bonus in it for you. You'd be shocked how easy it is to make a few bucks in here."

A few bucks, Clem thought after she and Dixon walked out of the filing room. Odette must have this whole place wired, a perk of being a trustee. Clem looked at Dixon and nodded at the money in her hand. She made a grossed-out face and said, "It's damp."

Dixon shrugged. "Twice the pay."

"And for doing what we were already doing anyhow."

"In this economy, too."

Clem pocketed the money. "Boob sweat dries same as regular sweat," she said, mentally spending that bonus.

In an echoing corridor of the courthouse, as deputies and lawyers and inmates, current and future, shuffled into and out of the sheriff's office, Clem paused to chew on a few items she'd learned from Odette. By "keep it in the family," had Turnip been referring to his criminal family or his actual one? Was Randy Hubbard the unintended victim in some turf war between the DM and the Matrangas? And why did that guy over there wheeling a yellow mop bucket into the janitor's closet look so familiar?

Clem found the answer to her last question in an exposed patch of bicep. The janitor had rolled his short sleeves like some 1950s greaser, revealing a tattoo of a cross draped with a Confederate flag. Clem never forgot a bigoted motherfucker. She had seen this one in the photograph Lenora Coogan had shown her of Turnip and his friends on the cockfighting circuit.

10

THE SPIDER LILY MEN

Meridian needed a better class of hot-pillow joint. That was for damned sure. Throughout his adult life, Christopher had sampled most of the hotels, motels, inns, and lodges in town—whether out of convenience, preference, or necessity, depending on who he was sharing the room with—and none of them ranked more than a notch or two above fleabag. The AC units wheezed and whirred, barely keeping the triple digits at bay. Eerie stains crept up from the undersides of strategically flipped mattresses. The complimentary drinking glasses had to be scrubbed clean before they could receive a snort of whiskey.

"And the irony?" Christopher once joked to his sister, Molly. The rooms rarely if ever had closets.

Of course, Christopher thought as he lay in bed, tapping his cigarette above an ashtray perched on his bare chest, the Elysian Motor Court was basically one giant closet for Meridian. It was a place to visit but not be seen. Lord knew how many wedding rings had been accidentally left on the nightstands. *Hi, yes, this is Mr. Smith. I stayed with y'all last night. Room 12. Did the housekeeper happen to find . . .*

"Time is it?" Christopher asked the man in bed next to him. "Checkout at the Elysian is nine if you check in before five."

"P.M.?"

"You're the one said you couldn't stay the night. That costs twenty extra. I can call the front desk and ask to extend, you want."

"No. I've got an early meeting. These small-town motels, though. Seedy."

Christopher scrunched out his cigarette and moved the ashtray to the carpeted floor. He ran his hand through the man's deep-pile chest hair. "Bet you say that to all the boys."

According to what he'd said at the bar that afternoon, the guy was in town for some kind of consult with the local audio equipment company that was quickly becoming a national one. They were thinking of going public. The guy said he'd flown in from New York. He had asked Christopher why he was wearing a camouflage jacket. "Are you on a hunt?"

Yeah, Christopher thought two hours later, but apparently not for big game.

The guy pulled the clicker from where it was Velcro'd to the headboard. "They got HBO?" he said, turning on the TV, its rabbit-ear antenna as plain as actual rabbit ears.

"HB-what?"

"Jesus Christ. I'm surprised this state has running water."

"I was fucking with you, asshole. We've got HBO in Mississippi, just probably not at a place like the Elysian Motor Court." Christopher turned up the dial on his accent. "We also happen to have running water, a whole river's worth. We even put our name on it."

"Bite my head off already. I didn't realize the yokels were so into *drama*."

Wow. So here was yet another jerk in a long line of jerks. Christopher didn't know why he put up with this shit. The yuppie assholes from out of town, in their repp ties and pinstripes, with their Cross pens and Rolexes, were no different than the young, non-urban professionals who tossed their napkins on the table, excused themselves from their family dinner at the country club, and cornered you in the men's room. Instead of cloak-and-dagger, these city queens were just dagger.

Christopher missed Flynn, the closest he'd ever had to an actual boyfriend. A pilot formerly based out of Atlanta, Flynn had first entered Christopher's life eight years ago, when Christopher was just seventeen. Flynn, twenty years older, had taught him how to maneuver through the scene. He'd taught him the signals, the hints, who to trust, who not to give the time of night. "The South is a minefield, a paradox of physics," Flynn used to say. "Being light in the loafers somehow makes you all the more likely to trigger one."

"Wait. Stop. Go back," Christopher said to the yuppie asshole, whose name he couldn't remember, a name that was probably fake anyway. "Back some more. The news channel."

WTOK's evening news anchors materialized from the weak signal like cross-stitch figures on a grandmother's sampler. Stacks of prop papers in hand, the sack-suited man and woman read from a teleprompter, oblivious that their words were sending one of the occupants of room 8 at the Elysian Motor Court into cardiac arrest.

"More news on the murder of real estate entrepreneur Randall Hubbard," said the woman, a photo of Hubbard appearing above her shoulder, at once taunting and accusatory. "An eyewitness has reported seeing two men the night of the murder. A sketch artist has provided the following rendering of one of the men. Unfortunately, the witness could not make out the accomplice."

His breath held and fists clenched, Christopher watched as a black-and-white sketch replaced the photo of Hubbard above the anchor's shoulder, a Jiminy Cricket about to whisper in her ear and rat out Christopher—to the news anchor, to all of Meridian. The face in the sketch, odd but familiar, confused Christopher for a moment, though he soon realized why. Those long ears, the acute brows, that cropped hair: it was Mr. Spock.

It was Mr. Spock! All his features had been diluted by the sketch artist, ears shorter, brows straighter, but staring at Christopher from the television set was none other than the chief science officer of the USS *Enterprise*.

"If you recognize this man," said the news anchor, "please notify the police."

The eyewitness must have seen Christopher and Jacob *after* they put on the *Star Trek* masks they'd brought for the job. It had felt logical at the time. Ski masks were hard to find in Mississippi.

"You okay?" asked the guy next to Christopher. "You look a little flushed."

"I'm doing great, actually."

"Done with your *news*?" the yuppie asshole said, the mustard he spread on that last word implying he didn't consider it as such, here in this city.

"Have at."

The clicking of channels mirroring the slowing pace of his heart, Christopher eased back into a semblance of calm, a simulacrum of peace. Never before would he have imagined he'd be so grateful for nearsighted neighbors. God bless you, Leonard Nimoy.

"Have you seen this yet?" the yuppie asshole asked after stopping on NBC. "Don Johnson is so fucking hot. I'd go for that stubble look myself if my senior VP wasn't such a Wharton prepster nelly."

On the TV appeared shots of the "vice" Miami had to offer, models in teensy bikinis, gleaming Rolls-Roycean grillwork, racehorses galloping to victory. Christopher barely paid attention. Ever since his dolt of a sister had told the PIs a man named "Flynn" had been Cassidy's partner on the Hubbard job, Christopher had been thinking more and more of the actual Flynn, who'd transferred to Chicago last year. Meridian's airport did not get any service from that city, but Flynn still managed to catch a jump seat and drop by once every few months. He'd bring Christopher silk button-ups and pastel scarves, neon tanks and linen sports jackets, clothes they both knew Christopher couldn't wear in Meridian. Queen City? Yeah, right.

"You need to get out of town more," Flynn said on his last visit. "Go to New Orleans, Atlanta, even Birmingham. Toss those Carhartts and *live a life,* baby. Promise?"

Promises, promises, Christopher told himself, standing from the bed, ignoring Crockett and Tubbs. He walked naked across the room, removed a pint of Jack Daniel's from his jacket, and took a much-needed gulp.

"Remember, checkout is nine," Christopher said as he got dressed. "That's an hour from now."

"You're leaving?"

At the door to the motel room, his back to the guy in bed, Christopher paused, raising his fist to the doorframe. He unclenched the fist and pressed his hand flat against the unvarnished wood. What the hell. It was worth a shot.

"Yeah, I got to split." Christopher turned back toward the yuppie asshole. "My aunt's in the hospital, and she's not doing so great. I promised I'd visit her. Actually, I'm supposed to pick up her meds. But they're expensive. Health care these days, you know?"

Neon and synthesized guitar pulsed out of *Miami Vice*. The yuppie asshole, looking away from Don Johnson in those rolled sleeves, sat up in bed.

"Oh, no. Will she be okay?" he asked, the concern on his face mutating with every change of scene on the TV.

"I just don't know. She needs those meds. Insurance lapsed."

Somehow the yuppie asshole's entire body seemed to smirk. "HBO, running water, and rent boys. Mississippi has everything." The corporal smirk turned into a sneer. "You think I'm some john off the street? Listen. If you can afford top-shelf you don't pay for well liquor."

It had been worth a shot. Money was tight. Christopher had missed the last two notes on his pickup. "And here I was going to ask you to explain what IPO stands for," he said.

Outside, in the crisp evening air, Christopher zipped his jacket. Traffic blurred past on the interstate. The Elysian's neon sign cast a red glow of VACANCY. Back in the old days, Christopher had read, Meridian's early settlers would move away so frequently, the townspeople that remained would paint GTT on the doors of the abandoned homes, GONE TO TEXAS, regardless of where the settlers had actually moved, regardless of where they could be found.

It was funny. All that mattered to the people left behind? Others were gone.

On a different TV the next day, after the yuppie asshole had joined the blurry ranks of forgotten assholes, Christopher watched Ronald Reagan talk to Barbara Walters about family values. They were his priority as he approached the start of his new term of office.

"You know me, Barbara. We go back. You know Nancy. You know the kids," said the president. "Father, mother, children. Husband, wife, children. Those three things make up the family unit, and they're as all-American as red, white, and blue. The family is my top priority in this second term the American people have so graciously given me. I will bring back family values. The only *nuclear* I'm concerned about is the family kind."

A derisive, incredulous laugh broke free of Christopher's throat. After quickly covering his mouth, he looked around the ranch, at the handful of guys playing poker at one of the card tables, at the pair of guys shooting pool in the back, but nobody seemed to have noticed. Christopher didn't want to blow his cover. Whereas most of his DM colleagues had bought into the ideological claptrap espoused by management, even when said colleagues were clearly being used as the levers, buttons, and triggers for what had to be non-ideological aims, Christopher only cared about the cash, cold and hard and on the barrelhead.

The ranch served as a DM headquarters of sorts. A former roadhouse in the outskirts of Kemper County, the communal part of the ranch included a well-stocked bar, a bunk room for anybody needing to sleep one off, a kitchen for anybody wanting to cook a meal, and a stock room that was now, Christopher had been told but never actually seen, an armory. A DM shell company had purchased the roadhouse and five hundred acres of land surrounding it to create what Christopher thought of as a financial oasis. The barn across the parking lot hosted cockfights. Tunnels running beneath housed various explosives.

"I said this throughout the campaign, Barbara, and in my heart, I believe it to be true," the president said after a commercial break. "It's morning again in America. A new day is here."

His smirk reflected in the mirror behind the bar, Christopher raised his pint of beer and, toasting himself, took a sip. *In my heart.* The man was always saying horseshit like that. What heart? Ronald Reagan only cared about certain people. Christopher's parents weren't any different. What the president called a sin, they called a plight. That phrase *nuclear family* was fitting. Christopher's parents had blown up theirs, fallout be damned.

Hell with them, Christopher thought, rotating on his barstool. He stared out a duct-taped window, where, in the pale afternoon light, it definitely did not look like morning in America.

Half a dozen dually pickups were parked in the lot. People so often said El Caminos were the mullets of cars: business in the front, party in the back. Christopher knew that to be way off. Duallies were the mullets, except the party in the back, around these parts at least, was a trailer with a false floor hiding kilos of heroin and cocaine, its cargo a dozen crates of unshucked corn and unshelled beans placed artfully on top of firearms, cash, and marijuana.

"Another beer?" asked the bartender, Toots McGonagall, a Vietnam vet and former safecracker sidelined by Parkinson's. DM management paid for the medication not covered by Veterans Affairs or Medicaid.

"Thanks," Christopher said. He could barely notice the hand tremors as Toots held a glass under the tap and drew the beer. "Heard of any jobs coming up? Sands of the Sahara, past few months."

Toots slid the beer toward Christopher. "Couple jobs. Jimmy Spatchcock and his brother are pulling a smash-and-grab in Mendenhall. Gas station, I think. Clement Redondo has a line on some kind of fake kidnapping? Don't know how that works. Tony Balsamic and Ray-Ray Jr. are talking about boosting a truck of VCRs passing through Hattiesburg."

"How do you fake a kidnapping?"

"The mind reels, my man."

After thanking Toots, rumored to be called that because of chronic childhood flatulence, Christopher looked back up at Mr. Reagan chatting with Babs. It was kind of ironic. That dude in his starched denim jacket and his cowboy hat without a sweat ring was the reason Christopher had been introduced to the DM and its own version of down-to-earth.

Five years earlier, at the Neshoba County Fair, near Philadelphia, Mississippi, Christopher had gone with friends to hear the Republican candidate make a speech while on his 1980 presidential campaign. What the hell else do I have to do today? Christopher, out of work, had wondered. Back then he still wore the political beliefs of his parents like the antiquated clothes from the backs of their closets he scrounged for Tacky Day. At the fair, Reagan focused less on the jobs Christopher and his friends so achingly, desperately needed and more on what it seemed the crowd just outside Philadelphia, Mississippi, so achingly, desperately wanted to hear. *States' rights this!* he ranted. *States' rights that!*

Christopher found a job that night at a bar, when he met a crew from the Dixie Mafia. They were drinking to the murder of three civil rights workers in 1964 that some of their older colleagues had committed near the fairgrounds. Christopher had been leery, especially at the relish the crew took in talking about the murders, but a paying job was a paying job. Later that night he helped them knock off a high-stakes poker game at a city councilman's hunting camp.

Only recently, after the shit show that was the Hubbard hit, with management calling the job off last minute, did Christopher begin to suspect the triple murder in Philadelphia, Mississippi, had been motivated by more than race. It also involved where the bodies had been buried.

"Almost forgot," Toots said, approaching from a corner of the bar. He flipped through the pages of a notepad. "You got a call yesterday. Guy sounded kind of frantic."

The slip of paper that Toots ripped from the pad and handed Christopher was scrawled with the message, *Call Flynn–URGENT.*

Those three words somersaulted Christopher across a threadbare gym mat of emotions: anger at Flynn, to whom he'd given the ranch's phone number *only in case of an emergency*; worry for Flynn, who might actually *be* in an emergency; anger at himself, for getting angry at Flynn when he might actually be in an emergency; and, finally, worry for himself—selfish, selfish worry for himself. He worried Toots might see in his face how much he cared for whoever had left the message. He worried the other guys at the ranch might figure out why exactly he cared so much for whoever had left the message. Christopher, who'd always taken pride in his ability never to fall victim to love, also worried—selfishly, God but how selfishly—he'd lost that "gift."

A dial tone greeted him when he lifted the receiver to his ear. In a dark, empty corner of the ranch, the phone line snaking across the floor and the cradle roosting on the table in front of him, Christopher punched the numbers he knew by heart. Screw the long-distance charges.

"Chr-is," Flynn half cooed, half scolded, somehow intuiting who had called.

This wasn't a time for kid games. "Is everything okay?" Christopher asked. "Are *you* okay?"

"For now."

"What's that supposed to mean?"

"The wheel goes 'round and 'round."

"I repeat."

"How are you?"

"Flynn."

On one of the TVs behind the bar, Barbara Walters turned to the camera, vivid California sun sharpening the lines around her eyes. "There you have it," she said. "From actor to politician, Ronald Reagan has remained one thing above all. He's a human being, a human being with conviction, with compassion, with, I steadfastly believe, heart. Please join us on January twenty-first for his second inauguration as the president of the United States of America."

Flynn coughed. "I thought it was a bruise at first. Purple spot on my neck."

"Oh God."

"They don't have a test for this thing yet, but my doctor says he's seen enough of it to know. He did his residency at San Francisco General."

"Flynn," Christopher tried to say, but his throat closed around the name, raising its pitch, turning it into a plea. His lower lids cupped tears. His hands forgot how to work.

"You know why I'm calling, right?"

Because you wanted the first person to know to be the man you love. But of course, Christopher knew, that wasn't the reason. "Yes," he managed to say.

"You're probably fine," Flynn said. "There's still so much they don't know about this thing."

Hope kicked and thrashed in Christopher's mind, a drowning swimmer not yet willing to give up. He couldn't lose Flynn. He couldn't lose Flynn. "You said it yourself! There's so much they don't know. You can beat this. You're strong. When have you ever lost a fight?"

"Baby," Flynn said, hundreds of miles away. "It's spider lily time for me."

Across the room, while one guy at the poker table raked in a pile of chips and another guy at the pool table called his shot, the front door to the ranch swooshed open. Jacob Cassidy surveyed the crowd, his thumbs hitched into his belt, a cigarette dangling from his parted lips. On spotting Christopher, Cassidy strolled toward him. "Well-the, well-the-well," he said, grinding out his cigarette on the floor with the scuffed toe of his boot. "You're not exactly a hard man to find."

Spider lilies bloomed in cemeteries. That was the first thing Flynn ever told Christopher about the flowers. Spider lilies bloomed in cemeteries, but not necessarily marked ones.

"Legend goes," Flynn said, "when you say goodbye to somebody you'll never meet again, spider lilies bloom along their path. Back in Georgia, my first boyfriend was beaten to death walking home. They say he made a pass at the wrong guy at the bar that night. Son of a bitch caved in the back of his skull. He bled out alone on the sidewalk.

"I had to look at the spot where he died every day on my way to work. Come the next fall, swear to God, these red, tendrily flowers sprang up right next to the spot on the sidewalk.

"Over the years since, I've heard about so many dying that way. Glance at somebody wrong, out comes the tire iron, the baseball bat, the Maglite. Have you ever been hit by a Maglite? That's pain. Beaten to death by light. Can you imagine?" Flynn shook his head. "Thousands of victims. Every fall I picture spider lilies blooming in the places where they died, where they were killed. America? It's covered in spider lilies.

"Now with this new thing, GRID, whatever, more spider lilies are coming."

In Jacob Cassidy's truck, Christopher stared out the passenger-side window, studying the roadside, looking for red flowers. *It's spider lily time for me.* The gray sky sapped color from the grass and trees, most of which were layered in dust from the latest dry spell. Piebald cows moseyed through piebald pastures. Old hay bales melted into the ground like dropped ice cream cones. Abandoned cabins dotted the ridges of abandoned farms.

"This won't take a while," Jacob said. "I'll get you back to the ranch after."

They had to knot a loose end from the Hubbard job, Jacob had said when he told Christopher to come with him. "Orders from management." Christopher had been too out of sorts to protest. He'd been too out of sorts to consider or care what the loose end might be.

"Why so glum, chum?" Jacob asked.

Christopher kept his focus on the posted property out his window. "Oh, I don't know. Maybe the fact you almost killed my sister?"

"And I feel awful about that," Jacob said. "I was after the PI. I had no idea the girl next to her was your sister."

"She's pregnant, you know."

"Seriously? Fuck."

With an aura of calm as deliberate as his use of a turn signal, Cassidy pulled onto the highway that led back south toward Meridian. Christopher had been able to tell from the second he met Cassidy that he was the type of professional who gave nothing to chance. No turn signal would go unused as surely as no prints would be left behind after a job. Only a fool would let worry lights fill their rearview because they were literally too lazy to lift a finger.

"Where we heading?" Christopher asked when Cassidy exited onto the interstate that ran through Meridian, an artery to more prosperous cities, what Christopher thought of as the real queens, the real kings, the bona fide royals.

"To clarity," said Cassidy.

Downtown entered the landscape, buildings of tan brick hunching toward the streets, their backs turned against the slate sky. That once-booming business district was foregrounded by the hotels, motels, inns, and lodges bordering the interstate. Christopher could almost smell the cigarette burns spewing cotton lint on those shabby bedspreads. "I want you to know I didn't tell Molly anything," he said. "Only that the job was called off, that we didn't pop anyone. Swear on my life, I didn't tell her what happened after."

"I'm hurt," Cassidy said. "Do you hold me in such low regard? Do you think I'd ever intentionally harm a woman with child? Only time I ever hurt a woman was back at Khe Sanh, and she would've done me if I hadn't done her. I'll tell you what I am curious about, though."

"Yeah?"

Cassidy nodded toward the side of the interstate, where the sign for the Elysian Motor Court streaked past. "I'm curious about your pillow talk. Do you ever get a little loose-lipped after? Want to brag what a badass you are?"

"I don't know what you're—"

"Christopher."

"Okay. Okay." Breathe. Inhale, exhale. "I assure you," Christopher enunciated more than spoke, "I have never said a word to anyone. Not. A. Single. Soul."

Outside of town, as they exited the interstate and then turned onto a dirt road, Christopher willed himself to stay calm, despite the sweat drenching his back. Cassidy had been keeping tabs on him. That was understandable. The man practiced caution. "You've got to believe me," Christopher said, staring at a faded green sign for Lost Gap beside the road.

"Know why they named this area Lost Gap?" Cassidy asked, ruts in the dirt road adding extra syllables to his words. "Underground iron deposits. An old railroad guy told me about it. Back in the 1800s, they're building one of the rail lines, and their compasses go haywire because of the iron deposits. Right where we are now. A lost gap in the line."

Cassidy pulled his truck to the side of the road, which, Christopher noted, was so overgrown it barely qualified as one. "How about let's take a walk?" Cassidy said, opening his door. "We can get some fresh air. No need to bring a compass, right? It'd be useless."

None of this shit made sense. Christopher didn't know enough to incriminate anyone! On the night of the hit, he recalled while following Cassidy into the thick brush of the woods, they'd followed protocol, switching out the tags on the Toyota that Cassidy had boosted the night before, wearing those Kirk and Spock masks Christopher had found in the back of his closet, but when Cassidy's radio pager beeped, they stopped at a pay phone. Orders came from management for them to stand down. Odette Hubbard, cold-footed, had canceled the job.

Later that night, though, Cassidy picked Christopher up again, saying they were supposed to clean up "some kind of mess." They drove to Randy Hubbard's house and found the man slumped in blood against his piano, slugs in his back, shoulder, and head, a nine-millimeter on the piano bench and, on the coffee table behind him, a whiskey glass perched next to a revolver. The glass still had ice cubes in it. Christopher had no idea who'd killed the poor bastard. He didn't want to know. Through the eyeholes of the Spock mask, Hubbard's corpse looked consolingly inhuman. He wasn't a person and couldn't be mourned as one. Under Cassidy's direction, he and Christopher wiped down the entire scene for prints, put the glass of whiskey in the sink, pocketed the revolver, and, before they left, did a cursory pass for incidentals. Afterward Jacob tossed the revolver in the attaché case he called his "kill kit."

"This really did come straight from the top," Cassidy said to Christopher in the woods, walking a few feet behind him. "It's nothing to do with what goes on over at the Elysian. That shit's a-okay with me. I got a cousin. But you know how management can get. Never too careful."

A numbness spread through Christopher's body with every step he took. He couldn't feel his arms or his legs, his hands or his feet, his face or the tears falling down it. Tree limbs overhead unthreaded the sunlight and wove it into a patchwork of shadows on the ground. Gray sky, gray leaves, gray bark—this world was a drawing by some kid who'd run out of all the fun crayons. Christopher figured he wasn't the first person to be punished for doing nothing wrong. He should have left this godforsaken town when he had the chance.

Next to the freshly dug hole lay a shovel and a bag of lye. "Right there's fine," Cassidy said. He motioned for Christopher to stand at the ledge.

Christopher did as ordered. Sunlight hit his upturned face, and nearby a wren began to sing. "If anyone asks," he said, the barrel a cold, hard dot against the base of his skull, "tell them I'm gone to Texas." He closed his eyes and saw beautiful clusters of red.

11

NEXT TIME, FIRE

The key to a proper stakeout? Junk food, loads of it, junkier the better. In her Jeep, as the morning sun breached the horizon, Clem sat next to Dixon, their feet hedged by wrappers for Snickers and Slim Jims, empty Doritos bags, crushed cans of Dr Pepper, Slice, and Diet Coke. Dixon had drunk the Diet Cokes. His wife, who had recently gotten into Jane Fonda's workout tapes, insisted he participate in what she called her spanking-new "lifestyle." Clem found it absolutely hilarious.

"Fucking Barbarella." Dixon crumpled his fourth can and dropped it into his already crowded footwell. "'Less than one calorie,'" he said, quoting the soda's gimmick from the commercials. "How do they know? What do you think gives it that one calorie?"

"Your manhood?"

"Har-har."

They were staking out the home of one Harold John Riggins. At the courthouse, after speaking with Odette Hubbard, Clem had recognized a janitor with the tattoo of a cross draped in a Confederate flag. She knew him from the photo Lenora Coogan had shown her of Turnip's friends on the cockfighting circuit.

Unsurprisingly, Harold John's rap sheet failed to surprise Clementine—two stints in juvie for possession, vandalism, assault, and disturbing the peace; postbacc work at Parchman Farm for similar offenses. The thirty-nine-year-old currently lived with his mother. In Clem's unadulterated opinion, Harold John was a sentient Pontiac Firebird, redneck trash with a souped-up engine, his exhaust fumes chokingly toxic with imbecility and hate. That ink on his arm might as well have been a business card. RACIST FUCK FOR HIRE.

Yes, Harold John was clearly Dixie Mafia, and Clem wanted him to lead her to wherever that esteemed organization congregated.

It was a quarter till seven. The neighborhood, typical of the depressingly blue-collar ones in Meridian, woke up at, Clem quipped to herself rather than out loud to her partner, the cracker of dawn. Funny how the blue-collar thing was sort of accurate. Men in navy jumpsuits left their houses swinging their coffee thermoses, followed soon after by their kids, looking downright depressed in their own collars to be heading for another day at school, and, finally, women left the house, dressed for the office grind in stilettos, skirts, and collared blouses, many of which were shades of cobalt or teal or sapphire.

Clem knew she shouldn't be so judgmental. These people were trying to get by like everyone else. Her antagonism came from what she'd had to endure last night, when damn near every single person who drove or walked past her Jeep in this overwhelmingly white neighborhood gave Clem the nastiest of stink eyes, until, of course, they spotted the overwhelmingly white man in the seat next to her. She'd long ago trained Dixon to notice and be duly offended. On their first stakeout, he had asked, with total seriousness, "Why do all these people have the hots for you?"

Still, Clem couldn't say she wasn't exactly used to this sort of shit. Before and after her father took his first fall, she'd lived in a white neighborhood in the northern hills of Meridian. The typical look she got back then was one of confusion more than fear, pity more than anger, curiosity more than suspicion, all of which disoriented her still-forming consciousness of self. *Where's your mother, sweetheart? Is she a maid around here?*

To think how much hurt can be done with a tone of voice. No little girl should be inflicted to feel that way.

"It's seven o'clock," Dixon said as he reached for the radio dial. "My turn."

While Dixon changed the station from the pop hits Clem liked to the country-western hokum she tolerated, he passed a news broadcast. "Wait, stop," Clem said. "Go back to that last one."

The anchor was talking about the thirtieth anniversary of the death of Emmett Till. Apparently, organized protests were being held throughout the state in opposition to any events scheduled to commemorate the anniversary. "Although as yet unidentified," noted the anchor, "the protests were spearheaded, according to various reports, by the Citizens' Councils in communities throughout Mississippi. We'll keep you up to date as this story develops."

Clem shook her head. "What happens to white supremacy deferred? Does it dry up, like a raisin in the sun?"

"Raisins are already dried up," Dixon said, changing the station to country.

"What?"

"The line doesn't make sense. Raisins are dried grapes. They can't dry up. They *are* dried up. Leave them out in the sun, they can't get any drier."

"You know I'm quoting a poem, right? A really famous one."

"Condescending."

"You're the one being—"

"It would have made more sense if Hughes had said, 'Does it dry up, like a grape in the sun?' But that's not fancy-sounding, so he went with nonsensical."

"It's also the title of—"

"Kind of ruined the play for me, too, Hansberry naming it after a line that makes no sense."

What the hell was in those Diet Cokes? Dixon must have been doing some extracurricular reading. It didn't really surprise Clem, once she thought about it. Dixon had always been a quick study, as eager to learn as he was to please, the former, in their partnership at least, often leading to the latter. That a white man would sincerely want to learn about the African-American experience was a rarity for Clem. During Dixon's first few weeks, Clem had pointed out the minor but insidious acts of racism they encountered on a job, from a client playfully calling her "homegirl" to a suspect saying, "You can *ax* me any question." Dixon said he'd never realized, and unlike the many other times Clem had heard that sentiment, she genuinely believed him. His keenness for homework went a long way in earning her trust. "What kind of books should I pretend to have read?"

Dixon had joked. Clem loaned him her copies of *Beloved* and *Their Eyes Were Watching God, I Know Why the Caged Bird Sings* and *Sister Outsider,* her Ralph Ellison and Alice Walker and Harriet Jacobs. She even gave him *The Fire Next Time,* referring to its author as Uncle Jimmy. Dixon fell for it as easily as she expected.

Throughout their partnership, Clem had, to her genuine shock, spotted those books on Dixon's coffee table and dashboard, tucked in his jacket pocket and gym bag, with the occasional bright yellow splash of a *Cliff's Notes* to prove that, in fact, nobody was perfect.

Now, apparently, he had been taking some initiative in the literature he read. Langston Hughes? Clem hadn't recommended any poetry. Although Dixon remained beholden to that ancient male pastime of going back to the well—"Well, actually," "Yes, but, well"—Clem supposed he was right about the Hughes line, however much she hated to admit it. Raisins couldn't dry up, just as ash couldn't burn, just as ice couldn't freeze.

"Are we wasting our time?" Clem asked before letting out a serrated yawn.

Dixon tilted his head. "Honestly? I wonder if we've lost sight of what we were hired to do."

"Meaning?"

"We were hired to find out who poisoned Turnip Coogan—and now, thanks to Odette's advance, who shot Randall Hubbard." The implication they were double-billing their clients tugged at a loose thread in Clem's conscience. She ignored it as Dixon said, "Do you really think it was Sir Harold John Riggins? Do you really think some poor bastard who doubled up on first names will lead us to either killer, assuming it's two of them?"

Her partner had a point, Clem conceded. Guy was a regular whiz kid today. "I think this case is bigger than we realize. The DM? Wouldn't you want to take it down if you had the shot?"

"They already had a shot at you, in case it slipped that sharp mind of yours."

From across town came the baritone susurrus of a train, most likely, Clem guessed, the Queen City Limited, which still bore this town's nickname but no longer stopped here. What a lovely, pathetic metaphor. Trains brought people to places as often as they took people away from them.

Cities teetered in that balance. Meridian had never given up being a frontier town, at first reliant on trains, now reliant on the memories of them.

Clem hated this place—her *home,* that four-letter word, a curse—but she also hated herself for hating it. She hated that she hated that she hated it. Clem supposed that made her a true Mississippian, *no,* a true Southerner, *no,* a true American. What was the word for a snake eating its own tail? Ouroboros. America was an ouroboros of prejudice. Everyone hated everyone. Only the reasons varied. The rich hated the poor for being too uneducated to get rich, while the rich made themselves richer by convincing the poor that education was elitist. Poor white people hated Black people because they wanted to feel better than somebody, because rich people's hate of their poverty had taught them to hate, to want to feel superior to abate feeling inferior. And men hated women, no matter the man's class or race, because that was how their fathers had felt toward their mothers, their grandfathers toward their grandmothers, so on and so on, ad infinitum, until—*stop it, Clementine!*

Clem clenched and released her toes, clench and release, clench and release, a method her father had taught her to relax whenever her mind became too incensed with rage. "You dropped nickels and dimes on the floor," he used to say, "and your hands are tied behind your back. Now pick up your change. That's my girl. Pick up your change."

Espousing the impossibility of a solution was yet another problem, Clem told herself as she watched Harold John Riggins's house down the street, as one more George Strait song played on the radio. Such fatalism had not worked out well for her in the past. She'd tried to walk away from the justice system but had only gotten as far as the private sector. Justice system. Pfft! The problem was right there in the name. Clem had witnessed far too much of that "system," Black men used as catchall plugs on leaky cases, suspects confessing through bloodied lips and broken teeth. Quotas had to be met! Paperwork had to be filed! The reality was so obvious to Clem. Systems didn't help people; they helped other systems. You couldn't redline without red tape.

"I feel like I must've asked you this before," Clem said to Dixon. "But do *you* think the DM is real? Or are we chasing a bunch of boogeymen?"

With a rueful, close-lipped smile, Dixon shook his head. "No, you have not asked me that before. I was wondering when you would." He looked out the window. "I never told you this—ashamed of it, I guess—but people used to say my grandfather was Klan."

"Jesus."

"That's pretty much what people in my family thought of him. Godlike."

"Did you ever see him—"

"Wearing a hood and lighting crosses? Hell no. Pappy died before I made it to kindergarten. But I felt a legacy in how people treated me." Dixon tongued a back tooth. "After the war, especially."

"Pappy."

"You don't have to be a jerk all the time, Clem. I know I'm white trash."

"I'm sorry." Clem lowered the volume on the radio. "You were saying, about after the war?"

"I got the sense of people feeling me out, wanting to know if I'd play ball."

"Did you?"

"That hurts. Seriously."

Clem once again said she was sorry. She once again meant it. "So you do think the DM is real."

"I think the DM is the latest name for something been around a long time."

For a moment, as she noticed the Rigginses' front door opening, Clem envisioned an ouroboros not only eating its own tail, but being fed it. "Get your game face on," she said to Dixon, while at the same time thinking, Fed by whom?

Both Clem and Dixon buckled their seat belts as they watched Harold John get into his car, take three turns of the ignition before the engine turned over, and peel out in a cyclone of exhaust. Clem followed him, keeping her distance. Occasionally, residential districts gave way to commercial districts, shotgun houses bleeding into strip malls, signs on empty lots printed with such slogans as BROUGHT TO YOU BY TIFFEE DEVELOPMENTS or COMING YOUR WAY FROM SOUTHWAYS ALLIANCE. Clem and Dixon followed Harold John past the foundation of some condo complex that had been placed on indefinite hold when human remains were unearthed by a bulldozer, then turned at an intersection bordered by stacks of construction material for some fast-food restaurant whose franchisee, Clem had heard, forgot to bribe the zoning board prior to their most recent meeting. They were just about to get on the highway that led north into Kemper County when a siren sounded off behind them and the red flashes of a gumball on top of an unmarked filled the rearview.

"Motherfucker," Clem said as she pulled to the side of the road. She watched Harold John's car fade into the distance.

"Think we've got a taillight out?" Dixon asked with a knowing but sympathetic smirk.

"That's not funny."

"I keep telling you, this wouldn't happen near as often if you let me drive."

"That doesn't make it right."

"But it makes it easier."

Clem shut her eyes. She picked up change with her feet, clench and release, clench and release, furious her tail had gotten away because some moronic plainclothes had seen a "suspicious" person driving a Jeep. Eyes shut and toes clenched, Clem asked her partner, "Do you know why they call it 'lighting' a cross and not 'burning' one?"

"No. Why?"

"The KKK are Christians, and a real Christian would *never* 'burn' a cross."

"Which word did I use?" Dixon asked, his tone implying he already knew the answer.

"You may be ashamed of the man," Clem said, ignoring the metallic tap of a drawn sidearm against her raised window, "but your pappy has got his language in you."

12

DENVER OMELET

"Oh my God, Clem. It was a joke," Samantha Bellflower all but screamed.

Sam, Dixon, and Clem were sitting in a corner booth at the Village Fair Grill, a greasy spoon not far from where Sam, twenty minutes earlier, had pulled over Dixon and Clem, pretending, "as a joke," to have stopped them for a traffic violation. Some joke, Clem thought. Sam should do stand-up, she was so hilarious. Get this lady in front of a mic.

"But did you have to pull your piece?" Clem asked. "That's beyond crazy."

"Dixon," Sam said, "will you talk some sense into your girl? The Clementine I used to know had a sense of humor."

"Thinking I'll go with the Denver omelet," Dixon said, focused on the menu open like a hymnal in his hands. "Though, got to say, waffles are looking mighty good."

Clem's partner had the right idea. Keep your eyes down. Still, however many times Clem told herself to let it go, she couldn't get over the fact Sam had so egregiously broken the code of conduct. For a stunt like that, the captain would have her badge, not a second's hesitation. Sam had never been by the book, true, but she'd at least thumbed its pages while at the academy.

"You have got to be more careful," Clem said. "You're the second woman to make detective in MPD history. Not to mention the first Native American? Every fuckwad who had to wait in line for his stripes would snap at a chance to take you down. Queen City's a small barrel, Big Fish."

"I'll always be second place to you," Sam said. "As long as we're talking MPD history."

"I got lucky, is all."

Between sips of coffee, Sam, a quarter smiling and, Clem could tell, a quarter meaning it, said, "But you're right. I promise I'll be on my best behavior from now on, Ms. Tibbs."

"Shut up."

"You're the famous one."

"Infamous, more like."

Clem knew what a sore spot that article had been for Sam, how it had turned a grain of competiveness into a pearl of resentment. Not only had Sam's best friend on the force beaten her to detective, but the case that made her career had also made her a minor celebrity. Clem definitely had not wanted the spotlight. Being in it, though, scrutinized by her colleagues, pushed by them to see what she would tolerate, had at least brought about one good outcome. After she'd been disillusioned enough to turn in her shield, Clem had gotten her friend back. She didn't know how lonely she'd been until she wasn't anymore.

"Have y'all made any new headway on the Hubbard case?" Clem asked Sam.

Sam turned to Dixon. "She sick and tired of you already? Wants her old job back?" She returned her amused gaze to Clem. "I thought you were hired for Turnip's untimely demise. Let us handle Hubbard."

Had Sam been talking with Dixon behind her back? He'd brought up the same point earlier that morning. Clem chose not to mention they'd been hired by Odette Hubbard, especially since she'd just scolded Sam about following the book. It wasn't her book anymore, Clem tried to convince herself.

"Oh, come on, Sam," she said. "Whoever clipped Hubbard has got to be the same guy who poisoned Turnip."

"You're making easy assumptions. What'd you always tell me about those?"

"Very least, same perp ordered both hits, no matter who carried them out."

Leaning back in the booth, Sam hitched an arm across the top of her seat. "We still like Jacob Cassidy for it." She sipped her coffee, steam billowing when she exhaled through her nose. "Which is why I want you to stay frosty. Everything I hear on how this guy handles business makes me want to stay out of his business, you get me? Cassidy is not a guy who misses twice. You got lucky, first time. So keep sure to be careful out there."

Sam paused. In a ragged voice, she said, "What would I . . ." before trailing off.

. . . do without you? Clem thought, finishing Sam's sentence. She felt the same way. Clem was about to tell Sam that when the waitress appeared next to the booth.

"Y'all about ready, or do you need a minute?"

After the three of them ordered, a Denver omelet for Dixon, pancakes for Sam, and nothing-but-coffee-thanks for Clem, a first-date sort of silence reared up at the table. Clem could barely even remember the last time she had been on a first date. She avoided thinking about it by looking around the diner, at an elderly man with a neck barnacled in moles, at a teenage girl with a Dimetapp-purple nail job.

All these fair villagers of the Village Fair, they were suspects, the lot of them. Clem could see only suspects. She needed a day off. She needed a week, a month, a year off.

"Go ahead and run it by her," Dixon said to Clem. "I know you want to."

"Run what by me?" Sam asked.

"Philippa Marlowe here has what she calls a 'Cocktail Napkin Theory.'"

"Clem with a theory that involves cocktails?" Sam scrunched one eye. "Checks out. Are you going to enlighten me?"

What the hell. Clem figured she might as well sling the pasta against the wall to see if it was done. "There's no evidence that Hubbard knew Cassidy, correct?" she asked Sam.

"None."

"So it's doubtful they'd be on sociable terms, sit around and have a drink, that sort of thing. 'Hey there, Mr. Hit Man! Have a seat. How about I play the piano for you?'"

"But Cassidy broke in. He snuck up on Hubbard while he was playing the piano."

"Easy assumptions, Ms. Bellflower." Clem pulled a napkin from the chrome holder and placed it in front of Sam. "Go back and check the crime-scene photos. There was a cocktail napkin on the coffee table, but I don't think it was Hubbard's. I think he had a guest that night, somebody he knew, somebody he was comfortable showing his back. An old college buddy, a business associate."

Sam leaned forward. "Girlfriend?"

"Maybe."

"Boyfriend?"

"Possible."

"Little green man from outer space?"

A self-righteous simper stretched across her face, Sam took her elbows off the table, either to allow room for her food that had just arrived or to fillip the point she had just scored. Bit of both, Clem supposed. Only a good friend knew how to be such a bitch.

Dixon, forking into his omelet, seemed to notice the tension. Even before her partner started, Clem could tell he was about to do his mom-and-dad-are-fighting routine. Dixon tilted his head, feigning deep thought. "Y'all ever wonder how Denver omelets got their name?"

"You have any better theories?" Clem asked Sam.

"I mean, were they invented in Denver, or were they invented by a guy named Denver?"

"Yeah, I got a better theory," Sam said to Clem. "Goes like this. Wife calls in a hit on her husband. Husband turns up dead. Who did it? Hmm, maybe it was the *hit man*."

"Paul Denver. Barry Denver. Donald Denver. Yeah, that sounds good. Donald Denver, master chef whose finest creation is known worldwide. But, much to his chagrin, nobody knows he invented it."

"Great police work," Clem said. "Just ignore that Odette called off the hit."

"Donnie's very bitter about this. Who wouldn't be?"

"Claiming to have called off the hit," Sam said, "is awful convenient, after the hit."

"The whole thing's tragic, really. Don Denver. That poor, pathetic bastard."

"A woman in your position not believing another woman," Clem said. "Why does that not surprise me?"

"But French fries were neither invented in France nor created by a guy named French."

"Hand Gloria Steinem a badge," Sam said. "See how far she gets taking prints from a DOA. See if she can out-hoof a runner on enough crack to fuel the space shuttle."

"Guess the world will never know where the Denver omelet got its name."

Clem had heard enough. She reached across the table, picked up the napkin she had used to illustrate her theory, and flapped it in the air like a flag. "Pancakes are getting cold."

Around the Village Fair, the morning rush had subsided, with only die-hard stragglers left. They sat at the counter, classifieds in one hand and a cigarette in the other, their ball caps Rorschached with grease and dirt, their eyes and mouths so lined they were as readable as newsprint. Two children shared a waffle while their mother sipped a cup of coffee and stared out the window toward the parking lot. Clem figured it was the father's weekend, and they were waiting for the handoff. Hubbard's kids were about the same age. His little boy and his little girl.

"What about the jewelry?" Clem asked Sam. "All Randy Hubbard's jewelry."

Some people should never play poker. Clem could see by the tiny crease at the corner of Sam's lip that the question had hit home. She chewed her last bite of buttermilk pancake and said, "Man liked his jewelry. What else is there to know?"

"I already talked to his insurance, so I know everything was accounted for."

"Yeah?"

"Yuh-huh."

"And?"

"You tell me."

With the napkin Clem had used as a white flag Sam wiped her mouth. She tugged a cigarette from her pack. "Couple of the pieces were hot."

"Really?" Clem said. "Hubbard doesn't seem the type who needed to steal."

"Hubbard didn't know they were hot, my guess. He bought them off a jeweler well-known to fence stolen goods."

"You don't mean—"

"He and the jeweler were business associates, actually. Owned a parcel of land together. They were going to do a subdivision. Upscale homes for upscale professionals."

"But that can't be—"

"The jeweler's doing a bid at Parchman. Problem is, he won't talk to us."

Sam lit her cigarette, tapped it over an ashtray, and glanced at Dixon. Clem said, "He won't talk with police, but he might talk to . . ."

"Someone he cares about."

The litany of cuss words that filled Clem's mind was soon drowned out by the cacophony of the diner. Eggs sizzled atop the grill. Silverware scratched against ceramic. Coffee slopped into mugs. The bell above the door jangled when a new customer walked in, a sound followed immediately by two children's voices hollering in unison, "Daddy!"

13

IN THE LAND OF GOOD & PLENTY

At a quarter past nine o'clock, having spent the entire day at the ranch, Harold John pulled into his driveway, decently buzzed, smoking a cigarette, nodding along to the final verse of "Girls Just Want to Have Fun." He adjusted the rearview mirror so he could see across the street. The two PIs were gone. The call he'd put in to management must've worked.

"Did you pick up dinner?" Harold John's mother asked when he walked in the house. "I was going to cook, but they're showing a rerun of *The Day After*. Got hooked."

It was their routine these days. Harold John's mom, Clara, pretended she had actually intended to cook a meal, and Harold John pretended to believe her. Ever since the car accident two years ago she only left her Barcalounger in front of the television set to use the bathroom and answer the phone. "Double meat, no onions, large fry," Harold John said, handing her a sack from Lonnie & Pat's.

Harold John's mother peered into the sack. "Think it could really happen?"

"What?"

"Nukes."

"Who knows? The Russians launch, we'd launch back. It's called mutually assured destruction. Keeps everybody on their toesy-wosies."

"Nuh-*uh*."

"I read about it in my semester at MJC," Harold John said. "Swear to God."

"Watch that mouth." Harold John's mother chewed a fry. "My son, taking the Lord's name."

After apologizing, Harold John walked to a window, two panes of which were duct-taped where some neighborhood kids had slung rocks. Talk about swearing to God. This whole damn town was tripping the light fantastic to hell. Meridian used to be a place of prosperity. A man could open a business and turn a profit in no time at all. Given a few years, he could be a city councilman, even the mayor! But now you had good-for-nothing little shits knocking holes in your window. Now you had colored women staking out your home! It was enough to make you sick, what had happened to this town. Swear to God.

Harold John studied the street outside. Still no sign of the woman. He walked through the house and into the kitchen, noting the dishes in the sink he'd have to wash. Lord knew his mother would never get to them. She hadn't been much of a housekeeper even before the accident. On top of which, her unemployment benefits would hardly have made a dent in her bills without his help, though, Harold John supposed, he owed her for supporting him after the war.

When he'd gotten home from Vietnam, Harold John hadn't been able to land a job anywhere. He considered it the lowest point of his life, how nobody would pay him to drive a cab or pour cement or even wash dishes, like that was somehow too difficult for a man who'd done three tours. He had an entire semester of junior college from before the draft. Not many of his brothers in Charlie Company or the DM could claim that much.

"Mama," Harold John hollered. "Did I get a call today? About anything?"

"No."

"You sure? Nobody called saying, like, *yes, it's a go* or *no, it's not a go*? You forget sometimes."

"I hope you're not getting mixed up in something illegal under my roof."

Her roof, Harold John thought as he picked up the phone and dialed Cassidy's motel. Harold John had been paying the mortgage for at least ten years now. This roof would belong to the bank if it weren't for his custodial job over at the courthouse and his well-needed supplementary income from the DM. A bunch of mongrel immigrants would be living in this house if it weren't for Harold John and all the opportunities the DM had given him, every truth the DM had taught him—each of the blinding scales the DM had peeled from his eyes.

"It's me," Harold John said after Cassidy picked up.

"Get my message?"

Damn it. "My mother. Her head gets foggy sometimes. The meds they got her on."

"Word came down from the top," Cassidy said. "You're on, firebug. Here's the thing. They want it messy. Nothing surgical. A scatter-and-splatter job, do you get me?"

"Affirmative. Still just the one? I could do both. The world needs less PIs."

"Don't question orders."

A dial tone replaced the voice on the line. Cassidy was not one for ceremony.

In the basement, Harold John jerked the chain for the overhead light and said hello to the Duke, his eight-by-ten portrait framed in real glass and given pride of place on top of Harold John's workbench. "Been doing okay, sir? Good. That's good to hear."

Along the walls of the basement stood old shelves lined with cardboard boxes, some of the bottoms of which were chewed away by mice, and along the ground lay piles of firewood, unused carpet from an abandoned renovation job, paint cans, a broken coffee maker, and pink dust bunnies of fiberglass insulation. Harold John, making a mental note about the fire hazard, put on his shop glasses, sat at his workbench, and removed a cloth from the device.

It still needed work. "That's the thing about scatter-and-splatter," he said to the Duke, grinning from his press photo, his gaze following Harold John like the *Mona Lisa*. "It actually takes more work. Mess is hard. Precision? That's easy."

Harold John plugged in his soldering iron. He clipped a wire. He unwrapped the C-4.

"Like back in 'Nam, right, Duke? I'm talking about that Green Beret shit."

During his second tour, Harold John had learned how to use C-4 to heat his rations, because unless detonated with a primary, it would burn like any class of fuel. He always made sure to keep his head away from the fumes. Harold John was one for caution. Not long after, he and the boys stumbled on an even better secondary use for the explosive. If you ate a tiny bit of it, say a teaspoon knifed from a claymore, C-4 gave you a smooth, mellow high. Harold John had been feeling no pain during the search-and-destroy on My Lai. But he knew to be careful. Eating too much could turn you queasy.

"Want to hear the worst thing?" Harold John said to the Duke. "It's that the journalists lied. You understand better than most. Newspapers, TV reporters. They lie. Flip on the tube, Mr. Cronkite says there weren't no VC in that village. Lies. Lieutenant Calley saw them, and Lieutenant Calley was God's mouthpiece. Does God lie?"

From its eight-by-ten frame, the photograph of the Duke silently, affirmatively stared.

"See? You get it." Harold John set aside his wire cutters and picked up the soldering iron. "But try explaining that to all the flower children we come home to, with their rallies and sit-ins and protests. Try explaining that to the people who interview you for a job. They watch the news. Cronkite should be ashamed."

A tiny mushroom of smoke, a chanterelle of burnt copper, rose from where Harold John soldered a wire to the device's rudimentary circuit board. He'd adapted it from a slot-car track he loved to play with when he was a boy. Back then Harold John's mother used to lavish him with toys, presents disgorging from under the Christmas tree, wrapping paper scuttling across the ground during his birthday parties at the carousel in Highland Park. In those days, before his mother's accident, before Harold John enlisted, they'd go to the picture show every week, and Harold John's mother would let him get *two* things of candy, his choice: Raisinets, Good & Plenty, Red Hots, Milk Duds.

"What I admire about you?" Harold John said to the Duke. "You're a cowboy. Same with me. I'm a gunslinger, holstered and willing. Lock, stock."

Soldering iron set aside, shop glasses growing foggy, Harold John rummaged through an old Maxwell House can, where he kept his spare detonators and blasting caps.

"You've got to be, this day and age." He looked at the Duke, who stared back, seeming to nod. "They give some spear chucker the job what should have gone to a white could use the paycheck. Out in the Delta they're holding fund-raisers every other week for those Black Democrats running for white seats. I know all about the Blackocrats. I've got a semester of JC. It's science, you know. Political *science*. But listen to me. Look at who I'm talking to."

Gospel truth? Harold John hadn't learned about the Blacks running for office from his time at the Meridian Junior College, where, if he was being honest, he'd only gotten through half a semester, but from the DM. That was what it offered. From the DM, Harold John had learned how the minorities were oppressing his people, taking their jobs, sleeping with their women, thefts ordained, if you could even fathom such a vile betrayal, by a Southern white man, name of James Carter. From the DM, Harold John had learned why and when and who to fight. As for how? The US military had taken care of that.

"Remember the synagogue?" Harold John said as he began to wire the firing mechanism to a 7.5V lantern battery. "Now, that had been precision. Orders came for me to take out *only* the rabbi, and as that stick-up-his-ass Cassidy said, 'Don't question orders.' Pre-ci-sion."

After the bombing, Harold John, either tempting fate or flipping it the bird, he wasn't sure, had decided to go to the funeral. He'd kept toward the back of the grave site congregation, necessitated by the condition of the synagogue, and he was shocked at how normal the whole thing was, with prayers, readings, and eulogies no more ridiculous than a Baptist service. Harold John couldn't look away from the rabbi's widow, seated toward the front. Mascara as dry and flaking as snot tracks on a toddler stretched a path down her pale, liver-spotted cheeks, and a lonely housefly buzzed around the melting soft-serve of her blue-gray hair. Harold John knew what was coming next even before the syncopated wails began to pour like heeltaps from her lungs.

As the widow slumped not forward or backward but down, her legs crumpling both into and across the grass, Harold John's heart kicked at his chest; she reminded him so much of his mother the first couple months after the accident. That capitulation to loss, a beat-down-ness by life. The engulfing resignation: resignation that had engulfed him as well.

But that wasn't the same at all, Harold John told himself, then as now as always. Go ask anyone in the DM. Suffering was not created equally.

"Damn it all to hell," Harold John said. He pushed back from the workbench, stood, and looked at the Duke. "Can you believe this? Battery's dead. It's Rayovac, too. American-made."

The device sat powerless on the bench. Around it lay filaments of wire casing, mounds of sawdust, and tapes electrical, masking, packing, and gaffer, a school diorama titled, Harold John tickled himself by thinking, UNFINISHED BUSINESS. He'd always loved making dioramas for his school assignments. They were so much easier than memorizing dumb facts and figures, evaluating this, analyzing that, all the critical thinking baloney.

Fists propped on hips, his shadow swinging on the ground in rhythm with the pull-cord light he'd bumped his head against, Harold John tilled his brow at the photo of the Duke. "I'm heading to the store to pick up a battery that works. Need anything while I'm out? Okay. I didn't expect so."

The photo had been taken of the Duke before his rise to the highest seat. Back then, with his trimmed moustache and in his tailored suit, he'd brought legitimacy to the organization. Harold John had met him when he first ran for a seat in the Louisiana State Senate. The man was his idol, his hero, the North Star of the American South, so much so that Harold John had never felt comfortable calling him David. The Duke deserved more respect than that. "Back in a few," Harold John told the photo.

Upstairs, after grabbing his keys from the pilgrim-hat wall hanger with hooks instead of a buckle, Harold John put on his favorite New Orleans Saints jacket. "Damn," he said after noticing a tear at the shoulder, little tufts of cotton poking through like some careworn teddy bear. He took the duct tape he'd used to fix the window those damn kids had broken and, figuring the jacket was good otherwise, put a square of it over the tear.

"Benny Hill's on," Harold John's mother called out. "Want to watch with?"

Harold John walked to the living room and kissed the top of his mother's head. She needed a fresh dose of the Aqua Net. He'd pick some up while he was out. "Another time, Mama. I got to run, take care of a thing."

"So late?"

"Go-getters go get."

"My college boy. I'm so proud."

"Thank you, Mama."

From the linen basket, Harold John lifted the plaid comforter his mother loved and—mindful of the stump of her right leg, any contact with which, even two years after the accident, made her flinch—draped the length of it over her body. "Think you'll want to sleep in your bed tonight?" he asked.

His mother, Clara Riggins, *the* Clara Riggins, yawned. "After my program."

Harold John picked up the crumpled hamburger sack from beside his mother's lounger. He was going to have to call that nurse again to come by and check for bedsores. The extra weight didn't help. *Poor white trash.* That was what those kids had yelled after breaking the window. Clara Riggins could never be white trash. She was only in a slump.

At the front door, after tossing away the hamburger sack, Harold John looked back toward the living room, where his mother was just beginning to snore. *It's not your fault,* he wanted to tell her. It was the fault of the Jews and the Blacks, the Mexicans and the Chinese. Harold John could recall a time when those damn people knew their place.

That time would come again. As God was his witness, it would come again.

14

BALDWIN GEMS

The Mississippi State Penitentiary was commonly known as Parchman Farm. That was what Clem had always called it, and that was how she had always thought of it. Occupying roughly twenty-eight square miles of flat, fertile land in the Mississippi Delta, with a decentralized layout of camps, the maximum-security prison could hold over four thousand inmates, many of whom worked the crops. "A prison without walls," Clem had often heard of it, and as she and Dixon sat on a bus taking them from the visitation center to her father's unit, Clem, looking out the window at the work crews with shovels, picks, and hoes, noted the race of most of the crew members and thought how, back in the days of antebellum plantations, "a prison without walls" would've described the lot of them.

"How is that different from slavery?" Clem asked Dixon, nodding toward the window.

A bump in the road made it appear as though Dixon shrugged, which Clem considered fitting, because it matched the fatalism of his tone when he said, "It's legal."

Ever since Sam Bellflower had pulled a chapter eleven on Clem, bankrupting most of her hunch about Hubbard's jewelry by revealing that some of it had been stolen not after but before Hubbard's murder, information that forced Clem to reorganize her hunch to credit the implausible fact her father had been in business with Hubbard, Clem had debated whether to make this trip.

She hadn't seen her father since he'd been put away—correction, since she'd *helped* put him away—four blissful, entirely too short years ago. *Too short* felt right, given how busy Clem had been in those four years, quitting the department, hanging her own shingle, but she might have been pushing it with *blissful*.

It was a living, Clem told herself while she and Dixon stepped off the bus and walked into the inmate housing unit, a squat, cinder-block structure as bland, she thought, as the saying, *It's a living*.

But she had quit the force in order to live, hadn't she, to free herself from that obsolete system of so-called law and so-called order? Clem had figured that as a PI she could be a ronin, one of those samurai without a lord, except in her case the lord was the belief in justice.

Look how far that attitude had gotten her, Clem thought, walking down a hallway painted bureaucratic taupe, the floors marked with lines for inmates to follow. She was going to speak with a man she'd put away back when she still believed in justice, her own flesh, her own blood, a man she'd promised herself, out of a sense of justice, never to speak with again. But still. She was only doing this because of the case she had been hired to solve. Her father was the quickest route to her next payday. Clem didn't actually care who had killed Turnip Coogan or Randy Hubbard, leaving one's mother without a son, the other's children without a father. Clem was still a ronin. She had no lord or master.

"Hicks, Dixon, and Baldwin, Clementine," said a guard holding a clipboard, of course checking in the man before the woman. "Here to see Lauder Baldwin. Y'all aren't kin, I take it, you and the Laud-Mouth. Though you seem a speck young for his missus."

"I'm his daughter."

"No fooling?" The guard smirked like they all did. "I mistook the likeness."

In the visitation room, where the guard led them, his face still pasted with that smirk Clem had seen a thousand times growing up, she and Dixon sat at a table near the center. The room reminded her of a school cafeteria, with chain-smoking inmates instead of students, ashtrays instead of food trays. Most of the visitors were wives or girlfriends or, at one table, an apparent girlfriend and a wife. The occasional toddler bobbed on the knee of an orange jumpsuit. Boyfriends posing as cousins held hands under their tables.

"You doing okay?" Dixon asked. "I know you're not ecstatic to be here."

She couldn't shake that fucking smirk. It had been a while since she'd seen it. "Yeah, I'm fine."

Clem's father entered from the far side of the visitation room. He brushed back his newly gray hair with a sun-cured hand. The suggestion of a paunch pushed against his waist chain as he shuffled across the room. "That's him over there," Clem said to Dixon.

"Where?"

"There."

"Him?" Dixon said. He turned to Clem not with a look of surprise or confusion, as she'd expected, but one of hurt, of wounded friendship. The look said, *Why didn't you tell me?*

To grow up biracial was to grow up in two worlds. Clem supposed that was part of what made her such a good detective.

In fact, Clem used to tell people before noting she had intended the pun, that wasn't even the half of it. She had to grow up in two worlds, no world, and every world, all at once. Around white people, including her father's family, she only on occasion felt completely at home, just as around Black people, including her mother's family, she only on occasion felt completely at home. Sometimes she didn't feel at home anywhere. Other times she felt at home everywhere. Not to be a part of one single thing was to be a part of everything. Not to be a part of one single thing was to be a part of nothing. The constant in Clem's childhood? She had to translate her own identity through the eyes of others.

Clem, age twelve. She and her father visit a restaurant, and the waitress, white, takes their order. Is that confusion, admiration, or suspicion in her look? Does she see her as adopted, a pity case, or as a shameful product of miscegenation?

Clem, age eight. She sits in the car while her father pumps gas. A man, Black, notices her as he pumps his own gas. Is that concern or anger in his look? Does he worry something untoward is going on? Does he hate her father for having dared to love a Black woman?

Clem, age five. Her babysitter, white, helps her pick out a crayon for her drawing of "a family." Is that helplessness in her look? Fear of making the wrong choice?

Clem, age nine. After her father, white, goes to prison the first time, her aunt and uncle, Black, welcome her to her new home for the next eighteen months. What is that look?

Clem, age thirty. Her partner and friend, white, gives her a look that says, *Why didn't you tell me?*

"Hi, Dad," Clem said, not bothering to follow Dixon's lead and stand from the table, "good manners" be damned. What were manners in the visitation room of a prison?

"My little girl," her father said. A streak of bright orange in a space streaked in orange, he remained standing beside the table, as tall as ever, as calm as ever, the look on his face one that could only be described as *beaming.* Clementine's father was beaming at her. Lauder Baldwin, his prison jumpsuit trussed in chains, was beaming at his only child, the daughter he had not seen in four years. He was beaming with utter, irrefutable love.

That motherfucker, thought Clementine.

Dixon extended his hand. "Mr. Baldwin, it's a pleasure. I'm Dixon Hicks."

While Clem maintained her marmoreal disposition, giving up nothing, a statue of cold reproof, her father shook Dixon's hand. He looked at Clem. "Boyfriend?"

"Partner," Dixon said.

"Aha. I thought I smelled MPD."

"Oh, shucks, not quite." When Dixon got flustered, Clem knew, he got goofy. *Shucks*? "You're looking at the brain trust of the Queen City Detective Agency." Dixon paused. "Clem is the brains, and I trust her." He ended with an even goofier laugh, *te-he-he*!

"You quit the department?"

"Dad, sit down. A lot tends to happen in four years, and I'm not in the mood to synopsize. What can you tell us about Randall Hubbard?"

Clem's father, after sitting, folded his thick forearms against the table, those quilted muscles Clem remembered lifting her as a child, bringing her favorite cereal at the grocery store within reach, now DIY'd in prison ink. The tattoo looked like a thorny rose or rosy thorns. All things left their mark, Clem was aware, incarceration more than most. "There's a name I haven't heard in a while," Lauder said. "How's Randy doing?"

"Dead."

"What?"

Once Clem had given her father the basics, from Hubbard's to Turnip's murder, eliding her run-in with Cassidy—concern for her safety, not his history with the police, had been her father's main objection to her career—Lauder said, "Yes, Randy and I were going to do a subdivision together. Subdivide and conquer, right? But it fell through last minute. The financing. It wasn't the roaring eighties yet. Not that I got to experience all that much of them, though I hear they're lovely. What's a Pac-Man?"

Ignore the bait, Clem told herself. "Did Randy have a nefarious side, too?"

"My girl, with the vocabulary. It's okay to say *criminal* around here. We all know what we are."

"Was Randy involved with anything illegal? Y'all were partners, after all."

Lauder turned to Dixon. "She was a remarkably pleasant girl growing up, if you can believe."

"I'm an honorary duck," Dixon said, grinning, "the volume of her water off my back."

While staring at her partner, Clem, scathingly blank-faced, said to her father, "Do you know of any reason someone would want to kill Hubbard?"

"I used to call her Halo when she was little. She was my halo. Inculpable."

"Clementine the Halo. I like it," Dixon said, as though daring her not to be.

"A good joke," Clem said. "Dad was always full of them. Wait. Did I say *them*? I meant *it*."

"Inculpable *and* clever. Thank God my Clementine doesn't take after me."

"Sounds like a country song," Dixon added, infuriatingly, then continued, to Clem's greater fury, in a George Jones croon, "Thank Gawd my Clementine don't take after—"

"Before starting his own company," Clem said, "Hubbard worked for Dixie Land Development, which we know had mob connections. The Matrangas out of New Orleans. Do you know if he maintained those connections? Did the Matrangas get their taste? Pull a trigger once in a while?"

His bright green eyes dimmed by an incarcerative squint, Lauder said, "Don't worry about the Matrangas. That organization has been infighting so long it's hollowed out. Besides, they were always more of the boogeyman than anything for real. A way to skirt blame for Kennedy. The president is killed, and red-blooded, hate-mongering Americans find it easier to handle if they blame all those Eye-talian gangsters and their Eye-talian mob."

Clem thought of her aunt Myrtle and uncle Hersh on the day of Kennedy's assassination, how devastated they had been, how cleaved of all the hope Kennedy had epitomized for them. Their voices broke when they recalled the civil rights speech he'd given on the day George Wallace stood in the schoolhouse door. "Such a fine man," they had said, in a reverential tone, but later, after rumors of the Mafia's involvement began to surface, they used the exact opposite tone when they whispered, "Those fucking wops."

Red-blooded, hate-mongering Americans. Was there no end to the cycle?

Dixon nudged Clem. "See? He just said it. Nothing more than the boogeyman. Same goes for that other Mafia you're obsessed with. I told you they're nothing to worry over."

"What *other* Mafia?" Lauder asked.

"It's nothing," Dixon said. "Clem is dead set on this hunch the Dixie Mafia had something to do with Hubbard's murder."

"I'm not dead set on anything," Clem said. "Our j-o-b, mind you, is to consider every nuance of a case. Good investigators should never abide their preconceived notions or prejudices. You more than anyone should know that, Mr. *Hicks*."

Clem was about to dig deeper into Dixon when she noticed her father's face. It had blanched of color, his prison squint now a chasmal stare, his forehead bunched into a pound sign of horizontal and vertical wrinkles. "Listen to me, Clementine. You are not to involve yourself *whatsoever* with the DM."

After looking at Dixon, who raised his eyebrows in return, Clem said, "It's real?"

"Yes, but not in the way you think." Lauder glanced over his shoulders. At the nearest table, a man with the Confederate flag inked in the crux of his neck and shoulder held a baby in his arms, the mother watching them, as doe-eyed, Clem thought, as Nancy gazing at Ronald. The same flag was tucked in a corner of the Mississippi state flag Clem could see flapping outside a barred window of the visitation room. "Promise you will not go near those animals," Lauder said. "I've got an idea who'd want to clip Hubbard, but first you have to promise you will never go near the DM. Those sons of bitches are hateful and stupid, the worst combination. You have to swear, Clem. I don't know what I'd do."

"You know I won't promise that."

"Sir, take my word, she won't promise that, much as I'd rather she would."

"And besides," Clem said, "if the DM was involved, how could I not go near them?"

With a sigh so weak it could have been a breath, slumping his shoulders to the point of caricature, Lauder looked from Clem to Dixon and back again. "What you think of as the DM are the attack dogs," he said. "And what, pray tell, do all attack dogs have?"

"Masters," said Dixon.

"Thing about being a master," Lauder said, "you get used to it. You like it. You want to stay one. The South? Certain people will always want it to rise again."

A round-edged corner piece appeared in Clem's mind, a hub ready to be fitted with other pieces of the puzzle, creating a much larger picture than she'd expected. "Are you saying the KKK is involved?"

"Different letters, same objective. Smoke screens at a puppet show."

"Wait, what?" Dixon said. "I'm lost."

"There's more to the Klan than wearing hoods and terrorizing Black folks. I mean, 'course, those are very much a part of it. Clem, ask your grandparents. They lived through the worst days. But look at slavery. What was the real motive behind it? Money."

"Who profited the most from Hubbard's death?" Clem asked herself out loud.

"Remember those Freedom Riders, got murdered outside Philadelphia?" Lauder asked, the question a camera flash bar that lit Clem's mind. Sam had mentioned the same murders back at the station. Lauder said, "The bodies were buried on some old, run-down farm, dammed up with a bulldozer."

Dixon nodded. "TV said they found clay in the lungs of one. Buried alive."

"What the TV probably didn't tell you?" Lauder said. "That farm happened to be in the path of progress, literally."

"I think you mean *figuratively*," Clem said.

"You're not the only Baldwin with a vocabulary, Halo. I meant what I said. That farm was in the direct path of Dwight Eisenhower's pride and joy, the Interstate Highway System."

"Y'all lost me again."

"He's talking about eminent domain."

"That noodle of hers," Lauder said to Dixon. "Can you imagine what hell it was convincing such a child Santa Claus was for real?"

"Dad."

"Right, sorry. Where was I?"

"Interstates."

In a string of words as clustered as the traffic that interstates were intended to eradicate, Lauder explained how two routes had been proposed for a major highway that would connect Mississippi to the greater South. The route most likely to be approved ran through the farm where the murder victims had been buried, but after the bodies had been found, the alternate route passed legislation. "Imagine the public outcry if they had paved over the sight of that tragedy," Lauder said. "No politician would come near an issue that piping."

"Not even the bigots," Clem said.

"Especially not the bigots. They may be foolish, but they sure aren't fools."

"So what's the difference?" Dixon asked. "Who cares which route passed?"

"There's money in transportation," Lauder said. "Gas stations, restaurants, any business next to the highway. Motels? Shipping? Come on, buddy row. The people what own the land alongside a major transportation route won the jackpot without ever having to slot a nickel."

"Bullshit."

It was bullshit. Clem didn't buy it for a minute. Interstates? The concept was similar to her father's attempts to exonerate himself. All hail the reallocation of blame! The same way Clem's father had only dealt in stolen goods and illegal drugs to "provide for his family," one of the South's most notorious acts of racial violence, according to his theory, stemmed from greed. She supposed the symmetry made a perverse kind of sense, the bullshit notion of states' rights as an excuse for slavery leading to the bullshit concept of interstates as an excuse for murder. "Are you saying," Clem said, "those racist fuckers killed three innocent people not because they're racist fuckers but to open a Pure Oil?"

"No, that's not what I'm saying. Attack dogs want blood. They like the taste of flesh and bone and gristle, have since they were pups. Their attack training sharpened that taste. But their masters? They're out for something a shade greener than blood, bit flimsier than bone."

"Smoke screens at a puppet show." Clem repeating her father's words from earlier. "What I don't get, where does Hubbard come in?"

"Good question."

"Not an answer."

Lauder looked at Dixon, as though to say, *An honorary duck, you said?* He flattened his hands against the table. "Deduction without imagination, Halo. You've got to broaden your mind."

"Yeah, that's my problem."

"Hubbard wasn't DM, I know for certain," Lauder said. "But I also know for certain a number of his rivals in the land-development game were."

That motherfucker. He knew for certain.

Inside Clem's chest, somewhere hidden, somewhere tender, a scab peeled off, birthing pain—pulsating, smoldering pain. A neon sign turned on in her mind, pulsating at the same frequency as the wound: BALDWIN GEMS, BALDWIN GEMS. YOU STEAL IT, WE'LL FENCE IT.

Clem said, "And just how in the shit would you know that 'for certain,' *Dad*?"

Squinting, Lauder said, "Well."

"Cle-em," Dixon said, his voice hitting a bump in the monosyllable. "He's only trying to help."

"By doing business with the Ku Klux Klan Jr.?" Clem turned to her father. "I always hated that stupid name, by the way."

"The DM?"

"Halo."

Lauder shrugged his chin, a tic Clem recognized too well. "You never told me," he said. "I only meant—I mean, it never occurred—I guess, well, you—is there a reason why—"

"Only angels have halos, and you are not an angel."

Of all the looks Clem had encountered while growing up—from concerned men pumping gas, from sympathetic waitresses asking if that would be all, from confused babysitters digging through a crayon box—her father's looks had always been the simplest to interpret, if only because they seldom needed interpretation. They were as plain and guileless as his jewelry business had not been. The look Clem's father gave her now, while a prison guard called out that his time was up, was not one of anger or vitriol. It was not one of pain or disappointment, confusion or sadness, shame or indifference.

After standing from the table, his face beaming the way it had when he first sat down, Clem's father needlessly put his look into words. "Your mother would be so proud of you."

The lanyard attached to the state flag snapped like a whip against the flagpole outside the inmate housing unit. While she and Dixon waited for the bus that would take them back to the prison entrance, Clem stared at those red, white, and blue stars and bars, thinking of someone she'd never known, a woman she only saw every time she looked in the mirror.

"She looks just like her, I swear it," her father's friends used to say, the few he hadn't lost after he and Clem's mother first got together.

To Clem, who arrived in the world at the same moment her mother left it, they might as well have sworn she looked like Julie Newmar or Eartha Kitt, for all she cared. Both had played her favorite character on her favorite television show as a child, and two Catwomen were as dear to her as some face suspended in framed Polaroids. To Clem, her mother wasn't a person but a series of platitudes and remarks from family and strangers.

"That poor child," said people in the checkout line at the grocery. "That poor father, too."

"Your mother was so brave," said Clem's doctor.

"What a brave girl you are," said Clem's teacher.

"Where's your mother, sweetheart?" asked a woman from her car window after spotting Clem playing skip-rope at the end of her driveway. "Is she a maid around here?"

To think what devastation could be wrought in a helpful tone of voice. Clem may not have known her mother, but she for damn sure knew what a maid was, even as a child. The lady in the car, before driving away, had "suggested" she might feel more comfortable playing in the backyard, "where you would have more privacy."

"I thought he was nice," Dixon said, squinting in the bright sun. "Helpful."

Sure, Lauder Baldwin could be genuinely helpful, thought Clem. He had been helpful the day she ran inside crying, her skip-rope abandoned in the driveway. He had been helpful when he quietly listened to what had upset her. He'd been helpful when he put her in the car and drove around the neighborhood where they'd only recently moved, periodically asking, "Is that it? What about that one? You said sky blue with whitewall tires, right?"

After Clem pointed out the woman's car, her father had been helpful enough to knock on the woman's front door and give her, if his body language was any indication, a severe talk about how his daughter could, should, and would be treated.

"He has his moments," Clem said to Dixon outside the housing unit.

Not a single tree was in sight for miles. A spinning net of flies blurred the vista like a smudge on the lens of a pair of glasses. Dixon prodded a crack in the sidewalk with the toe of his mud boot. "He wasn't what I expected, your dad. You've spoken about him enough, all things being equal, but he wasn't what I expected. You picture people in your head."

Even though Clem knew exactly the topic he was trying to broach, she couldn't bring herself to discuss it at the moment, not with everything piling up in her brain, from seeing her father for the first time in years to learning the DM was a real organization and clearly, undoubtedly involved with the case.

She nonetheless had trouble shaking Dixon's look from earlier: *Why didn't you tell me?* Clem supposed she owed him an apology. It had hurt to see the hurt in his eyes, the wound she had inflicted on their friendship. Clem put a down payment on the apology by offering a different one instead. "I'm sorry about that 'Mr. Hicks' thing. It was rude."

"It's okay," Dixon said. "I am one."

"A hick?"

"A hick and a Hicks."

"You've got the title. Now write the memoir."

Clem rubbed her finger. In the distance, past a cemetery and a concertina-wire enclosure, stood one of the little red houses she knew were used for conjugal visits, a gun tower looming beside it. Mississippi had been the first state to allow conjugal visits, Clem had read. Originally only Black prisoners were allowed the "privilege." Prison authorities believed it kept them docile, that it made them more productive in the fields, like beasts.

"What's our next move?" Clem asked Dixon, her nail digging into the pulp of her cuticle.

"I could go for some lunch."

"I meant with the case, hayseed."

Dixon laughed. "I know. It's fun to mess with you." The guy had skill, Clem thought. He always knew when she was on edge. He always knew how to pull her off it. After a breath, Dixon said, "I think we take your dad's advice. His warning, more like."

"Remind me."

"Forget the buttons. We go after who's pushing them."

The Murphy bed of a plan lowered into the cluttered apartment of Clem's mind, sheets freshly pressed and folded back. "See what you can dig up on Hubbard's competition in the real estate game."

"Yes, ma'am."

"Not just who they are. I want to know what projects they have in development, whether Hubbard made competing bids recently, names of execs, names of support staff, tax records, what brand of toilet paper they stock in their office john. Everything, I'm talking. Got it?"

"The partridge *and* the pear tree," Dixon said, repeating what Clem had told him on one of their first cases. "Check the stone *and* the ground beneath it."

"But stay low-key. We don't want these shitheads to know we're coming."

The bus to carry them out of the prison rounded a corner. Headed their way, it crept past fields that, come summer, Clem knew, would teem with cotton, soybean, and corn. Men in white shirts and white pants that amplified the blackness of their skin stood to each side of a ditch. They chopped at weeds with rusty hoes. They stabbed at dirt with blunt shovels. White men on horseback, shotguns propped against their hip bones, trotted beside the ditch. Neither guard nor prisoner looked at the bus as it passed them, a funnel of grainy dust marking the path of its wake, and above Clem's head, a canton of thirteen crisscrossed stars, one for each state that seceded from the Union, knuckled in the warm breeze.

15

A LAUDERDALE COUNTY AFFAIR

At an intersection of Confederate Drive, Molly turned onto Old Country Club Road—confederates and country clubs, she thought, went together like Nazis and Alpine redoubts—passing a dead deer in a ditch, its neck kinked at a nauseating angle. A freshet of tears rose at the thought that it might be a mother. Hormones. They were getting to Molly.

The rolling hills of the road's namesake came into view out her driver's-side window. Instead of golfers and caddies, the former eighteen-hole course was now spangled by cows and hayricks. The dilapidated mansion on a distant hilltop, a reproduction of either George Washington's Mount Vernon or Thomas Jefferson's Monticello (Molly always got the two mixed up), had once been the clubhouse but in the early '70s had been repurposed as Wayward Straits, a group home for "troubled" youths.

Molly's parents, it hurt to recall, had sent her brother there for an excruciatingly long month, to "straighten his ways," according to the brochure. It didn't take, to Molly's relief. Then again, Molly thought as she turned into the Big Easy RV and Mobile Home Village, if it *had* taken, maybe Christopher would be knocking back a cold one at home right now.

He'd been missing for days. Despite her hope that Christopher had taken an out-of-town job last minute and without telling her, Molly couldn't shake the feeling that what she had worried about her entire life had finally, horrifyingly happened: that he had hit on the wrong guy, that he'd been seen leaving one of those seedy motels down by the interstate;

in other words, that the quacks at Wayward Straits had been proven right, that everything she hated most about this town, this state, hell, this whole damn country had finally, horrifyingly turned personal.

Her only solace? Her only hope? A body had yet to turn up. Molly ached even to think it, but the kind of monster who would hurt someone like her brother typically didn't get rid of the body. They wanted people to know what they had done—as a warning, as a validation. At least she had that, Molly told herself, knocking on the door to her mother-in-law's trailer, refusing to admit that, if only she'd tried harder to get him to quit working for the DM, her brother might be standing by her side.

"Good gracious!" Lenora Coogan said after opening the door. "You're about to burst. Come in out the cold. Babies need that warmth. You go settle down in my chaise."

"Couch's fine."

"Nonsense."

In the living area, which stank of cigarettes and shone dully in the hue of their ash, Molly ignored her mother-in-law's order and sat on the couch. Directly across from her sat that same old decrepit lounger, its fabric arms of tufted cushion flanked by a standing ashtray to one side and a magazine rack to the other.

"Oh, thank you so much," Molly said, accepting a glass of milk from Lenora.

"Nutrients. That's what my grandchild needs. Turnip used to drink milk by the gallon."

"Good thing it comes in that size."

Molly didn't understand why she was so prone to being rude with this woman who'd shown her nothing but kindness. Her knee tended to jerk toward the catty remark. She supposed private school had left its stain, all those years of Tacky Day teaching her that its titular adjective was a synonym for *poor.*

But recognition was not absolution, Molly told herself, nor did it automatically, effortlessly bring about improvement. That required work. Part of Molly had always resented the fact her mother-in-law lived in a trailer park, that her husband had never lived in a house with stairs, and if she wanted to get over that resentment, she would have to see herself as the tacky one. "Heard from the PIs?" Molly asked Mama Coogan, over there in her lounger.

"They're still on the scout for those sons of bitches who killed my boy."

"I spoke with them. The boss lady seemed sharp."

"I thought so, too," Lenora said. "Surprises come in all sizes. And colors."

"Mama Coogan," Molly scolded. She figured she should say more, maybe give a little speech about how recognition was not absolution, how improvement required work, but Molly had other work to do on this visit. "Have they said anything about who they are looking into? Solid leads? Prime suspects? Any of that *Hill Street Blues* kind of stuff?"

"They're more like *Simon & Simon*. Or *Cagney & Lacey*? No, wait. They're a man and woman. Simon & Lacey. Cagney & Simon."

Already exhausted from this conversation, Molly said in monotone, "Who do they think poisoned Turnip?"

"They still think it was Jacob Cassidy. He shot at you, didn't he? He's got to be the one. Clem said a friend of hers in the department said Cassidy has been spotted all over town."

That was just what Molly needed but had been afraid to hear. Cassidy had to be the guy who'd killed her brother. He was cleaning house, that motherfucker, mopping up the blood by spilling more of it. Satisfied and relieved, however oddly, given the knowledge that, if Cassidy was still hanging around town, she might very well be next on his list, Molly took a sip of her milk. She held the milk in her mouth, trying to decide whether it had gone bad. She then made a face at her mother-in-law, who smiled her rejoinder, close-lipped, sly.

"My pregnancy with Turnip. All those years raising Turnip. Fifteen years with Turnip's father, who could throw a punch, may he not rest in peace. None, I mean, *none* of that would've been possible had I not learned to pour a little nip in my coffee, my iced tea, my milk."

"Brandy?"

"Just a tiny bit. I'd never put my grandchild at risk."

On the couch in an uncluttered trailer, sipping a desperately needed milk-and-brandy from a chipped glass, Molly felt, for the first time, that she understood her mother-in-law. A flower of kinship bloomed hydroponically inside her chest, its roots thriving on a solution enriched by the nutrients of respect, admiration, and cognac. Molly imagined her mother-in-law over the years, living with a brutal husband, raising a son without help, her tools the same ones Molly herself had acquired in her journey through the world of men: a cunning charade of ignorance, a guileful pretense of naiveté. Some doormats lay on top of trapdoors.

Molly's late husband had been a true Southerner, umbilically reliant on his own past, an unwitting creation of that hidden matriarchy, the one empowered by every good ol' boy's love and fear of his mama. Now she could see how carefully that part of Turnip had been groomed throughout his life. Ms. Lenora Coogan was a woman after Molly's own heart. Mississippi born and raised, Mama Coogan, Molly realized, understood the term "Ole Miss" was feminine for a reason. Southern men worshiped their mothers as much as they did the corrupt idea of the Old South. It seemed Lenora had figured out how to game that glitch, giving men time only till it was time to get hers. Why hadn't Molly recognized that sooner?

Before Molly could answer her own question, Lenora asked one that proved its validity. "Has the insurance money come through yet?"

Molly had never told her about the insurance money. True, she'd convinced—or *thought* she'd convinced—Mama Coogan to hire the PIs, hoping they'd prove Turnip had been killed, thereby entitling her to the life insurance, but Molly hadn't told her mother-in-law any of that. "How'd you—"

"Come on, honey," said Lenora. "I'm not a buffoon, and I'm certainly not a monster. Turnip wasn't perfect; I'll raise my hand there. I know how he treated you. But he was my boy, and if he was killed, whoever's responsible will pay, God's my witness."

"But I—"

"And if, as a perk to making those sons of bitches pay, some fat-cat insurance company has to pay my daughter-in-law money she'll use to raise my grandchild? Like I said, I'm not a monster."

With the back of her hand, Molly wiped off her milk-and-brandy moustache. She placed the empty glass on the coffee table. "It hasn't come through quite yet, the money."

"I'm sure there won't be any problems. When have insurance companies not happily paid out?"

"Are you going to want any of it?"

"Molly," Lenora said, to Molly's relief. The look on her face repeated, *Like I said, I'm not a monster.*

And she wasn't. Over the five years Molly had been married to her son, Lenora Coogan had been kind and forbearing and, unlike most mothers-in-law, mindful of when to butt out, especially after Molly lost her first pregnancy, the one that'd brought about her marriage to a man like Turnip. "It's seventy-five thousand," Molly said. "Plenty to share."

"Don't you worry about me," Lenora said. "I came into a recent windfall."

"Mm?"

Last week, Lenora told Molly, a man knocked on her door and offered what he described as a "severance package" for Turnip's years of employment. Lenora could see he was not from Pathrite, the freight company listed on Turnip's W-2. The man made one stipulation. Lenora could keep the severance, $15,000, but she had to be more discreet in voicing her opinion that Turnip had been killed. "He was DM; I'm no fool," Lenora said. "I figured, what the hell? I'll keep quiet and use the money to pay my two detectives."

"Using the DM's money to take down the DM," Molly said. "I'm impressed."

Molly had to use the bathroom, a necessity that owed less to the glass of fortified milk she'd drunk and more to her own takedown of the DM. She excused herself without mentioning the latter motivation.

Behind the thin, accordion-style bathroom door, all that separated her from the living area, where Lenora remained in her chaise, Molly gripped the sink counter, listening to her mother-in-law talk. The woman had few boundaries. "Another little windfall?" she said. "Because of Hubbard's mishap, my rent here at the Big Easy went down by a hundred a month."

"How's that work?" Molly said, kneeling in front of the sink.

"Hubbard Developments has been liquidating assets, including this place. The new owner lowered the rent. Kept everything else the same, except they evicted the one co—I mean, the one Black family."

Molly opened the cabinet beneath the sink. "Really?" she said, thinking, Only one Black family? It sounded depressingly typical for Mississippi.

"I don't see why, neither. They were considerate people. Better than a lot of the degenerates we got around here."

Inside the cabinet, Molly found the old Kleenex box Turnip had told her about. "Who's this new owner anyway?"

"I forget. Southways something."

Southways? What a surprise, Molly thought, reaching into the Kleenex box and removing the snub-nosed revolver Lenora kept there "for appearances." She put the gun in her purse, flushed the toilet, ran the sink, and, after rubbing her dry hands with a hand towel, walked out of the bathroom.

"Have you thought about reporting this Southways something?" Molly said, not sitting back down on the couch. "That's blatant discrimination."

Lenora swatted a dust mote. "We're outside Meridian. It's a county affair."

In the middle of the room, a stolen gun pulsating heat from her purse, a nip of brandy coursing slipshod through her veins, Molly paused, the brandy dulling the anxiety educed by the gun. *A county affair.* Molly had heard that little euphemism so often during her life. Originally meant to describe activities, legality notwithstanding, outside the ken of city officials, especially the police department, *a county affair* had evolved past any relevance to jurisdiction. The phrase grew into an acknowledgment of Meridian's origin as a community of outlaws and scofflaws, of frontier justice, of vigilance committees, of codes greater than law. Your neighbor stealing your chickens? It's a county affair, dealt with by poisoning your neighbor's cow. The cartwright beats his children? It's a county affair, solved by giving the man a what-for of stern words or, if need be, sterner fists.

But times change, Molly understood. Whereas *It's a county affair* had once implied forthcoming action by the locals of Lauderdale, Clarke, and Kemper, the three counties that constituted the Queen City's micropolitan area, the phrase had become one of resignation more than action. *What can you do?* it now meant. *The whole thing is out of my hands.*

"I should be heading on." Molly kissed Lenora on the cheek. "You take care."

"So soon?"

"Yes, ma'am."

The air outside had dipped to an agreeable chill. Molly felt alive to see her own breath. "A county affair," she whispered inside her car, staring at a sign across the street that read THESE GOOD TIMES CAN ROLL. Molly had written off far too much of her life as a county affair, something beyond her control, from the pregnancy her parents had forced her to keep, to the man her parents had forced her to marry, to the miscarriage her parents had pretended never happened. Now her brother, the only person she truly cared about in this world, had probably been killed, had *likely* been killed, given the line of work Molly had failed to convince him to quit, and she could, she might, she would be next.

From her purse, Molly removed the snub-nosed revolver, its heavy solidity like a paperweight to her thoughts. She was through waiting around for something to happen to her. Molly decided to show that son of a bitch Cassidy the true meaning of a county affair. He wouldn't get away with what he had done. Molly placed the gun in her glove compartment. She cranked the engine, shifted to reverse, and pulled out of the parking spot. It was time to get hers.

16

SOUTHWAYS ALLIANCES

Honey?" Dixon yelled over his shoulder as he stood in the open doorway to his apartment. "Lock the liquor cabinet!"

On Dixon's front steps, Clem crossed her arms and tapped one foot against the pavement, a pantomime of annoyance. She almost sprained her eyes from rolling them so hard. "I just about sprained my eyes," she said to Dixon, "from rolling them so goddamn hard."

"I guess I can let you in," her partner said. "But you promise to behave?"

Dixon's invitations to have dinner with him and his wife were as common as Clem's refusal of them. Tonight was an exception. He had coerced her into accepting the invitation by promising new information on the Hubbard case, despite, as Clem had claimed earlier in the day, that being "your job—for now, at least."

The smell of pot roast greeted Clem as Dixon led her into the living room. A cassette player spilled slide guitar across arts-and-crafts furniture. Atop built-in shelves, relegated to the back corners, sat framed photographs from what Clem liked to think of as her partner's Springsteenian glory days: Dixon puffing his chest at prom, Dixon throwing for a touchdown, Dixon at a graduation podium, midspeech, mortarboard on his head.

"Drink?" Dixon said, giving it, Clem noted, more period than question mark.

"Yes, thanks."

Two and a half sips later, Dixon's wife, Heather, walked in from the kitchen, a towel draped over her shoulder, longneck hooked between her index and middle fingers. "Oh God, yes," she said before taking Clem's glass of whiskey, downing what remained, and handing it back to her. Their subsequent hug reminded Clem how hard it always was to turn down any chance to hang out with this tiny, blond, psychotic bundle of egoless id.

"Thank you, Heather. I was worried I wasn't going to be able to finish that."

"I am owed. The late nights you get to spend with the ol' ball and chain? I am *owed*."

Heather, Clem knew, had put up all those photographs of Dixon's glory days. Heather, Clem knew, was ridiculously, cartoonishly in love with her husband, whom she had first started dating at the peak of those glory days. It would've been enough to make Clem sick, if only it weren't so frigging adorable.

"*Garçon*, fetch us another round of 'freshment," Heather said. She shoved her empty beer bottle toward her husband and led Clem into the kitchen, where they gathered plates, silverware, and pots to set the table. *Boy* was insulting enough in English, Clem paused to think, but deliciously more so in French. She had to hand it to Heather Hicks.

"It beats Denny's Build-a-Breakfast, you have to admit," Dixon said as he placed drinks in front of his wife and partner, each of whom had already sat down.

"I'd rather it were a Dixon's Rebuild-a-Carburetor." Heather, while scooping butter beans onto her plate, made a face at Clem. "I've been trying to get Spark Plug here to fix my truck for three months. Three. Months."

"It's not the carburetor. Squirrels chewed up the fuel line. I've told you."

"Squirrels," Heather said to Clem. "I go three months without my Chevy, and he blames squirrels."

"You've got my VW whenever you need it," Dixon said.

That the Hickses were a two-car family had never seemed of note to Clem. That petite little Heather drove a Chevy pickup and good-ol'-boy Dixon tooled about town in a VW Bug? Now, that Clem found hilariously noteworthy. Whenever they were on a job, she insisted they use her Renegade. The Bug was a cover-blowingly bright red.

Dixon forked a cut of pot roast onto his plate. "Who's going to say grace?"

"Very funny." Heather buttered a roll. "Give Clem a coronary, why not?"

Although Clem hated clichés along the lines of *It's been so long I can't even remember the last time,* she genuinely had to think in order to remember the last time she'd eaten a home-cooked meal. She was always too busy working a case, the thought of which reminded her she was currently too busy working a case. "And now, Mr. Hicks," Clem said between bites, "what have you got for me?"

"Can we at least enjoy our dinner first? It feels rude not to."

"Heather?" said Clem.

"Don't mind me," Heather said. "Y'all do your thing. I'll listen pensively."

Hands steepled above his plate, his face pointedly expressionless, Dixon said to Heather, "Thank you so much for your support."

"Love means never having to offer support."

Gravity got confused in its work on Dixon's shoulders and head, pushing down the former and raising the latter. Dixon looked plaintively at the ceiling, as if praying for mercy. "You asked I look into Hubbard's competitors," he said, lowering his gaze to Clem.

"And?"

"He's got—excuse me—he *had* a number of them. But most aren't local. I'm talking companies based out of Jackson, Birmingham, as far off as Atlanta. One or two from New Orleans."

"New Orleans?" Clem said, thinking, Matrangas.

"I know what you're thinking. The Matrangas. But that's a blind alley, gut says. Hubbard had one tippy-top, king-of-the-heap nemesis, and he happens to be based right here in Meridian. Ever heard of Southways Alliance?"

Within the record crate of her mind, Clem did her usual, flipping through LPs, looking for a title or artist named Southways Alliance. Funny, she thought before finding it, how that name could work as a euphemism for the Confederacy. "I've seen their signs around town." Clem pictured the slogan COMING YOUR WAY FROM SOUTHWAYS ALLIANCE on billboards next to vacant lots, beside bulldozers, excavators, and track hoes, in front of mounded dirt; the words painted beneath the picture of a housing subdivision or fast-food restaurant, a gas station or grocery store. "Were Hubbard and Southways competing on any projects before he died?"

"When *weren't* they competing on any projects?" Dixon pensively chewed his last bite of pot roast. He took a sip of his drink and fingered a fork tine. Guy knew how to milk a moment. "But that isn't the best part."

"The chase. He finally cuts to it!" Clem said.

"The paper chase? Yes, ma'am. The best part is Southways has been acquiring Hubbard properties since the man's untimely, unseemly demise. Including the mobile home park where our client lives."

"Lenora Coogan?"

"One and same."

That was interesting, Clem had to admit. Theories drifted through the dogtrot breezeway of her mind, heating it up rather than cooling it off. Did whoever owned this Southways Alliance have a grudge against the Coogans? To answer that question, Clem would have to know who owned the Southways Alliance.

Apparently a psychic, Dixon said, "The guy's name is Hamilton Delacroix."

Clem knew the name without having to shuffle through any LPs. She had first heard it in a story told by the man she had plans to get a drink with as soon as she left the Hickses'.

"Russ Clyde told me a story about this Delacroix," Clem said as she took her plate to the sink, half her food untouched. "He owns Le Saloon, that dive bar and grill?"

"It's a rough joint." Dixon, always so flagrantly polite, nudged Clem aside, a St. Bernard with a sponge and dish soap clutched in hand instead of a keg of brandy strapped under his chin. He began to do the dishes.

Aware that Dixon would not allow any help at the sink, Clem, who would have preferred the brandy, sat back down at the table. *It was wonderful, thankyousomuch,* she mouthed to Heather before saying to her husband, "Russ mentioned Delacroix owns near half the whole town, but he keeps a low profile. Which explains Southways Alliance and not Delacroix Developments, I guess you can suppose."

"I can and I will," Heather said. "And you're welcome."

"For what?" Dixon said over his shoulder.

"My forbearance at letting Clem be the Dabney Coleman to your Dolly Parton, Lily Tomlin, and Jane Fonda."

"Honey, my hours are a hell of a lot worse than nine to five."

One thing nagged at Clem. In the story Russ had told her, he'd made Hamilton Delacroix out to be a proponent of justice, a man insistent on Russ doing his utmost to put away the kind of thugs, hoods, punks, and goons who patronized Le Saloon. Would such a person have his primary business competition taken out by a professional hit man? That was a question best answered by the assistant district attorney, a date with whom Clem was already running twenty minutes late for.

"Hey, y'all, I need to be heading out. Thank you so much. This was great."

At the front door, where Heather demanded she handle the goodbyes without Dixon present, the woman Clem used to jokingly refer to as Mrs. Dixon tossed her well-maintained armor to the floor, its clank found in her newly somber expression, its clatter present in her newly serious tone of voice. "How're you doing?" she said. "I mean with what happened at the John Wesley Hardin."

Clem tilted her head with what she hoped was a playful grimace. "I'm fine."

"Clementine B. A. Baldwin."

"B. A.?"

"Bad Ass."

"Thanks, but seriously. I've never been better."

Inside her shoes, Clem clenched and released her toes, *clench and release, clench and release,* the way her father had taught her to relax as a child. The movement helped her not to hear the gunshots from that night. It helped her not to see the cold-eyed killer across the room. Soon the clenching of her toes became the squeezing of a fist became the curling of a finger became the pulling of a trigger. Wasn't that the hardest lesson to learn? Sometimes you had to pull a trigger. Clench. Release.

"You don't have to worry," Clem told Heather, facing her in the doorway.

"I know. Not with you looking after him. But we have to look after ourselves."

We. Clem understood what Heather meant, how the two of them were alike. She nodded with her back turned to the closing door.

The night had grown cool. A tabby cat scowled from the window of a house across the street. A man in a New Orleans Saints jacket with a patch of duct tape at the shoulder stepped from the curb, his back facing Clem, his head angled toward the cat in the window. Clem figured the cat must be an Atlanta Falcons fan.

At the end of the driveway, its meager square footage occupied by Heather's Chevy pickup and Dixon's Volkswagen Bug, Clem got into her Jeep and, clenching and releasing her toes to calm and steady her fingers, turned the ignition. The engine roared.

Ten minutes later and half an hour late, Clem arrived at the Skyview Club, a flophouse located at the former site of the Evangel Temple. Its heritage as a temple, to Clem's mind, accentuated the club's un-temple-like plywood floors, newspaper-covered drywall, exposed wiring, and overall sacrilegious atmosphere, that last part accentuated further, Clem noted as she walked through the club, by its clientele. Although not nearly as rough-and-tumble as the John Wesley Hardin, the Skyview still attracted the kind of folks Clem wouldn't have been surprised to see in a lineup or described in an APB.

The irony? Clem thought as she passed a woman taking a shot, unaware of the baby spit-up crusted on her shoulder, slightly more aware of the baby in a carrier basket next to her feet. Most of these people drinking, smoking, and God-knew-whating here in the former Evangel Temple probably attended the church's new location every Sunday.

"I got no idea why you picked this place," Russ said as Clem joined him at the bar.

Clem knew why, but she was saving it for later. "What are you drinking?"

"LA Beer."

"It's from LA?"

"Stands for *light alcohol*. It's new."

"Jesus."

After ordering a bourbon on the rocks, Clem lowered her hand surreptitiously toward Russ's thigh, which she squeezed. He squirmed exactly as she'd expected him to, as someone made at once uncomfortable and titillated, a combo of states that induced the latter in Clem.

They'd only been sleeping together for a week. At first, especially the night he turned down Clem's advances because she'd had too many, Russ had been unrelentingly nice and obnoxiously kind, and that had not changed. Clem's attitude toward those traits? That had changed. If the worm wouldn't turn, she figured, maybe she shouldn't step on it.

Clem *deserved* to have someone nice and kind in her life. She *deserved* to be looked at with unabashed adoration. And if, in the process, she could get inside access to information from the district attorney's office, well, all good jobs came with perks, didn't they?

"I was thinking about that story you told me last week," Clem said to Russ.

"Yeah?"

"The one about—"

From overhead, drowning out the jukebox's reverb, the nasal clatter of ice in plastic cups, the offbeat percussion of pool balls against bumpers, and the incipient cries of a baby, came the rumbling, sustained whoosh of the Skyview Club's namesake. Once the plane had landed at the airfield half a mile away, Clem finished her thought. "I said," the words coming out louder than she intended, "the one about *Hamilton Delacroix*!"

Clem could have sworn half a dozen heads at the bar pivoted in her direction when she said that name. Then again, given the ideologies typically found at a bar "out by the airport," the half-dozen heads might not have been filled with interest in the name but the color of the woman who'd spoken it. That, Clem edited herself, and the color of the brazen, traitorous man beside her.

"What about Hamilton?" asked the traitor.

"Have y'all kept in touch?"

"Sure. He cooks me a burger at Le Saloon time to time. Still insists I eat it in the kitchen."

"You're friends?" Clem asked.

"You could say."

"He ever talk about his business ventures?"

Russ, exaggerating exasperation, leaned back on his barstool. "Clem, what's this about? You clearly want to ask me something specific."

Okay, fine. He could have it his way. Clem said, "Did you know Delacroix, via Southways Alliance, has been acquiring properties from Hubbard Developments?"

Exasperation giving way to bemusement, Russ, whose face made like Charlie Brown declaring, *Good grief!* returned his barstool to its original position, the front two feet chirping against the floor. "Clementine," he said, in tune with the chirp. "That's what Hamilton does. He buys and sells properties. Now, as for Hubbard? That's a coincidence."

"You know what I say about coincidences."

"Actually, yes. You're right. It's correlated, not coincidental. A developer dies. What do other developers do? They acquire his developments. You're overextending the causality."

"'Overextending the causality.' They teach you that in law school?"

"Well."

"All I *do* is overextend causality. I overextend different causalities until I can *prove* one." Clem finished her drink and rattled the remaining ice cubes at the bartender. Fucking law-school jargon. It drove her nuts. In college, Clem had given serious thought to law school, to the extent she registered for the LSAT, but she ultimately decided she'd had enough of academia, that climbing the ladder at a law firm would entail even more of what she'd had to endure as an undergraduate. All those interns and associates and junior partners would look at her the same way her classmates and TAs and professors had.

What did all of them see? A cheater, a fraud. They saw somebody who had the advantage of both worlds: white privilege and that most scalding of buttons in the South, affirmative action.

Never mind Clem scored stratospherically on all her standardized tests. Never mind Clem consistently ranked near the top of her class. Never mind her law professors would most likely have been legacies at Harvard or Dartmouth or whichever college they had gotten into with their B average at Groton. Never mind the senior partners at her law firm would most likely have gotten out of their latest DUI by calling in a favor from their stepson's fraternity brother who, without having tried a single case as a lawyer, had been appointed municipal judge.

Clem had thought the police department would be different. All those working-class cops, none of them born with the privilege Clem's Black friends in college secretly suspected her of, all those boys and the occasional girl in blue, they were the key to a life of bringing law and order to a world in dire need of both, Clem had incorrectly believed.

"You're absolutely right," Russ said, peeling the label off his LA Beer. "I came across as condescending. I know I can do that sometimes. I'm sorry."

"Don't be sorry. I was being defensive."

"With good reason."

"What do football people like to say?" Clem asked. "The best defense is a good offense?"

"I think you mean war."

Over Russ's shoulder drooped a cuff-linked, gold-watched wrist, followed by a slurred voice that could have also been wearing cuff links and a gold watch. "Prosecutor!"

Russ turned, his expression more resigned than curious. "Chaunce," he said.

"What brings you slumming these parts? Ho Jo's run out of bitters and soda?"

"Clementine." Russ motioned to the man standing behind them. "Do you know Chaunce Lattimer?"

"Nope."

But she'd heard of him. Everyone in Meridian had heard of Chaunce Lattimer. Proud Mississippian, Phi Deltan, Rotarian, American, father, and husband, in order from most proud to least, Lattimer owned car dealerships across the South. The rollback of gas prices after the oil crisis in the 1970s had given him the foothold to build a motor empire. In interviews, Lattimer often claimed, with regard to the pronunciation of his given name, that he put the ch-ching in *bonne chance*.

Clem knew his type. Lord, did she. Chaunce Lattimer believed, like all white Southern men with money, that luck was forged, not given, that success was earned, not born into, that all it took to make a single malt sessionable was a splash of water. He had the entitled white Southerner's move of flipping the first two letters in *what*. "H-wat we got here is a failure to communicate!" Guy even looked like the warden from *Cool Hand Luke*.

"My, my," Lattimer said after introducing himself to Clem. "But it seems our Russ is going for a new make and model."

"Okay, Chaunce," Russ said. "That's enough."

Lattimer was still holding Clem's hand from when he'd shaken it. He trailed his pinkie finger over her wrist. "Such a lovely complexion. Such beautiful skin."

Disgusted not only by Lattimer's pathetic line but also his limp hand's oppressive girth, Clem pulled her own hand away and used it to take a necessarily large gulp of her drink. She despised this guy's particular genus of flirt. If Clem had been a couple shades darker, she wouldn't have caught his eye. She would have been invisible to the son of a bitch.

"Brings you to the Skyview Lounge, Chaunce?" Russ asked perfunctorily.

"Club, not lounge," Lattimer said. "You really are new around here." He was speaking to Russ but staring at Clem. "This afternoon I'd been looking at a possible site for a BMW dealership nearby. I got thirsty just thinking about those little Kraut cars and how much bread they'll—wait a second, are you Clem Baldwin, the private eye?"

"Investigator," said Clem.

"Excuse me. The investigator eye. A little birdy told me you're looking into the Hubbard murder."

"Oh my God. You know a *bird* that can *talk*?"

Lattimer smiled at Russ. "And I do admire a woman gives good as she gets."

"Did you know Randy Hubbard personally?" Clem asked.

"I knew him socially, as far Meridian society would allow." Forehead dewed in whiskey sweat, cheeks rosy with whiskey burn, Lattimer swilled from an aquarium-size tumbler full of the source of his sweat and burn. He said, "The Queen City of Mississippi loves a success story, but only certain kinds of success."

Clem recalled how Hubbard's membership application had been denied by the Lakeshoals Country Club, that bulwark of striped sweatbands, chlorinated hair, branded visors, golf balls, tennis balls, and soggy swimsuits, with a staff made up almost exclusively of Black men and women, each in all-white, heavily starched uniforms. Her dad had been a member. "Why exactly," Clem said to Lattimer, "was Hubbard's success the wrong kind?"

"'Wrong kind.' Did I say that? Doesn't sound like me. So pessimistic."

"He wasn't Irish. He wasn't Jewish."

"Wouldn't have mattered. Some of Meridian's most prominent are Jewish, Lil' Miss."

"Lil' *Ms.*"

"Ma'am?"

Cognizant of Russ beside her, teetering on his stool like a nervous motorcycle passenger leaning against the sissy bar, Clem asked, "Are we talking extralegal success? That why he wasn't well-liked by the Junior Auxiliary?"

"Junior Auxiliary's coffers would be running mighty damn low, it weren't for extralegal success." Lattimer finished his aquarium of whiskey, ice cubes bouncing like suffocating goldfish. "Naw, Hubbard shot straight, poor bastard. It was the type of element his projects catered to. Certain folks don't want that element encroaching, you get me."

"Element?" asked Clem.

"Hubbard built dollar stores, fried-chicken joints. You know."

You know. Yes, Clem knew. The ease with which Lattimer had admitted to that kind of bigotry shocked her. It felt like a sorority girl cheerfully asking if she could touch her hair.

"Chaunce, ol' boy," Russ said, gripping Lattimer's shoulder. "I do hate to bear bad news, but Clem and I were in the middle of something. Would you do me the favor?"

"I get you," Lattimer said. He placed his aquarium on the bar, pulled a ring of keys from his pocket, and twirled them on his finger. "It's time for me to be getting home anyhow. Miss Baldwin, a pleasure. G'night, Russ. Y'all don't sleep too tight, you hear?"

Light winked from Lattimer's cuff links and watch as he shook Russ's hand.

Once they were alone, Russ apologized to Clem, explaining that Lattimer had contributed "substantially" to his boss's campaign for DA, that some "light" ass-kissing was a regrettable part of his job. Clem didn't bother mentioning Lattimer could easily get a DUI on his way home. He'd already contributed his way out of that sort of predicament. "Is what he said true?" Clem asked instead.

"About the Jewish population in Meridian? Absolutely. Look at the names on the buildings downtown. Lowenstein, Meyer, Rosenbaum, Lichten—"

Clem punched Russ's shoulder. "You know that's not what I was talking about. Was Hubbard looked down on in Meridian because he developed businesses patronized by, by . . ."

"Poor people?"

"No."

"Black people?"

"Yes."

"Eh." Russ, after swigging from his beer, slumped against the sissy bar of his stool. "My opinion, it's both. Poor *and* Black, two categories that, unfortunately and not coincidentally, tend to overlap in a place like Meridian."

"A place like Meridian. A place like Mississippi. A place like America."

"Now there's an extension of causality that's sound."

Why hadn't Clem considered racism as a factor in the murder before now? It hadn't occurred to her, not once, most likely due to the fact the victim and prime suspect were white. Still, the motive felt too simple, too pat, a square puzzle piece in a jigsaw of wild, unruly shapes.

To both distract and focus her thoughts, Clem looked around the bar, thinking about her actual reason for meeting Russ at the Skyview. She'd first spotted Jasper Potts five minutes after she'd arrived. Slight of build, five foot four, trim-bearded and round-gutted, Mr. Potts was sitting across the room, sipping a beer, studying a waitress who was clearly out of his league. Clem watched Jasper Potts stand from his table, pretend to stretch, gesture toward the waitress, and then lose his nerve. He shuffled moodily toward the restrooms.

"Excuse me," Clem said to Russ as she stepped away from the bar. She slipped her extendable out of her purse, the baton's weight soothing in her hand, its rubber grip a balm to her fingers.

Clem hadn't handled a skip trace by herself since she'd hired Dixon. Even as a team, they rarely handled these kinds of jobs, only resorting to them in slow months, when Clem needed the agent's fee as a quick fix to pay her office rent or E&O premium. Dixon was typically the muscle, but Clem didn't want him around tonight. She needed to get her nerve back. She needed to walk into a joint full of Jacob Cassidys and walk out with one of them bound in her shackles.

Besides, Clem thought as she pushed open the door to the men's room, Jasper Potts was your basic contempt trace. She'd studied his sheet. It was on the mild end, nonviolent this and misdemeanor that; the playlist of a perp who would not put up a fight.

"Wrong door, Mama," Jasper said after glancing over his shoulder at Clem.

He was pissing with poor aim into a freestanding, stall-less commode. He and Clem were the only people in the room, its walls bright red, lit by a naked bulb above the broken sink. "Jasper Potts?" Clem said.

"Yeah?"

"Mr. Potts, you've contemned a court order, and as such, I have the authority to take—"

Clem had been wrong about the not-put-up-a-fight part. The snick of a blade's spring action preceded its appearance, the suddenness of which forestalled the usual housekeeping: as Jasper lunged at Clem with the knife, his dick was still hanging from his zipper, snub-nosed, dripping, and pink as a piglet.

Jasper's poor aim from earlier had left the floor around the toilet hazardous. He slipped in his own urine, the knife falling from his hand. *"Oof!"* Clem kicked the knife aside. She wedged her knee into Jasper's back, shoved her extendable into her purse, and pulled out her handcuffs.

"I'm not your mama," Clem said after shackling Jasper. She stood him up.

At the door to the bathroom, Jasper shuffled to a stop. "You got me, okay? But would you please help me out?" He nodded toward his crotch.

Clem, who briefly considered embarrassing the guy by marching him through the bar in his present condition, succumbed to compassion. She reached down and tugged at his trousers until he was tucked away. "You owe me one," she said, elbowing Jasper out the door.

"I owe you shit."

"Boy."

"Yes, ma'am."

Initially, as Clem guided Jasper through the club, one hand on the back of his neck and the other inside her purse, holding her baton, nobody paid them any mind. But soon heads began to turn. Voices quieted. Drinks lowered. Someone turned off the music. By the time Clem reached Russ at the bar, every patron of the Skyview was staring at her, a Black woman with a handcuffed white boy in her custody. Clem stared back at all those hateful faces, as if confronting the entire gamut of history and saying, *That all you got?*

Clem turned to Russ. "I'm bringing my new friend here down to Twenty-Second Avenue. Shouldn't take more than an hour to process the paperwork. I'll stop by your place for a nightcap?"

Ante meridiem was an unusual period for Clem to spend time working in her office. Start kind of late, finish very late: That was her typical routine. The morning after her impoundment of one Jasper Potts, however, Clem had woken bright of eye and bushy of tail. She hadn't bothered saying bye to Russ before leaving his house, the morning sun greeting her like the friend it had once been. Her lack of a hangover, due to Russ having only had club soda on hand when she'd gotten to his place late last night, also helped.

Clem's mood faltered when she found her office door unlocked. Drawing her piece, she silently turned the knob, and after taking a step back, she eased the door open. Clem, in that rush she always felt when her training and years of fieldwork merged into a single, fluid motion, kept her elbows locked and both hands on her sidearm as she cleared the room, one corner at a time. Snap, slice, slice, scan. Snap, slice, slice, scan.

The economy of movement ticking in her blood, Clem lowered her weapon on confirming everything in the office was clean, her double-pedestal desk with its fluttery stack of invoices, her wood-grain television with its crooked set of rabbit ears, everything except her sleeper couch, which was commandeered by a passed-out, snoring Samantha Bellflower.

Clem holstered her piece. She raised the window blinds, spilling winter light across the room. "Wakey, wakey," she said to Sam, who writhed against the sun in her face.

"Time is it?" Sam asked.

"When I gave you a key to this place, I assumed you'd only use it in case of my suspicious curtain fall or exit stage something-don't-smell-right."

Sam sat up and stretched. "'I assumed,' says the dissenter of assumptions."

"Only the easy ones."

At the kitchenette, Clem put a two-day-old pot of coffee on the hot plate. She waited for it to heat up by interrogating her friend, who had apparently tied one on after the guy she'd been seeing stepped out on her. Sam had managed to stumble her way into the office without, she promised, throwing up in it. "I did that in one of the trash cans on the street."

"You still take two sugars?" Clem asked.

"Mm-hm."

Unfortunately, Clem had about as much sugar on hand as she did fresh coffee. She did, however, have a bottle of ibuprofen. Clem decided that, given Sam's condition and those little brown tablets' sugary coating, she'd grant them a battlefield promotion to coffee sweetener. She felt like being back in college, when an apple could rise to the rank of bong, a paper clip to bookmark, a pencil eraser to earring back, a slap of a boy's face to birth control. "Here you go," Clem said, handing Sam a hot mug of hangover medicine.

"Perfection."

Clem sat behind her desk with her own steaming mug. "So who's this guy?"

"Piece of shit I thought might not be a piece of shit. How's the Hubbard case shaking out?"

From her desk chair, Clem looked around the office, at mementos of her past cases: receipts from background checks, blown-out fingerprints, ziplocked strands of hair, a framed parking ticket from her first tail-and-surveil. "It's going okay," Clem said to Sam, "but I can't seem to grip it. Investigating the case feels like trying to hop the QC-LTD."

"The Limited doesn't stop here anymore."

"That's my point, dumbass."

"*Detective* Dumbass, thank you."

"I'm still not convinced Cassidy is our guy," Clem said. "It feels too easy."

"Heaven forbid a case be easy."

Clem swiveled in her seat. "Who was first at the scene? The Hubbard murder, not Turnip's fall."

"Poissant."

"God."

"Right?"

A bouquet of whiskey and aftershave wafted past Clem's mental nose. She pictured Detective John Poissant sitting across from her the night of the shoot-out at the John Wesley Hardin Club. Of course an asshole like that would be primary on this kind of case.

"Was he sober the night of?" Clem asked.

"Pffft!"

"How bad?"

"I heard the bartender at Ho Jo's eighty-sixed him. Would have been right about the time the call came in."

Remembering her Cocktail Napkin Theory, Clem asked, "And he didn't take note of a second drink somewhere at the scene?"

Sam leaned into the couch. She draped an arm across the back of it. "I've been chewing on that little theory of yours. Had a look at the file, and I'm thinking you may be onto something. Second cocktail napkin? Yes. Second cocktail glass? That's a yes, too."

"A second glass? Shit a brick. Where?"

"The sink. And before you ask, the answer's no. Forensics didn't recover any prints."

"Residue?"

"Minimal. Brown liquid. Whiskey, my guess."

"Poissant didn't take a whiff?" Clem asked, already knowing the answer.

"Says he didn't think to."

"Classic Poissant. When has that merit scholar ever remembered to think?"

Do some thinking of your own, Clem told herself as she turned in her chair to look out the window. What were the ledges of this case she could hang on to, ledges she could dangle from, climb, or peer over? Fact: on March 27, 1984, Randall Hubbard was shot and killed by a .38 Special, four slugs in his back, two in his shoulder, one in the back of his head. Fact: at the scene of the crime were two cocktail glasses, one holding the vodka and rocks with lime that Hubbard favored, the other holding a brown liquid residue that was most likely whiskey. Conjecture: Hubbard was murdered by an acquaintance, somebody he'd made a cocktail for and felt comfortable with. Conjecture: the murder was an impromptu act of passion, not necessarily premeditated, given the typical Mississippian's tendency to have a gun on their person at any time. Conjecture: the murder was motivated by racism. Conjecture: the murder involved Hubbard's real estate business. What did they say about geography as destiny?

Clem sipped her coffee. An orange-breasted bird landed on her windowsill. "Did you ever watch *Batman* as a kid?"

"With Adam West?" Sam asked.

"And Burt Ward as Robin. Cesar Romero as the Joker. Burgess Meredith was the Penguin."

"Zap! Ka-pow! Of course I watched it."

"Every time one of the villains was on-screen, the camera angles were skewed. Tilted, not horizontal. To show us the villains were, you know, crooked." Clem turned to her friend. "That's what this case feels like. Everything's tilted a few degrees. Nothing is on the right axis. Capitalism and prejudice, all tied together, misaligning the big picture."

"Maybe that *is* the big picture."

Leaning back, Clem propped her feet on her desk. "My all-time favorite villain was Catwoman," she said. "Julie Newmar played her at first. Last season the role went to Eartha Kitt."

"I love Eartha Kitt."

"I didn't. Least not at first. That's not *my* Catwoman, I thought. She grew on me, but it still felt wrong. How everyone, my dad, my friends, assumed I'd like seeing a Black woman on television. And I did. What I didn't like? How people assumed because a Black woman played her, I'd see Catwoman as a role model, someone to aspire to be."

"What's so wrong with that?"

Clem shrugged. "Batman was my role model."

After Sam excused herself to use the bathroom, noting as she stood from the couch, "This coffee's got a weird taste to it," Clem entwined her fingers, situated them against her stomach, and, with her feet still propped on her desk, studied the Queen City skyline, that EKG of prosperity and depression, prosperity and depression. How suitable: The Queen City wasn't a real queen. But it still clung to the ostentatious title of queen. Only a place like Meridian would refuse to give up the superiority of that monarchial monosyllable. Then again, Clem chastised herself, what had she chosen to stencil on the frosted glass of her office door, right above DETECTIVE AGENCY? Titles could be empowering to those in need of power.

As much as Clem loathed about this city, it was her home, the place she'd been born, the place she'd been raised—abiding, ineluctable truths that on occasion made her proud. Nowhere was that more evident than the federal courthouse visible from her office window. In that blocky limestone structure, not to be confused, Clem reminded herself, with the county courthouse from which Turnip had taken his fall, James Meredith had filed suit against Ole Miss, a legal campaign that eventually led to the Supreme Court as well as the state university's integration. In that courthouse, too, after the death of those three civil rights workers in Philadelphia, an all-white jury convicted seven people, including a white deputy sheriff, for deprivation of the three victims' civil rights. The verdict marked the first time in the history of Mississippi a white jury had convicted a white official on civil rights charges.

"I never really understood the saying 'Piss like a racehorse,'" Sam said as she walked out of the bathroom. "A palindrome like *racecar* works better. Spelled the same backward and forward? Symbolizes the backsplash. You're out of toilet paper, speaking of."

"A real class act, my girl Sam is. Ever consider trying out a verbal filt—"

That Sam's father had been Philadelphia PD at the time of the Freedom

Riders' murder, coupled with the sensation in Clem's fingers, still laced across her stomach, sent her mind unwillingly, confusingly back to the previous night. She watched a sped-up film reel of the time she'd spent at the Skyview Club. The reel froze, grainy and tremulous, on one image: Russ shaking hands with Chaunce Lattimer, silver cuff links glimmering, gold watch shimmering, and, barely visible in the dim bar light, both men's pinkies entwined.

17

BLACK AND WHITE

"The greatest tragedy in this world? Everything is beautiful in black and white." Heather Hicks remembered those lines from an otherwise unremarkable short story, one she had carefully read, earnestly considered, and ever so politely, ever so constructively destroyed in a creative-writing workshop as an undergraduate at Vanderbilt.

She supposed the line about black and white had come to her because, at the moment, colors were very much on her mind. Two in particular: pink and blue.

From the kitchen, where she opted for a glass of water instead of the wine she could actually use right now, Heather meandered through the living room, momentarily quiet while Dixon was out running his usual day-off errands. She walked past her bedroom, down the hall, and into the guest room, which, based on the news she'd recently gotten, wouldn't be so for long.

The guest room's decor, Heather liked to joke, was Midcentury Goodwill, its bed frame void of a headboard, its lamp fixtures absent of shades. A secondhand dresser stood in the corner, capped by a clock with a wonky second hand. The walls were as bare as the closet. Terra-cotta stains blended into the terra-cotta carpet. When Heather and Dixon had first moved in, not long after their wedding, her parents had offered to furnish the entire place, every room. "It's just a starter," her mother had said with a verbal shrug, and by the way she'd glanced at Dixon, Heather could tell she didn't mean the house.

Of course, Dixon, who would readily cede any measure of his pride to give his wife the home he believed she deserved, had wanted to accept the offer of financial help, but Heather refused. She never told him why.

"Just a starter." Heather shook her head at the memory of those words. Jesus, Mother. Sometimes. Near the one untreated window of the guest room, Heather gave the space another look, assessing the square footage, the layout, the side of the room where a crib would fit perfectly. They wouldn't even have to get rid of the bed. Heather imagined taking a nap on it, listening to her cradled baby sleep while she was being cradled by her husband, Dixon's funky-sweet barnyard breath trailing along her ear, his arm a trestle to hers.

Heather sipped her water, but it didn't do any good. She was still a wreck of nerves. One bundle of them involved money, that lurking but invisible specter haunting every unexpected child, a ghost made all the more sinister by Dixon's anemic salary from the agency and Heather's slightly less anemic pay as an English Lit professor at the junior college. Yes, it was true, Heather's father, a retired contractor who, during his career, had built nearly half of Meridian, including the junior college, would gladly help out. Heather supposed her friends would sneer at her "predicament," how she refused to eat humble pie while others starved.

But money wasn't the real reason Heather's glass of water splashed a sprinkle onto the floor as she raised it to her lips. The real reason was Dixon. After the war, when he'd come home, so many of his friends gone, the last of his family dead, Dixon had been unusually but understandably taciturn. "I just can't imagine," he'd said, "bringing a child into this world," and from the look in his eyes Heather couldn't tell if he meant the world he'd left or the one to which he'd returned.

"What are you doing in here?" Dixon asked, standing at the door to the guest room.

On the terra-cotta carpet dilated an arterial-red blotch of water. Heather's glass dangled from her fingers. "We need to do something about this room," she said, nudging past Dixon, heading back toward the kitchen.

Dixon followed. "I keep saying. But when has anybody even used it yet?"

"Nobody has because it's embarrassing." Heather placed her empty glass in the sink. "That's probably why Clem prefers the couch."

"Clem 'prefers' the couch because that's where she happens to pass out."

To distract herself, Heather took a rag to the kitchen counter, cleaning its clean surface. "What's she doing today? How come you're home? Weekdays my lover likes to visit."

Dixon, shrugging out of his jacket, walked into their bedroom. "She's got a date," he said, loud enough to be heard from the kitchen. "Remember those?"

"Of course. Dried fruit. They killed that lil' Nazi monkey in Indiana Jones."

"The women in my life!" The screech of their closet door opening underscored Dixon's sarcasm as he added, "So good with wordplay!"

From the bedroom walked Dixon, changed into a ratty T-shirt and that pair of jeans he refused to toss, regardless that they had more holes than the plots of those paperback whodunits their accountant said he couldn't write off. He held up a plastic bag. "Got that part I've been needing to fix your truck."

"Finally. I'm about sick of driving your Volkswagen."

"Zee people's cah?" Dixon asked in his sad excuse for a German accent.

Heather completed their usual joke about how Germans in movies always said *no* in triplicate. "*Nein, nein, nein.*"

"And as a bonus . . ." Out of the plastic bag Dixon removed what looked like a tiny spray bottle of Binaca. "Squirrel deterrent!"

"They make a spray specifically for squirrels?"

"Rodents in general." His eyes creased by a smirk, Dixon circumnavigated the kitchen island, kissed Heather on the cheek, and said, "I promise not to spray it on myself, baby."

In the silence after Dixon's exit to the driveway, where he went to work on her pickup, Heather gripped the kitchen counter, her mind a narrow, damp cave echoing what Dixon had called her. He would be happy about the news. How in this world could he not be? *This world.* Heather thought again of that bit from her fiction workshop in college, an attempt at profundity so weak, so awful she didn't want to admit she'd written it herself.

"The greatest tragedy in this world? Everything is beautiful in black and white."

An irrefutable truth? Nothing was black and white. Another irrefutable truth? Everything was black and white.

"Where's my head at?" Dixon said, startling Heather for the second time that afternoon. "I forgot the most important tool for a job like this," he said before grabbing a High Life from the fridge. He tossed the bottle cap in the trash and walked back out to the driveway.

Through the kitchen window, Heather could see Dixon, squinting against the sunlight, carry his tool kit from the garage, his image superimposed by that of Heather's face, stenciled with fear, blanched by doubt. She turned away from the window. After the war, had the fatalism, doom, and resignation she'd seen in Dixon's eyes been a reflection of her own? He'd always been so much more perceptive than people allowed him credit. Had his thousand-yard stare been a sympathetic amplification of her hundred-yard one?

Stop thinking that way, Heather told herself. That house had no basement.

Out of habit and instinct, Heather pulled a wineglass from the incongruously expensive rack hanging above the kitchen island. She shook her head at the mistake and returned the glass to its rack, a housewarming gift from her mother, who knew all about the occasional necessity and unnecessary occasions for wine.

Heather was smiling at those thoughts of her mother, whose shaky balance of failure and competence now felt unavoidable if not essential to the job, when every wineglass hanging from the rack shattered, spilling shards across the counter. The light fixture on the ceiling shattered as well, and so did a pair of lamps sitting by the breakfast nook.

Glass tattered mutely on the tabletops, mutely on the countertops, mutely on the linoleum, hardwood, and area rugs. Heather could only hear a shrill, deafening hum inside her ears. A spray of broken glass from the kitchen window pinged against her back. A small object blew past her face.

Heather dropped to the floor.

On her hands and knees, with her mind now an echo chamber filled with the internal reverb of her own breath, she crawled around the puddles of shattered glass, past what she groggily registered as her truck's sideview mirror. She checked for heat before opening the front door.

"Dixon!"

Heather's husband was lying on his back in the yard, flocked by torn metal and ragged patches of flame. Heather's truck had been flipped on its side by the explosion, its undercarriage peeled apart in husks like a bud bloomed into some gruesome, oily flower.

"Dixon!" Heather screamed as she got to her feet, tears warping her vision the same as the heat rising from the wreckage of her truck. "Get up, baby, *please*!" She clung to the door handle to steady herself.

Dixon's foot twitched, Heather sobbed to see, happily, gratefully. She watched, still happily, still gratefully, but also greedily, as Dixon sat up, touched the red hashtag of a scrape on his forehead, surveyed the smoldering ruin of the truck, and looked at Heather, his face shifting between concern and confusion, confusion and concern, over and again.

As his gaze rose to meet hers, the expression on Dixon's face turned from a question mark to an exclamation point. He smiled so wide more gum showed than teeth. His eyes, framed by smeared streaks of blood, bulged either from excitement, joy, or a concussion.

Heather should've known better than to try to keep secrets from a detective. The son of a bitch had seen that she was instinctively clutching her belly.

18

MIBURN

The afternoon was threatening rain. Across the sky that capped Highland Park, clouds meandered past the sun, each as ominous, misshapen, and unrelenting as Clem had begun to picture the embodiment of her current case. A storm either was or was not on its way.

To wit, the man currently walking beside her. Was he bad weather or good?

"You're still mad about the handshake, aren't you?" Russ asked, a reminder that Clem needed to work on her poker face. Of course she was still mad about the handshake.

Yesterday, after Clem asked Russ about the odd way he'd shaken hands with Chaunce Lattimer, how their pinkies had entwined, Russ had acted confused at first and then quipped he must be terrible at shaking hands. They had been having lunch in public; Clem knew very well when and with whom *not* to make accusations behind closed doors. "That handshake," Clem said, her voice sliding effortlessly into cop mode, "I have reason to suspect may be linked to a conspiratorial organization responsible for the triple murder of Messrs. Andrew Goodman, James Chaney, and Michael Schwerner, in Philadelphia."

"MIBURN?"

Clem knew he was referring to the FBI's case name, shorthand for Mississippi Burning. "Yes."

"Clementine." Russ's tone grew frustratingly calm. "That grip is a fraternity handshake. I was hesitant to tell you because it's supposed to be a 'big secret,' all that fraternity bullshit. Chaunce and I were in the same frat at Ole Miss, though a decade or two apart. I'm kind of embarrassed to have been in one, honestly. I didn't want you to know."

A day later, beneath clouds fighting against sunshine, Clem answered Russ's question of whether she was still mad about the handshake by using the same tactic her father had wielded on her as a girl. "No. I'm just *disappointed.*" Clem avoided clarifying who or what had disappointed her by looking around Highland Park, at the bandstand and gazebo, at the terraced amphitheater and stone bridge, at the swimming pools, arboretum, and picnic shelters. A bronze statue of Israel Marks, one of the park's founders, posed on a pedestal, watching squirrels rummage through waste bins. A vintage steam locomotive sat behind a fence, a tribute to Jimmie Rodgers, the Meridian-born country singer called the Singing Brakeman.

This town had its virtues, Clem had to admit, thinking of all those times she'd tossed bread to the ducks in that pond over there, how she used to vault from the swing set in the playground, landing on the damp cushion of cedar mulch.

Another thing she had to admit? Clem wasn't disappointed in Russ about the handshake thing. She was disappointed in herself. Clem should have known the handshake was a blind alley. Secret handshakes for a secret cabal? Come on. Real life wasn't some pulp novel.

Still, Clem wondered as she spotted their destination up ahead, Russ's excuse, however reasonable, however rational, pissed her off, unreasonably and irrationally. She got pissed off remembering the fraternities and sororities from her time at Ole Miss, with their elaborate pageantry and indistinguishable members, their unchecked enthusiasm and outmoded traditions, a bunch of mostly white kids pretending they lived in the Old South. Russ's excuse for the handshake pissed Clem off because it reminded her of how excited she had been for rush, how over the moon she had been when three sororities had given her bids.

"Clementine?" said her aunt Myrtle, emerging from a crowd gathered for a birthday party in the park. "Is that really my little Clem I'm looking at? No, it can't be."

"I wouldn't miss this for the world. You know how I feel about sheet cake."

The birthday party was for Clem's seven-year-old cousin Regina. It was being held at the Dentzel Carousel, one of the oldest in the country and, Clem wanted to forget, the site of the bust that had, consecutively, ratified, aggrandized, destabilized, and obliterated her career on the force.

Inside the shelter building, dozens of party-hatted second graders sat at picnic tables devouring ice cream, popcorn, and birthday cake, while on the carousel itself, less-enthused children sat atop hand-carved giraffes, deer, tigers, horses, and antelope, slowly revolving in a circle. Parents stood around the carousel, and over the thunderous barrage of merry-go-round music, they yelled, "Smile, honey, please! One time for the camera!"

Clem dreaded going into that building, both for the migraine the music would inevitably induce and the memories the carousel would inevitably draw forth. She didn't want to think about a serial killer at a child's birthday party. "Aunt Myrtle, I'd like you to meet my friend Ru—"

"Hershel!" Aunt Myrtle hollered toward a group of adults gathered around a barbecue grill. "Come look who's—Hershel. I *said* no *cigars*. The hell kind of example?"

Across the cracked swath of concrete in front of the carousel house, pausing to extinguish his stogie in an empty Coke bottle, which he then shoved into an overflowing trash can, ambled Clem's uncle Hersh. He'd lost weight since Clem had last seen him, at least twenty pounds, but he still had the juggernaut frame of the center lineman he'd once been. In his late fifties, Uncle Hersh, so slimmed down, with a hint of gray, barely looked different than he had when Clem had lived with him and Myrtle, for that year and a half, starting at age nine, after Clem's father had taken his first fall.

His hug pleasantly suffocated Clem. "Where've you been, girl? We haven't seen you in forever."

"It's only been a couple months."

"It's been a year, at least, and you know it."

Clem did not know it. She'd always told herself that keeping in touch with her aunt and uncle was important, especially after they'd shown her so much generosity and kindness by taking her into their home all those years ago, and until this moment, she had honestly thought she'd seen or talked to them at least once every few months. Where was her head at?

Where it usually was, of course. Dredging the dark, murky depths of a case.

"Oh, Hersh. You know she's been busy." Aunt Myrtle laughed. "Off doing her *Beverly Hills Cop* thing. Living in that other world."

Other world? Clem thought. Before she could consider the phrase, Russ, who Clem was embarrassed to have forgotten about, introduced himself to Myrtle and Hersh.

"I'm sorry," Clem said before reiterating Russ's name. "He's the assistant district attorney. We've been seeing each other a bit."

Uncle Hersh and Aunt Myrtle exchanged a glance that, Clem knew, had nothing to do with Russ's distinction of office. "It's lovely to meet you," they both said, nearly in unison.

Handshakes were exchanged. Fruit punch and birthday cake were offered and accepted. At a circular, fiberglass picnic table, where all four of them sat with their tiny paper plates and tiny paper cups, Hersh squinted at Russ and, with a streak of icing at the edge of his mouth, said, "Assistant DA, is it now? You know, Russ, I've got this parking ticket, a few of them, in fact, and I sure would be appreciative if you could help a man out."

"Well, I, the thing is, uh," Russ said, his mouth as wide as his eyes, two dirty plates tittering on the edge of the drain in the kitchen sink.

Not breaking eye contact with Russ, Hersh elbowed his wife. "Almost had him, didn't I?" The scale progression of his laugh peaked at the resounding clap of his thickset hands.

"You're scaring the poor thing," said Myrtle.

Clem sipped her fruit punch. Band-organ music, a torturous arrangement of pneumatically operated instruments, coiled from the carousel shelter. A toddler inhaled and exhaled into a kazoo as though it were an asthma puffer. Fringe blowouts blew out fringe. Confetti poppers popped confetti. Why in the Lord's name had Clem left her flask back in the car?

Across the table, Aunt Myrtle was saying to Russ, "How'd you two meet?"

These were her mother's people, Clem reminded herself. Family was important. Both sides of it. Clem had spent her life constantly swimming from one shore to another, never finding purchase, never treading water—always swimming, forever in motion. She'd say she was tired, but what was tired to someone who'd never known rest: a foreign idea, the gossamer of dreams, fairy tales, bedtime stories. She was tired like a fish was wet, like a volcano was hot.

"But our first real date? *Skyview*," Russ was saying to Myrtle and Hersh.

Therein lay her problem, Clem considered. Within the Venn diagram of her world, the Cartesian equation of her life, she didn't know what or whom to call home.

"And so out of the bathroom comes Clem, with this lowlife in handcuffs!"

Clem's experience with the Greek system at Ole Miss exemplified her entire problem. The sorority had been another shore to swim toward after her life in Meridian. Tri Delta had felt like a community. Clem's sorority sisters weren't ashamed that life was one long pantomime of pageantry. Going out for a nice dinner? Pageantry! Decorating a float for homecoming? Pageantry! Although it hurt now to admit, the sorority satisfied one of the gender conventions (Intro to Sociology, freshman fall) that Clem had learned society imposed on women, not excluding herself, when they were girls: in the sorority, Clem got to play with dolls, except those dolls happened to be living, breathing people, her "sisters."

During her six months in the sorority, Clem's sisters never once acknowledged she was Black, which almost hurt worse than if they'd said or done something blatantly racist. It felt like she had some terminal disease that made everyone too sad to address outright. The closest Clem's sisters came to acknowledging her race happened when they were considering party ideas, and one especially obtuse girl suggested "Antebellum Flower Power," in which boys would dress in tie-dyed Confederate uniforms and girls in bead-studded, fur-trimmed hoopskirts. Nearly half the sisterhood looked surreptitiously at Clem. The suggestion was rejected by a majority show of hands.

How fitting, Clem had thought at the time. She'd gone from being just another sorority girl to being just *an other* sorority girl with proper parliamentary procedure.

"What was Clem like as a child?" Aunt Myrtle said slowly, contemplatively, repeating the question Russ had asked seconds earlier. "This one time, Clem was nine, ten years old, about the same as these kids here, and she decided to be Amelia Earhart."

"Oh Lord," said Hersh. He pushed up from the table. "I'll let you tell that one. I'll be right back. Going to find the birthday girl, let her say hey to her cousin."

After Hersh had left, Myrtle continued, "I know what you're thinking, Russell. Amelia Earhart? So she wanted to be a pilot, break records, be what I call a First Woman To."

"First woman two?" Russ asked.

"First woman to fly across the Atlantic. First woman to be a US president. First woman to walk on the moon."

"I see."

"But that's not what Clem had in mind," Myrtle said, looking at Clem with a close-lipped smile. *Get it over with,* Clem smiled back. Myrtle said, "See, my girl here, she loves a mystery, the legendary kind. Bigfoot, the Bermuda Triangle. Mr. James Hoffa."

"Checks out," Russ said to Myrtle.

"Watch it now," Clem said to Russ.

Myrtle slabbed her forearms on the table and S-hooked the fingers of each hand together. "Every day after school, Clem would march out to the backyard. She'd say over her shoulder, 'I'm Amelia Earhart today, Aunt Myrtle. Wait five minutes. Then come out, help me solve the mystery of my disappearance.'"

Lines of incredulity and amusement stenciled onto his forehead, Russ looked at Clem. She shrugged one shoulder. What was there to say? She'd been a weird kid.

"Every day she played out some different theory," Myrtle said. "She might be lying there on the ground, which she said meant her plane had run out of fuel somewhere over the ocean and she crashed and died. One time she'd surrounded herself with GI Joes, which she said were the Japanese soldiers who'd captured her because she was secretly a spy for FDR."

"Sweet Jesus," Clem said. "I forgot about that one."

"And me?" Myrtle said. "God help me if I was ever able to make head or tails what all she was doing. Come suppertime, Clem would sit down at the dinner table, all pouty and woe-be, and she'd go, 'I'm still missing,' with this great big depressing sigh."

Russ said, "That's so sad."

But had it been sad? Clem wondered. She'd felt so alive while trying to figure what had happened to that missing aviator, whether by borrowing her uncle's Walkman and pretending to be a Tokyo Rose, one of the radio broadcasters of Japanese propaganda some believed to have been Earhart, or by pretending to be Becky Cuthbert of Santa Rosa Beach, Florida, or Sara Worthmire of Monson, Maine, or Wendy Flatts of Nebraska City, Nebraska, Clem's made-up aliases for Earhart, should she have, as some theorized, faked her death in order to start a life beyond the glare of flash-bulbs, free from the demands of fame.

Aunt Myrtle had left out the one truly sad part about Clem's investigation of Amelia Earhart. At the birthday party in the park, staring at puddles of melted ice cream on the concrete, shining milky white like oil spills from a kids-cartoon car, Clem thought of what she used to say after she'd said, "I'm still missing," during those times when she conflated herself with Ms. Earhart, unable or unwilling to distinguish between the two.

My daddy will find me.

"Regina, you remember your cousin Clementine," Hersh said. He was standing behind Regina, his hands on her shoulders, both of them standing next to the picnic table, looking at Clem.

In a ruffled denim skirt over hot pink leggings and an oversize T-shirt under a faded denim jacket, her braided hair pigtailed in beaded ties, Regina proved to Clem that time travel existed. Only via time travel could this young lady in such adult clothes be the little girl Clem used to know. "Whoa, Regina. You grew up so fast!" she told her cousin.

"Are you the lady cop?"

Clem leaned back. "You don't remember me? It's only been—uh, yeah. I mean, no. I used to be police. And you don't have to prefix *cop* with *lady*."

"Regina's staying with Myrtle and me a little bit," Hersh said from over Regina's shoulder. "While her mom's busy handling the . . ." He mouthed *divorce* to Clem.

Without looking over her shoulder at Hersh, Regina said, "Are you mouthing *divorce*, Grandpa? I *know* what it is." She rolled her eyes at the same sluggish pace and with the same flexibility and control of motion Clem knew she herself would have had at that age.

"Happy birthday," Russ said. He introduced himself as Clem's "friend." "How old are you now? Wait, wait. Let me guess. Thirty-five?"

Regina raised her brows at Clem, far too adultlike for comfort. "You're dating *him*?"

Incapable of conceding a rhetorical point, especially not to her cousin, more especially not to a bratty kid, most especially not to a facsimile of the bratty kid she had once been, Clem propped her elbows on the tabletop. "Nope," she said to Regina, batting her eyes and exaggerating a smile. "He's dating *me*."

Yes, Clem didn't add, *he's a milquetoast white man in Dockers and an Izod. Jealous?*

Russ wasn't the only white person at the party—Clem had spotted two kids, a brother and sister, going by their matching tennis shoes, and two or three adults—but he was absolutely one of the few. Above the ball field of Clem's mind floated the Goodyear Blimp of a memory, its flank proclaiming those three words Aunt Myrtle had said earlier. THAT OTHER WORLD. She'd said Clem had been doing her *Beverly Hills Cop* thing, living in "that other world."

By *other,* had Aunt Myrtle meant *white*? It wasn't as if Clem had a choice. Sure, her partner was white. Sure, her boyfriend was white. Yes, sure! White men filled her world as trees did a forest, but what choice did Clem have? She couldn't simply chop down the forest. She couldn't simply toss a match into a pile of pine needles, could she?

"Next year I get to do the roller rink," Regina was saying to Russ, in answer to some question Clem had missed. "I'm getting too old for carousels."

If Clem wanted to make a living, she told herself, if she wanted to succeed, she had to acclimate to "that other world." Acclimate, she stressed in her mind, not acquiesce.

"I wanted an Atari," Regina was saying to Russ, again to a question Clem had missed, "but Uncle Hersh said wait. He said he read about a new thing, Nintendoodle or something."

"We should get going," Clem said to Hersh and Myrtle while looking at Russ.

"But I was learning what a 'bit' is!" Russ said, referring to still more of a conversation Clem had missed. He turned to Regina with a straight face. "So there's eight of them in this new console? Whoa. I'm not totally sure I get it, but eight's a lot, sounds like."

On their walk through the park, after saying goodbye to Myrtle and Hersh and wishing Regina a happy rest of her birthday, Clem and Russ held hands, like the couple she was starting to admit they'd become. Today Russ might have even earned a promotion above the rank of Family Buffer.

Sunlight dappled the pathway. The sky had cleared of clouds. "I'm proud of you," Russ said. He squinted one eye, the way he always did when he was about to make a joke.

"Why?"

"You made it a whole entire afternoon, a social event, no less, without an adult beverage."

"Right?" Clem said. "Shame they didn't have any club soda and angora."

"Angostura."

"Are you sure? I feel like it's angora. They're both made from rabbits, aren't they?"

Clem loved poking fun at Russ about his drink of choice. The man enjoyed his club soda and bitters. He had those little eyedropper bottles of bitters lined up on a shelf in his home bar, the existence of which Clem found absurdly laughable, a *home bar* for a guy who preferred nonalcoholic cocktails, whose favorite, in fact, mimicked the taste of alcohol without giving you any benefits. The hell was the point of that? Virgin cocktails were like taking a placebo when you were deathly ill. Bitters tasted godawful, anyways.

"Uh-oh," Russ said.

"It was a joke, okay? Mocktails deserve to be mocked."

But Russ hadn't been referring to her angostura joke, Clem realized on seeing Samantha Bellflower leaning against the hood of her unmarked, the only car aside from Clem's in the parking lot. Sam had been waiting for them the time it had taken to smoke three Salems, the third of which she finished in a long drag and rubbed out with the ball of her foot, next to the first two. "I hate to spoil the party," she said, "but this's urgent."

Clem said, "What is it?"

"Prosecutor." Sam nodded at Russ.

Russ nodded back. "Detective."

"*Sam,*" Clem said, choosing to ignore the Kirby Krackle she suddenly sensed. Sam tended to get equally possessive and protective whenever Clem started dating a new guy.

After running her tongue behind her bottom lip, Sam said, "First, know that Dixon and Heather are *o-kay,*" elongating that last word by shortening it to two letters.

"What?"

"In fact, Dixon made me promise not to come tell you. He said he didn't want to ruin your date."

"Jesus, Sam. What happened?"

Sam exhaled. "An explosive device was planted in Heather's truck. The device detonated at approximately—"

The sound of children at play drifted from some distant corner of the park, the screech of swing sets rising above the walla effect of skinned knees and caught Frisbees, of hiders hiding and seekers seeking, of time-outs, of snack times, of "it" transmogrifying from tagger to tagged. When Clem had been one of those children, the swing set had been her usual haunt, a perpetual motion machine she never wanted to leave, and only after her father yelled, "Just let go!" had she been able to unclench her fists and launch into the air.

Rushing toward her car, frantic to get to her partner, Clem felt as weightless as she'd always felt when flying from the swing. Her breath came and went on a lag. Her eyes forgot how to blink. Clem had to get to Dixon. She had to make sure he hadn't been hurt.

"Clem!" yelled Sam, reaching for her arms. After Clem slipped out of her grip, Sam went full cop, pinning Clem to the hood of her car. *Articulate suspect's wrist. Apply pressure to neck.*

Face pressed against cool metal, her breath fogging the paint, Clem surveyed Highland Park. She'd never seen the world from this angle. A blue songbird landed on a plaque of Jimmie Rodgers. A yellow Labrador chased a tennis ball beneath a picnic table. In the old days they called these places pleasure parks. "I'm okay," Clem said, the damp of her breath obscuring RENEGADE. "Ease up already."

"Are you calm?"

"I'm calm."

After taking Clem's car keys from her pocket, Sam released the hold and lifted Clem away from the car hood. "Now listen," she said, handing Russ the keys. "I'm going to let your date drive. You're in no condition. That suitable with you, ADA Clyde?"

"Where am I driving us?" Russ asked.

"They've already been released from the hospital. Scrapes and scratches. *Hear that, Clem?* Scrapes and scratches. Obvious reasons, they can't go back to the house, time being."

"Heather's parents," Clem said, knowing Dixon didn't have any family left.

Sam raised her arms like a referee calling a touchdown. "She's back! I assume you don't need the address."

"I know where they live."

Once Clem and Russ had gotten into her car and pulled out of the parking lot, Clem peered out the passenger window. How could she have let this happen? Clem had made peace with risking her own life. But Dixon's? Heather's? Some lines shouldn't be crossed. Some lines couldn't be uncrossed, and the shape that made was aptly biblical.

"You okay?" Russ asked.

"What do you think." Not a question.

At a bend in the road, Clem and Russ passed the carousel, where the party was still going strong. Uncle Hersh stood in front of the barbecue grill, prodding burgers with a spatula, flames leaping toward the grease. It was fitting, Clem thought. From a distance, when large and hot enough, a fire looked like a sunrise—light emulsifying the dark, color birthed of a void, climbing higher and illuminating wider, Mississippi burning into a new day.

19

THE SILLY PUTTY SOLUTION

At Weidmann's, two hours later, after Clem had made what she now admitted was a bit of a scene at the home of Dixon's in-laws, a breathless inquiry about her partner and his wife's well-being followed by an equally breathless admonition for his not having contacted her sooner, she and Dixon sat at the lunch counter, waiting on a take-out order.

"My best guess?" Dixon said. "It was the squirrels. They set the bomb off by chewing on it. Don't that beat all? Saved by squirrels."

"You mean you hadn't even started working on the truck yet?"

"Nope. I was ten feet away. The blast turned those feet to yards. Came to on my back."

"You're lucky."

"It kind of felt good to get a first down after all these years."

"This isn't funny, Dixon."

It was odd. Despite having survived, hours earlier, a literal attempt on his life, evident in the bandage covering a laceration on his forehead, Dixon seemed untroubled, laid-back, if not outright happy. Clem couldn't square it. Her partner should have been a puddle of fear. He should have been building up his nerve to request a furlough from this case, one that Clem, given the involvement of Dixon's wife in the assassination attempt, would have gladly granted, and with pay.

Instead, Dixon sat there, sipping his iced tea, hands as steady as Clem's had not been after they'd survived the same kind of attempt at the John Wesley Hardin. Clem didn't know why they'd only gone after one partner this time. Probably assumed the white guy was the boss.

"Where are we at in the case?" Dixon asked, motioning toward the waitress at the other end of the counter and pointing at his cup, now more ice than tea.

Clem sipped her own iced tea. "Sure you don't want to take a few days off?"

"You're the one said I'm on a hot streak."

"I said you were lucky not to be dead."

After thanking the waitress for his refill, Dixon said, "Cassidy got any priors for arson?"

Priors for arson. Look at this guy, ready to rodeo. Clem had to hand it to him. "Man has got no priors, period. He's a ghost. My guess? Cassidy is but one name of many."

"Any new info on the partner? Flynn or whatever his name?"

"Good point."

Clem grabbed the copy of *The Meridian Star* she'd noticed earlier sitting on a stool nearby. An advocate of visual props ever since her days of rigging evidence boards in the squad room at the MPD—the collage effect made her feel like seeing her own mind braced by pushpins and labeled in Sharpie—she turned to the LOCAL NEWS section, folded the paper, and placed it on the counter between her and Dixon. Staring from the grayscale place mat was the sketch artist's rendering of a man seen outside the Hubbard residence the night of.

"Ring any bells?" Clem asked Dixon. "Have you ever see him walking around your neighborhood? He might've pulled a meterman. Slip the clerk a twenty, anyone can get the uniform from that supply outlet on Frontage."

Dixon's face morphed into italics, every feature slanted inward to emphasize *concentration*. HAVE YOU SEEN THIS MAN? read the caption beneath the sketch, its tone, Clem imagined, similar to those brow-beating PSAs—"Do you know where your children are?"—that evening news shows used to telecast. The tone of the caption worked on Clem the same as the PSAs had on parents. *Do your damn job!* the caption seemed to say.

"Our meterman isn't nearly this photogenic," Dixon said. "Almost looks like a movie star, you know it?"

"Your meterman?"

"Guy in the sketch."

He was right. The guy in the sketch had a cinematic symmetry to his face, the eyebrows a little too acute, the hairline a little too plumb. Clem, figuring the artist must have unconsciously given the suspect a movie-star makeover, allowed her focus to graze the newspaper free-range, skimming its ads and headlines. Lost Gap Homes was offering a luxury lifestyle at affordable prices, financing available, and later this week, the revival of Meridian's famous Calf Scramble Parade, which last took place in the late 1950s, would be held downtown. Everybody was welcome!

Clem turned from this veritable map of the city that had made her and looked around Weidmann's, at her grandfather's photo on the wall, at the stock room where he used to hide her as a girl, always supplying Hot Wheels and Legos and other toys to keep her occupied while he finished his shift. Yeah, geography was destiny, Clem thought, and what were cops and detectives but glorified cartographers, except for the "glorified" part.

"Hold on," she said, picking up the paper. Clem ignored the four instances of a misplaced apostrophe in *y'all* and one egregious insertion of the letter Q in *barbecue* and squinted at the sketch of the suspect. Those ears, that hairline, the eyebrows. Could it be? Clem considered using butcher paper and a pencil, but then she came up with a better way to test her theory.

"What is it?" asked Dixon.

After telling her partner to make like Deep Purple and hush, Clem flagged the waitress, who, by the cross around her neck so new it aggravated the skin at her clavicles, the cigarette divot between her twitchy fingers, and the shell-shocked manner of someone not accustomed to an unlubricated world, Clem guessed to be a former Lover of Jack and current Friend of Bill.

"I was wondering if you could do me a favor," Clem said to the waitress.

"Mm-hm."

"In the stock room? There's an air vent in the corner near the floor. Its screw threads are so worn it pops right out the wall. Inside that vent? There's a little hamster's nest of toys. Old issues of *Highlights*. Jacks, GI Joes. And a small, flesh-colored egg."

"Flesh-colored egg?"

"I used to play in there when I was a kid. My grandfather worked here. Would you please bring me that egg?" Clem, on realizing the waitress was about to say no, went for the kill shot. "My sponsor says I should 'interrogate childhood trauma,' whatever *that* means."

It worked like a charm—or a chip, Clem supposed—though not to her partner's approval. Once the waitress had left for the stock room, Dixon made a clenched, scolding face, one directed at Clem by way of his iced tea. "Sponsor?" he said to the iced tea. "Do you ever feel guilty about manipulating people?"

"Nope."

To be in this line of work, Clem wished she could explain to Dixon, you had to adopt the flexible morality of suspects, perps, and doers—the same flexible morality, for that matter, of cops and junkies, the nuance being that suspects, perps, and doers were the tarry, overcut junk of cops. The key to a quick fix of getting shit done? Relativity. If you were trying to catch a killer, Clem wanted to explain to Dixon, a killer who, in addition to ending the career of a real estate developer, had in the process left two children without a father, and let's say, Clem couldn't figure out how to articulate to Dixon, that by catching said killer you'd nail the piece of shit who'd tried to murder your partner and his wife, an attempt that, regardless of your partner's strangely nonchalant demeanor, you cannot, you *will not* abide, and if, Clem couldn't admit to Dixon, telling some waitress a tiny white lie could protect your partner's, no, your *friend*'s life, then guess what, ladies and gentlemen?

Clem had almost figured out how to tell her partner and friend all those things when the waitress returned from the stock room and placed the pink egg of Silly Putty on the counter.

"One day at a time," the waitress said.

"You know it."

As Clem split the two halves of the putty's plastic container, Dixon, doing a poor job of hiding his gotcha face, said, "'Flesh-colored,' huh?"

"I said flesh, not skin. There's a difference."

The Silly Putty had dehydrated to the density of a squash ball. Clem supposed twenty years in an air vent could do that. She used a cube of melting ice to massage the putty back to life, prepared, in its renewed malleability, to manipulate a false reality into a true one.

Clem thumbed the putty onto the newspaper like a school kid disposing their chewing gum under a desk, and then she peeled if off to reveal, on the side that had been pressed to the paper, a copy of the sketch of the incongruously handsome suspect spotted outside the Hubbard home. "Remember what Molly Coogan said her dog was named?" Clem asked Dixon as she gently tugged and pulled and stretched the thin sheet of Silly Putty.

"Checkers?"

"Chekov. Named after Pavel, not Anton."

"Pavel?"

"From *Star Trek*," Clem said, still tugging, still pulling. "Molly said her brother was a big fan of the show. He'd go as a different character every Halloween. What kind of priors did we pull for the brother?"

"Pop Warner shit. Possession with intent. One count of B and E. You said he was a blind alley, why bother."

"Let's say he wanted to jump leagues, go pro." Clem studied the sheet of putty. She stretched it a bit more. "Let's say Molly's brother partnered up with Jacob Cassidy for a hit."

"Okay. Let's."

"If you're smart, you do it in ski masks. But you have trouble finding them."

"Not a lot of skiing in Mississippi."

Satisfied with the putty, Clem turned from it to look at Dixon. "So you go to the closet where you keep your old childhood Halloween costumes."

"You think the witness saw this guy *after* he put on a Captain Kirk mask?"

"No," Clem said, showing Dixon the putty, the image on which she had tugged and pulled and stretched, elongating the ears, peaking the eyebrows. "I think the witness saw this guy after he put on a Mr. Spock mask."

Dixon, whom Clem relied on to keep her honest, revealed zero admiration for her clever bit of problem-solving. He parried the way Clem had anticipated. "And how do we know it wasn't Molly in the mask?"

"Hermetic alibi. She was at work. Manager and time sheet confirmed."

"So that means—"

"We've got a new lead on where to boldly go."

Before Dixon could respond, whether by declaring Clem's deduction highly illogical or perhaps saying he'd rather they live long and prosper, the waitress placed a stack of Styrofoam to-go boxes on the counter. "Y'all be careful," she said. "These are hot."

20

QUEEN OF THE GYPSY NATION

Her name was Kelly Mitchell. On January 31, 1915, she died at the age of forty-seven from complications during the birth to her fifteenth child. Queen of what was then known as the Gypsy Nation—Romani people who'd immigrated to America—Mitchell's funeral in Meridian, Mississippi, drew more than twenty thousand members of the Mitchell, Bimbo, Costello, and Marks clans. Queen Mitchell lay in state for twelve days before the funeral. Camped all over hell's half acre in Meridian, the Romani celebrated her passing with loud, festive music and a boisterous procession that many locals, according to what Jacob Cassidy had read on microfiche at the library yesterday, believed left an indelible mark on the town's culture, given how many Romani had decided after the funeral to put down roots.

"Gypsies ain't nothing but con men and thieving fortune-tellers, the entire lot of them!" *The Meridian Dispatch* quoted a septuagenarian veteran of the Civil War. "That's why in this town you can't flip a nickel without some swarthy bastard snatching it out the air."

On his walk through Rose Hill Cemetery, cloaked by a starless midnight sky, Jacob thought about that newspaper quote from the veteran, who of course had fought for the Confederacy. Sons of bitches like him would blame anyone for a crime so long as it wasn't themselves. *Swarthy.* Jacob knew what that word not-so secretly meant. *Not white.* Lord almighty, if Jacob wasn't sick to death of this town, this job, this outfit.

It had been such a simple job at first. Odette Hubbard wanted someone to kill her husband, Randy. Turnip Coogan called Jacob. Jacob accepted the offer of thirty-large to kill Odette Hubbard's husband, Randy. Odette got cold feet and called off the job. Jacob received orders from management to stand down. Jacob stood down. So how in all hell, Jacob wondered as he reached the grave of Queen Mitchell, had Randy Hubbard still wound up dead?

The headstone was draped in colorful plastic beads, the kind Jacob had seen tossed from Mardi Gras floats hundreds of times over the years. The wolf stone, fissured by all the vandals trying to plunder the gold coins apocryphally tossed in the casket at the funeral, was covered by soggy decks of cigarettes, unopened six-packs, unopened bottles of whiskey and wine and vodka, bouquets of wilting flowers, piles of pennies, and rusted cans of Orange Crush, thought to have been the queen's favorite. Lit candles quivered in the cool wind. Ambient light from downtown paved the surrounding grass in white.

Who killed Randy Hubbard? It didn't matter. Jacob had long ago learned not to question leadership in the Dixie Mafia. His job was to take orders. Prior to his promotion to management, Jacob's DM mentor, Remy the Bolt-Cutter, a consummate professional of the hit, had said to him, "Ours is not to reason why. Ours is but to do—and lie."

Even the hierarchy of the DM was a mystery to Jacob, and he knew he wasn't alone in the dark. Decades ago, back when the DM went by different initials, its leaders were known to all its members, with those ridiculous costumes and even more ridiculous titles. Grand Wizard? For the love of God. Now, though, after the Klan's rebranding and its hostile acquisition of the Matrangas' operations, Jacob and his fellow soldiers knew little to jack squat about the executive branch of the Dixie Mafia. They took orders from management, who supposedly took orders from leadership.

Jacob sometimes wondered if leadership was only a smoke screen to keep operations in order while mitigating any legal exposure. There was a certain elegance to it.

"We used to do Halloween here as kids," said Harold John, sidling up to the queen's grave, on the opposite side from Jacob. "Hide-and-seek, shit like that. Got to be teenagers, we never stole any of her whiskey or beer. Tempted, but we never dared."

"How come?"

"They say she haunts this place."

"Smart kids."

"No wonder they call Meridian the Queen City."

"Actually," Jacob said, "it's just a coincidence. This place is called the Queen City because it used to be number two in the state, not because of her."

"No shit? Huh. And I'm the guy grew up here. The things you don't know about home."

With one of the votive candles from the grave, Jacob lit a cigarette. He gave her majesty a little nod in thanks. "Speaking of things you don't know."

"I told you on the phone! How was I supposed to know it was the wife's truck? Kind of man drives a VW Bug anyway?"

"They call it due diligence."

"And that C-4 must've been defective. I had it wired pristine."

"It doesn't matter now. We've been ordered to stand down with those two."

Harold John slipped his hands into the pockets of his Members Only. "Fine," he said, curling his shoulders against the January night. "You ask me, we should've targeted the colored one from the start. She's the honcho. Why stand down?"

"Ours is not to reason why."

"Huh?"

"Tennyson."

"Is that the white one's name? It sounds Hebrew. I had a feeling. The nose."

Another true acolyte of the DM. Jacob cherished his hatred of their kind. How else was he supposed to stay sane in his line of work? Good ol' boys like this fella here, with their cultivated, flourishing racism and their pedigreed, withering entitlement, made for the most susceptible recruits. It was standard operating procedure for the Dixie Mafia, which turned criminals into believers by providing them with an ideology. To people like Harold John Riggins, Jacob understood, the DM wasn't an enterprise for profit, but an association, a movement, a crusade to reclaim the white man's sovereignty in America.

Jacob had to perform Olympic feats of mental gymnastics whenever he was around other DM members. So long as his wife, Min, didn't know what he really did for a living, Jacob told himself, he would keep doing it. He would keep providing for what remained of their family. People could call him a nihilist, but Jacob sided with that old cliché: he was a pragmatist. Jacob had made his peace with God, the one who'd taken his daughter, and that peace could be summed up, *Go fuck yourself, where's my money?*

"So why'd you bring me out here?" Harold John said. Arms folded across his chest, he bounced on the balls of his feet. "My mama's not doing so well. I need to check on her."

"I'm sorry to hear that." Jacob took a drag of his cigarette. "You still work at the courthouse?"

"Custodial," Harold John said, as if the word were dog shit yucking his boot.

"I'm here about the friend of Turnip."

"Yeah?"

"Management wants her taken out."

"What?"

"She's considered a liability, and management has decided to minimize their exposure. Understand?"

Harold John, clutching the back of his neck with one hand, keeping the other stuffed in the side pocket of his jacket, toed the flowers, cans, bottles, and coins piled on the grave in offering. According to legend, they enticed the queen to answer the prayers of those who left them. "But why?" Harold John asked. "Odette hasn't done anything wrong."

"We both know that's not true."

Across the cemetery swept a pair of high beams from a passing car, two bright circles the size of dining-table chargers that duly sent Jacob's and Harold John's trigger hands toward their waists. Jacob, after letting go of his weapon, said, "You got any of that poison left from Turnip's last meal? That'd be the ticket. Especially fitting for her, too."

"Used it all."

"Not a problem."

Jacob had come prepared. He reached into his jacket and removed a vial of poison, which he then tossed toward Harold John. "You can pick up a syringe at any local pharmacy."

Pocketing the poison, Harold John mumbled, "Mama's got plenty to spare."

"There you go. Saves you some time."

"Mm-hm."

"Come again, Private?"

"Yes, sir."

"Chin up, soldier. Orders are orders."

Despite his distaste for the ideologies of DM recruits, Jacob, who had been Special Forces in Vietnam, respected their skill sets. Jacob's mentor, Remy, once told him, "Before 'Nam, our boys were a bunch of untrained bozos. They botched bombings, had no fucking clue how to handle a piece. A passel of dumb-fuck rednecks with nothing but chips on their shoulders. But then, after the war, with our boys coming home to boos and jeers, all that disrespect from the hippie kids, we realized America had given us just what we needed: an army."

Again with such elegance, Jacob thought while climbing into his truck. The South raised its children to hate, the US military turned them into weapons, and then the DM weaponized their hate. Jacob watched Harold John drive off, knowing that, like any soldier, he'd do the job without questions or doubts, without complications from ethics or morals or brains, without any awareness his situation was as absurd as someplace called the Queen City *not* being named after the famous royalty buried right there in its heart.

Jacob opened his kit lying next to him on the bench seat of his truck, the contents of which, reflecting moonlight, included walkie-talkies and ammunition, brass knuckles and handcuffs, throwing stars and a can of Mace. Beggars couldn't be choosers, people said. Jacob chose not to beg. He'd take lives in order to ensure the livelihood of his family. That poor kid who frequented the Elysian Motor Court, and soon enough, that admittedly formidable PI who, for whatever reason, management had ordered Jacob to let continue with her investigation. *Ours is not to reason why. Ours is but to do and lie.*

From his kill kit, Jacob removed the revolver he'd taken from Randy Hubbard's house. The rest of tonight would be easy. Committing murder was so much less palatable than planting a murder weapon.

21

LAKESHOALS COUNTRY CLUB

In the fruit basket that was Mississippi, only certain types of people were so fragile they came wrapped in tissue, and they sure as hell weren't the Black folks. Clem came to that conclusion as she and her partner drove onto the kempt grounds of the Lakeshoals Country Club.

"Look at these jerks," she said to Dixon, nodding at the women in their tennis whites and store-bought tans, the children in swim trunks sucking on Ring Pops, the men in tasseled golf cleats propped on the hoods of waxed golf carts. "No bruises on them!"

"Bruises?"

"This place is one giant Harry & David fruit basket," Clem said, "and all these people are those fancy pears that come in special wrapping. It keeps them from bruising. I was making a metaphor."

"Who's David and Harry?"

Clem, unclear if Dixon was fucking with her, decided to drop the subject. She parked in the visitor lot. The Lakeshoals Country Club, located north of Meridian proper, sprawled across a few hundred acres of rolling hills, its eighteen-hole golf course studded with enough dogwoods and magnolias amid the less desirable pines to warrant the sizable cost of membership. Blue hydrangeas encircled the six clay tennis courts. Trumpet vines capillaried the brick wall surrounding the pool and outdoor grill.

FOUNDED 1927, read a sign out front, though, Clem noted as she and Dixon walked by, the claim was not exactly true. The original clubhouse, located on Old Country Club Road, had been built in 1927, but these facilities, the result of Meridian's early, unspoken years of white flight to less "urban" environs, opened in the late 1950s.

"Urban," Dixon repeated. "Now there's a metaphor I think I understand."

"More of a euphemism, but I do appreciate the effort." After stepping over a scuffed golf tee that she mistook for a cigarette butt, Clem asked, "What's the word on Flynn?"

"You mean Mr. Spock?"

"Or Molly Coogan's brother, Chris, if our hunch is right."

"Christopher, not Chris," Dixon said. "Christopher-not-Chris is in the wind. But that's not even the juiciest bite of this steak. Heather's sister's friend? She handles bags at the airport. She told me our Christopher-not-Chris is close with a flyboy, name of Flynn."

"Close?"

"Exactly."

"You think Molly tried to protect her brother by framing his boyfriend?"

"Or punish him for having one."

"Maybe we need to have another chat with Ms. Coogan."

"I tried," Dixon said. "She's MIA, too."

"Christ. That could mean—"

"I think she's gone to ground. Cassidy out there tying off loose ends? I would."

Clem supposed Molly Coogan might be savvier than she'd thought. Maybe she should have given her more credit. "You don't see that many *female* baggage handlers," Clem told Dixon as they passed a gleaming row of golf carts. "It's actually kind of impressive."

In front of the driving range loomed Lakeshoal's main clubhouse, a modernist jumble of asymmetrically cut wood, colossal panes of glass, and boulders imported from Tennessee. Clem guided her partner up the main staircase, past the ballroom, through the grill dining room, through the Sunday dining room, past the private dining room, through the billiards room, and into the bar, along the way spotting a bulletin board near the entrance to the kitchen.

CELEBRATE PRESIDENT REAGAN'S INAUGURATION AT LAKESHOALS! noted one bulletin. The celebration, to be held January 21, 1985, was only four days away.

From the bar's far southern wall, built of partitioned glass and overlooking a seemingly endless stretch of golf links, seeped the afternoon sun, its amber hue making the entire room feel trapped in it. Mahogany dominated the decor. Cigar smoke hovered above the brown tufted leather of wingback chairs. A deer's extravagantly antlered head overhung the fireplace mantel. Behind the bar, a mirror doubled the number of bottles as well as the sunburnt faces, all men, steadfastly decreasing the contents of those bottles.

Clem vaguely recollected running into this place as a child in a soaking-wet bathing suit and asking her father if she could get an order of cheese fries from the pool grill.

"Can I help you?" the bartender asked Dixon, unsurprisingly ignoring Clem.

On spotting the chance to identify the person they had come to see, a person neither of them had ever actually seen, Clem said to Dixon, "I told you he wouldn't be here. On the phone, Hamilton's secretary said meet him in the parlor, I could've sworn."

"Mr. Delacroix?" the bartender said. "He's right over there, past that lamp."

"Thank you," Dixon said before turning to Clem with a put-on glower. "You could've sworn, huh?"

Clem, who an hour ago had called the offices of Southways Alliance and in a squeaky, frantic voice told the receptionist she had "that affidavit" from "Hapless, Mark & Sons" for Mr. Delacroix to sign, led the way to a corner of the room, where Hamilton Delacroix sat alone on a half-moon suede-upholstered sofa.

"Mr. Delacroix?"

The man was staring at a sheet of paper, one corner of which had been burned. It could have been a prop for a pirate movie, the burn marks gave the paper such a treasure-map feel. "I'm sorry." Delacroix, shaken from the grip of his thoughts, pocketed the paper. "Yes?"

"Good afternoon," Clem said as she and Dixon sat in two chairs across from the sofa, in front of an oblong cocktail table. She introduced herself and her partner. "Would you mind if we ask you a few questions?"

"This is a private club."

"It won't take long."

Hamilton Delacroix checked the Rolex Yacht-Master on a forearm obviously tanned by eighteen holes a week and chiseled by a round-robin every other Saturday. In his late sixties, the man could have passed for fifty, with swept-back gray hair left frizzy from dried sweat, a lean face that for most white Southern men his vintage would've been jowled to the point of caricature, and a chest so barrel-like it drained all banality from the cliché "barrel-chested." To Clem, Delacroix pulsated filthy wealth and filthier privilege, and she loathed how attractive she found the guy.

"What's your poison?" Clem asked.

Unfazed, without even a twitch of an eyelid, Delacroix lifted his cocktail glass and, before taking a sip, said, "Tanqueray and tonic."

"I can't do gin. It goes straight to me. Like a bullet to the back of my head."

Again unfazed, Delacroix said, "Is that why you two came here? To talk about hooch?"

Dixon crossed his legs, some of the few in the entire bar not covered in material engineered for breathability and pleated to offer an unrestricted swing. He said, "That and Randy Hubbard. Where were you the night of his death?"

"That one's easy." Delacroix leaned back on the sofa. "I was at his house."

Despite her usual efforts never to show her ass or her hand, Clem revealed the latter when she gave Dixon an expressly pointed look. Delacroix was at the scene of the crime on the night of the crime? And he'd just flat-out admitted it to the PIs investigating the case?

"Have you told the police this?" Clem asked.

"No," said Delacroix.

"Why not?"

Delacroix shrugged his forehead. "They haven't asked."

"Why were you at Hubbard's residence on that particular night?" asked Dixon.

"Business." After setting his cocktail on the table, Delacroix sucked the glass's condensation from his ring finger. "Randy was overextended on a project. I offered to take it off his hands. He refused. I could tell you the meeting was cordial, but that would mean you don't know Randy Hubbard." Delacroix's ring finger, now damp with saliva instead of cocktail sweat, drooped from a hand perched on the sofa's arm. "That retail plaza was the reason he took out the insurance policy the press is saying got him killed, if you ask me."

"I didn't," Clem said. She gave the world a Dutch angle by tilting her head. "What time did you leave the Hubbard residence?"

"Before he was murdered."

"Mr. Delacroix."

"Ms. Baldwin."

"*Ms.* Baldwin."

"Is that not what I said?" asked Delacroix.

"Oh, uh, yes. I'm used to—would you please be more specific about what time you left Hubbard's home?"

"I got home in plenty of time to catch Carson. Best estimate, I left at nine."

The medical examiner had put Hubbard's time of death at approximately 11:00 P.M. Noting the discrepancy, Clem decided to get straight to her point. She wanted to test this Harry & David pear's bruisability. "Are you a racist, Mr. Delacroix?"

"Ex*cuse* me?"

"Are you a racist? Do you not like Black people? That's why you and your cronies looked down on Hubbard, isn't it? Because he developed businesses and projects that catered to Black people?"

After glancing toward the bar behind Clem, where she assumed his gaze was met and understood by the bartender, Delacroix said, "That is not even remotely true."

"What I don't get," Clem said, "is why, if you so abhor the types of businesses Hubbard developed and the type of people they served, what I don't get is why you're going around and buying them up. Now that Hubbard is conveniently no longer among the living."

The bartender's voice detonated behind Clem's shoulder. "Ma'am, I'm going to have to ask you to leave."

"I have a right to be here," Clem said without turning to look at the man.

"Ma'am, this is a private, members-only club. We've a strict policy that—"

"Nine-two-six."

"Pardon?"

"Nine-two-six. My membership number is nine-two-six. You'll find that all my dues have been paid, are never late, that I am a current member of the Lakeshoals Country Club in good standing."

"I, um," said the bartender. "I beg your pardon. I didn't know. Mr. Delacroix, would you like another cocktail? Ma'am, uh, may I offer you or your friend a beverage?"

All three of them declined. Once the bartender had left, Clem, ignoring her partner staring at her, met Delacroix's less persistent stare and said, "My father has kept the membership active for years. I have no idea why. I always hated this place as a kid."

"Then why keep it active?" Dixon said. "He can't exactly visit these days."

"The membership isn't in his name," Clem said. "It's in mine."

"Lauder was always generous." Delacroix rotated the Yacht-Master on his tan, striated wrist, either mindfully or absentmindfully, Clem couldn't decide. "He wants the best for his girl."

The best. Talk about a euphemism. Clem's unpleasant attraction to this guy was dissipating pleasantly fast. "You know my father?" she said.

"Of course. Everybody in Meridian, Mississippi, knows Lauder Baldwin."

Maybe, Clem reflected, she should have ordered a drink. Simply hearing her father's name dragged a match across her mind and dropped it into the pool of gasoline gurgling deep in her psyche. It wasn't like alcohol was flammable or anything, right?

A concussive thump against one of the partitions of glass overlooking the golf course yanked Clem back to the world outside her mind. It was followed by another one. Thump. An oily streak of imbricated splotches grew in length each time the bird flew into the glass. Thump, thump. "Have you been acquiring Hubbard's developments?" Clem asked Delacroix.

"Yes."

"Why?"

"Profit." Thump. "You say I'm a racist? I say I'm a capitalist. An American, more specifically." Thump. "Take California, which I've had the displeasure to visit a time or twice. Out there, they see the rest of the country as being full of a single type of person: descendants of those who gave up early. I admire that mentality. Manifest destiny doesn't mean put down stakes in Nebraska." Thump. "Mississippi Deltans such as myself feel the same way about people from New Orleans. Their ancestors quit at the mouth of the river, got cozy and fat among all that luxury and decadence, while my ancestors ventured upriver, into a dangerous, untamed frontier, and wrested the country's most fertile land from its most pestilent swamps." Thump. "Randy was a visionary. People in this town don't cotton to visionaries. He saw a market, and he made money off it. Who cares what color people his properties served? Their money's still green." Thump. "But I am nonetheless a Deltan. I don't give up, and I don't back down, and I sure as hell wasn't going to let some fuck from New Orleans take over the city I have spent my life wresting from pestilent swamps." Thump. "Did I kill Randy Hubbard? No. Am I glad he's dead? Yes. Am I going to back down from a profit in order to honor the man's memory? Fuck you."

At least a minute of silence followed. Clem didn't know what to make of what Delacroix had revealed to her and Dixon. Was it a confession masquerading as a diatribe? Was it a cri de coeur pretending to be a battle cry? Was it a challenge wearing the glasses and fake moustache of a rebuke? Clem couldn't say. Instead, looking out the newly quiet window, she said, "I guess that bird is dead." A single white feather twirled in the wind outside.

"Only the foolish try to bust into places they're not wanted," Delacroix said, to which Clem responded, "Only the wise try to bust out of places they don't belong."

Dixon looked from Clem to Delacroix and back again. "Y'all still talking about that bird?"

From his tone of voice, Clem could tell Dixon was making a joke. It didn't help. Delacroix's speech nagged at Clem. Meridian may be a swamp, sure, okay, but it was *her* swamp. This swamp at the center of not only

Mississippi but the entire South had created Clem. She had this swamp to thank for her fortitude and shortcomings, her bitterness and joys, her cunning and stupidity, her blind spots and farsightedness, her good, her bad, her everything and all. Despite her usual resentment with her hometown, Clem was a swamp creature, and at rare times not unlike this one right now, it surprised her to learn, proudly so.

Delacroix stood from the sofa, said he had dinner plans, and excused himself. Before leaving the bar, he turned to Clem and said, "What are they not making more of? Land. What is there an inexhaustible supply of? Hate. I have had to balance those two my entire career. My guess: Randy tipped the scales and chapped the wrong person's ass." He winked in a way that somehow made it not seem corny. "Happy hunting, *Ms.* Baldwin."

On their walk through the club, Dixon said to Clem, "Charming motherfucker. You don't see a lot of people can make senselessness seem to make sense." He side-eyed Clem. "You liked him. I could tell."

"Gives you that idea?"

"He kind of reminded me of somebody I met for the first time not long ago."

"Shut up."

Clem didn't want to think about her father. She didn't want to feel that sort of anger. Navigating the world of white men, whether Lauder Baldwin, Chaunce Lattimer, Russ Clyde, or Hamilton Delacroix, was beginning to take its toll, regardless that the one currently walking beside her she trusted with her life. To distract herself, Clem focused on the club.

Being here for the first time in so many years panned forgotten memories like gold from a stream. At the pool in the summer, Clem used to eat an ice cream sandwich every afternoon, the sun conjuring wriggles of heat from the apron of beige concrete that surrounded her chaise longue, threads of chocolate-flecked vanilla inching down her arm. On the main staircase, plush-carpeted, broad, gently helical, Clem and her friends used to ride the stair lift for elderly and disabled club members, up and down, up and down, until one girl broke her ankle on the lift's track, spawning a legend among the younger kids.

Clem had to remind herself she hated this place—*you hate it here, you hate it here*—a sentiment bolstered when she and Dixon passed a busboy,

Black, pushing a tray cart topped by a plastic tub of dirty dishes. The busboy nodded at Dixon and, on noticing Clem, made that face she could never forget from all the time she'd spent at the club as a girl. At once curious and confused, shaded with concern, begrudging just enough to make Clem shrivel into herself with shame, the face always seemed to say, *What are* you *doing here?*

22

ALL THE KING'S MEN

Pricks. Odette was surrounded by pricks. She lived on a mountain of pricks.

Actually, Odette thought as she walked down a circuitous, echoing hall of the Lauderdale County Courthouse, "a bureaucracy of pricks" fit better. She'd always liked those fun collective nouns. A waddle of penguins. A horde of hamsters. A pod of whales. *A bureaucracy of pricks.* Yeah, that phrase worked. It fit this city, this state, this entire world.

An embodiment of bureaucracy, the courthouse was populated by pricks, and Odette had been dealing with them every day since she'd been booked six months ago. The prick known as the sheriff chose her to be one of his trustees early in her tenure as an inmate. One of the deputy pricks joked the old man sure did like blondes as he watched her fill out a stack of paperwork. In the stairwells of the courthouse, Odette shouldered past the same kind of lawyer pricks who half a year ago had told her she wouldn't be detained more than a couple weeks. In the courtrooms, where she mopped the floors, Odette had to be supervised by the security pricks, who afterward would pause a little too long at her ass when patting her down. Pricks checked her wristband for proper clearance. Pricks made her sign her initials every time she returned a mop bucket to custodial.

A bureaucracy of pricks loved bureaucracy, and none more so than the new clerk in the sheriff's office. "Name?" he said, ink pen poised above a clipboard.

"You know my name, Jeff. How many times we have to go over this shit?"

"I'll have you please refrain from such language," said Jeff, a thirty-something who, like all Baptists Odette had met, looked and acted as though he were in his fifties, in *the* fifties. "I ask again. Name?"

"Odette Hubbard."

"Mrs. Hubbard—"

"Jeff, you damn well know I'm not a Mrs. anymore."

"Your assignment for today, per the sheriff's orders, is in the filing room. Same as—"

"Yesterday. I know."

"Please sign here."

In the filing room, the same one where not long ago Odette had met with those two private investigators, she pulled a chair up to one of the filing cabinets and removed a pile of disorganized files. The previous sheriff had been in the pocket of every criminal in the city who had a pocket. With his double-digit IQ, the guy had considered subterfuge as simple as the ABCs—in other words, that by keeping his files in alphabetical disorder, no one would find out he'd sold out.

Odette, who'd heard the indictments had been surprisingly swift, not out of any kind of justice, but because the sheriff had forgotten to give a certain city councilman his taste, placed today's batch, L–P, on her lap. On the floor around her feet lay stacks of files for each letter of the alphabet, onto which she tossed, at a calculatedly dawdling pace, the files from the L–P batch. An E file onto the E stack. An R file onto the R stack. B to B. Q to Q.

What was she still doing here? Turnip had been dead for nearly three weeks. Without him, the prosecutors didn't have a case against Odette. Without him, they only had the records of unsubstantiated statements from a petty crook who, after having taken a swan dive from the roof, could never testify in court. Odette couldn't be placed at the scene of the crime. Odette no longer had verifiable ties to Jacob Cassidy or his cronies in the DM or whoever ran their operation. Those ties had been snipped clean along with Turnip.

An F file onto the F stack. Plop. Two V files onto the V stack. Plop. Plop.

Yesterday had been her daughter's eighth birthday. Her little girl, Leslie

Ann, eight years old. It grieved and overjoyed Odette even to think such a thing. Her little girl had turned eight years old, for the first, only, and last time in her sweet, precious life, and her own mother hadn't been there. Her own mother hadn't woken her by singing, "Happy Birthday to You," hadn't carried the sheet cake out of the kitchen, hadn't helped her blow out that last stubborn candle, hadn't watched her open presents, hadn't kissed her eight-year-old cheek and whispered, "I'll always love you, my sweet girl."

P onto P. Thwop. R onto R. Thwop. G onto G. Thwop. S onto S. S onto S.

Ever since the arrest, Odette's parents, who'd never wholly forgiven her for leaving home at fourteen and marrying some guy twice her age, had been keeping Leslie Ann and her brother, Philip. They'd promised to bring Leslie Ann to visit for her birthday, but Odette's mother had called the night before. "Your father and I decided we cannot let our grandchild see her mother like that. It wouldn't be proper. A child visiting her mother in jail?"

Thwack. Thwack.

"I'm going for my lunch break," Odette said to Jeff when she walked out of the filing room at noon.

"Sign out here, Inmate Hubbard. Please mark the time as 12:03 in the P.M."

The noon hour had sieved the courthouse of its usual crowd. A public defender sat on a bench, saving a few bucks by eating a sandwich from home instead of heading to one of the few restaurants that remained downtown. A mother spooned yogurt toward the shaded part of a stroller, the legs of her child, clearly too old for a stroller, sticking out of the frame like the handles of a wheelbarrow.

Despite Odette's orange jumpsuit, nobody looked at or noticed her as she got on the elevator, which she rode to the jail on the top floors of the courthouse.

"What's for lunch?" Odette asked the cook after she walked into the kitchen.

"We're just past the midpoint of January," the cook said, "and I'm already at the end of my budget for the month. Heard of chicken du jour? This is chicken *du hier*."

The cook, Odette knew, was taking night classes in French, both literature and language, at the Meridian Junior College. He had a thing about Julia Child. Odette asked him, "You got me?"

"I got you."

From beneath the counter the cook retrieved a paper bag from McDonald's. He gave Odette the bag, and she palmed a J into his hand, payment for not making her eat his food.

"No onions, right?" asked Odette.

"Yeah, I remembered. You know, onions are an essential part of French—"

"Hasta mañana!"

Odette walked out of the kitchen, down a hall, and around a corner, toward the door that led to the roof. She slipped a deck of Marlboros into the front shirt pocket of the guard on duty, who kept his eyes straight ahead as she walked past him, through the door.

Another day in paradise, Odette thought, taking in the sunshine that struck her face when she stepped onto the roof. She figured the temperature for midsixties. A gust of wind frisked her hair.

Since Turnip's death, Odette had been eating lunch on the courthouse roof, her mind clinging desperately, blissfully to the hope, no, the *belief* she'd get out of this place any day now. That poor bastard's death couldn't have been in vain. Something good had to come of it. What was the old saying? Two wrongs don't make a right? Horseshit.

Odette sat on the ledge, allowing her legs to dangle, the same as she imagined Turnip must have on New Year's Day. *Humpty Dumpty sat on a wall. Humpty Dumpty had a great fall.* After taking a bite of Quarter Pounder, knuckling a shred of lettuce from the corner of her mouth, Odette glared at Meridian, her hometown, the city where she'd lived her entire life. Over there, past the newest rings on the tree stump that was downtown, sat Anderson Hospital, where Odette had teetered beside her youngest during that awful bout with pneumonia. It was also where Odette, after the first time Randy broke her wrist, had told the attending, "I fell down some stairs."

Could you really blame her for what she'd done? Odette wondered, pinching a fry from the bottom of the bag.

Odette's second marriage, unlike her first, was more practical than romantic, the decision of an adult. Randy was supposed to have been her way out of this place. He was supposed to have been a sensitive, considerate man of the '80s, the kind Odette had heard about on *Donahue*. Instead, he turned out to be the other kind of '80s man, on the come-up and up and coming, his gosling-green eyes focused on that other green thing, the one with a dead president winking in its center. Odette had wanted only what she was owed. In the Wild West, you were either a gunfighter or a bank robber, and Odette didn't know a damn thing about guns. Randy was a bank, she'd figured, easy to be knocked over.

Except she'd been wrong. Randy, always more ambitious than sensible, was an alchemist of money; his assets were so not liquid they moved beyond solid to some fifth state of matter. Odette wouldn't have gotten any of the life insurance.

With a napkin, Odette wiped her mouth, trying to disinter a modicum of pity for her deceased husband. It was no use. She could never feel sorry for that man. Odette may not have killed him, but she wasn't sorry he was dead. A man like that, who brought home bouquets but not of flowers, a man like that, whose "love taps" left bruises and necessitated casts in the same floral shades of purple, green, and yellow, a man like that, he deserved exactly what he got. In fact, Odette would have liked to thank whoever had killed him, if only she knew who'd done her the favor.

It certainly hadn't been Turnip. That traitor only cared about himself. When the heat came down, he'd given Odette up without pause, thinking only of his own ass. What kind of man takes a mother away from her children? A prick. That was what kind. Turnip deserved what he'd gotten, the same as Randy. They'd both had it coming. Odette felt even less pity for Turnip than she did for Randy. Some wrongs had to be righted with a wrong.

On the roof of the courthouse, sitting on the ledge from which that prick had fallen, Odette closed her eyes against the sun's warm, palliative glow, remembering how free of guilt, how happy she'd felt when sprinkling the poison onto Turnip's breakfast of scrambled eggs, toast, and bacon.

Humpty Dumpty sat on a wall. Humpty Dumpty had a great fall. All the king's horses and all the king's men couldn't put Humpty together again.

The rooftop door groaned as Odette pulled it open. After checking the time, she took the elevator to the basement, where she had her usual one-o'clock appointment. She was running a few minutes behind. "You're late," Harold John said when Odette stepped into the janitor's closet.

"Lost track of time."

Roughly the size of the nurse's office Odette used to visit in elementary school, with a cot exactly like the one on which she used to lie "sick" until gym class had ended, the janitor's closet fit two people with surprising comfort. A utility sink loomed from the back wall. Pairs of nails choke-held mops and brooms by the axes of their handles. On a grid of shelves, beside boxes of trash liners, sat bottles and commercial-size tankards of cleaning fluids, each gleaming a chemical neon: bright blue, bright orange, bright green.

Odette had never been able to get used to the smell in this place. It gave her a headache. "Any trouble with the order?" she asked.

"Nope." Harold John removed a gym bag from beneath the wobbly worktable that he called his desk. He unzipped it to reveal three cartons of cigarettes, a plastic lunch bag of mealy weed, rolling papers, six pint bottles of rotgut vodka, and the latest issue of *Good Housekeeping.*

"Thank you, honey," Odette said. She slipped her arms around Harold John. He'd smoked a menthol earlier.

Throughout her six months of detainment at the county's pleasure, Odette had assembled what she liked to think of as her own version of a Reagan-era economy within the courthouse. Hers did not trickle down. It trickled up and laterally, but it did not trickle down, because it began with her, an inmate and a woman, here at the bottom of this entire sexist, chauvinist system. From where she was situated, Odette reckoned, everything was up.

Odette-onomics integrated the distribution and trade of cash, liquor, cigarettes, marijuana, and the occasional specialty item—Teddy Bethlehem in cell D2 believed he could handicap the cockfights in Kemper County based on cabalistic signs gleaned from the ads in *Good Housekeeping*—goods the scarcity and affordability of which made them well sought after among the inmates, clerks, guards, deputies, and other staff members of the courthouse. Although Odette gave herself credit for the economy and her consequent network of influence, none of it would be possible, she reluctantly acknowledged, if it weren't for the help of a man.

At least Harold John wasn't a prick. He was one of the few men Odette had met during her stint who actually treated her like a human being, a flesh-and-bone-and-blood, thoughts-and-feelings person. "What's a matter, honey?" she asked, touching the back of her hand against his bristly cheek. "You seem distant."

Harold John stepped back. "I'm fine. I'm okay."

"I've got half an hour before I'm due back." Odette nodded toward the cot.

"I don't really feel like it about now. I haven't really been in the mood. Want a drink?"

Without waiting for an answer, Harold John took two paper cups from a shelf, filled them with vodka, and handed one to Odette. "What are we drinking to?" she asked.

"Our time together."

"You say that like it's about to end."

The rotgut did as that name foretold. Her stomach wrenching at the vodka like one of the mop wringers over there in the corner, Odette sat on the cot and took a breath, the fumes from the cleaning fluids making the room tilt askew. God, she hated those fumes.

Harold John refilled their cups and sat next to her. He leaned back against the wall. "I was thinking," he said, suddenly, adorably wistful. "They call this place the Queen City, right?"

"There's that semester of junior college at work."

"Funny."

"Sorry."

"I was thinking," Harold John continued. "They call Meridian the Queen City because we're number two in the state. We're second place, or we used to be. But who's number one in England?"

"The queen?"

Eyebrow raised to a comical peak, Harold John said, "Shit makes you think."

Odette, curbing the urge to double down on her bit about that one semester of junior college, sipped her vodka. She was going to do things different when she got out. Life in jail, with its endless routines, with so much repetition, had taught her the value of variety. She needed to diversify her life. *Carpe* her some *diem*. Turnip hadn't been Humpty Dumpty. The old Odette had been. The person she used to be, Odette thought as she stood from the cot, was shattered into bits and pieces, and only she, this new self, could put that woman back together again. All the king's men could ride all the king's horses straight to hell.

"I should get going," Odette said. "I promised my daughter I'd give her a call soon as she gets home from her dentist appointment. It can make her anxious. That drill."

Harold John, one hand in his pocket, walked toward her. "Hey, come here."

Due to the pressure of Harold John's embrace, the sincerity of which reminded her she needed to be sweeter to the poor guy, Odette tried to ignore the sting in the lower part of her shoulder blade, near her armpit. She grimaced through the pain, not wanting to ruin the moment. The shoddy underwires in these jail-issue bras were always tearing free of the cheap fabric. "Queen City Queen," Harold John whispered, his breath hot against Odette's ear.

"Oh, honey."

In the service elevator Odette had to grip the handrail. Those fumes from the cleaning supplies were really getting to her. The elevator's rise through the courthouse, floor by floor, magnified gravity, pressing down on Odette's head, arms, waist, and legs with greater and greater force. She could barely stand, the force was so great. It took all her effort to watch the numbers change, to count the hours from one floor to the next.

"It's all going to be okay," Odette said as her knees buckled. "Mama's here. Hold my hand. I'm right here. Everything's going to be fine."

23

THE CALF SCRAMBLE

Meridian had become a rodeo, with gunslingers trolling its alleys, their rowel spurs clinking, their leather holsters weighted by six-shooters. Cowboys in fringed chaps coiled their lariats. A herd of cattle stood behind a series of corral panels arranged around an intersection. From a designated area of the sidewalk, children wearing yoked Western shirts and with murder in their eyes studied a calf, steeling themselves to wrestle it to the ground.

On her walk to the courthouse, Clementine had to navigate the Calf Scramble Parade, a former Meridian tradition—Elvis attended it before he was the King—recently revived by a heritage-minded mayor. Crowds of onlookers clogged the downtown streets. Stetsons bobbed on an ocean of ball caps, boots scudding a seafloor of tennis shoes. Clem had to sidestep a troop of Boy Scouts chasing a greased pig, pass a cart vendor selling that poor animal's slow-roasted siblings, and shoulder through an idle marching band in order to reach at last the courthouse steps. Rarely had she felt such relief to enter the building.

The reason for Clem's visit to the Lauderdale County Courthouse was also a rarity. It involved the ethics of her trade. Clem had decided she couldn't abide billing two clients for her work on a single case. Today she would give Odette Hubbard a brief report on her case and then explain that she could no longer keep her on as a client, that she needed to focus on what Lenora Coogan had hired her to do.

"Ma'am?" said an octogenarian security guard, looking up from his crossword. "You can't go that way."

Over her shoulder, Clem said, "This is a public facility, isn't it?"

"But, ma'am!" the guard yelled as Clem rounded a corner. She mistakenly heard him say something about the "crimes" she'd "seen."

The crime scene was cordoned in yellow, patrol cops off their usual foot posts keeping watch that nobody crossed the color. Weegee could have shot it: EMTs lifting a gurney, the vic already bagged and tagged, now more shape than person; first responders inside a service elevator with their forensic kits, collecting evidence and control samples, including a gum wrapper, a cigarette butt, and a strand of blond hair; the coroner, whose surgical-gloved fingers held a lit cigarette, telling the team not to bother with the butt.

Crimes seen. The crimes Clem had seen could fill one of those thick law books lining so many of the courthouse offices. Regardless of the tropes, witnesses straight out of central casting, murder weapons direct from the props department, crime scenes never failed to rise above the generic and into the rarefied, conscience-slaying firmament of the particular. Take this one, Clem thought. It was so typical for this town. Only in Meridian, Mississippi, could some poor bastard get himself killed inside a literal bastion of law and order.

"Clem?"

With a start, Clem turned around to see Russ Clyde, haggard in his rolled shirtsleeves, a five-o'clock shadow cast on his face a few hours early. "Hey," she said, unable to come up with anything clever at the moment.

"How'd you find out so fast?"

"Find out what?" Clem stepped aside as the EMTs rolled the gurney past her. Nodding toward it, she asked Russ, "Who is that?"

"Where's Dixon?"

"Day off." Clem again nodded toward the gurney. She again asked Russ, "Who is that?"

Russ settled his hands on his hips, shoulders sagging, gaze directed toward the floor. "What a mess."

"Russ?"

"Officer Head Up His Ass," Russ called to someone bagging evidence in the elevator. "Yeah, you. Don't forget the chain-of-custody receipt. I won't tolerate another mistrial on account of you can't be bothered with paperwork."

"*Russ,*" Clem said.

Hands still on his hips, Russ pondered the ceiling, then his wing tips, then Clem. "Odette Hubbard."

"The hell?"

"She was found DOA—in that elevator, in my courthouse. What a mess."

"COD?" Clem asked, her cop brain resorting to sterile acronyms.

"Nothing conclusive until the ME report, but we think poisoning. Administered with a syringe. Right armpit."

"Jesus."

"That's not all."

After checking they weren't being watched by anyone working the scene, Russ took Clem by the arm and guided her into a corner of the hall, next to conspicuously dual water fountains. "We did a sweep of Odette's cell," Russ said, "and we found a stash of a different poison. Water-soluble and tasteless. Often administered in food. Slow onset."

"Botulinus?" Clem asked.

"Looks like."

"That means . . ."

"Odette killed Turnip. You got your man. Or woman, seems. Case closed."

Clem stepped back from the water fountains. On the wall hung a metal sign for shelter from nuclear fallout, its capacity number illegible after more than two decades. A yellow custodial notice stood above a mound of pink sawdust. The night she'd gotten the call from Lenora Coogan, Clem had watched the woman's son plummet in slow, televised motion from the roof of this very courthouse. The sight of Turnip falling through the sky, both free from and subject to physics, had made Clem feel incorporeal, diaphanous, with nowhere to land. Those two words from Russ, *case* and *closed,* had the same effect. They unmoored her.

"Where're you going?" Russ asked after Clem turned to walk away.

"Home."

"Want me to come with?"

"You've got work."

Her steps echoing sepulchrally in front of, behind, and around her,

Clem let the news seep by trying not to dwell on it. She almost didn't notice the footsteps as her own. At the courthouse's entrance, the security guard, without looking up from his crossword, asked, "What's a five-letter word for *Told you so*?"

"Gloat."

"Hey. That's actually pretty good."

Outside, where she hoped for fresh air, Clem inhaled the smell of barnyards, a reminder she hated barnyards. The Meridian High marching band led the Calf Scramble Parade toward Union Station, followed by Shriners on motorbikes, Miss Mississippi in a Mustang, and the 4-H club, with prize goats, hogs, ducks, and sheep. A group of children chased a calf around a section of the street cordoned by corral panels. The crowd erupted in applause when a little boy in chaps wrestled the animal to the ground, and nobody but Clem seemed to mind that a wrangler had already roped the calf's neck to slow it down.

24

CASE CLOSED

So that was it. In Clem's apartment, her bottle of bourbon lowering at the same rate as the sun, she tried without success to square her ego with failure. She had failed. It was over. The case she'd been hired to solve had been solved, thanks in no part to herself.

A lightning bolt tore down her throat as Clem finished the whiskey left in her glass. She poured herself another one. Failure didn't come easy to Clem. Success was her true addiction, not the booze, not her anger at a world that refused to align with any sense of justice or morality, with any system of ethics, integrity, or common, no-duh decency.

Clem needed to win, regardless of collateral, and with this case, she'd lost.

Yes, sure, Clem thought as she ambled toward her record player, the case had been solved. To some people, that constituted a win, a straight-up victory. Those people were morons. Ask a professional boxer how they feel about TKOs. Watch any competitor react when they hear those two little words, *Opponent disqualified*. Winning by default was winning with an asterisk. It was a victory the opposite of Pyrrhic, one with too paltry a cost.

On her knees, drink by her side, Clem flipped through her record collection, trying to decide between the Clash's *Sandinista!*, Bowie's *Scary Monsters*, Lou Reed's *The Blue Mask*, or Big Star's *Third*. All white men, Clem noted, just like her excuse of a career, her joke of a life. To honor the DM, that union of power, corruption, and lies she had failed to bring to justice, Clem settled on New Order's *Power, Corruption & Lies*.

The opening chords of "Age of Consent" provided Clem a score as she stood, walked to the center of the living room, closed her eyes, and, swaying with the rhythm, began to dance. She hoped it would help her think, dancing, movement of body spurring movement of mind, the physics of deduction.

Odette Hubbard. How had Clem not seen it? The logistics made so much sense. Odette, as a trustee of the jail, had easy access to Turnip, particularly his food. Trustees went into and out of the kitchen all the time, from what Clem knew of their duties in the jail. Covertly slipping a fatal dose of botulinus toxin onto a plastic tray of powdered eggs, burnt toast, rubbery bacon, and grits oleaginous with margarine would have been simple. It wouldn't have mattered if botulinus weren't already tasteless. Jailhouse cuisine was a perfect conveyance for poison.

Now, with regard to a motive, that made even more sense, if Clem was being honest, and the answer had been dangling in her face like a cat's toy this whole time. Odette had been in jail because of Turnip. He'd given her up to the prosecution. The other week, when Clem and Dixon questioned her, Odette had admitted flat-out that, because Turnip had taken her from her children, leaving them alone without their mother, she would have killed him if she could. Those had been her exact words. "I would have killed Turnip if I could." Clem, who had never been one and had never had one, knew well enough not to mess with a mama bear.

One serious question lingered, and it excruciated Clem. Who killed Odette?

Before Clem could torture herself further by asking again, and again not being able to answer that question, the phone rang. She placed her cocktail on the coffee table. From the hallway, she grabbed her rotary phone, wedging her fingers into the cradle and propping it against her hip. She lifted the handset to her ear, the black coils of the spring cord dangling along her torso. "Hello?" Clem said, walking back toward the coffee table.

"Good afternoon, ma'am. I'm a telephone services agent from the Mississippi State Penitentiary. Are you willing to accept a call from inmate 749012, name of Lauder Baldwin?"

Clem used her shoulder to keep the handset against her ear. With her free hand, she picked up her bourbon from the coffee table. "Yes," she said after relieving the drink of its contents. "I'll accept the call."

A series of clicks and beeps from the phone mimicked the clicks and beeps in Clem's head as the sour mash did its much-needed work. "Hello?" her father said from a plantation-cum-prison that used to be and, so far as Clem was concerned, remained a site of slave labor. "Clementine, are you there? This is important. Please answer, honey. It's serious."

"I'm here," Clem said.

"Thank God. ThankGodthankGodthankGodthankGod."

But rarely had Clem heard such apprehension in her father's voice. It rippled through her body, taking inches off her height, loosening wrinkles, plumping her cheeks, assuaging the ache of an old knee injury. It sent her back to a time as a little girl when she naturally adopted the emotions she saw and heard in her father, his joy becoming her joy, his pain her pain, his fear her fear. Into the phone she whispered, "What's wrong, Dad?"

"You have to drop the case we talked about."

"What? Why?"

"Clementine Rosemary Baldwin, listen to me. You have got to drop the Hubbard case. The hit is back on."

Clem didn't know what stung worse, hearing her mother's name, which also happened to be her middle name, or hearing that prearrangements had been made for her murder. "How do you know this?" she asked, trying to keep her voice calm, willing it to stability.

"Lot of the guys in here are ex-DM, which means they're current DM, because nobody quits the DM. Lot of the guys in here talk. I've had my ears pricked, and they've been talking about some lady PI—"

"Just say *PI*."

"—who's been getting too close to some DM business got to do with a land developer out of Meridian. You're the shamus, not me, but I know a bell when it rings."

"What about the hit?"

"The hell didn't you tell me somebody shot at you? The John Wesley Hardin Club? Clem, you're too smart to waltz into a place like that, even with your country-boy sidekick."

"Partner."

"The kinds of lowlife they've got in that joint? I probably went to high school with half of them, least until they dropped out. Stupidity, hatred, and whiskey don't mix."

"Dad."

"Thank God you weren't hurt. I don't even know what I would have done."

"Dad."

"My little girl at the John Wesley Hardin. I mean, Jesus Christ, Clem. I suppose I can only blame myself. If I weren't locked up in here like some poor excuse for a—"

"Dad!"

"Huh?"

"WHAT ABOUT THE HIT?"

Clem's father inhaled and exhaled through his nose before saying, "What I've heard, the hit was called off, but that's no longer the case. It's back on. I don't know why it was called off, but I do know why it's back on. You're no longer of any use to them."

Therein, Clem figured, lay the answer to why the hit had been called off in the first place, why they had gone after Dixon with the car bomb instead of her. The DM had thought she could be of use to them. She'd been a tool this whole entire time. Implements worked best, she knew but too well, when they didn't know they were implements. Call a slave a "prisoner" and watch them swing that hoe. See them harvest that cotton crop.

Contrary to her own expectations, Clem didn't care that she had been used. She only cared about *how* she'd been used. What had she inadvertently done to help the Dixie Mafia?

"Any word on who's handling it?" Clem asked as she wandered through her apartment, the phone cradle pressed to her hip like a service weapon, the handset tucked against her shoulder. Her anxiety melted with each step she took. She didn't know why.

"My guess? The same guy took a shot at you at the John Wesley Hardin."

"Okay."

"Okay? Clementine, this is serious. Somebody's going to try and *kill* you if you don't drop the case."

"I've already dropped the case," Clem said. "Or it dropped me. We know who killed Turnip. She was DOA by the time we could ID her as the perp, so. Case closed."

Once again, Lauder Baldwin, a devout atheist his entire life, thanked God.

In the kitchen, Clem poured herself another bourbon, then dumped it into the sink. She needed her faculties to dodge bullets and bombs and Lord knew what else Jacob Cassidy would come after her with. Absentmindedly, Clem opened and closed the kitchen drawer where she kept her binos, print kit, Mace, ankle holster, handcuffs, pocketknife, and bullet dump. Open, close. Open, close. The sound veiled that of dribbling whiskey.

"Dad?"

"Yeah."

"Before you went away this last time, why'd you pay to keep my membership going at Lakeshoals?"

Clem's father, two hundred miles and a twelve-year sentence away, most likely dressed in orange and looking at a wall of cinder block, said, "You honestly don't know?"

"I honestly don't know."

"You honestly don't remember?"

"Remember what?"

The silence that followed slotted a handful of dimes into the parking meter of Clem's patience. She appreciated her father was giving the inquiry thought. "During my first bid," he said at last, "you went to live with Hersh and Myrtle. They're family, after all, and they love you."

"I know."

"But they didn't have all the advantages in this world I had. They couldn't give you everything I was able to give you, much as they wanted to, and that's not their fault."

"I know."

"Some of my advantages were ill-gotten, true, but others came from me simply being—"

"A white man in America. I know this. Dad, what is it you're trying to say?"

Typically, to Clem's mind, everybody who spoke to her, if they knew she was investigating a case, spoke to her in sentences riddled with ellipses.

Her skill . . . was in . . . reading . . . between . . . the dots. At the moment, though, she had no idea what to make of the string of periods coming from her father. She had no idea what he was going to say next. He broke the ellipsis with, "You hated living with your aunt and uncle. Loathed it."

"That's not true." Clem leaned against her refrigerator. "I was happy there."

"Every time I called to see how you were, you'd cry and cry over the phone. 'I hate living in a trailer!' 'These people are poor!'"

"I *did not* say that."

"You were a whiny little brat, but that doesn't mean it didn't break my heart."

"I would have *never* said those things."

"Worst of it came that summer. 'I want to go to Lakeshoals!' You wanted your cheese fries from the pool grill. Your Mickey Mouse ice cream bars."

It wasn't true. Clem had always hated Lakeshoals. Whenever she'd visited she was shoved into the role she abhorred, That Poor Thing, the Black staff tilting their heads at a Black member, the mothers of her friends being extra-special, super-duper nice to the little girl without a mother. "That poor thing," they all said, sometimes in words, other times with a look. *That poor, poor thing.*

The refrigerator, so cool against Clem's sweat-damp back, began to whir. The opening synth beats of "Blue Monday" pulsated from the record player. Clem longed for a drink.

Among the many discrepancies between pop-culture PI work and real-life PI work, one had always stood out to Clem: no one *ever* had amnesia. Amnesia was a lazy plot mechanism, a way for pulp writers to trick their readers. It was hackney for hacks, a red herring on the trail to black hats.

Yet apparently, if she were to believe her father, Clem suffered from selective amnesia. Lakeshoals reminded her of a time she'd wanted to forget. The name alone ambushed her with memories of living with her aunt and uncle, that time when every night she'd decant her tears into the downy folds of her pillow, missing her father, aching for home.

Clem had wanted to go home, and Lakeshoals had felt like a part of home.

Over the phone, Clem's father said, "Some people say it's wrong to spoil a child. Those people are idiots. Every child deserves to be spoiled. Your mother would've spoiled you every day of her life."

The record player across the room, as the lyrics of "Blue Monday" finally got started, asked in monotone how did it feel. Clem switched the handset from one ear to the other. "So you've been paying for my membership all these years because I was a spoiled brat?"

"It was one of two promises," Clem's father said.

"What was the other?"

"I wouldn't go away again."

Classic Lauder Baldwin. Of two promises he'd made to Clem, he'd kept the one about making it always possible for her to patronize the antiquated, discriminatory, and, Clem thought now as an adult, downright silly center for dining and recreation, and he'd failed to keep the one about not breaking the law and being sent to prison and leaving his only daughter alone in the world. But at least she could get cheese fries at the pool grill!

"Dad, I have to let you go." Clem slowly spiraled out of the phone cable she'd accidentally wound herself into.

Her father asked, "If I call again, will you take it?"

"Yeah, I guess I'll take it."

"Thank you. It really means a lot. I've missed hearing your—"

"Bye, Dad."

After hanging up, Clem carried her empty lowball glass into the living room, where on the coffee table she had stacked her files for Turnip Coogan, Randall Hubbard, and everybody else involved with the case. She flipped the page on a legal pad and started to take notes for her case report. With each bullet point, Clem organized the corresponding receipts for expenses, wedging them into paper clips and attaching Post-it notes labeled BACKGROUND CHECKS, GAS/MILEAGE, AMMUNITION, and BUSINESS MEALS/BEVERAGES.

Clem always kept track of her receipts.

The next day, January 19, 1985, Clem sat beside Dixon in Lenora Coogan's trailer, making small talk, Clem's least favorite kind, about one of Clem's least favorite subjects, the reelection of Ronald Reagan.

"Do they call it a re-inauguration," Dixon said, "or just an inauguration?"

Lenora, sitting in her lounge chair, shrugged. "Why do they need to do a whole other one anyway? It's a lot of sugar for a dime. The man hasn't been un-inaugurated, has he?"

"What I'm saying," said Dixon, holding a cup of Sanka. "When is it again?"

"January the twenty-first," Lenora said. "I'll be watching it, I can ever get my TV to work."

Clem knew from broken TVs. While sitting on Lenora Coogan's shabby couch, Clem looked around Lenora Coogan's shabby trailer, recalling what a shabby person she, Clem Baldwin, had once been.

Uncle Hersh and Aunt Myrtle's mobile home had been a lot like this one here, with the same rabbit-eared TV, perpetually on the fritz, the same brown/tan/beige/khaki carpet, its color spectrum corollary to the season's muddiness and the vacuum's efficacy. Even the pattern of linoleum in the kitchen was the same. Clem wanted to shrink into her own body in shame whenever she thought of what a horrible little shit she'd been as a child. Reminded by her father, she now remembered all those petty comments she'd made to her aunt and uncle, about how she used to live in a house with actual stairs, that her daddy always bought the name-brand chocolate-chip cookies.

Capitalism turned everything into capital, including prejudice. America had no chance.

"That's quite a bill," Lenora said, looking at the sheet Clem had handed her.

"Everything's clearly spelled out, I hope," Clem said. She leaned forward, the couch cushions squeaking. "You paid for the first week in advance, as you can see noted. Hire date, January second, means we worked a total of seventeen days, at two hundred dollars a day. This bill is for ten days, because of the advance, plus three hundred forty-seven dollars in expenses, itemized at the bottom. I'm happy to go over each of them, you'd like."

"I trust you, Ms. Baldwin," Lenora said as she reached for her checkbook.

After accepting the $2,347 payment, a sum desperately needed for office rent, insurance, and last month's American Express bill, Clem thanked Lenora. "Do you have any questions, ma'am?" Dixon asked. "I know it can be upsetting that your son's death wasn't an accident."

"Upsetting? It's comforting." Lenora lit a Viceroy. Her next words hid behind clouds of smoke. "I knew my Lewis never would have took his own life. He was always too headstrong for it. He was my sweet boy, but he'd get a temper at times. You can bet I tried to give him every chance, but it can be hard to give what you don't have, you know? Did my best." Lenora waved her cigarette diagnostically, a piece of chalk with no blackboard. "So that Odette Hubbard woman poisoned his food, and she was found dead of poisoning?"

"Yes, ma'am," Dixon said, to which Clem added, "As for who poisoned Odette, they remain at large."

"At large?" Lenora said. "The DM killed that woman, dollars to donuts."

Clem leaned back, coughed, and flared her nostrils. The flippancy of Lenora's comment was a dash of salt on a paper cut. The DM most likely had killed Odette, yeah, sure, but something didn't fit. If only Clem had more time, she could solve the rest of this case. She could feel it. This case was a Lite-Brite with missing pegs. It was a Trivial Pursuit set with some of the wedges long ago swallowed by couch cushions, fallen down floor vents, slurped up by a Dustbuster. Clem hated to leave a game unfinished. Without a loser there couldn't be a winner.

"You know what?" Clem said, clenching and releasing her toes. "I think I will take that cup of coffee after all. If it's not too much trouble?"

Lenora said, "Of course!" She scrunched out her cigarette and walked into the kitchen. From her seat, Clem listened to the sounds of cabinets opening and closing, of a Sanka jar twisting off and twisting on, of the water tap turning on and turning off, of the door to the microwave opening and closing.

With his eyes, Dixon asked Clem, *You okay?*

I don't know, Clem said by creasing her chin.

"Here you go." Lenora handed Clem a cup of instant coffee, silky gray steam rising from its grainy black surface. The chipped mug had the satisfying weight of those used at Waffle House. Clem, after taking a sip, recognized a flavor other than coffee. She looked inquiringly at Lenora, who responded, "A special blend. My daughter-in-law, she takes it with milk, account of the pregnancy. Even decaf has caffeine, I read somewhere."

Brandy made for a nice coffee additive. Clem would have to remember that. A momentary break from her recent vow of celibacy from the sauce didn't matter too much.

"Thank you both," Lenora said, returning to her lounge chair, "for not turning down this case because the kind of man my son was. Takes integrity, thing like that. I'm grateful."

"We just did what anybody else would've done," Dixon said.

"Not exactly, Mr. Hicks."

"Are you saying," Clem said, "we weren't the first agency you attempted to hire?"

"Y'all were the fourth. The first three said no, flat-out. Scared of the DM."

In Meridian, Clem knew, there wasn't a fifth private investigation agency. She and Dixon had been the only PIs in this godforsaken town willing to take the case. Clem could imagine the referral. *You might try Queen City. But fair warning, they're a salt-and-pepper op.* That referral would've come from some retired desk jockey who supplemented his pension by handling child-support spats and interviewing witnesses for civil disputes, with the occasional pretext call to a utility company for intel on a no-priors jumper. Put another way, Clem thought, someone who'd left his balls in a drawer at Twenty-Second Avenue.

"Your special blend of coffee is to die for, Ms. Coogan." Clem placed her empty mug on the table between her and Lenora. "I'll have to get the recipe sometime. Feeling it already."

"Do as I can. I like to say I can always tell whenever somebody can use it."

Outside, in the radiant noon light and the brittle winter chill, Clem and Dixon wished Lenora a good day. They walked toward Clem's Jeep, the trailer park's thruway, graveled in shredded asphalt roof shingles, keeping their footsteps quiet. Clem stopped at the second E of the RENEGADE scrawled on her hood. She turned to look at the pasture across Old Country Club Road.

The pasture used to be a golf links, Clem recalled, in the original iteration of Lakeshoals. That had been before white flight sent the whites into flight, like clean little golf balls soaring toward a "less urban" area outside town. Cattle now grazed the fairway. A foreclosure sign stood near the road, with a note painted at the bottom—POSSIBILITY TO REZONE! That old poem had been wrong, Clem thought. So much did not depend on a red wheelbarrow. So much depended on zoning laws. They were a means of putting people in their place, by skin color, by tax bracket, so nobody could cross those fictional, arbitrary divisions. The road to progress wasn't paved in bureaucracy. It was ripped apart by it.

"Clem?" Dixon asked, standing on the other side of the Jeep. "You good?"

Clem turned to look at her partner. "How are you on money? Think you can handle a few days of pro bono?"

"Jesus Christ, Clem. You can't honestly be thinking of going after whoever's behind all this." Dixon placed both hands on the Jeep's hood, as if he were being patted down by a beat cop, though of course that was a rarity for someone with his complexion. "Need I remind you, Ms. Baldwin, it is literally a matter of life and death. The hit is back on. Your dad told you all this. We go after the DM, they might kill you. They might kill *us*."

He was right, the lunkhead. Dixon was always right, much as Clem loathed to admit it. She could put her own life at risk, but she could never do that to Dixon. Hands on her hips, Clem toed a clod of dirt. Why was she even thinking of keeping on with the case? It wasn't like her. She'd gotten her paycheck. That was all she cared about, wasn't it? To go after the DM would be worse than free labor, worse than potential suicide. It'd be an affirmation of all she'd disavowed, proof of the misguided belief that in this world lay any distinction, however poorly, haphazardly defined, between right and wrong.

Around a bend of Old Country Club Road barreled a big rig, its cargo trailer emblazoned with a campaign ad for Reagan/Bush '84. Was it morning again in America? Clem wondered as she watched the rig turn onto the interstate. Of course it wasn't. Had it ever been morning in America? That interstate might well be the one, if Clem's father was correct, at the heart of the Freedom Summer murders in Philadelphia, Mississippi.

What the hell. Clem didn't care that America had no chance. The world may be fucked, but it was her fucking world.

"You deserve a vacation," Clem said to Dixon. She walked around the hood of her Jeep, so that she and her partner weren't separated by a RENEGADE. "Why don't you and Heather go down to Gulf Shores? Take a long weekend."

Dixon shifted his weight from one foot to the other. "I have been meaning to catch up on some reading."

"Yeah? Where are you on the Reebok Syllabus?" Clem said, in reference to the shoebox of books she'd loaned him after he asked to learn more on the Black experience.

"Last week I finished *If Beale Street Could Talk*."

"What'd you think?"

"Beale Street is in Memphis."

"Huh?"

"First line of the book, 'Beale Street is a street in New Orleans.' Seems like they should've made sure its first line was accurate."

"You're still going back to the 'well, actually.' It might've been a metaphor. Like an intentional nod toward—"

"Clem, what's the plan? How're we going to find the people behind this?"

We.

Adjacent to the parking area stood a community mailbox hutch. Clem walked toward it. She studied the grid of mail slots, how their lines intersected, the way each of the tiny gray doors created a pattern, a system of entryways. An empty whiskey bottle sat beneath the boxes. A bird feather floated past a keyhole. "I don't have a plan," Clem said, turning to look at her partner, "but whoever's responsible, I'm going to Marple their ass."

Dixon raised his upper lip. "Ew."

"Not my best wordplay."

"And besides," Dixon said as he walked around the Jeep to the passenger side, "Odette did pay us an advance. We can say we're putting that money toward solving her own murder."

"Well, actually, we don't have her advance anymore."

"What?"

"I mailed the money to Odette's parents. They're her kids' guardians now."

"You did?"

"Yup."

"Huh."

Clem said to Dixon, "Wipe that goofy smile off your stupid face. Shut up."

They both got into the Jeep. With a steady hand, Clem cranked the engine and shifted into first. She adjusted the rearview and slipped the clutch, thinking about another book by the author of *If Beale Street Could Talk*.

Baldwin had been right. The next time was now, and Clem was bringing fire.

25

MISSISSIPPI GODDAMN

And Alexander wept, Hamilton Delacroix thought as he saw the breadth of his domain. Plutarch had the right idea. It wounded the heart to run out of worlds to conquer.

Hamilton was sitting on what as a kid in the Mississippi Delta he would have called a porch. His second wife called it a veranda. "Darling, let's have our cocktails on the veranda, no?" Although Sheila had moved out ten years ago, a decade that followed two of the worst in Hamilton's six and a half of them, her influence persevered in his use of that particular term and his routine of drinking the occasional cocktail on the *veranda.* At the moment, he was enjoying a mint julep, heavy on the bourbon, light on the simple syrup.

The key was to spank the mint leaves. Muddling them gave it a bitter taste.

Silver tumbler in hand, its sides frosted and cold, Hamilton looked across the hundred acres that constituted his backyard, colossal magnolias heaving their shadows onto slopes of weekly serviced grass, the pristine, mirrored surface of a stocked pond waiting to be broken by the hook, bob, and line cast from a little boy's fishing pole. Purple-tinted cirrus clouds feathered the blue afternoon sky. A bird peeked into the open mouth of a feeder like a dentist asking a patient to say, *Aah*. Hamilton sipped his julep, utterly happy, supremely at peace. Today was the day.

The letter sat signed and sealed in his lap, SOUTHWAYS ALLIANCE nestled in the creamy white envelope's top left corner, *The Meridian Star*'s address printed neatly at its center.

"Can I get you anything, sir?" said Lorraine, his housekeeper, cook, and all-around help. She was standing at the French doors that led onto the veranda. "Another?"

"I'm still working on this one, Lorraine. Feel free to head out whenever."

"I'll leave your dinner in the oven. Mrs. Delacroix said she's having hers with friends tonight."

"Lorraine?" From his lap Hamilton lifted the letter. He held it out. "Would you mind dropping this in the mail?"

"Of course. Good night, Mr. Delacroix."

Hamilton took another sip of mint julep slushy with crushed ice. Who'd have thought he would make it this far in life? Certainly not Hamilton. In World War II, as a scared little thing who, before enlisting, had never been west of the Mississippi or east of the Yazoo, he'd resigned himself to death, which in turn made living a hell of a lot easier. To have nothing so much as your own life at stake meant you had nothing at all to lose.

The war made Hamilton a risk taker. The GI Bill hedged those risks. The baby boom escalated their reward. Through the '50s, '60s, '70s, and now the '80s, Hamilton took Southways Alliance from a fledgling company based out of a veritable utility closet at the Threefoot Building and nursed it into an empire whose residential and commercial assets *included* the Threefoot Building.

Had it been difficult? Hamilton was recently asked by one of the few people he considered a confidant. Therein lay the rub. Hell no, it hadn't been difficult. It had been shockingly easy.

Hamilton called that ease the Mississippi Goddamn. In drastic need of a cash influx to float the construction until a mixed-use would be ready for market, Southways is granted a balloon loan by Piney Woods Bank, no financials required, a handshake deal. Goddamn, Mississippi. Southways bypasses its first zoning issue, and all it takes is a wad of cash, a cheap envelope, a rubber band, an elegant table at an elegant restaurant, and the surreptitious passing of said cash in said envelope bound in said rubber band beneath said table at said restaurant. Goddamn, Mississippi. Hamilton receives notice of an impending tax audit. Hamilton gives a call to the governor. Audit goes away. Goddamn, Mississippi. Goddamn.

Only ice left in his tumbler, Hamilton set it on a side table, stood from his rattan chair, and stretched, taking one last look at his beautiful, empty landscape.

In the kitchen, Hamilton opened the oven, a wave of hot air caressing his face. Lorraine had made what he jokingly liked to call her quiche Lorraine. It was a traditional quiche with a couple modifications—chorizo for ham, Swiss cheese for Gruyère. Hamilton didn't know what he would do without Lorraine. Originally named Veronica Dominguez, she starched Hamilton's shirts and pants hard as cardboard, kept Hamilton's house tidy as a barracks, and worked for a quarter of the pay and none of the benefits of a housekeeper who wasn't an undocumented Marielito refugee from Castro's Cuba wanted by the INS.

Hamilton closed the oven. He didn't want his quiche Lorraine getting cold.

"What are you doing for dinner?" Hamilton asked his wife after he walked into the living room, where she was sitting on the couch, tidying up her works from the glass coffee table. Cecily looked at him through the floor-to-ceiling mirror hanging on the wall opposite them both, her frothy, teased hair banana-clipped into a side ponytail, her hands skittering along the saliva-daubed top of the coffee table in their fingerless mesh gloves.

"Heading out with my girls," she said. "That new club opened downtown? I figured we'd see what's swaying."

Despite being in her thirties, Cecily behaved as though she were still a twenty-something, Hamilton was wont to note. Her *girls*? Come on. They were her lackeys. But at least they helped keep her out of trouble, dragging her home when it got late, stopping her from doing that last shot or hit or pill or bump, slapping sense into her if she made the mistake of making out with her side piece in public. Cecily was a woman of impulse, part of what Hamilton loved most about her, but she was a handful, like all of life's rewards.

Spoils deserved to be spoiled, he often reminded himself. "Promise you'll be careful," Hamilton said. "I'm running out of favors with the MPD."

Cecily sprang from the couch, an understandable bounce to her step. She crossed the room. "Yes, Daddy."

"Don't," Hamilton said. "Makes my stomach turn." From his money clip, he peeled three $100 bills and handed them to Cecily, and after giving her a kiss, he thumbed clean what she'd missed on her upper lip. Hamilton didn't want his trophy covered in dust.

"And what are you doing this evening?" Cecily slid the money into her purse.

"I don't know. I thought I'd maybe call up some friends. Get a drink."

"*Friends.*" Cecily pecked Hamilton on the cheek and patted his butt. "You're cute."

Once alone, after listening to the garage door creak open and the sports car he never used squeal out of the driveway, Hamilton walked into his humidor and selected a cigar. He got it lit, *puff, turn, puff, turn,* thinking about that movie with the candymaker.

"Don't forget what happened to the man who suddenly got everything he always wanted," the line went. "He lived happily ever after." How very true, Hamilton thought as he meandered through his house, smoking a fine cigar, hearing the echo of his footsteps. So very true.

He walked past his study, down a hall, and into the parlor. At the center of the parlor stood a grand piano. Hamilton couldn't play. He'd always imagined it would one day be played by a daughter who'd turn out to be a prodigy. He could see her now, seated on the bench, pastel as a Jordan almond, in a blue dress with a yellow sash, a pink bow in her hair. She'd play some impossibly difficult piece, and afterward, she'd give a curtsy to her applauding father. Instead, the piano had become the world's most expensive coaster, its black varnish constellated with interlocking drink rings.

Hamilton checked his watch, thinking, Never enough time. He perched his cigar on a Rotary Club medallion and entered his study.

On his desk lay the photocopy of a marriage certificate that had arrived at his office last week. He had no idea who'd sent it. Hamilton picked up the certificate and ran his finger against the burnt edges of a corner, where, after receiving the copy, he'd held a lighter for the few seconds it took him to realize the futility of that, for the few seconds it took him to realize the futility of everything. What good was an empire if you had no one to inherit it?

The bottom of the certificate drew Hamilton's gaze as irrevocably as it always did. On the last line, next to the X that Hamilton had marked himself at the Circuit Court all those years ago, his ink intersecting that of his bride: Odette's tiny, delicate signature.

His first love, ruined by a lie that could've become a scandal. His child bride. Goddamn, Mississippi.

The night Hubbard got what he deserved, Odette had shown up at Hamilton's door, her nose bloodied, her lip ruptured. "This is the last time," she'd told him through her tears. "I won't let that man touch me again." After getting Odette to sleep with a shot of Jim Beam and a Valium, Hamilton had loaded his gun and, numb with rage, driven to Randall Hubbard's house.

Now Odette was gone, too, Hamilton thought as he laid the certificate back on his desk.

In his bedroom, beneath rafters he'd repurposed from the sharecropper shack where he'd been raised, Hamilton pulled back the curtains on the custom bay windows and took in the gorgeous light from the end of another gorgeous day. The bedsheets had been turned down perfectly, their high thread count giving them a liquid gleam. A slight chill from the overpowered AC unit hoisted the hairs on Hamilton's defined, tan, round-robin forearms. From a high shelf in the closet he retrieved the rope.

He'd fastened the knot the day he was sent the marriage certificate, an accusation of murder and a reminder of the last time he'd been happy.

Hamilton, after tossing the rope over one of the rafters and securing it to the doorknob across the room, situated a chair. He stepped on it and placed the knot. Aware neither that a revolver had been planted in one of his air vents nor that an anonymous tip had been phoned into the Meridian Police Department, Hamilton rocked the chair side to side, back and forth, until it fell over, the flashing lights of a police cruiser swerving into his driveway, coloring the walls of his bedroom red and blue, red and blue, red and blue.

26

DARK FEAR ROAD

At the same moment Detective Samantha Bellflower discovered the body of Hamilton Delacroix, Clem and Dixon were staking out, once again, the home of Harold John Riggins. A stakeout was a bit of a letdown, Clem had to admit, after her decision to bring fire to this case. But most detective work, truth told, was waiting for a lead to grow legs.

They'd been parked down the street from the Riggins house since leaving the Coogan place earlier that day. The time was near 5:00 P.M., Clem didn't have to glance at the console clock to know. She could tell by the men and women returning home from work, tired looks on their tired faces. Children, some literally with latchkeys around their necks, roamed the neighborhood, barreling into and out of back alleys, cluttering every sidewalk with their cars Matchbox and their Joes GI.

To clear her mind, Clem turned toward Dixon, whose feet were entrenched by beef jerky wrappers and Diet Coke cans. "I like your shirt," she said, nodding at Dixon's oversize, vertically striped button-up. The stripes alternated between fuchsia and cream.

"Thank you."

"You look like you're being fumigated."

Dixon huffed, clearly amused but trying not to give Clem the satisfaction. "Okay, Miss Thing."

"*Ms.* Thing."

"Heather gave it to me for Christmas. She said stripes are slimming. Not one for subtlety, I tell you what."

Heather. Clem didn't want to be reminded of her. The guilt was too much.

Clem had sworn to this man's wife she'd always look out for him. She'd told Heather not to worry, that Dixon would be safe under her watch. Yet here they sat, on a stakeout for a nonpaying case, one that had already led to an attempt on their lives and, based on reliable intel, could lead to another. Clem had to be cautious. She could never abide making Heather Hicks a widow. She'd already come so close to that unbearable eventuality with the car bomb. Clem had to be present. She had to be vigilant. She couldn't make any mistakes.

After adjusting her side mirror, Clem looked up and down the block, where the ambient evening light had consolidated into dim, hazy pools beneath the streetlamps. The Riggins house remained quiet. Harold John's nigh-past-its-prime muscle car hunkered in the driveway, same as it had been the past few hours.

The house was as depressingly battered as the rest of them on the block. A blue plastic tarp covered part of the roof. A front window had been duct-taped, one long strip intersecting the other, cracks threading from the letter made by the two. *X marks the spot,* thought Clem, an attempt to stifle her nagging empathy for this son of a shit Harold John, with his Confederate flag tattoo. He had to have been involved with Odette Hubbard's murder. The guy was a janitor at the courthouse. He was a known associate of the DM.

Clem tried to find more promising news by changing the radio station. "And expect high temps for the rest of the week, with a slight chance of rain tomorrow," said the anchor. "In other news, events scheduled for this summer to commemorate the death of Emmett L. Till have been canceled in various counties throughout the state. Officials, noting that safety at the events could not be guaranteed, expressed hope that observances both public and private remain peaceful. The Citizens' Council of America could not be reached for comment."

As he crumpled another Diet Coke can and dropped it near his feet, Dixon said, "Wonder what happened."

"A Black boy got killed for whistling at a white woman."

"I meant with the commemorations."

"So did I," Clem said. "You know another name for the Citizens' Council? The *White* Citizens' Council. They got their way. This is Mississippi."

"This is America."

"The Twilight Zone."

"Hmm?"

"We got *The Twilight Zone* because of Till." Clem kept her eyes trained on the Riggins house. A stray cat slinked through a fence. "Rod Serling came up with the show because of the Emmett Till case, how infuriating he found it. He decided the best way to get across his social criticism was to sneak it into a TV show with space aliens and time travel."

"Like putting dog medicine in a hunk of cheese."

"You know the name of the street Emmett Till was killed on?" Clem asked.

"Nuh-uh."

"Dark Fear Road."

"Really?"

Clem had always loved the singer Jesse Winchester, a Mississippian by way of Louisiana. He'd gotten it right in his song "Step by Step." Only an idiot wouldn't want to know how come the devil smiles. Problem was? Clem had been born knowing how come. "When you're Black in Mississippi," she said to her partner, "every road has the potential to be Dark Fear."

The high beams of a passing car stretched and shrank the shadows around the neighborhood. Dixon fingered the door handle like a loose tooth. Clem could tell what he was going to ask next. It was time, she figured. They'd put off this conversation for long enough.

Dixon stared straight ahead as he asked Clem, "How come you never told me about your dad?"

"Because what does it matter?" Clem asked the question with more vehemence than she'd intended. With less force she said, "I am what people see."

"That's not true."

"When people look at me, they see a Black woman, so that's what I am."

"Clem."

"If I weren't Black, then why do I live in deathly fear of people like you?"

Like me, Clem could tell Dixon was thinking, and she felt terrible about it. "I don't mean you-you," she said. "I mean *like* you, you know?"

"Mm-hm."

"And what does it matter I have a white father? I stand in front of someone, they don't see my parents. They see me."

"But—"

"It's easier, to be honest, him being at Parchman. That's made my life a hell of a lot less confusing."

"Confusing?"

"Ellison had it wrong. Being invisible isn't the worst thing. The worst thing is being confusing. Being a question mark. Being a knitted brow. Being a tilted head. Being a problem to be solved. I saw that look all the time growing up. A look that said, *What is she?*"

"God."

"Right?" Clem said. "My dad can go to hell, for all I care. I didn't tell you he's white because he isn't now. He's a criminal."

In the quiet that followed, Clem, who knew all about know-it-alls, worried that was how she'd come across with her screed. She didn't mean to imply her experience of race stood for everyone's experience of race. Monoliths always made for the most boring structures. And a black dahlia in a bouquet of white lilies was still just another flower.

Dixon looked at Clem. "Why is it you have so much anger toward him?"

"My dad?"

"Yeah."

Because, Clem wanted to say, *I need somewhere to put it.* Because the world wanted her to be a stereotype. Because she couldn't let the world have the satisfaction.

Before Clem could make any of those claims, however, Harold John Riggins marched out of his house, swinging a key ring on his finger. He had a patchy chaparral beard and wore acid-wash jeans, mud boots, and a Saints jacket with duct tape along the shoulder. Clem, realizing who'd planted the bomb in Heather Hicks's truck and deciding not to upset her partner for the time being, cranked her engine. After Harold John pulled into the street, Clem tailed him, the length between their respective vehicles a consistent city block.

"To be continued?" Dixon asked, returning to the subject of Clem's father.

"If you want, but I made my point. Just know I'm sorry for not having told my friend about that part of myself. He deserved better."

Friend, Clem could tell Dixon was thinking, with a faint smile, and she felt happy about it. Dixon wasn't some good ol' boy. He was the best.

As they followed Riggins across county lines, Clem patted the lump of her Beretta where it was snugly shoulder-holstered. If Lauderdale County was the Old West, Kemper County was the Wild West. Drug distro was rampant. The local badges tended to be pocket cops for whatever redneck kingpin had crowned himself of late. Clem had even heard rumors back at the squirrel cage that the DM had some sort of compound out here.

"Easy," Dixon said as they tailed Riggins onto a dirt road. "Keep it steady."

A line of traffic lay ahead, unusual for the backwoods. Pickups prevalent, the congested traffic snaked around a corner, brake lights giving the tree canopy and gravel and roadside ditches an unearthly red glow. Clem had no choice but to stop directly behind Riggins, far too close for a tail, as the traffic inched forward. She and Dixon instinctively held their knuckles to their brows and turned their heads in an effort to keep from being made.

On spotting the line of traffic's destination, a driveway that led toward a large, spotlighted pole barn in the distance, Dixon said, "Looks like a party."

"And on a school night, too."

They were flagged to turn into the driveway by what looked to be a guard or ticket taker or bouncer. Probably all three, Clem thought as the guy, wearing sunglasses and a baseball cap despite the hour, leaned toward her side window. "That's four dollars a head," the guy said. "And trust me, ma'am, it's worth it. The birds are feisty tonight!"

Clem looked at Dixon, and Dixon looked at Clem. Both looks said, *Birds?*

27

KEMPER COUNTY COCKFIGHT

Molly had never been to the ranch before tonight. She couldn't claim the place surprised her all that much. In a parking area filled with pickups whose beds were filled with beer cans, surrounded by good ol' boys in sleeveless flannel and good ol' gals with stretch-marked midriffs, Molly readied herself for what she had to do, taking a deep breath and checking that the snub-nosed revolver she'd borrowed from her mother-in-law was still in her purse.

Earlier that day, she'd gone to pick up her last check from the John Wesley Hardin, and her friend who worked the bar warned her Jacob Cassidy was back in town. "The hit's on again for the PI. Maybe you, too. Definitely steer clear of the cockfights."

"Where are these fights?"

The beau and haute monde of Kemper County had turned out for the occasion: hard-ass farm-boys drinking six-packs of light beer; prom queen runners-up in Jordache, Benetton, and Vuarnet; security agents, replete with earpieces, guarding what Molly could have sworn was the governor's eldest son; teenaged world-beaters with pupils the size of Krugerrands, who'd obviously been smoking or popping or snorting that ceremonial-grade shit; loudmouths, bigmouths, poormouths; a woman with a crimson mohawk; and even a few men in the Southern "power suit" of pleated pants, suspenders, dress shirt, and bow tie.

Of all the people here, regardless of how strangely egalitarian, Molly only cared about one: the man who'd likely killed her brother, the man who likely wanted to kill her. Tonight she was going to take care of that son of a bitch before he could take care of her.

She approached the pole barn, one of the biggest she'd ever seen, the kind that would usually store a dozen tractors, combines, bulldozers, and track hoes. Instead, it was broiling with hundreds of people in stadium seats overlooking a circular arena. The fights hadn't started yet. The arena, its dirt floor dappled in green shit dried white and red blood dried brown, with the occasional, heart-wrenching feather gamboling across the mess, sat empty. Three-toed tracks choreographed past horrors.

Molly had never seen a cockfight. She would have gladly kept it that way but for the small matter of her life being at stake.

As with the football games Molly had gone to in high school, satellite clusters of people had formed around the bleachers, passing whiskey bottles and smoking cigarettes, the various breezes being shot. Molly roved from cluster to cluster, spotting friends she had not talked to since her days in private school.

Wealth didn't buy class, Molly was thinking when Harold John Riggins brushed past her, carrying a travel coop occupied by his money bird, Clara.

Harold John hated the cockfights. They attracted all the scum of Meridian, the rich kids playing redneck, the poor kids playing gangster. The rich ones were the worst, of course, with their uncalloused palms and consciences. While Harold John had been in the shit, killing the gooks for his country, these pampered kids had been off at Ole Miss, where they learned to be the assholes they were now.

Used to be, he hated the coloreds most all, but lately he'd been "rethinking his position," as a professor from his half semester of junior college once said. The coloreds had fought alongside Harold John in Vietnam. The rich boys had stayed home. He saw a lesson there. Bullets leveled the playing field, and Harold John was ready and willing to play.

"Hundred-dollar entry," said Toots McGonagall, sitting behind a fold-out table next to the chain-link gate to the cockpit.

"Toots, it's me," Harold John said. Members of the DM didn't pay entry.

"Shit, HJ. Don't know where my head's at. You're all set. I've got you on for the seventh pitting."

"Seventh? Nothing sooner?"

"Don't worry. The first six will go quick. These birds are mean. I'm talking peak beak."

"You say so."

"What've you got for me?"

Harold John placed his travel coop on the table. "This is Clara. He's new."

"Ain't that your mama's name?" Toots asked. Harold John didn't answer. He watched Toots, always an honest and respectable judge and referee of the fights, inspect the gamecock. He was a novice Whitehackle. Harold John had renamed the rooster after his mother because of the importance of tonight's pitting. He needed the money. They'd found a blood clot in his mother's one good leg, and the surgery was going to cost some serious cash. Despite his past few jobs for the DM, Harold John was strapped for funds. He planned to bet his entire roll on this Clara in order to help save the life of the other.

"I can give you two to one," Toots said. He turned to the blackboard standing behind the table and chalked the odds. "That's a friend ratio."

As he placed a fold of hundreds and twenties on the table, Harold John said, "I'm down for one thousand, seven hundred eighty dollars."

"Mr. Big Money. Luck to you and yourn."

In the designated prep area on the other side of the pit, Harold John placed his coop on the ground and squatted next to it, fuming about management. They could go to hell, whoever they were. How could they have asked him to murder Odette? She had been the love of Harold John's life! Not a second had passed since her death that he did not see her trusting eyes, her gorgeous smile, the furrow in her brow as he shot her full of poison.

Harold John opened his gaff case. It held a bottle of rubbing alcohol, a piece of flannel, waxed string, chamois coverings, a set of short spurs, a set of long jaggers, and a SIG Sauer. He trailed the tips of his fingers over the piece. Management was the same as all these rich folks here tonight. They stood by as people like Harold John did their filthy work for them. They earned a fat wad while people like Harold John had to bet their life savings to pay the mortgage, the car note, the hospital bill.

She's considered a liability, and management has decided to minimize their exposure.

Orders were orders, Jacob Cassidy had said, referring to Odette. Harold John was done taking orders. He slid the SIG between his belt and his back, opened the door to the travel coop, and lifted Clara from the bed of peat moss. "First we win some money," he whispered to the rooster, "and then we settle a few scores."

While Clara clucked in affirmation, Harold John looked through the bleachers, studying the crowd. People loved a bit of bloodshed. In one row, a father offered his son a grab from his bucket of popcorn, and behind that row, a fistfight broke out between two women in cutoffs, and on a top row a teenager made out with his girlfriend, and between two sets of bleachers—*shit, shit, fuckitty shit, shit*—walked that lady PI and her partner.

"It's like Hieronymus Bosch on Dexedrine," Clem was saying to Dixon. She hadn't noticed Harold John noticing her.

"Anonymous who?" Dixon asked, a joke Clem chose not to acknowledge.

They'd been wandering the crowd for twenty minutes. Her rookie year on the force, Clem had helped break up a dogfighting ring, but she didn't have experience with the cockfighting circuit. What she had seen thus far boded damn far from well. The rows of bleachers were like venetian blinds over a window to some netherworld of Mississippi culture, one that combined a country music fan's jingoism with a stock car fan's hope for a crash. To Clem, the entire spectacle felt so proudly, horrifically American. That she was the only Black person in attendance only compounded the feeling.

"I cannot believe you're eating that," Clem said to Dixon. He was halfway done with a hot dog he'd bought from a cart vendor by the parking lot.

"Stakeouts are my cheat day." With his thumb, Dixon wiped a spot of mustard from the corner of his mouth. He took the last bite of hot dog and threw away the napkin.

"What's a cheat day?"

"I asked my wife the same thing. She got a tad upset at how excited I got about what I thought they were."

Clem had a hunch her partner would be a vegetarian by the end of this evening. She was telling him so when, as the crowd grew quiet, a man who looked familiar walked to the center of the pit.

"Jesus Christ," Clem said after she figured out who the man was. "You've got to be kidding me. Kemper County cockfights have corporate sponsorship?"

Chaunce Lattimer wore a ball cap inscribed, LATTIMER MOTORS. A toothy grin smeared across his rosaceous face, he was holding a microphone, its cord trailing behind him. "Y'all ready for a night of fights?!" he hollered into the microphone, after which the crowd erupted in thunderous applause, cheers, and four-, two-, and no-fingered whistles.

"That's what I thought," Chaunce said as he took a card from the pocket of his suit jacket. "First up, we've got Warlock, a fourteen-win bird out of Whynot, Mississippi, pitting against First Pancake, a seven-time champ from Toomsuba. And remember, folks, at the top of the pecking order you'll always find Lattimer Motors. Across this great state, we've got the best deals on all your favorite vehicles. Birds of a feather . . . flock together . . . to Lattimer Motors!"

"Is this for real?" Dixon asked, putting into words Clem's exact thoughts.

"I honestly have no idea."

Despite knowing she needed to find Harold John, who they'd lost while Dixon was buying his hot dog with the works, Clem couldn't keep herself from watching these strange proceedings in the pit.

"Bill your cocks," the referee said to two men, each with a bird cradled in his arms. The men approached each other. They stopped a few feet apart and turned side to side. Within their handlers' arms, both birds thrashed, feathers bristling, combs flapping, each with a fury, a thirst, a rage, a hunger to trammel the other to death. "To your lines," the referee said after the birds had been sufficiently stoked to kill each other. "Release on my say."

The two men retreated to lines on different sides of the pit, roughly eight feet apart, enclosed by a circle of wooden boards, nearly two feet in height and about twenty feet in diameter. Clem tapered her breath. Her pulse sloshed through her veins. "Pit your cocks!" the referee yelled.

From each handler's arms the birds sprang into the air, their wings blurring to clouds of brown and red and black, at the bottom of which their gnarly yellow feet spit out like lightning bolts. They met midair, two clouds becoming one, and plunged to the ground. Dust swelled. The crowd fell quiet until they could see who had the advantage.

Neither did. The birds retreated to opposite sides of the pit. They shook their feathers and began to circle each other. Clem marveled at their training, how much like actual, human boxers they seemed, bobbing, feinting, keeping their heads low and their feet nimble.

One of the birds made a rush at the other. Only when it rose to a short flight did Clem see what differentiated this fight from a human one, what, in fact, humans had done to these animals to enable the violence they would do to each other.

The metal spurs tied to the birds' heels glinted in the harsh floodlights. Blood scattered across the dusty pit when one of the spurs pierced a wing. The bird then pecked at its opponent's head. Clem wanted to look away, but she couldn't shift her gaze. If only she'd had slightly more willpower, she told herself seconds later, she wouldn't have seen the losing bird's eyeball, pecked from its socket, fly through the air and thud once, twice, three times before rolling to stop in the blood-streaked dirt.

"Match winner is Warlock of Whynot, Mississippi!" the referee announced.

Clem and Dixon only heard the announcement. They hadn't stayed to watch it. They hadn't stayed to see the crowd in the bleachers applaud such a display of savagery. Hearing them was hard enough.

"I don't want to talk about it," Clem said before Dixon could say anything.

Behind the bleachers, surrounded by empty beer cans, stray kernels of popcorn, cigarette butts, and ketchup-slicked hot dog wrappers, Clem breathed through her mouth. And here she'd thought Dixon would be the one to have his stomach turned. She gagged.

The sound caused people in the bleachers to peer through the seat gaps at the newbie losing a meal. Among them was Jacob Cassidy, who had to admit the luck, good for him and poor for her, of Clementine Baldwin's timing. Rarely had he run into a target by accident.

Jacob cracked a peanut between his thumb and trigger finger. He tossed the shell over the side of the bleachers. From his seat, while keeping an eye on Baldwin and her partner below him, Jacob watched the ref check that the next two birds hadn't been greased, peppered, or soaped, that their hackles, crests, beards, primaries, and coverts had been trimmed to regulation. Jacob knew his "Cocker's Code of Conduct." In his garage could be found boxes of back issues of *Southern Cockfighter* and *The Gamecock*. Jacob had been a cocker himself for a short time after 'Nam, before he'd joined the DM, before he'd met his wife. He supposed that was part of why he'd come to the fights tonight—to revisit a time when he was alone, unburdened by a family. What was left of his family.

Sue June would have hated the fights, of course. She'd adored all animals.

"Pop quiz," Jacob said to a guy sitting near him. "Which US president was a cockfight referee in his youth?"

The guy looked at Jacob as though he'd farted. *Well, fuck you, too,* Jacob thought. He stood from his seat and walked down the bleachers.

On the ground level, Jacob leaned against the railing, facing the pit but with enough of a slant to glance inconspicuously at the private investigators behind him. The guy was patting his partner's back as she cleaned her mouth. Poor thing. Jacob felt for the kid; after canceling her from the equation, he'd be glad to be done with this job.

This fucking job. Jacob was starting to lose faith that management had the slightest clue what in all hell they were doing. First they want Randy Hubbard dead. Then they don't want Randy Hubbard dead. What happens next? Randy Hubbard turns up dead. "Fix it, Jacob," they say, so Jacob fixes it. Then they want the revolver used to kill Hubbard planted in the home of Hamilton Delacroix. And for what? Jacob had no clue, and he suspected management had no clue, either. This scorched-earth mentality was like Khe Sanh all over again. Management was using Jacob as napalm on the operation.

Even the cockfights, Jacob thought as he followed the private investigators through the crowds, as he listened to the emcee introduce the birds for the fourth pitting, even this whole scene testified to the DM losing control. The cockfighting circuit used to be for members only. The DM would have never let the general public so much as see the ranch. Why did they now? Economics. Jacob had learned all about that subject during a short stretch at Parchman Farm when he had a tax-accountant-turned-money-launderer as his cellmate. Adam Smith's invisible hand now controlled the KKK's invisible empire.

It was time to retire, Jacob knew in his gut, tracking the PIs as they left the main crowd, headed toward the roadhouse a hundred yards away. Management, Jacob thought, had lost sight of its objective, which was to give poor, uneducated white folks an ideology of hate and bigotry. Money was management's ultimate goal, obviously, but the poor, uneducated white folks didn't know that. There would be trouble when they found out.

Jacob and Min could start over, he told himself, closing in on the pair of PIs. They could even try for another baby. That was what they needed, a fresh start, a second shot at being a family. Their life together could be perfect again. They could be so happy.

"Psst," Jacob said, standing behind Baldwin and her partner in the deserted stretch of field between the barn and the roadhouse. He held his gun at hip level. "Let's take a walk."

Clearly old pros of the stickup, the PIs stiffened professionally, which was to say unnoticeably. They kept their hands by their sides but in sight, and they kept their heads on and aimed forward. Jacob was impressed. He valued competence in anyone being held up.

The air smelled rotten. On their walk to the ranch's roadhouse, the two PIs and Jacob passed what Jacob knew to be the source of that smell, a trench where cockers tossed their birds after they lost. It needed a fresh dose of lye. Another example, Jacob thought, of the Dixie Mafia shirking its discipline.

Even Molly, sitting in the bleachers over fifty yards back, could smell the trench. She caught a whiff of it laced into that yeasty scent of draft beer from the guy behind her. Molly turned toward the roadhouse in time to see Jacob Cassidy leading the two investigators through its saloon-style doors.

Goddamn it to hell. Molly, besides the rot and the draft beer, smelled trouble.

"Enjoying the fights, little lady?" asked the man behind her. Molly had felt him eyeing her for the past fifteen minutes as she had studied the crowd in search of Cassidy.

She turned to let the guy see how soon she was due. "This little fellow is."

That shut him up. But it also concerned Molly. She was about to begin her third trimester. What was she doing out here? Pregnant women didn't carry guns to cockfights to shoot the men who'd killed their brothers. Pregnant women were supposed to stay home eating chocolate pickle ice cream smothered in bacon grease and rainbow sprinkles. They were supposed to sit on the couch with cotton balls between their toes while their devoted husbands applied new coats of Periwinkle Sky. What in God's good name had Molly been thinking of?

Saving her life, that was what. From her seat in the bleachers, ignoring the pit below, Molly reminded herself that, in fact, two lives depended on what she was going to do tonight. Her child superseded any inklings of morality she might have. Molly's soul did not matter, but another one did. Tonight wasn't about revenge for her brother's murder. It was about the safety of her child's life. Born under a bad sign? From an even worse seed? None of that compared a whit to not being born because your mother had caught a bullet.

Screw all whether this situation had begun when Molly failed to stop her brother from joining the DM. Molly may or may not have started it, but she sure as hell was going to end it.

She'd show these folks about class. She'd prove it was more than money.

"Now for our seventh pitting of the night!" that car salesman hollered into his microphone from the middle of the pit, his redneck accent as unflattering as under-head lighting, his cheeks glowing sixty watts from eighty-proof. The man continued, "We've got Rooster Cogburn, a four-time winner from Lost Gap, pitting against Clara, a novice bird out of Meridian, Mississippi."

Molly stood from her seat. She groped her purse to reassure herself of the hard lump of snub-nosed steel at the bottom of it. On her trudge through the bustling mass at the bottom of the bleachers, she spotted what looked like a plainclothes cop, lingering in the area where the fighters readied their birds. The sight of the guy in his sack suit and cheap oxfords quickened Molly's pace as she left the cockpit and headed toward the roadhouse.

The cop was only there to get his taste. In the prep area, Harold John watched Officer What's His Face collect his $100 sin tax, a bargain for the DM, given the money they made on these fights. It figured. Not even the crooked flatfoots got a fair shake from management.

Who really believed in honor among thieves? Harold John wondered, holding Clara in the air and gently blowing cigarette smoke into his face, a trick to get birds riled for a fight. He tucked Clara in his elbow. He looked at the other handler across the pit. At two-to-one odds, Harold John stood to make $3,560 if he won tonight, which would bring his total roll to $5,340. That would just about cover his mother's medical expenses for the blood clot. If he lost, though, Harold John would be down to his car title in one hand and his dick in the other. His mother, bless her soul, would fare even worse, likely losing the leg.

But this bird wouldn't lose, Harold told himself when the ref yelled, "Bill your cocks!" In the center of the pit, as the shadows of flies orbiting the floodlights overhead orbited his shadow on the ground, Harold John held firm to Clara, who thrashed madly at the other bird, like a summer thunderstorm in the crook of Harold John's elbow. "Now go back on your lines," the ref ordered both handlers.

"You've got this," Harold John whispered to his Clara. "You can make it."

Originally bought from that poor bastard Turnip Coogan, a top-drawer breeder before his "accidental" spill from the courthouse roof, Clara exhibited the instincts of a true fighter. Harold John had trained the rooster himself. Every morning, he ran the little guy on a treadmill. In the evenings, he tied weights to Clara's legs and got him to leap for treats. He was flying ten feet high as of last week, at which point Harold John had given him time to rest before the fight. With enough rest, any bird would come back stronger, faster, more beautiful, ready to take on and conquer the world.

"Pit your cocks!"

Clara shot from Harold John's embrace as though spring-loaded. Instead of an aerial fight, the birds attacked on the ground, their sharp, metal jaggers wheeling toward each other like the flails of a combine. Clara's opponent, Rooster Cogburn, pounced with a swift downswing of beak, landing a solid blow to the chest, enough that a daub of blood leached into satiny down. Harold John mirrored Clara's movement at scale, his feet doing in inches what Clara's were doing in yards, sprinting from one side of the pit to the other, falling back, pitching forward.

Each bird's contour feathers were a comic book's stylization of motion. Those streaks of red, brown, white, orange, and black seemed to vibrate even when still.

The birds took the fight to flight, Harold John thanked God to note. Clara was good in the air. He dove toward Cogburn and sliced his wing with a jagger, but Cogburn pivoted, sending Clara off-balance and, while turned to the side, double-tapping his beak. *His beak.* Harold John felt it happen more than he saw it happen, the seam fissuring down that hard ridge of keratin. He could feel his own mind dangling from a pink string of gristle.

The bird staggered back, too stunned to dodge the pounding, concussive blows from his opponent. If Harold John had been clutching a towel, he would have thrown it into the pit, but these fights only ended one way. He stared at his bird refusing to give up. *Let go,* he could not say.

Clara tried in vain to peck the other bird. Throughout the bleachers people drew into silence. In a bottom row, as one bird meekly stamped coins of blood onto the breast of the other, a laid-off AC repairman pulled away from his wife, the newspaper dowel of his erection descending fast, crumpling headlines, abbreviating bylines. In a top row, a group of teenage boys finished their beers while Clara took his last, tottering step. A black-eyed dental assistant whose request for a restraining order against her ex-boyfriend had been denied by a judge who'd gone to law school with her ex-boyfriend watched as Harold John gathered Clara into his arms. The governor's eldest son, high on shrooms, stared at a Rankin/Bass version of Harold John carrying Clara out of the pit. "Dude!" the governor's son said. "Christmas!"

Harold John was not seeing, feeling, tasting, smelling, or hearing the world in stop-motion animation. Near the parking lot, he tossed Clara's limp body into the trench he'd helped dig, the bottom of it sloshy with rainwater, dozens of carcasses bobbing in a soup of rot. From the pole barn cracked an escalating cacophony of applause for the next fight.

A drink. That was what Harold John needed right now. He resituated his piece behind his belt, ran a fist across his cheek, and headed toward the roadhouse.

Normally, on fight nights, the roadhouse was supposed to be closed, but when Harold John got near, he saw the lights were still on. He looked through a window to see Jacob Cassidy chatting with the PIs, his demeanor oddly pleasant, given that the PIs were hog-tied to chairs in the middle of the roadhouse.

"Oh, yeah?" Jacob said to Clem and Dixon, out of Harold John's earshot.

"Two tours," Dixon said.

"Semper fi, brother."

Clem couldn't get a read on this guy Cassidy. In a rickety chair, her hands roped together with electrical tape, she watched him pull a barstool toward her and Dixon and sit down, casual as Sunday brunch. He held a longneck in one hand and a semiautomatic in the other. "Look at us now," Cassidy said to Dixon, his eyes, in the dingy light of the bar, evincing what Clem could have sworn was soul. "We're two monkeys dancing," he said. "Same tune, different fiddler."

"Your fiddler's the DM," Dixon said. "What's mine?"

With the barrel of his pistol instead of an index finger, Cassidy depressed his lips, staring at a far wall in thought. "I traded up after the war. You didn't. Uncle Sam's your fiddler yet still."

"How original," Clem said. "Blame America." She shuffled her electrical-taped feet along the corduroy of narrow-planked, soft-wood floorboards, though not out of anger, as she hoped Cassidy thought, but to see if she could wrench them free. She was only able to push one shoe an inch off her heel.

Still on the barstool, Cassidy sipped his beer, a soulful gleam to his eyes. Clem couldn't decide if he was pumping them for information or if he simply wanted to have an amiable conversation with someone. She suspected the latter, which frightened her worse. Warm-blooded killers could be unpredictable. Cassidy asked, "What'd you think of the fights tonight, Baldwin?"

"A horror show," Clem said, trying not to recall the horror show.

"Pop quiz." Cassidy lifted an eyebrow. "What former United States president was a cockfight referee?"

Clem hadn't the first clue, but her partner did. "Abe Lincoln," said Dixon.

Clapping his hands in rhythm to each word, Cassidy said, with a slow, singsong lilt, "Winner, winner, chicken dinner." Clap. Clap. Clap.

Across the room, Molly, who'd snuck into the roadhouse through a back door, peered over the top of the bar, her feet sticking to a rubber mat on the floor, glassware obscuring her view. What in all hell was going on in this place? Jacob Cassidy was sitting in front of the PIs, saying something about Abraham Lincoln having been "soiled of conscience."

It didn't matter. All that mattered was what Molly had come here to do tonight. From her purse she removed the snub-nosed revolver, allowing her fingers, her hand, her entire body, it seemed, to conform to its shape. She sat on the sticky floor mat and leaned back against the underside of the bar. She rested the revolver on the curve of her stomach and eyed the liquor bottles lined on the wall. A vodka tonic would have hit the spot about now. Molly hadn't had a drop since she'd gotten official notice that Turnip's life insurance would pay out. She'd celebrated with half a glass of wine and a promise to see this thing through.

The presence of the two PIs entangled Molly's admittedly underdeveloped plan. They were about to be witnesses to a murder. Molly briefly entertained the idea of popping them as well, but she could never live with three deaths, one deserved and two not, riding shotgun in her already dilapidated conscience.

Shit. This whole situation had slipped from Molly's control; even worse, it had never been in Molly's control. She felt like a ribbon being wrapped around a maypole by someone she couldn't see, her path here, she realized, a winding course around a straight, direct line from which she'd never had a chance to deviate. Actually, Molly thought as she gripped the handgun, lifted herself into a crouch, and got ready to spring from behind the bar, a maypole was too gentle an analogy. She was a pinball slapped by flippers, banked against ramps, slung from spinners, and all the points she racked up went toward a high score with initials that were not her own.

Molly had never had a chance. She decided to go on three. *One. Two. Three!*

At the moment Molly jumped from behind the bar, gun raised, a man covered in feathers walked into the roadhouse and, without saying a word, shot Jacob Cassidy in the head.

Blood went everywhere, onto the floors, onto the tables, and worst of all, given she didn't have hands free to wipe it, onto Clem's face. She had to blink her vision clear. Clem turned to Dixon, the question of her look reflected in his own: *What just happened?*

The sketch artist of Clem's overwhelmed and reeling mind drew the picture in front of her. It appeared line by line, shading by shading, one figure at a time. Cassidy lay sprawled on the ground, inarguably deceased, a pool of blood guttering around the ragged hole in his head. Harold John loomed over the body, gun in hand, feathers stuck to his shirt, and blankness in his face—bright, livid vacancy.

"She can't lose it," he whispered. "She can't lose it. She can't lose the leg."

Again, Clem wordlessly asked Dixon what had just happened. She twisted her hands, trying to free them, but the tape was too tight. As soon as Harold John came to his senses, Clem knew, he'd clean up his mess by making more; age-old criminal logic.

Clem managed to get one shoe off. She was about to pull her bare foot out of the tape when Harold John turned to her and Dixon. He blinked once, twice, and then raised his gun.

"STOP."

Adjacent to Clem, Dixon, Harold John, and Cassidy stood a woman Clem slowly recognized as Molly Coogan. She was pointing a snub-nosed revolver at Harold John. The gun shook in her grip. Clem could read her inexperience with the weapon as easily as she could the fear in her face. "Put it down," Molly said to Harold John, "or I'll use this thing."

Harold John did not make any acknowledgment other than to stare at Molly. A silence reared between them. Without turning her head, Clem stretched her shoeless foot toward Cassidy's pistol, which lay on the floor near the pool of blood. She used her big toe to drag the gun in her direction, careful not to make any noise, careful not to accidentally pull the trigger.

"How about let's talk this out, y'all?" Dixon said. "I'm sure we can find some, some common ground. I mean, you know?"

"Shut up, Dixon," Clem said.

"There's a, a pregnancy involved here, right?"

"Dixon," Clem said.

"What'd you say you were at, Molly? Twenty-six weeks? Think about that, for starters. I mean, right?"

"Dix-on."

Her heartbeat in her ears, Clem navigated the gun between her toes, so that she could wedge one into the trigger guard. She clocked the piece, still flat on its side, to aim at Harold John's feet. She braced for the recoil by pressing her heel hard to the floor. This was going to take crackerjack timing and dexterity and a whole fiery hell of a lot of luck.

"Molly," Clem said. "Don't do it. That's not you. The asshole isn't worth it."

"That one on the ground killed my brother," Molly said, her voice serrated with anger.

"Okay," Clem said. "Okay. This asshole did you a favor by killing that asshole. Y'all are square. Mr. Riggins? Do me a favor and put the gun down. Then Molly puts hers down, okay? Can you do that for me, Harold John? Put it down, and we're cool. Just put it down. Put it down. Put it—"

In the seconds that followed Harold John raising his gun to fire on Molly, Clem performed the mental trick she'd learned at the academy, melting time into slow motion, every discrete moment elongating into a single, fluid event. She fired the gun beneath her foot by clenching her toes, the recoil flinging the piece out of her reach, keeping her from firing a second round. Harold John's boot exploded into hunks of leather, beads of blood, and shards of bone, and as he fell, dropping his gun and crying in anguish, the hunks and beads and shards of leather, blood, and bone twirled in the air like confetti jubilating his descent.

Harold John lay curled on the floor, clutching at the carnage of his foot. Molly stood in shock, still holding her revolver. Clem spotted the gun she had fired. The recoil had knocked it by Dixon. He kicked it toward her.

"You fucking bitch!" Harold John screamed. Still on the floor, his face pressed against the dusty boards, he reached for where his gun had fallen.

Clem's sweaty foot wrangled with the piece Dixon had kicked toward her, its barrel hot from the last round, its trigger guard difficult to find with her toes. Finally, she gained purchase.

"Goddamn fucking bitch," Harold John said as he got hold of his own gun.

He might have said more if it weren't for the bullet that obliterated the bottom half of his jaw. The recoil sent the gun spinning away from Clem. She didn't care. It was gruesomely evident a third shot wouldn't be needed. Due to where she sat, still tied to the chair, Clem couldn't brush away the tooth, a molar, that had somehow flown from Harold John's mouth and landed in her lap. A mercury filling glimmered at her from its yellowed crown.

On the floor, Harold John gargled blood. Clem forced herself to stare at him, counting the seconds until she officially, immutably became a killer, a taker of life. One . . . two . . . three . . . four . . .

He stopped breathing on five. A blood bubble marked his last exhalation.

"Molly," Clem said. "Molly, look at me. It's okay. Look at me. I'm going to need you to cut our hands loose. They're taped behind our backs. Go find a lime knife at the bar."

From her chair, Clem watched Molly, dumbfounded by such violence, wander toward the bar. Clem turned to Dixon, whose pants, to his obvious embarrassment, were covered in his sick. "Semper fi, eh?" she said, trying to give him a twinkle of eye, a little soft-shoe to distract from his vomit-covered shoes. "Two tours didn't leave a callus?"

Dixon shook his head. "I thought I'd seen it all."

The lime knife quivered in Molly's grip as she staggered her way back from the bar. "Careful," Clem said. "Easy now." After Molly cut them loose, Clem and Dixon said thank you, rubbed their wrists, and stood, both mindful to keep their feet out of the blood. Clem pointed at the revolver that Molly looked startled to notice was still in her hand. "I'll take that," Clem said.

"No."

"Molly."

"No."

Shaking her head but keeping her chin hinged to her chest, Molly put her hands behind her back, her gaze turning toward the scene on the ground: two dead bodies, one without a jaw, the other with a hole in the head and an eye bulging from its frayed socket. Clem looked at the scene as well. "Fine, hang on to it, in case," she said. "You did good, Molly, not pulling the trigger. You did great."

"I couldn't do it."

"Like I said." Clem turned to Dixon. "Think anybody heard the shots back at the pit?"

"Sons of bitches would be busting the door this minute if they did. It's what, a football field away? I think we're okay. But it's a lovely mess we got on our hands."

"And feet."

With a whimper, Molly shifted her own feet, still staring at what lay before them. Clem regretted making her flinch by touching her shoulder. "Go out the back door," she said. "I'll wait five minutes before putting in the call to MPD."

Molly wrenched more than shook her head. "But, but I'm involved. I can't—"

"You were *not* involved. Molly, look at me. *You were never here.* Do you hear me, Molly? You were never here."

"But."

"You go out the back door and you get in your car and you go home and wait for that baby to arrive."

Exhaustion sank into Molly's shoulders, her knees, the strings of her lower back. "Eat pickle ice cream?" she said. "Paint my pinkie toes?" As the PI nodded, Molly rubbed those strings in her back, a terrible violinist playing the most soothing song. She nodded.

On her way through the rear of the roadhouse, Molly, tired but intent, breathless and relieved, bumped into a freezer, rattled a box of liquor, banked against the door to the stock room, slung past a prep table, and looped around a mop bucket, until she reached the back door, beyond which, she knew, lay a road that would take her anywhere she wanted to go.

28

SHENANIGADES

The next night, after being detained for questioning at police headquarters for almost an entire day, Clem and Dixon sat at the Howard Johnson bar. Ho Jo's was seldom frequented by anyone staying in the motel, which, to Clem's mind, made it the most Meridian bar in all of Meridian. The notion of permanent transience encapsulated this entire damn town.

"Another?" asked the bartender, who poured a bourbon without waiting for a reply.

On a TV mounted behind the bar rolled footage from earlier that day of Ronald Reagan taking the oath of office as president of the United States, one hand on the Bible, the other raised in the air, his professional actor face silently mouthing some variation of *I do solemnly swear* on the muted screen.

"So help me God," Clem said before she took a long pull of her third drink.

"That eye of yours. A patch of duct tape?" Still registering what Clem had just told him about Harold John Riggins, Dixon shook his head. "May the poor bastard R in P."

"Maybe not too much peace," Clem said. "The guy tried to murder you."

"*And* he was a Saints fan." Dixon tapped his bottle of beer against her glass. "Don't go too fast on me. The Renegade can't handle more of your bourbon swerving."

The Renegade? It was more like the Shenanigade, for all the wrong turns, false steps, and bad moves Clem had taken on this case. She and

Dixon had gotten themselves into one shenanigan after another, all of which culminated in two dead bodies at an illegal cockfight.

"What's the boyfriend doing tonight?" Dixon asked.

Her partner needed better bait, Clem thought after deciding not to take it. Who cared if Russ was her boyfriend? She had more crucial things to worry about. "He's got a brouhaha at Lakeshoals. Some inauguration-party-slash-campaign-fund-raiser-slash-great-big-circle-jerk. I declined the invitation."

"I like him. Heather, too. She says he's a nice, steady presence in your life, you know it?"

"Yeah."

"Brouhaha. I haven't heard that word in a while."

Clem said, "You think they'll toe-tag the brother as Cassidy's partner?" She was referring to Molly Coogan's sibling, Christopher, the one she said Jacob Cassidy had killed. His body had been found near Lost Gap when a construction crew began the dig for some "lifestyle" housing subdivision. To protect Molly, Clem had left him out of the account she gave the two catching detectives, neither of whom were enthused to be working a double homicide, even with the OT it would bring.

"Doubtful," said Dixon. "That would require deductive reasoning."

"*In*ductive."

"I was just testing you."

Clem fingered her cocktail napkin. "Let's run down the events in sequence. Top to bottom, soup to nuts."

"Again?"

"Humor me."

"The Pope, a rabbi, a monk, and Christie Brinkley are on a lifeboat, lost at sea, when—"

"Stop trying to outclever me, dickhead."

"—they spot this dolphin swimming by—"

"Dixon, you're out of your element." Clem flagged the bartender and pointed at her drink and Dixon's beer. "Can we get some more of our element?"

As she slowly tore a strip from her napkin, Clem looked around the bar, at the ardently intoxicated and the desperately getting there, at the locals who had never been anything but, at the off-duty cops mingling with the off-duty crooks, at the evergreen and deciduous winners and losers of whatever con had been played on or by them. For some here, the only comeback was the sauce, and Clem loved this place the more because of it. For others here, all they needed to take the pot was to place a bet, and Clem still loved this place with them in it. Outside Meridian, in her experience, barflies were like canned fruit cocktail. Everything wound up tasting the same: fruit-flavored peaches, fruit-flavored cherries, fruit-flavored pear.

In this city, despite its gratuitous faults, a grape tasted like grape. Ask any wino sucking on fortified in one of its alleys.

"Everything began with Odette Hubbard," Clem said to Dixon as she tore another strip of napkin. "She asks Turnip Coogan to kill her husband. He hires Jacob Cassidy, whose co-killer was likely Molly's brother, Christopher, aka Flynn, aka Mr. Spock."

"But what does it matter, aka-wise, given the brother's untimely death?"

"Correct. So Cassidy, with Chris/Flynn/Spock, is all set to do the job, but then Odette calls it off. At this point, Hamilton Delacroix pays Randy Hubbard a visit. The man told us this. He also told us he paid that visit to make an offer to buy the retail center Hubbard had in development. What didn't he tell us?"

"That he had a history with Odette."

During their sojourn at the police station, Clem and Dixon discovered on their release, reams of newsprint and hours of bandwidth had been occupied by the suicide of Hamilton Delacroix. Clem understood why. Gossip was like a steak, the juicier the better, and that was especially true in the South. The story, Clem had to admit, was sensational, with secret marriages, clandestine trysts, domestic abuse, murder, and even child brides.

"Our kindly Mr. Delacroix," Clem said to Dixon, "was previously wed to the good Miss Hubbard."

"Ms."

"But upon learning his wife was only fourteen years old, he had the marriage annulled and, using his GOB network, most but clearly not all records of it scrubbed."

"GOB?"

"Good ol' boy."

"Was Hamilton still holding a flame for the original Mrs. Delacroix?" Dixon asked.

"Better yet, was this a different kind of flame? Police report notes that at first questioning, Odette exhibited signs of battery. Told us herself Hubbard beat her. Say she came to Hamilton's house like that. Hamilton decides to keep it from happening again."

"Either way."

"Either way," Clem said. "And so, after popping Hubbard, Delacroix does a sweep, cleaning up best he can. He takes the murder weapon and hides it in an air vent in his home. Yesterday, the MPD gets an anonymous tip about said weapon. They arrive at the Delacroix residence, only to find him at the business end of a noose. No indication of foul play."

"Guy didn't want to spend the rest of his life behind bars."

"Or he was a deeply unhappy man."

"Being rich doesn't guarantee happiness."

"Neither does being white," Clem said, "but you don't see a lot of people wish they weren't."

"Either way."

"Either way."

Dixon sipped at his beer. "Who called in the tip on Delacroix?" he asked.

"That's the loose end keeps bugging me." Clem shredded more napkin. "If this boils down to a lovers' quarrel, why perforate the walls at the John Wesley Hardin trying to take us out? Why turn your wife's pickup into yard art? Why clip Molly's brother?"

"In other words, is our kindly Hamilton Delacroix nothing but a fall guy?"

"Thing is?" Clem said. "I kind of always had Delacroix pegged for DM."

"He does fit the profile of how your dad described the DM's executive branch, all its puppet masters, all its button pushers, and your dad did mention he knew that some of Hubbard's friends in the real estate game were DM."

"And that would explain why so many buttons have been trying to kill us."

Food chains all start from the bottom, Clem told herself, despite what those politicians on the TV behind the bar would have the public believe. The economy didn't trickle down. It got sucked up. The people at the top of the DM used people like Jacob Cassidy, Harold John Riggins, Turnip Coogan, and even Odette Hubbard to make them money, to clean up their messes, to bulwark their citadels of wealth and power. People like those politicians in their navy suits and red ties manipulated Harold John into poisoning Odette. People like those politicians applauding their reaffirmation of power manipulated Harold John into shooting Jacob Cassidy.

Speaking of entitled white men, Clem thought as Detective Poissant sat next to Dixon.

His red smudge of a face relaxed by the standard end-of-tour glut of whiskey, Poissant, who, Clem recalled, had been a wide receiver for Dixon in high school, patted his shoulder. "That was some shit y'all got into out in Kemper County, Captain. I'm sorry I wasn't the catching on it. I wouldn't have detained y'all that long. Case is open-shut."

"Let the animals kill each other off?" said Clem. "That how you view it?"

"Baldwin!" Poissant said. "I didn't see you there, they got it so dark. Blended right in."

He was a funny fuck all right. While Poissant and Dixon chatted about the old days, which for guys like them were always the glory days, Clem stared ahead, studying the color spectrum of liquor bottles lined against the wall. Something bothered her about Delacroix. She didn't like him for this, but she couldn't articulate why.

Clem looked down at the bar, where, nestled beside her cocktail, there now lay a tiny nest of shredded napkin.

"Hey, Poissant," she said, "you were primary at the Hubbard homicide, yeah?"

"Yeah."

"What was in that second drink?"

"Second drink?"

Leaning back on her barstool, Clem recalibrated her focus on Poissant.

She wanted to work some magic on his twenty. "Let's take a walk through the scene, okay? After getting eighty-sixed from this very establishment for being too hosed up to sit in a fucking bar, you get the call and decide to go to work. Smart. Industrious, our *Pissant.*"

"Out your ass, Baldwin."

"You get to the Hubbard residence and find the man slumped at his piano, DOA, with a vodka lime sitting beside him. The ice is still good, this guy was popped so recent. And I bet that drink sitting there got you thirsty. But as we know, you're smart. The drink is important evidence. You've sobered up just enough to know that."

"Clem," Dixon said, giving her a look that said, *Pull back a little bit, okay?*

"Scene secure, you've established. The actor is in the wind, and the vic has no vitals. You call it in. And that's when you spot a second drink in the kitchen sink." Clem saw the man flinch, a screw tightening around the lips. She had him. "This drink is brown hooch, none of that girly vodka. You decide, What the hell? It won't be missed. And you knock it back."

"Bullshit. I would never contaminate forensics at the scene of a homicide."

"What was it, Poissant? Scotch? Bourbon?"

"Put a leash on your girl, Captain."

"Crown? Beam?"

"I'm serious, Baldwin. You're walking a thin line."

"Jack? SoCo?"

"I'm not even joking. I've heard enough, fuck's sake."

"Maker's? Jameson? Turkey?"

"It was nothing, all right?" Poissant slapped the bar. "It tasted like nothing!"

After giving Dixon a glance that said, *Now, that's how you bait a motherfucker,* Clem took a celebratory swallow of her drink. She said to Poissant, "What do you mean, nothing?"

"I mean it wasn't liquor. It was just, I don't know, rusty water." With his eyes Poissant searched the ceiling. "Bad plumbing, I figured. All it tasted like was, was bitter."

"Bitter?"

"Yeah."

A clammy hand inched across Clem's scalp, its reach growing with each pulse. The feel of it sent her back to childhood. *Crack an egg on your head and let the yolk drip down, let the yolk drip down, let the yolk drip down.* Her stomach catapulted onto its side. Clem was going to be sick. She gripped the edge of the bar top and willed it to suffice for the edge of the world.

"You okay?" Dixon asked, placing his steady palm on her quaking shoulder.

"We've got to go."

"Where?"

"I don't know why I didn't see it."

As Dixon and Clem stood to leave the bar, Poissant, jarred to his senses by a swallow of real whiskey, without bitters, said, "Dixon! I almost forgot. Congratulations! You think it'll be a boy? Shit. Who am I kidding? Of course it'll be a boy. Tell Heather I said happy, happy."

The clammy hand gripping Clem's head ignited in smoldering heat. How could Dixon not have told her that kind of news? Why the hell would he keep that a secret? She and Dixon were going to have words, but she didn't have time to think about it right now.

Right now Clem needed to pay a visit to the Lakeshoals Country Club.

29

HOW COME THE DEVIL SMILES

I planned to tell you, I swear!" Dixon said to Clem on their way to Lakeshoals. "We only just found out. Remember dinner the other day? Heather was drinking! Would she have been drinking if she'd known she was pregnant? And you're supposed to wait to tell."

"Then how did Detective Fuckface know?"

"Heather and his wife are friends. They had lunch, and Heather turned down a glass of wine, which you know is not something she does often. Outed by Pinot Grigio."

It was half an hour until midnight. Clem didn't have time to explain to Dixon precisely why she cared, how the onus of responsibility weighed heavier on her because she was his boss, that it had been hard enough for her to put his life in danger and that her responsibility had been compounded because he was soon to be responsible for a life that was not his own. God's sake. Men could be such idiots, but only on those rare occasions, like when it was sunny or cloudy, warm or cold, raining or not raining.

In the Lakeshoals parking lot, Clem took her piece from the glove compartment and secured it in her shoulder rig. "No," she said to Dixon, who was reaching for the door handle.

"What?"

"You stay in the car. I was worried enough about making someone a widow. Now I got to worry about making someone an orphan? Stay the fuck here."

"Cle-em."

"*Stay,*" Clem said, thinking that Dixon did in fact look like a puppy dog staring at her from the Jeep window as she walked into the club.

Along the front entrance to Lakeshoals hung red, white, and blue bunting and tattered pennants that read REAGAN/BUSH '84. Confetti with a similar nationalistic color scheme traced Clem's way up the plush-carpeted, helical staircase that always reminded her of *Gone with the Wind,* of its bygone era that people loved to pretend had actually gone by.

The event, which had been held in the main ballroom, was on its last, drunken legs. Exhausted waiters watched the usual stragglers—men in tuxedoes literally hanging on to the bar, women carrying their heels in whichever hand wasn't occupied by a martini—proof that the Grand Old Party could always be relied on to have itself a grand old time. Clem spotted Russ near a buffet table, glad-handing his way toward what she knew was going to be a run for district attorney. His smile faded quick when he saw her face.

"You and your stupid bitters," she said. "You didn't even need a real drink to murder someone in cold blood?"

"Jesus, Clem, *what*? Here, let's go out to the pool, okay?"

"Don't you touch me," Clem said after Russ tried to guide her by the elbow.

Underwater lights the color of urinal cakes shimmered onto the empty lounge chairs lined around the pool. Blatantly nonindigenous palm trees listed in the winter breeze. A partly deflated beach ball floated in the long shadows beneath the diving board.

During the day, what at night became the pool bar served as the pool grill, an open area with tables and stools and a Sisyphean-to-keep-mopped array of puddles. The pool grill had been Clem's favorite part of the club. It had offered her an endless supply of cheese fries, Ring Pops, orange sherbet push-ups, and Mickey Mouse ice cream bars.

Now it offered the man who'd murdered Randy Hubbard. "You're clearly upset about something," Russ said.

Clem drew her weapon. "You don't say."

"Holy Christ, Clementine! Have you lost your mind? Put the gun away."

"Why'd you do it?"

"Do what?!"

Russ had raised his hands, though not above his shoulders, as most perps did instinctively. He was stretching his hands toward Clem. It almost looked like he wanted to give her a hug. Obviously this wasn't going to be an easy confession. All Clem had on Russ was a sip of bitter-tasting water that had long ago been pissed out by the not exactly reputable detective who'd contaminated a crime scene by mistaking it for the whiskey he was already sloshed on. Russ needed to confess to the murder, and to get him to do that, Clem had to ease him off his heels. If anything, she wanted him to kick those heels up.

After lowering her piece and relaxing her shoulders, Clem lifted the bar flap, walked behind it, and grabbed a bottle of bourbon. "How about a shot?" she asked Russ.

"You know I'm not much of a drinker."

"That's not what I meant." Clem placed her Beretta on the wooden bar top, its leprotic varnish peeling in strips, its grain reticulated by water saturation. She slid the gun toward Russ, still standing on the other side of the bar, roughly eight feet away. The piece came to a stop inches from him.

Clem poured herself the other kind of shot, willfully not looking at Russ but sensing his gaze shift from her to the Beretta and back again. It took crackerjack control to keep her hand from shaking as she drank the whiskey. "I used to love it here as a kid," Clem said.

"I don't know what you're trying to—"

"Not just the pool, but this, the grill. In the summer, I ate here every day."

"Clem, these theatrics—"

"They did these amazing cheese fries. To wash them down, I'd always go for a mix of all the sodas. Coke, Sprite, Dr Pepper, Mountain Dew. Know what the kids called that?"

"Suicide."

While staring at Clem, Russ fingered her gun. He circled the trigger guard, stroked the barrel, and thumbed the muzzle. With a pitch of his wrist, he sent the piece sliding back to Clem. She caught it by gently raising her fingers, the firearm sliding into her palm like a ball into a mitt. "Why'd you kill Randall Hubbard?" Clem asked Russ.

"I didn't."

Clem slid the gun back to Russ. "You got lucky. You happened to kill the man same night two hit men hired by his wife were supposed to do the job."

"Or unlucky," Russ said, sending the gun back to Clem. "If Odette hadn't called off the job, Delacroix wouldn't have been able to do it himself."

Gun to Russ. "Why'd you frame Hamilton Delacroix?" Clem asked.

Gun to Clem. "I didn't."

Gun to Russ. "Play what-if."

Gun to Clem. "Hypothetically?" Russ said. "He's an easy mark. The secret ex-husband of Odette? He's either jealous of the man who's with her now, or he's angry at that man for battering the woman he still loves. The present wraps itself. Hypothetically."

If it weren't for the eight feet of bar between them, Clem and Russ could have arm-wrestled. Clem looked around the grill, at a bird's nest tucked into one of the rafters overhead, at a fly sitting on the spill mat behind the bar, sipping what might as well have been suicide. She was close. The son of a bitch wanted to admit it. He was eager to brag, to claim ownership.

"Lakeshoals Country Club," Clem said, shoving her Beretta back to Russ, its sound against the warped, flaking bar top like chalk on a cracked blackboard. "Up until recent I thought I hated this place. I guess in hindsight we have twenty-twenty virtue, you know?"

"You think it's virtuous to hate this place?"

"But now I understand why I loved it here. Being here made me feel better than other people. I was part of a club. I was part of something *exclusive.*"

"If only Hubbard had understood that," Russ said, his voice resigned but pointed, his expression pointed but resigned.

The admission hadn't been a slip-up, Clem could see. It also wasn't a boast, as she'd expected. Russ's admission was a request. He wanted Clem's understanding. And she'd be damned if she was going to give it to him.

"Know what everybody at the courthouse calls you?" Clem said, crossing to the customer side of the bar. "Forty-Watt."

"Why?" asked Russ.

"Because you're not too bright."

Clem, standing in the seating area of the grill, facing the pool area with her back to the bar, looked over her shoulder at Russ.

"Know what everybody at the courthouse calls you?" he asked, flat-toned.

Her feet shrieking against the damp floor, Clem turned to look at Russ, still leaning against the bar, casual and carefree, as if waiting for a drink order. Clem didn't have to answer his question. She could see the answer in the mirror behind the bar, where her face stared back, reflexively steeled to the blow of that word and all the variations she had heard her entire life. She could see the answer in Russ's face, patiently impassive, the face of someone whose question had been rhetorical.

Russ pushed off the bar and sauntered toward Clem. A sort of cowboy bravado edged into his posture, a looseness of limb and uncoiling of spine manifest in the way his shoulders drooped and his hips swung and in how Clem's Beretta dangled from his slack fingers.

"Nice to meet you," Clem said.

"You're so melodramatic, Clementine. I think you might get off on it, even."

"Never managed that with you."

"Low-hanging fruit." Russ waggled the Beretta near his hip bone, as if jangling coins while studying a vending machine's selection. "I really do care about you, Clem. I know this must be a shock."

"I can't believe I was so stupid," Clem said. "You were DM this whole time."

His head tilted, sympathetically and condescendingly, Russ stepped toward Clem, the gun still waggling at his side. "The DM? Please. The DM's the grunt division of something much, much bigger. Something much more powerful."

"What?"

"America. The real one."

In the rafters overhead, a dove returned to its nest, the beating of its wings in rhythm with Clem's thudding heart. Tonight could only end one way—unless she came up with a clever move out of it. Clem scoped the spatial layout. Both she and Russ stood within the seating area of the bar, Russ with his back facing the glass-walled dining room. Whoever was still at the fund-raiser would hear any shots fired and, from what Clem could tell, scurry to those glass walls to check things out. If Russ was going to kill her, he'd have to take her to a second location.

Clem looked around the pool area. A layer of steam floated above the heated water. The submerged pool lights distorted shadows in the folds of the closed umbrellas, between the thorns of hedgerows, and onto the lineaments of Russ's face, shifting it from partially to comprehensively sinister. Clem, after seeing a door open in the back of the kitchen behind the bar, said, "Why even kill Hubbard? You wouldn't get any insurance money. He didn't batter your ex-wife."

With the barrel of Clem's gun Russ relieved an itch at his temple. "Hubbard wasn't playing by the rules, bringing 'certain elements' into places certain elements don't belong. Me? I could give a shit about all that. But the lowercase mob? The ah-doi polloi?"

"Every year's an election year."

"Smart girl."

"So you tried to talk sense into Randy," Clem said, studying gaps in this William Carlos Williams jigsaw. *Oh, look. A red wheelbarrow.* "Was Delacroix part of America, the real one?"

"Not that he knew. But his interests were aligned with ours." Russ hefted Clem's Beretta in his open palm. He seemed to consider its weight. "Thing about Clyde men? We have a temper. I made a bit of a mess, but it cleaned up nice. Sometimes things just work out in your favor," Russ said in the manner of someone used to things just working out in his favor.

"Meaning you had Hamilton Delacroix framed and killed?"

"Framed? Yes. Killed? That marriage certificate was a helpful find, but I didn't know it'd have such an effect on the man."

"Some friend."

"It was you led me to realize I could turn the Hubbard mess to my professional advantage. Taking down somebody as high-profile as Hamilton Delacroix, it's my meal ticket here on out. Might even take me to the governor's mansion."

That explained why Clem had been kept around. Her work investigating the Hubbard murder would be used by Russ to pin everything on Delacroix. She'd brought him the verdict on the kind of platter only appropriate for a man raised with a silver spoon up his ass. "I've got one more question," Clem said to Russ.

"What?"

"Is it Dan Marino?"

"Huh?"

"In your joke," Clem said to Dixon, who was standing behind the bar, not yet noticed by Russ. "The Pope, a rabbi, a monk, and Christie Brinkley are on a lifeboat, lost at sea, and they spot a dolphin swimming nearby. Is the dolphin Dan Marino? Is that the bit?"

"Now's not the best time, Clem."

With a jolt, his face an unnatural blue in the chlorinated light, Russ wheeled around to face the barrel of Dixon's gun. Dixon took the Beretta from Russ and tossed it to its proper owner, after which Clem proceeded to draw a bead on Russ. "Thought I told you to stay in the car?" she said to her partner.

"You forgot to put the window down. Haven't you heard that's dangerous?"

Russ, now with his hands raised up instead of out, sneered at Clem. "Coward."

"Says the guy shot a man in the back."

"Gun was never even loaded, was it?" Russ said. "Your little game of chicken, sliding it back and forth. All for show. It was never even loaded."

Clem checked that Dixon still had Russ in his sights. She turned to the pool, aimed, and fired a round. The splash in the deep end produced a single, elegant note: blip.

As Clem ordered a suddenly quiet, suddenly pallid Russ to walk to the back of the bar, where she hoped to find some piece of plumbing to handcuff him, she tamped down the need to vomit, everywhere and forever. She'd *slept* with this man.

Clem, as she chose a sturdy pipe connected to a sink, recalled the crime-scene photos and, despite willing herself to stop, rewound and pressed PLAY on the events that led to what they portrayed. In Randall Hubbard's living room, Russ sat on the couch as Hubbard, his back to Russ, sat on the piano bench. "Are you sure you won't change your mind?" Russ asked, to which Hubbard, instead of shaking his head or saying he was sorry but no, started to play.

The fucking nerve, Russ seethed at Hubbard. How dare this man turn his back to him. Russ was a Clyde! His ancestors had conjured an invisible empire with nothing but their wits. George Washington and Thomas Jefferson had nothing on the Russells Clyde III and IV. They'd seen through the illusion of "democracy" and, rather than be outraged, grasped its genius, how it gave a few people power by making most people *feel* powerful. The brilliance! The simplicity! Everybody wanted to feel better than somebody. Let them have it! And now this shit-ass, over there in his silly white sports jacket emblazoned with I LOVE AMERICA in purple and gold rhinestones, this hovel monger with no inkling of the exquisite lie behind "We the People," he had the te*mer*ity to say no to Russell Clyde VII?

"Not so tight!" Russ said, wringing against the handcuffs. "My circulation."

Behind the bar, noting how quickly an unrepentant murderer could start to whine like a street-level collar, Clem stepped back to ponder her handiwork. Russ, both wrists in iron, stood stooped toward the pipe through which Clem had run the bracelets, next to a chest freezer she knew to be full of orange sherbet push-ups and Mickey Mouse ice cream bars.

Involuntarily, despite trying to stay in the present, Clem found herself back at Hubbard's house. She saw Russ stand from the sofa, gun in hand, rage scrambled across his face. The shots rang out, one and two and three and four, each deafening salvo consonant with a jerk of Hubbard's body, as if Russ were a macabre, synesthetic puppeteer, with sound for strings, violence for art. Hubbard, slumped against his piano, had once been a father and husband. Now, a body.

"You okay?" Dixon asked.

"Premeditated." The word crawled through Clem's mind, leaving a slimy trail. Russ hadn't gone out to his car, retrieved his gun, and gone back into the house to shoot Hubbard. He'd had the gun on him. Clem couldn't decide if that meant he'd planned to kill Hubbard or he always, regardless of the situation, kept a gun on his person.

"We should pat him down," Clem said to Dixon seconds before Russ lifted his ankle toward his hands.

The revolver glinted in the darkness behind the bar. It rose toward Clem. She could have shot Russ. She *should* have shot Russ. Instead, disregarding her instinct and years of experience, deciding that to kill two people in half that many days was too much for her conscience, Clem lurched toward him and grabbed his forearms, tucking them into her armpit like a football and aiming his gun away from her as though stiff-arming a blocker, a move her instructor at the academy used to call the Heisman. Russ grunted into Clem's neck. His teeth clamped down, a circle of contracting heat. Drop it. Let go. Clem yanked his arms back and forth. She banged his fist against her knee until—damn it—a wild shot fired.

When Clem managed to twist his wrist, Russ dropped the gun, which clanged across the floor, sliding to a stop in a puddle next to a cigarette butt, two soggy fries, and the green-veined, desiccated sleeve of a lemon-lime Fla-Vor-Ice.

Sweat soaking her shirt, out of breath, with her heart racing, Clem reared back from Russ. She kicked his gun farther away and trained her own piece between his eyes. All the entitlement he must have repressed during their time together oozed out his pores in the form of defiance. Russ, panting as if the air were his property, slit-eyed Clem with a smirk. His cuffed hands clattered against the pipe as he straightened into his full height.

She should have shot him. The son of a bitch deserved it. So many people had died as a result of this man's belief in his hereditary right of privilege, his preordained, tautologically meritocratic seat at the head of every political, cultural, social, and economic table. Not only had he built each table, always placing himself at the head, he'd convinced everyone else at the tables they were playing a game of musical chairs. Clem should have shot him.

"Listen, honey." Russ gave her a smug, let's-make-a-deal face. "We both know how this is going to end. So how about we call a spade a spade?"

That pointedly blank look underlining his wiseass joke pushed matters too far. Without giving herself enough time to second-guess, Clem kicked

Russ behind the knee, knocking him to the floor, then down-cut his chin with the steel-hard flank of her Beretta.

Impenitently on his knees, Russ held a hand to his bleeding, broken mouth.

"Thanks for all your help, partner," Clem said over her shoulder. On not getting any response, she turned to see Dixon slumped against the wall, tying his torn shirtsleeve around his gunshot thigh.

"Shit, shit, shit, shit."

"It went clean through." Dixon grimaced as he cinched the tourniquet. "But I am a little worried you may have nicked an artery."

"We're getting you to a hospital."

As Clem positioned his arm around her shoulders, Dixon nodded toward Russ, still shackled to the pipe. "What about him?"

"He'll keep."

Dixon, heavier than Clem expected, made a lopsided trail of red footprints on their walk away, evidence that Clem, as a harebrained, wild-haired rookie cop, probably would have deduced to have been left by a one-legged perp or a vic who liked hopscotch. *Nope,* Clem told her younger self, *you shot your partner. He's also your best friend.*

"You think this means anything?" Russ yelled at Clem. "None of this means one goddamn thing." His words were misshapen by a mouth that Clem was proud to have misshapen. His genteel Delta accent shriveled to a Hill Country twang. "I could kill ten more Randy Hubbards, a dozen more, and I'd still get off scot-free. Scot-goddamn-free!"

Such a blatant confession registered as an echolocative blip within the radar of Clem's mind, but that blip grew into a giant green blob when she saw the crowd gathered at the door to the dining room. The fund-raiser guests must have heard the gunshots. "Y'all hear what he said?" Clem looked from tuxedo to cocktail dress, cocktail dress to tuxedo, none of whom acted more human than a set of clothes. "You heard him, right? You heard what he said? Did any of you hear Russell Clyde confess to the murder of Randy Hubbard?"

To look into their eyes was to look into the eyes of the woman who had asked Clem if her mother was a maid in the neighborhood. It was to look into the eyes of every professor in college who'd asked if she'd had any help on her paper, all the cops who had joked about whether the sniffer dogs could tell her time of the month. Those eyes pushed Clem away from the shores that had never felt as her own. They set her blissfully adrift.

"I heard him."

Clem had to part the crowd by walking through it in order to reach the person who'd said those words. In her sixties, she wore a Lakeshoals uniform, its starched white cotton miraculously clean after what must have been a long night waiting on this group of world-beaters. "Call the police," Clem said to the woman. "Tell them Clem Baldwin was here, and she's driving her partner to the hospital. Tell them she'll answer any questions they have."

"Okay."

"Tell them everything you heard. Got that? Tell them everything you heard."

In the Renegade, after getting Dixon into the passenger seat and lurching over every speed bump in the Lakeshoals parking lot, after ignoring Dixon's yelp of pain and gunning the Jeep back toward Meridian, Clem said, "It's funny. I almost phrased it, 'Tell the world.'"

"What?"

"Never mind."

The black ribbon of asphalt spooled into the two yellow bars of her headlights. Beside the road, pine trees whipped past, their blurry streak out the window stenciled by utility poles. It was either very early or very late, judging from the surrounding darkness.

"So what was the answer to the joke?" Clem said. "The Pope, a rabbi, a monk, and Christie Brinkley are on a lifeboat, and they see a dolphin swimming nearby. What's the punch line?"

"I guess you'll never know."

Dixon's coy little chuckle, regardless of the blood-soaked tourniquet, told Clem enough. He was going to be okay. No arteries had been nicked. "Asshole," she said.

"This one learned from the best. Watch the road."

Clem did as told, pressing the gas. They crested a hill. Ahead in the distance, beyond the struggling farms still run with pride by fifth-generation families, lay the city that had never faltered in its pride of being second best. At the center of that city, a queen was buried, her grave covered in coins, whiskey, and beads. Farther downtown, an area stitched by the rail lines that had nourished the city, stood Weidmann's Restaurant, where Clem's grandfather used to give her peanut butter and saltines, but only in the stock room, far from sight of the white clientele. A few blocks up the street sat the federal courthouse, where, after the death of three Freedom Summer workers in Philadelphia, Mississippi, a white jury made history by convicting a white deputy sheriff.

From the driver's seat, Clem watched Meridian, Mississippi, take shape in the distance, a jagged silhouette beneath the night sky. A hazy, golden light crowned the city, pushing against the dark.

It wasn't dawn, Clem both regretted and was relieved to note. It was home.

LOCAL NEWS

Sunday, February 17, 1985 The Meridian Star

HEADS ROLL AT CITY HALL

Four of the six members of the Meridian City Council have resigned their positions. The development is a direct result of a letter received by the *Star* from local business magnate Hamilton Delacroix, now deceased and, according to District Attorney Will Pickett, no longer under investigation for the murder of Randall Hubbard.

As previously reported, Mr. Delacroix's letter described, with explicit evidentiary citation, various acts of malfeasance. Council members are alleged to have embezzled funds, accepted bribes, and allowed unethical influence of their votes. Indictments expected. Further information as this story develops.

LEGAL EAGLE FLIES THE COOP!

Former assistant DA Russell Clyde is still at large after being released on bail following his arrest for the murder of Randall Hubbard. DA Pickett said a thorough investigation is ongoing. He expressed regret for the conduct of his ADA. "He has a sharp legal mind," Pickett said, "which means, unfortunately, he knows all the non-extradition countries."

Clyde's alleged involvement in the Hubbard murder was brought to light by the Queen City Detective Agency. The *Star* reached out to the agency for comment. "You'll have to ask my boss," said Dixon Hicks, a former Meridian High quarterback and decorated Vietnam veteran who sustained (cont. B5)

CALF SCRAMBLE SCRAMBLES TILL MEMORIAL TILL

Last month, Meridian citizens celebrated the return of one of their city's most heralded and historic traditions, the Calf Scramble Parade. The event was an indisputable success. Unfortunately, the same cannot be said of its financial due diligence and oversight. The parade was financed, the *Star* has discovered, with funds granted by the state legislature expressly for the purpose of holding a memorial for the death of Emmett Till, who was murdered near Money, Mississippi, thirty years ago this year. In a written statement, the mayor's office apologized for the dereliction and assured that the memorial will be held unimpeded.

CINEMA 5–SHOWTIMES

Beverly Hills Cop - 2:15, 4:30, 7:00
Witness - 2:05, 4:15, 7:10
The Breakfast Club - 2:30, 4:45, 7:30
Vision Quest–2:15, 4:20, 7:00
The Killing Fields–2:00, 4:10, 7:00

ACKNOWLEDGMENTS

The John Wesley Hardin Club was an actual bar in my hometown of Meridian, Mississippi. Although the bar closed before I was old enough to patronize it, my father loves to tell the story of the one time he did. "Sir," the woman covering the door said to him, "are you *armed*?"

"No, ma'am."

The woman handed my father a revolver and said, "You can borrow this one. I think you'll need it, honey."

Regardless of its veracity—my father stands firm, despite my suspicions—that story and others like it inspired this novel. So, thank you, first of all, to Meridian, Mississippi, for your tales tall, short, and in-between. Thank you as well to my parents, Charles and Becky Wright, for raising me in such a crime-rich city. I feel like a fantasy author who grew up in Middle-earth.

I'm grateful to the arts residencies that provided generous support while I wrote this novel: Yaddo, the Hambidge Center, the Kimmel Harding Nelson Center for the Arts, Escape to Create, Monson Arts, and Tusen Takk. I'm especially grateful to the Carson McCullers Center for Writers and Musicians, where I was honored to be the 17th Annual Marguerite and Lamar Smith Fellow, and to the Longleaf Writers Conference, for each summer giving me a time and place to avoid working on this book.

Among the early readers of *Queen City*, thank you in particular to Leona Sevick, who put each sentence to the ancient torture device known as the poet's eye. I'm also indebted to the algorithm that placed Matt Burgess and me in the same dorm our freshman year of college. My friendship with such a brilliant novelist has been a pleasure to exploit.

My wonderful agent, Eve Attermann, is owed gratitude as unquantifiable as it is deserved. The vig is forever running on my debt to you, Eve, and that's the type of bad credit it's good to have.

I'm deeply beholden to everyone at the Williams Morrow and Morris Endeavor, all of whom have been as guiding and supportive as a muscadine trellis. Those who helped this scuppernong of a novel to grow include Nate Lanman, Janet Rosenberg, Owen Corrigan, Liate Stehlik, Sharyn Rosenblum, Kaitlin Harri, Stephanie Vallejo, Andrew DiCecco, Rivka Bergman, Sian-Ashleigh Edwards, and Eric Reid. Special thanks to David Highfill, whose insightful notes were necessarily critical and unnecessarily generous—in other words, the best kind a writer can receive.

Finally, thank you to my magnificent editor, Jessica Williams, for always doing her best to get me to do mine and whose faith in my work is matched only by my faith in hers. It was a joy solving this second case with you.